THE TH

"This brilliant, heart-tugging exploration of the tragic consequences of youthful mistakes and the power of redemption had me crying and sighing and wishing for more. Rexanne Becnel knows how to peel back the layers of human folly to get at the kernel of hope within."
—*Sabrina Jeffries, New York Times best-selling author*

"THE THIEF'S ONLY CHILD is the deeply moving story of two mothers battling to save one child—a story that lingers long after the last page is turned."
—*Carla Buckley, author of The Things That Keep Us Here*

...AND FOR THE NOVELS OF
REXANNE BECNEL

"A fascinating look at New Orleans in the early days after the storm."—*Times Picayune on Blink of an Eye*

"Becnel deftly captures the way actual women think. Brisk and entertaining, with a welcome focus on middle-aged sexuality, this tidy tale proves that Becnel is just as much at home writing high-quality contemporary fiction as penning the historical fiction for which she's known."
—*Publishers Weekly on Old Boyfriends*

"Humor, smart women, adventure, and danger all add up to a book you can't put down Constant surprises and characters that will win your heart."
—*Romantic Time BOOKreviews on The Payback Club*

"Darker than the typical Regency fare ... warm and well-paced and will please new readers and longtime fans alike."—*Publishers Weekly* on *The Troublemaker*

"Run, don't walk to buy The Matchmaker. A thinking reader's book."—*Romantic Times* on *The Matchmaker*

"Brings the middle ages to life with an elaborate plot, daring adventures, and satisfyingly complex characters."
—*Publishers Weekly* on *The Knight of Rosecliffe*

"This Victorian gem is perfect."—*The Atlanta Journal / Atlanta Constitution* on *Dangerous to Love*

"An absorbing, sexually charged tale of revenge and redemption."—*Publishers Weekly* on *The Maiden Bride*

"Not to be missed."—*Literary Times* on *Heart of the Storm*

"Skillfully blends romance and adventure in a seamless narrative."—*Publishers Weekly* on *When Lightning Strikes*

"A brilliant medieval novel."—*Denise Little, B. Dalton Booksellers* on *The Rose of Blacksword*

"Even if you don't like romances, you'll like this one."
—*Times Picayune* on *A Dove at Midnight*

"I cried through the whole book. If you loved It's a Wonderful Life, you'll love The Christmas Journey."
—*Michele Hearn, B. Dalton Booksellers* on *The Christmas Journey*

THE
THIEF'S
ONLY
CHILD

THE THIEF'S ONLY CHILD

REXANNE BECNEL

»vantage
POINT→

This is a work of fiction. Names, characters, places and incidents are the product of the author's imagination or are used fictitiously. Any resemblance to actual events, locales, or persons, living or dead, is coincidental.

Vantage Point Books and the Vantage Point Books colophon are registered trademarks of Vantage Press, Inc.

FIRST EDITION: September 2011

Copyright © Rexanne Becnel, 2011
All rights reserved, including the right of reproduction in whole or in part in any form.

Published by Vantage Point Books
Vantage Press, Inc.
419 Park Avenue South
New York, NY 10016
www.vantagepointbooks.com

Manufactured in the United States of America
ISBN: 978-1-936467-18-1

Library of Congress Cataloging-in-Publication data are on file.

0 9 8 7 6 5 4 3 2 1

COVER DESIGN: Victor Mingovits

FOR PAMELA AHEARN WHOSE FAITH IN ME
AND MY BOOKS HAS NEVER WAVERED.
THANK YOU DOESN'T BEGIN TO SAY ENOUGH.

PROLOGUE

"I'm so proud of you, Alyssa." Diane Leftwich glanced in the rearview mirror and smiled at her five-year-old daughter. "Tall enough to sit in a booster seat, and grown up enough to stop sucking your thumb. So," she went on, turning her attention back to the traffic. "What are you going to name your new teddy?"

"Um. Well. I was thinking ... How about ... Pinky? 'Cause she's three colors of pink?"

"Sounds perfect."

"Mommy? Can we take Pinky to the Dairy Queen? She never had ice cream before."

Chuckling, Diane stole another quick peek at her blond, blue-eyed cherub of a child. "Nice try, missy. You know it's too close to dinnertime for ice cream."

And yet as Alyssa started up the predictable litany of "Please, Mommy. Please, please, please, can we?" Diane felt her resolve falter. What harm would it really do? They could just eat dinner a little later than usual. "Okay," she conceded. "But with all this rain, let's go someplace with a drive-through window."

"Yay!" Alyssa crowed from the backseat. "McDonald's?"

"I thought you liked the frosties at Wendy's best."

"Oh, yeah. Wendy's. Wendy's."

"Wendy's it is," Diane agreed, bypassing her regular exit and heading further east on Highway 90. Today's trip to Gulfside Toys and Teddy World was a reward for Alyssa going an entire month without sucking her thumb except in her bed. That was a big first step, according to the book Diane had consulted. First make thumb-sucking a bedtime-only activity with a reward attached. Then move on to ending it completely with an even better reward. Diane and Jim had already decided on a beautiful 16-inch pink- and- purple bicycle with handlebar streamers, a big horn, and training wheels. If everything worked out as planned, by the time Alyssa started kindergarten she would no longer be sucking her thumb at all.

In the backseat Alyssa carried on a one-sided conversation with Pinky. "I like chocolate the best, and Mommy likes vanilla. But you're all pink, so pro'bly you'll like the pink ice cream best. Mommy, I forget. What do you call pink ice cream?"

"Strawberry." Diane switched the windshield wipers to high.

"Strawberry," Alyssa repeated as Diane hunched her shoulders, squinting through the increasing downpour. She was anxious to get off the main drag and onto a slower side street. People always drove like maniacs in the rain.

And then it happened. Fast, like everything does at fifty-five miles per hour. A truck hurtled across the grassy median, as if aimed at her car. At her and Alyssa.

Yet in Diane's brain, in the infinitely brief split-second before adrenaline flooded her body, and fear and panic became her only reality—in that merest slice of time, she saw it all so clearly. A slow-motion ballet. A blue truck back lit by two lanes of glaring headlights. The truck had lots of chrome on it, and even airborne, all four of its tires kept spinning.

·····

Diane jerked awake to the shrill discordance of sirens, then shrank back to darkness. To quiet. Until a violent crack of lightning burned away the foggy safety of unconsciousness. The thunder, the sirens, and the panicked shouting of too many people assailed her uncomprehending brain, all of it excruciatingly audible despite the muting roar of the unrelenting rain.

What sort of nightmare was this?

Then came the breaking glass. She heard it crack and dimly felt it shatter over her. But it didn't hurt. The shards didn't cut her. A rush of cold water sluiced over her numb body. Ice cold water. She tried to open her eyes, but it was so hard....

"C'mon, sweetheart. Stay with me."

Stay with me. Diane didn't recognize the voice, or the way he touched her. Her wrist. Her eyelids, pulling them open.

"No ..." She tried to twist away—and felt an explosion of pain behind her eyes, a pain buried in the deepest center of her head, erupting despite the bone and flesh trying to hold it in. A pain so awful she could not breathe through it.

"Relax, sweetheart. Try to relax. We'll get you out of here. Just keep still. Don't fight me."

"Cut the seat belt," someone behind her said. "Don't worry about the child seat."

"Looks like we'll need the jaws of life up here," the man in the windshield said.

The windshield.

The child seat.

And then came the screaming. Screaming that would not stop, which smothered Diane, which came from inside her. "Alyssa! Alyssa!"

They were in her Jetta. She remembered the blue truck, and now she was lying on her side, crushed against the side door, and a man lay halfway through her windshield, trying to check her vital signs.

"Alyssa!" Diane screamed for her little girl but received no reply from the backseat.

"Stay still." The man caught her head between his hands. His eyes bored straight into her eyes. "You'll hurt yourself."

But she didn't hear him. She only heard the cryptic words and grunts of effort from behind her.

"Easy. Lift that."

"Okay. Here."

"I've got her."

"Watch out! Okay. Okay."

Then the whole car shifted and a voice outside yelled, "Brace it. Brace it!"

The car stilled, but inside the cab the rearview mirror swayed, dangling from its bent stem. As Diane's eyes fixed on the unbroken surface of that narrow mirror, she saw a movement in it, a flash of denim and white lace, and then a lavender, sock-clad little foot: Alyssa wearing her favorite jeans and socks, but no shoe.

No shoe.

Where was her baby's shoe?

They were out of the backseat, the rescuers. Did they have Alyssa? Was she all right?

The mirror gave no answers.

Diane tried to twist her neck, to see more of her baby than only her foot, to see her outside the smashed-up car. Alyssa would be so scared without her mother. But the man in the windshield held her head rigid, his hands iron clamps on either side of her face. Desperately pleading, she stared into his dark eyes. "Is she okay? Is she?"

He blinked once, then looked away, not answering. "Hurry up with that neck brace," he called to somebody outside the car. Then to her, "You need to cooperate, okay? It's gonna take a little while to get you out but we'll—"

"Is Alyssa okay? Tell me!"

He hesitated, and in that moment Diane's heart froze. He looked over his shoulder, beyond her metal and glass prison. "They got her out," he said slowly. "They're working on her. That's all I know." He turned back to her. "Can you move your fingers?"

She swallowed hard, willing him to tell her more. But he was busy with the neck brace, and his eyes wouldn't meet hers.

"Can you move your fingers?"

"Yes—. I—I don't know." It took all her strength, every bit of her will to flex her right wrist. The rain on her neck was cold, but her hand felt warm and slippery. Blood?

Then a shudder wracked her, another earthquake inside her head and radiating outward. First that same blinding pain, then an odd flood of ... of relief, and a strange, heated lethargy. Her eyelids drooped closed. She struggled to open them, to see, but she failed.

"Alyssa," she said, or tried to say. *Alyssa has to be okay*. That man in the windshield, he would have told her if she wasn't.

"Find her shoe," she murmured into the heavy darkness that enfolded her. "They're her favorites. And her new teddy ..."

AUGUST 17, 1989

TEENAGER KILLS TODDLER ON HWY. 90

MOTHER IN INTENSIVE CARE

Thursday morning on rain-slicked Highway 90 in Gulfport an eastbound Ford truck skidded across the center line and collided with a VW Jetta, instantly killing five-year-old Alyssa Leftwich. Her mother, Diane Leftwich, 28, was transported to a local hospital where she is reported to be in critical but stable condition. The 17-year-old driver of the truck was also hospitalized with lacerations, a broken nose, and a broken leg. When released from the hospital she will be charged with driving without a license, driving with no insurance, and vehicular homicide. Pending blood tests, she may also be charged with driving under the influence.The dead child was the only daughter of Diane and Jim Leftwich of Gulfport. When the father reached the scene he had to be forcibly restrained from beating the abandoned truck with a golf club.

HANCOCK COUNTY JUVENILE FACILITY RELEASE REPORT 6/30/1990

Roberta Anne Fenner, age 18. Vehicular homicide. Released to mother's custody

SEPTEMBER 3, 1991

CIVIL DISTRICT COURT DIVORCE AGREEMENT

James Warner Leftwich vs. Diane Haines Leftwich

Insofar as the above-referenced parties are in agreement as to the dissolution ...

COMPASSIONATE FRIENDS

For anyone who has suffered the loss of a child

7 PM 12/03/1991

St. Joseph's Annex, Room 103

MARCH 4, 1992

CIVIL DISTRICT COURT
PETITION FOR CHANGE OF NAME

Insofar as Diane Haines Leftwich is no longer wed to James Warner Leftwich, she hereby petitions the court to restore her name to its original form ...

TRIAL SUMMARY: PARISH CRIMINAL COURT
MARCH 15, 1996

Bobbie Davis, 23, AKA Roberta Anne Fenner Davis Illegal possession of Class A narcotics: GUILTY
3rd Felony arrest: sentencing to be under Multiple Offender Guidelines

PART ONE

DIANE
SPRING 1996

CHAPTER 1

JAN. 20, 1996
PARISH PRISON, WOMEN'S UNIT

Dear Mom,
I am going CRAZY here! It sucks SO bad!! The other prisoners are awful. A bunch of losers. The guards are worse. And the infirmary is a torture chamber. Three days in withdrawal and they just leave me there laying in my vomit!! Nobody helped me clean up. Then in the shower some dyke tried to jump me. I punched her lights out but now I'm scared what she and her butch gang will do. You have to bail me out of here. Please Mom. Please!
Bobbie

3/15/96
PARISH PRISON, WOMEN'S UNIT

Dear Mom,
Why weren't you at the trial? My public defender was no help.
Fucking asshole! They found me guilty!!! A 3 hour trial and then that stupid jury found me guilty! I won't be sentenced for a week maybe, but my lawyer says they're using

the three strikes law against me so I could be locked up a lot longer than before. I'm so scared.

You got to help me. Find me a better lawyer or something. It's not like I hurt anybody this time.

Your daughter,
Bobbie

3/24/96
PARISH PRISON, WOMEN'S UNIT

Mom,

Where are you? I got 10 years and no parole!!! 10 years!!!

This is so bad. And all because of your stupid scumbag boyfriend!

He told me the dealer was a friend of his. And now I'm totally screwed. Ever since Ken died everything has been so fucked up. That's why you got to get a fast appeal. Find me a new lawyer, tell him about Lissy. She needs her mom, right? And maybe if you bring her to court with you. Dress her really cute too. You have her, right?

I'll call you Sunday, but it has to be collect. Find me a new lawyer by then. Because after that they're shipping me to a state prison!!!

Hurry Mom!
Bobbie

DIANE

I know the difference between right and wrong. Credit Sister Clara, the principal of St. Leo's School, for imprinting that on my brain and that of every other kid who spent kindergarten through eighth grade under her eagle eye. There is this line. Right is on one side; wrong is on the other; and the line drawn down the middle is very, very narrow. Not much wiggle room.

Little has changed in Catholic schools, although there is more help for kids wavering on that razor-sharp middle line. WWJD. What Would Jesus Do? Wear it on a beaded bracelet. Put a WWJD sticker on your math notebook and when you face a tricky choice, stop and consider what Jesus might do. But what people forget is that Jesus was a rebel. That he broke the rules, especially the ones that held good people down. He was the Rebel Jesus, like in the Jackson Browne song.

I haven't thought much about Jesus lately. Not since that day over six years ago when Roberta Anne Fenner rammed her truck into my car.

The weeks that followed Alyssa's death are a blur. I spent ten days in ICU and missed her funeral. My baby was laid to rest in our family tomb in New Orleans, and I wasn't there! It nearly killed my mother to go, and Jim never could talk about it. Never. But still, I should have been there. I'm her mother.

Was her mother.

On the surface it's such a little thing, that change from present tense to simple past. But it still has the power to suck the breath out of me, to send me spiraling down into that black emptiness I lived in for so long after Alyssa died. I *am* Alyssa's mother and always will be. But I no longer have a daughter.

Mother never recovered from her only grandchild's death. Nor did Jim. Not really. Mom died ten months after the accident, from a massive stroke. A year after that, my husband divorced me.

It was nobody's fault, that awful cycle of events.

No. It *was* somebody's fault. But Roberta Anne Fenner's name never appeared on my mother's death certificate or my divorce papers. In theory it was a no-fault divorce, one more shuffle of papers through our arcane legal system. No indication in our swiftly buried file that an entire family had died. First an innocent child, one with a penchant for dancing, who loved blowing bubbles, and slept with an entire teddy-bear family in her white Cinderella bed.

Then a marriage died, a happy, eight-year union based on love and respect, and a shared obsession for old houses, primitive art, crawfish boils, and zydeco music. And for our daughter. But she was gone. The glue that made us work was gone.

None of that appeared in any file, though, except for the one in my head. Jim and I both cried when our divorce was final. We still loved each other. That was the worst part. I think we love each other even now. But some tragedies are mountains too high to climb over. Or maybe we each recover at a different pace, in a different way. Not that I feel recovered from Alyssa's death. I'll never recover from that. And I know in my heart that Jim hasn't recovered either. Alyssa was everything to him, and she adored her daddy so much. He lost that, the pure, uncomplicated and boundless love only a child can give. We both did.

But Jim was ready to get on with life, while I was way too mired in grief to see my way out. So we got divorced and I moved back to New Orleans into Mom's old apartment. Neither of us was right or wrong. We were simply no longer in step.

Which blows Sister Clara's theory of right and wrong and its skinny separating line all to hell. What would Jesus do in a case like ours? I don't know. But I knew what he would do with the astounding information I'd just discovered in the CAJA caseload overview in my hand.

Three years ago I'd started volunteering with the Southeastern Louisiana Chapter of CAJA—Court Appointed Juvenile Advocates. We're supposed to advocate for children caught in the Bermuda Triangle of dysfunctional families, the juvenile justice system, and Child Protective Services. It's a terrifying responsibility, and when I'd started I'd been petrified. I'd been hiding from the human race since Alyssa's death—especially from children. To see them play, to hear them laugh and watch them run into the arms of their mothers—it was too painful, too much to bear. But something had drawn me to the program, something primal, as if emanating from my bones, my marrow. My DNA. I couldn't help Alyssa, but I could help these kids.

And lo and behold, helping them had given me a reason to go on, a way to regain a fragile hold on my wildly fluctuating sanity. I help them settle into a healthier, more stable family situation, and in turn they've helped me find a foothold back into the world, a place to be productive. To be needed.

I stared now at the paper in my hand, at the name and brief bio of our newest case. Lissy Anne Davis. Jesus would do what was best for this child—especially this child—no matter what the rules said. And so would I.

I glanced around the overheated office with its mismatched file cabinets, battered oak desk with three phones, and long football-shaped table stacked with files for today's meeting. The thick files were heartbreakers, the sad proof of way too many years of some child's life spent in and out of the system. But the skinny files were just as sad, clean and crisp with no folded-down corners or ancient coffee stains. They represented kids recently introduced to the system—and our purview.

And then there were the brand-new files, the empty stack still wrapped in plastic, just waiting for the familiar tales of misused children to fill them.

I split the plastic wrapper with my thumbnail and slid a fresh file out. Then I found the labels we used. Red for JV cases; blue for CPS. On a blue one I printed her name with special care: *Lissy Anne Davis.*

My heart pounded; my chest hurt; I could hardly breathe. Just writing her name dredged up all the excruciating pain of that first day, of the first everything. First morning waking up childless. First Halloween without my Little Princess or Tinker Bell, or Good Witch to take trick-or-treating. First Christmas without a pajama-clad imp staring wide-eyed at the mound of gifts Santa had left under our tree. First anniversary of her birth without her there to blow out the candles.

First anniversary of her death.

How are you supposed to commemorate the death of a child? I didn't know then. I don't know now.

But as I held that empty file in my hand, I realized that here might be the way. This file. This child. And for the first time since the beginning of my endless nightmare of a life, I felt an emotion I thought I'd lost, one I barely recognized: Satisfaction. And a sense, finally, of justice within reach.

I aligned the label and carefully smoothed it onto the file as a new world of options flashed through my head. Yes, it might be a misuse of my powers as a CAJA. But it was only right. Sister Clara knew nothing about right and wrong. Some situations were neat and clean. Black and white. And in Sister Clara's K-through-eighth world, maybe that worked. But this was the real world, where people made horrible choices, where they wrecked other people's lives. Killed other people's kids.

And neglected their own kids too.

The details in the child's bio were stark and all too common. Lissy Anne Davis, almost four, an only child whose mother had been convicted for the third time on some minor drug charge and now faced a full ten-year sentence. Father deceased. Child remanded to Child Protective Services for possible placement in foster care if the maternal grandmother couldn't adequately care for her. A paternal uncle had petitioned to take her in too. That's where CAJA came in—where *I* came in—to determine what was best for this child.

The mother was listed as Bobbie Davis, wife of Kenneth Davis, who'd overdosed two years ago. But I knew her as Roberta Anne Fenner.

My hand shook as I slid the empty file to the side and made a label for the next file. Corinne Hotard. Except that I wrote *Lissy Anne Davis* again.

I tore off the label and crumpled it up. How dare she name her child Lissy, Jim's nickname for Alyssa! The blood roared in my ears, throbbing in my neck, and the room kept getting hotter. I closed my eyes and made myself breathe, in through my nose, out through my mouth. Relax. Relax.

I'd learned this technique during Lamaze classes when I was pregnant with Alyssa. I'd relearned it at the grief sessions I'd attended after she died and again from the therapist I went to after Jim left, when I'd been suicidal, dreaming of finding that compelling white light people talk about.

But deep, slow breathing didn't work today. How could it? She'd named her child after my dead child. The child *she'd* killed!

She shouldn't even be allowed to *have* a child, let alone give it my Alyssa's name. So, no, I couldn't relax. Roberta Anne Fenner, aka Bobbie Davis had been angry with her mother and her mother's new boyfriend that awful day. So she'd taken his truck for a joyride to the beach. Why is it called a joyride anyway? Where was the joy? She'd been drinking and had no license when she'd lost control of that truck. Even worse, she didn't get any serious jail time for murdering my daughter, destroying my marriage, and killing my mother. She was a minor, and was released when she turned eighteen. Now all these years later she was getting a ten-year sentence under the Three Strikes Law for carrying a bottle of Xanax not prescribed for her. Ten years for a lousy forged prescription but only a few months in a juvenile facility for killing my baby. Where was the justice in that? Where?

My hand shook as I flattened it over Lissy Anne Davis's empty file folder. My other hand reached for the locket I always wore, the one with Alyssa's pictures in it. "Okay, Alyssa," I whispered. Her name had become my only prayer, my only connection to the hereafter. I didn't believe in God anymore. How could anyone believe in a God who let children suffer and die while trash like Roberta Anne Fenner went on her merry way, wreaking havoc everywhere she went? I did believe in Jesus. That is, I believed he lived, that he did good things and that we should emulate him. But for me he was the Rebel Jesus, the one who stuck up for the meek and the poor and the children, and didn't hesitate to break the rules if that's what it took. WWJD? He would help this poor little girl, no matter what it took. And so would I.

"Okay, Alyssa," I repeated, and kissed the locket. I could do this. I had to do it. For Alyssa. For myself. And for three-year-old Lissy Anne Davis. The best thing I could do for this child was to wrest her away from her pitiful excuse for a mother and the dead-end life that promised—and give her the kind of life every child deserved, the kind I'd tried to give my Alyssa.

Only this time I would not fail.

· · · · ·

"She hasn't said much about her life up to now," Linda Zito told me as she led me through her house. Linda was a temporary foster parent to kids just coming into Child Protective Services. When kids were removed from their parents' custody, they went first to homes like Linda's. She was a social worker by training, not too high up the food chain. But twenty-five years working in the field gave her an insight no amount of bookwork could ever impart.

We stood in the doorway and watched the three kids Linda currently housed. A boy about five or six stacked blocks into towers nearly as tall as himself. Then using a small military figurine, he smashed them down. "Die! Die! Die!" he chanted as he squatted down and battered the figurine against the terrazzo floor.

An older girl sat curled up on a love seat, her head buried in a book, oblivious to the noisy little boy. I recognized both their behaviors. Some kids acted out. Others turned their grief and pain inward. Then I saw Lissy. She sat behind a curtain, cross-legged with her back to the room, staring through the sliding doors into the back yard. She wore a pink T-shirt, with matching pink ribbons on her blond pigtails, and clutched a shabby teddy bear to her chest. She was sucking her thumb.

For one wrenching moment I hurtled into the past. Alyssa had loved teddy bears. And how many times had I matched ribbons to her T-shirts when I combed her silky blond hair into pigtails? What cut the deepest, though, was the thumb in Lissy's mouth. On the day Alyssa died, we'd been returning from her favorite toy store with a new teddy, a reward for her not sucking her thumb except when she was in bed.

If only I hadn't urged her to quit sucking her thumb, Alyssa would still be alive. If I'd just let her grow out of it at her own pace instead of bribing her—

"Diane?"

I flinched when Linda touched my shoulder.

"You okay?" she asked.

"Fine." I nodded. "Fine. It's just that sometimes ..." I shook my head. "Hard to believe the way some people neglect their kids."

"Yeah. Tell me about it." She crossed the room, stopping to calm the little boy with a hug, and to stroke the older girl's cheek. Then she squatted down next to Lissy. "Hey, sweetie. How would you like to go outside for awhile?"

Without a word Lissy stood. But the thumb stayed put and she clutched her teddy even tighter.

I guess a part of me was in denial, because it took a while before I admitted the truth to myself. The first day I met Lissy— the day I pushed her on the swing, asked her about her teddy, and gently probed her about her old life—that day all I felt was outrage at her mother, profound sorrow for the child, and determination to get justice for both Alyssa and Lissy. But I know *now* that I felt something else. It was a crack in the black vacuum that had taken the place of my heart. A tiny crack, and then the slow hiss of life leaking back in. And all because of Lissy.

I ignored the feeling at first, lumping it in with the satisfying feelings I got from helping every child I worked with. They were all so innocent, so in need of the love of a stable set of parents. Whose heart wouldn't feel for them?

With Lissy, though, there was more.

She was a cute little girl. But I'd seen cuter. She'd been neglected, of course, and who knew what else. But I'd seen kids in far worse shape. In spite of the similar hair color, she looked nothing like Alyssa. Alyssa had been pink and full-cheeked, with sparkling blue eyes and a rushed, breathless way of talking. She'd been bursting with enthusiasm, bursting with life.

Lissy was a waif, a skinny, wan little thing, with muddy-colored eyes and a solemn demeanor. Not frightened, exactly. More ... resigned. Which is just so wrong. No child should be resigned to her lot in life. Had she ever been breathless with enthusiasm? Bursting with curiosity about life?

Probably not. But like every child, she deserved to be.

So yes, I think maybe my heart began to heal—just a little—on that first day. I visited her every afternoon, and a week later I took her out to lunch for her fourth birthday. "What's your favorite thing to eat?" I asked as I buckled her into the backseat of my Honda CRV.

"French fries," she lisped around the ever-present thumb in her mouth.

"Okay. French fries it is." I got into the driver's seat. "Anything else?"

Her serious eyes met mine in the rearview mirror. "Coke."

Coke. I knew Linda didn't allow soft drinks or fast foods in her house. But this was Lissy's fourth birthday. When we got back there would be cake, ice cream, and juice. What was a little more sugar and useless carbs?

We went to one of those McDonald's with a playground in front, all red, blue, and yellow with slides and hidey-holes and a swaying wooden bridge. We ate outside, and I watched as she climbed to the highest spot on the play equipment and just sat there.

"Having fun?" I called.

She nodded. Then she took her thumb out of her mouth. "Mommy used to bring me here."

I stiffened. This was the first time she'd brought up her mother. "She brought you here? To this McDonald's?"

She nodded, but she didn't look too certain. She stuck her thumb back in her mouth and stared down the slide. But she didn't move until a pair of little boys ran onto the playground and began to climb up to where she sat. That's when she pushed her teddy under her shirt and shoved herself down the slide. Then she ran to me and sat down.

"Don't you want to play anymore?"

She shook her head.

"Okay. Are you ready to head back to Miss Linda's?"

That's when she removed her thumb from her mouth. "Can we bring French fries and cokes to Darryl and Jeannie and Miss Linda?"

And that's when I felt the first pangs in my heart. I told myself it was admiration, not love. I stared down into her round eyes—they were hazel, not mud-colored—at her petite features—not solemn, but piquant—and saw the generous spirit hidden inside her, the caring soul that remembered others even though her own mother had obviously spent four years forgetting about her.

Such a precious little girl. I leaned over and hugged her with one arm. "Of course we can bring them French fries and Cokes. As much as you want."

She hugged me back, the first time she'd done that. Her skinny little arms wrapped warm and fast around my waist, squashing teddy between us, and in that moment I was once and forever a goner.

I didn't want to admit it, even to myself, because it felt wrong, traitorous to my own, long-absent baby. Lissy was a sweet, needy child, like all my CAJA clients. But Alyssa had my heart. For over six years all that pent-up love I'd missed showering on my Alyssa had twisted inside me into a smothering anguish, a desperate love denied an outlet, mingled with a drowning despair for myself.

But now I had this child, this motherless little girl named after my baby. I still despised Bobbie Davis/Roberta Anne Fenner. She was a waste of space, a human train wreck who'd robbed me of my greatest treasure. Robbed me without a second thought. But now she'd given me this child, whether she knew it or not. She'd given me Lissy to nurture and guide and protect from the horrors of life, and I didn't mean to ever give her back.

.....

"*Don't you have* enough with the Henderson case?" my supervisor, Kate Lawson had asked that first day when I claimed Lissy's case.

"It is a complicated case," I agreed. Both sides of a family fighting for custody of twin boys. Father in jail; mother in long-term rehab; and not one responsible adult among the rest. What both families wanted was the state's monthly allotment for raising the twins, who were both officially wards of the state. But my job was to make sure Samuel and Steven were placed in a home that would allow them to thrive. "It's complicated," I repeated. "But it's coming to a close. Judge Holmes has my report." I handed her a copy. "I expect it to be settled by the end of the month. Meanwhile the bulk of my work is done."

"Okay, then. Lissy Davis is all yours. What else do we have?"

We went over the caseload. In the past three years I'd moved up the CAJA hierarchy. I wasn't paid to do this. None of us were. But I was dedicated to the children in my care. Driven. People come and go in CAJA. It's hard, emotionally draining work, and not everyone can take it. Especially when the courts place a child you've come to love back in a situation you know is far from ideal.

You're not supposed to love them. You're supposed to care about them and be diligent on their behalf. But you're not supposed to love them. The potential for heartbreak is just too high. Unfortunately we too often fall in love with our clients. Our kids. And we each had a child or two we still worried about, children who'd disappeared from the radar. Were they thriving or were they being neglected? Or abused? Or dead?

We didn't know. Despite all that, a few of us persisted. Hardcore CAJA, we're a small group. But we trust each other implicitly when it comes to our kids.

And though I was violating procedures by getting involved in a case where I knew any of the principals, I also knew that Kate and the other hardcore CAJA would understand—*if* they ever found out, which I would make sure they never did.

. . . . .

Once Lissy's case was assigned to me, I moved onto step two, starting the process to become her foster parent. It took almost three months, and I sweated every one of them. If Child Protective Services called me on even one of my lies I'd be rejected. Lie number one? That I didn't have any children. After my divorce, when I'd moved back to Louisiana and returned to my maiden name, I'd decided not to share my past with anyone. It's just too hard to explain your loss, to suffer the well meant but awkward murmurs of condolence. Nobody can understand your pain except for another parent who has lost a child, and even they can't offer any relief. I'd tried Compassionate Friends, but I could never get to a point of acceptance, of peace with God. All I ever felt when I went to the meetings was pain and rage, so I quit going.

It was easier to just be one more single, middle-aged woman instead of a divorcée with a dead daughter. None of my coworkers or neighbors needed to know about Jim and Alyssa. That was my private hurt to nurse.

Lie number two? I didn't reveal to CAJA or CPS that I knew any of the principals in this case. That is a very big deal at CAJA, one I understood. But this was different. I'd have lost access to Lissy if I'd admitted our connection, and *that* I refused to do.

Lie number three? That I would encourage whatever level of connection the child wished to continue with her parent. I even told CPS I might take in another child in the future. And who could tell? Maybe someday I would. But the only child I really wanted was Roberta Anne Fenner/Bobbie Davis's child. She *owed* me a child. I needed Lissy, and she really needed me.

Who says lying doesn't pay? Thanks to my excellent reputation as a CAJA, the powers that be were only too glad to let me take a child out of their overburdened system. I was already one of them, one of the good guys. Besides, we all knew the odds for kids like Lissy. If she'd been younger, not yet walking or talking, or at least with no living relatives, her chances of finding a permanent home would have been better. But she was already four, with relatives—albeit lousy ones—who might challenge any eventual adoption. The cold, hard statistics supported what I was doing. If I didn't give Lissy a permanent home, no one else was likely to. She would probably spend the next fourteen years of her life in foster care, moving from home to home, until at eighteen they cut her loose to make her own way in the world, and probably turn out just like her mother and grandmother. But I could break that grim cycle of misery. I could give her the life Alyssa was supposed to have, a stable home, a good education, and a parent she could rely on to guide her through life.

Surely that was more important than any rules I might be breaking.

"Congratulations," Linda said the day I arrived to take Lissy home. "You and Lissy are such a good match."

I nodded and averted my eyes, as if I was looking for something in my purse. "Thanks. I hope you're right." Of all the people I'd had to lie to, Linda was the one I most hated deceiving, even though I suspected she wouldn't care. She was all about getting kids into good homes. For her that was the beginning, middle, and end of it.

She smiled at me. "I'm right." Then she called up the stairs. "Lissy! Diane's here."

Lissy edged down the stairs, one slow step at a time, clutching her teddy and sucking her thumb. In the past three months we'd formed a bond, but she was still more attached to Linda. I'd told myself that was fine. Now though, as I hefted her My Little Pony suitcase and reached out a hand to her, I wanted her to love me best. Or at least like me best.

Instead she burst into tears, ran to Linda, and buried her face in Linda's lap.

"It's okay, Lissy. It's okay," Linda said, even as she sent me a sorry-'bout-this look. She rubbed her palms up and down Lissy's back. "I know you're tired of moving so much. And scared too. Right?"

A lump formed in my throat when I saw the almost imperceptible nod of Lissy's head. Was I making a huge mistake? Could I be any better a mother to this poor little girl than her own grandmother? At least Lissy knew her grandmother.

While Linda soothed Lissy, I recalled meeting Lissy's grandmother, Bobbie's mother. It had occurred three days after I took over Lissy's case, and I'd been a nervous wreck. Had the woman seen me during any of the legal proceedings that followed Alyssa's death? I didn't remember meeting her. But I'd been operating in a fog back then, oblivious to everything but my loss, my pain.

So the day before the interview I had my hair cut and colored. From a lanky, dirty blond, to short and sassy champagne gold. I bought a pair of teal-framed glasses, wore a rust-colored suit with a cream-and-orange polka-dot blouse, and high-heeled sandals. Nothing like my post-accident, who-gives-a-damn style, which ran to Dockers, twin sets, and loafers. Once upon a time I'd worried about my hair and my clothes. I'd loved manicures and pedicures and the occasional facial. But I'd been young then, and in love with my husband, my child, and my life. After the accident it just hadn't mattered.

But interviewing Bobbie's mother and rejecting her as a caregiver to Lissy did matter. So there I'd stood at the sagging trailer door, shaking in my three-inch heels, but smiling like this was just one more case I hoped would end happily.

"Come in," I heard someone shout.

I entered through the unlocked door. Strike one. Doors need to be locked if there's a toddler in the house, especially with a busy state highway one short block away. Inside the trailer was dim. But not dim enough to disguise how dirty and cluttered it was. "Mrs. Simpson?" I said to the faded-looking woman who sat in a bulky recliner. Anne Marie Grundle Loomis Fenner Simpson.

"That's me," she said, squinting in my direction. "Sorry I can't get up. Hip trouble. What can I do for you?"

Strike two. It would be hard to keep up with an active little girl if you couldn't get out of your chair because of hip trouble. I smiled at her. "I'm Miss Haines, Lissy's court-appointed juvenile advocate."

"Lissy's what? Oh." Pulling on the recliner's arms, she sat upright. "Oh, yeah. What's your name again?"

"Miss Haines." I didn't give her a business card just in case my first name raised her suspicions. "Because you've filed a request to raise your granddaughter, I've come to interview you and inspect your home for suitability."

Her eyes darted around her crowded trailer before returning to me. "I wish you'd called first. I would've neatened up some. Ever since Bobbie went and ruined her life, everything's gone to hell in a handbasket." She reached for a pack of Virginia Slims, but then thought better of it. "She was always wild, you know. But I still can't believe she's goin' to jail for ten years."

"She should have—" I bit down hard before I put voice to the rest of my thoughts. *She should have gone to jail six years ago.* I grimaced. "She should have thought about what she was doing before she got caught. May I sit down?"

"Sure. Sure. Just ... move that laundry basket off the couch."

A laundry basket full of men's clothes. Carpenter jeans, boxer shorts, a few T-shirts and socks. And beneath the basket a rumpled blanket and a tired feather pillow, as if someone slept on this couch every night.

I pulled out my folder. Even if I hadn't already decided to adopt Lissy myself, I wouldn't have approved this place for any child to live in. But I did the interview exactly as I'd been trained. And I wrote copious notes, transcribing her precise words.

" ... yes, I live alone. Oh, these clothes? They ... they belong to a friend of mine. No. He doesn't live here. He just sleeps here sometimes."

"Where does he live when he's not here?"

"Oh, he has an apartment over near Pearl River."

"So he lives there? In an apartment of his own?"

She sighed. "Yeah. Mostly."

"And does he have a job?"

"He works offshore."

I nodded. "I'll need his phone number, legal address, and the name and number of his employer."

"Why?" she asked, frowning at me.

"Because he obviously lives here with you part of the time. I see clothes, these sheets. That can of shaving cream on the kitchen counter." *Shaving in the kitchen sink? Gross!* "That case of beer under the table." I stared at her. "Unless you're the drinker in the family?"

"I don't drink beer any more. I can't," she said. "Beer and my pills don't mix."

I nodded. "And speaking of your pills, let's move on to the health portion of the interview."

Suffice it to say, Bobbie Davis's mother would not pass muster as a guardian for a four-year-old, not by my standards, or anyone else's. I almost felt sorry for Bobbie, being raised by this woman and her series of husbands and live-in boyfriends. You could see she'd been pretty once, just like her daughter. But hard living ages a person. As would prison. Still, I could see why Bobbie had run wild as a kid and had ended up in jail.

It didn't begin to make up for what she'd done to my baby. But it did reinforce why a stable home was so important for a child. The last thing Lissy needed was to relive her mother's erratic childhood. My report would ensure that never happened.

The interview with Lissy's paternal uncle was cancelled before it began. It turned out that Hal Davis had a record. No felonies. But marijuana possession, a DUI, and one domestic abuse charge made him easy to dismiss as a guardian to a four-year-old. I submitted my report; the judge accepted it; and now here I stood, foster parent to a little girl who didn't want to go home with me.

Despite my confidence that adopting Lissy was the best thing that could happen to her, as I watched Linda with her, doubt gained a toehold in my head. Linda had this way with kids, loving yet firm. What she said went, and that was that. But Jim and I had never been that firm with Alyssa. There'd been no need. We'd loved her without limits, and probably spoiled her too. But she'd been such a sweetheart, so eager to please her mommy and daddy. And she'd worked so hard to stop sucking her thumb—

My throat filled with painful emotion and it took all I had to stifle a sob. I needed to stop thinking about Alyssa and start focusing on Lissy. And yet the child I really wanted was my baby. My Alyssa. Last night I'd packed Alyssa's things into boxes and shoved them up into the attic. Her teddies, her Cinderella sheets and favorite pajamas and scuffed red Buster Brown shoes. And the photographs. So many pictures of my angel baby. Even my locket, taped now under cardboard in the hot, dark attic.

It had nearly killed me, no doubt the reason I'd left that task to the very last moment. My chest had hurt from the tumult of emotions, swelled with sadness and loss and guilt for packing her away, as if she didn't exist anymore. "I love you, Alyssa." I'd whispered those four words over and over. But still I'd done it. I'd tucked the mementos of my old life away so that I could start anew with Lissy. And so there would be no questions from anyone, ever.

"Okay," Linda said, bringing me back to the moment. "Better now?"

I started to nod, until I realized she was talking to Lissy.

"Can you come too?" the child begged Linda. "Please?"

Please. Such a plaintive word when whispered around a thumb.

It was exactly what I needed to tuck Alyssa's memory back deep into my heart so that I could deal with this sad little girl.

"No, hon, I need to stay with Jeannie and Darryl. But here." She handed Lissy a package wrapped in lavender paper with a white bow. "This is for you."

Curious now, Lissy picked open the paper to discover a little camera and a photo album. "For you to start making good memories," Linda said to us both.

It was such a perfect gift. I helped Lissy take pictures of Linda and the other kids, plus one of the swing set in the back yard. Then it was time to go. Before Lissy could protest I squatted down in front of her. "I have an idea. How about after we get you settled into your new bedroom, you and I go shopping for a present for Miss Linda?"

For a moment she didn't look too taken with the idea. Then slowly the thumb pulled out of her mouth. "And one for Jeannie? And one for Darryl too?"

There it was again, that generous nature of hers. I smiled. "Of course for Jeannie and Darryl. And maybe something for you too."

A tearful Jeannie gave Lissy a long hug good-bye. Darryl glanced at her, but he was frowning and quickly turned his back to us. At thirteen, Jeannie's chances of being adopted were almost nil. And Darryl, with both learning and behavioral problems, was equally doomed. Seeing a younger child leave, if only to a more permanent foster parent, had to be hard for them. But I couldn't save every kid. As a CAJA volunteer I'd been forced to accept that sad, heartbreaking fact.

But I *could* save Lissy.

I carried her suitcase to my car, helped her into her car seat, and then with a quick wave to Linda, we left. The sooner I got

Lissy settled, the better for both of us.

When I glanced at her in the rearview mirror, however, and saw that blank hollow-eyed stare above the thumb in her mouth, doubt crept back over me. I'd gotten custody of Lissy, just like I'd planned. And now step three was underway: to adopt her and wrest her completely away from her mother. But then what?

Then what?

A rush of panic threatened suddenly to swamp me. I needed Jim! I couldn't do this without him. How had I ever thought I could? We'd been good parents—together. But apart? The truth is, so much of the joy of parenting comes from sharing it, the glances that meet and cling over your child's every new accomplishment. A multisyllabic word learned, a Velcro strap on a pink tennis shoe attached. Though brief, those glances managed to multiply the love—for the child and for each other. The real payoff to parenting is just being there for those mini-miracles and to relish them together.

But I didn't have Jim anymore. We were divorced, my parents were dead, and I'd moved back to Louisiana, shrugging off all the friends we'd once had. It was just me now, alone with my new daughter. Me and Lissy.

The panic swelled to a tsunami, staggering me with the full implication of what I was doing. Lissy was only four. My fingers tightened around the steering wheel. If I couldn't manage this first day, how would I ever manage the thousands yet to come?

That's when Lissy pulled the thumb from her mouth. "Teddy's hungry," she said in a small, tentative voice.

"Teddy?" I willed down the knot of panic swelling in my throat. "What about you? Are you hungry too?"

Silently she nodded.

Our eyes held in the mirror, a long, steady connection. She

needed me. She truly had no one else in the entire world to turn to. Just me.

Knowing that somehow restored me. I could do this. I could feed her and unpack her clothes and take her for a walk to see her new neighborhood. I could show her the playground two blocks away and take her shopping for gifts for Jeannie, Darryl, and Linda. One little event at a time; I could get through this.

I'd been a good mother to Alyssa. A loving mother. Eventually I'd learn how to be just as good a mother to Lissy.

CHAPTER TWO

MAY 10, 1996

Mom,

    Thanks for fucking nothing! You can't find me a lawyer, and you don't know where Lissy is? Your own granddaughter and you can't make a few calls to find her? And you can't show up at my trial to tell the judge what a lousy childhood I had? I'm going to jail for 10 years. 10 FUCKING YEARS!!! All because of YOU!! You're a selfish bitch and I HATE you!!!

    Bobbie

MAY 16, 1996

Dear Bobbie,

    None of this mess is my fault, so don't go blaming me! I done everything I can do to get Lissy to come live with me. Some lady already come to talk to me about her. She is in some kind of foster home right now but since I am her granny I think they will give her to me.

    Meanwhile just try to behave for once in your life.

    Your truly, Mom

OFFICE OF CHILD PROTECTIVE SERVICES
MAY 21, 1996

To who it may concern:

I am Roberta F. Davis, mother of Lissy Anne Davis. I am in prison and I won't be out until she is 14 and she needs a real mom who can be with her. So I am giving up my parent rights so that she don't have to be a foster child or live in a orphan home. I want her to have a real mom who will love her, not just a baby-sitter who only wants to get her state check. Please make sure you give her to a real good mom, not one like mine.

Respectfully,
Bobbie Davis LA C3-0092

C-BLOCK INCIDENT REPORT
5/27/96

A verbal altercation in the mess room escalated into a physical altercation in the exercise yard. Inciting participants were Leonard C2-3111 and Davis C3-0092. Three officers were able to separate the two before it became a riot. Prisoner Leonard sustained a scraped elbow. Prisoner Davis sustained a bloody nose, a black eye, and a scraped knuckle. After topical treatment in the health clinic, both prisoners were referred to Block F for solitary confinement.

DIANE

A week passed, a calm week, all things considered. Lissy seemed to be settling in and she'd already made a friend at the half-day preschool I'd enrolled her in. While she spent the mornings at school, I took care of my CAJA cases. Then we'd spend the rest of the day together.

I was trying to wrap up my old cases, and needed to inform Kate that I wouldn't be taking on any new ones. That morning I wasn't three steps into the CAJA office, however, before the hair prickled at the back of my neck. Something was wrong. Kate stood, arms hugging herself, staring out the window, so still, as if she were frozen. Kate was never still.

At the copy machine one of the clerical volunteers made copies, methodically slapping documents onto the glass plate. Lift the cover, remove the paper, lay another sheet down, close the top, and press the green button. She hunched over her work, like it was the most important task in the world. Or like she was hiding in mindless activity.

I dropped my purse on the table. "Kate?" My heart raced. "What's going on?"

The copy machine sang its mechanical tune: squeak, swish, slap, squeak; *ca-chung, ca-chung, ca-chung.* Three full cycles before Kate turned, moving like it hurt, like she was an old woman, so weary of the world's machinations.

"Bad news," she said, her dark eyes gone dull in a face gone ashen. Even her voice, her robust, gospel-singing alto, merely parodied its real self. Which taken together sent a jolt of blinding panic through me. Was this about Lissy and me? Had someone discovered my lies, my connection to Lissy ... My former life with Alyssa?

For a long, suspended moment I couldn't catch my breath,

couldn't hear anything past the freight train of blood roaring through my head—except for the sob that came from the copy machine, from the volunteer who didn't know me or Lissy, and who, my numbed-by-fear brain belatedly realized, wouldn't be crying for us.

With that solitary sob, I knew it was a different sort of black hole, into-the-abyss bad news.

"Bethany," Kate said.

One word only: Bethany. But in it I heard all the rest, the words she didn't say: every god-awful atrocity that had ever been committed against all the children who had passed through CAJA's office. Neglected, abandoned, abused. Every kind of abuse there was. But that happened *before* CAJA got involved, not so much after.

What happened to Bethany?

I didn't say the words aloud, but Kate heard me. She blinked hard, though not hard enough to hold her tears back. "That bastard of a stepfather."

Of course.

"He snatched her and ran. But she fought him. That's the only reason that poor child isn't dead! She fought—"

But he raped her. Again.

I stared at Kate, hearing the quiet weeping at the copy machine.

"He was caught," she went on. "In jail in Bogalusa. She's being transferred to Children's Hospital."

"But she'll be all right?"

Kate shuddered. "Physically." She paused. "He planned to kill her, Diane. And Bethany knows it. She's thirteen years old, a multiple rape victim—" She couldn't go on.

"And now nearly a murder statistic," I finished for her. "But how did he find her?"

"The mom. He followed her to the safe house CPS had her in."

"That stupid bitch!"

Out eyes held a long moment. "I'm so glad you're adopting Lissy," she finally said, surprising me.

I nodded, trying to compose myself. "Me too."

"What Bethany has suffered … that will never happen to Lissy, because she'll have a mother who thinks beyond her own immediate needs, someone who puts love and safety, and honesty and truth above carnality and revenge and addiction. Parenthood is about sacrifice, not selfishness!"

A resounding "amen" came from the copy machine volunteer. As for me, I managed another nod, then ducked my head.

The copy machine was the only sound in the office. Tomorrow was the bimonthly recap so there were lots of reports to be copied. Eventually Kate returned to her office. I sat down at the table with my files and began to assemble the papers pertinent to tomorrow's meeting, but I couldn't focus. Bethany wasn't one of my cases, but we were one for all and all for one in CAJA. Every child mattered to all of us, no matter how broken and difficult they were. It only made it worse that the most severely traumatized of them were the most likely to grow into traumatizers themselves. That was the whole reason CAJA existed, to interrupt that torturous progression before it was too late.

Would this latest atrocity be one too many for Bethany? Did she have any chance of becoming a truly healthy adult?

Without warning my eyes filled with tears. I wiped them away, but still they came. And came.

Who was healthy anyway? Me? Not so much. Kate was probably the healthiest person I knew, yet she'd been sexually abused as a child. Meanwhile I, with my idyllic childhood and doting parents, had become a cold, bitter person, cut off from everyone I'd ever loved. How could I possibly believe I was up to raising a child like Lissy, helping her become a positive, useful adult, when I was so not that kind of person myself?

To make matters worse, I was adopting her as an act of revenge against her mother. Kate might not know that, but I did. And I knew it was wrong.

Blindly I dug in my purse, searching for a tissue, and searching for some remnant bit of altruism in my soul. That's when someone thrust a mini-pack of tissues at me. Kate.

"Thanks." I sniffed, wiped my eyes, and blew my nose.

She cleared her throat. "When you've got it back together, I need to talk to you."

I nodded and pulled out another tissue. *If* I got it back together.

"It's about the adoption."

That got my attention. I followed her into her office and closed the door.

"First off," she began. "You can't use Lissy as a reason to quit CAJA."

Brow creased, she studied me from across her cluttered desk. "You're too good at this job, and we need you. You know how much we need you."

I grimaced. "You can say that after that awful news you just gave me about Bethany?"

"Hey. Bethany is the clearest reason we have to keep on doing what we do." She leaned forward, and that church-trained righteousness returned to her voice. "You do good work, Diane. You save kids—"

"Like Lissy. I need to focus on her now."

She sat back in her chair, her hands flat on the desk. "So you *are* planning to quit."

My mouth opened, then closed. Finally I said, "Yes. I've been thinking about it ever since I got Lissy."

She just shook her head. "You could be a part-timer, Diane. You're the one who's made CAJA a full-time gig. Look." She leaned forward again. "Just work while she's in school."

"I don't know. It's just ... I'm really nervous about the adoption proceedings."

"Nervous? Girl, why should you be nervous? If ever there was a perfect candidate for adopting a child, it's you."

"That's what you say. But you're not the one making the decision. I wish you were."

"Come on, Diane. All mothers work nowadays. CPS knows that. And they don't expect married couples anymore."

"I know." *But they do expect honesty.*

The foster parent review had been harrowing, and the adoptions review was no different. I knew that on the surface I was a good candidate. But my lies hung over me like a guillotine blade, just waiting to fall and sever Lissy from me forever. All anyone had to do was run a really thorough background check on me. The Diane Haines who grew up in Louisiana and lived there still was not the problem. She'd graduated from a New Orleans high school with honors, gone to college, and after working out of state for a while she'd returned to tend her ailing parents. After their deaths she'd decided to volunteer with CAJA. But if someone got nosy and poked around in Florida state records they would find a marriage between Diane Haines and James Leftwich. Then if they followed her by her married name to Gulfport, Mississippi, they'd discover all those newspaper articles about the accident. And if they connected Roberta

Fenner, teenaged child-killer in Mississippi, to Bobbie Davis, neglectful mother of Lissy Davis in Louisiana ...

But as long as they stuck to Louisiana records, I was simply Diane Haines, a single woman with good credit who did a lot of volunteer work. I reassured myself that no one would probably dig too deep, thanks to CAJA and the criminal check I'd undergone when I'd signed up for that. Plus none of my acquaintances knew much about me beyond me the simple facts that I was single and my parents were deceased. I owned a five-plex in New Orleans that I'd inherited from my mother's side. A real estate management company took care of it, and I lived simply off the rents. That's why I could give so much time to CAJA.

But now that time would go to Lissy—Lisa once the adoption was final. Lissy Davis would become Lisa Haines and we would leave Louisiana. I'd thought about it a lot, how I was going to raise Lissy, and how despite her pitiful family tree she was going to grow up into a perfectly lovely young lady. I would teach her proper manners, make sure she excelled at school, and shape her into a smart, productive, well-educated woman, something her birth mother never could have done. She would never be Alyssa, but she could be the next best thing.

"Look," Kate said. "I'm sure we can work this out. Tell me about your current cases."

I sighed. She wasn't giving up without a fight. "Okay. Let's see. The court portion of the Telford case should be over by the time the adoption proceedings are finalized. That leaves me only two other cases, and since I just received the LeBlanc case, I was hoping you could hand it off to one of the new CAJA's."

Her eyes narrowed. "So you could stay on the other case?"

I could. I *should*. Finally I nodded. "Yeah. I could stay on it."

She laughed. "Hallelujah! Thank you, Jesus."

"But just because I'm following through on that case it doesn't mean a lifelong commitment."

"I know, honey. I know. Your lifelong commitment now is to that lucky little girl you're adopting." She gave me a sly look as she pushed up from her chair. "You know you'll be getting a superlative reference from this office, don't you? No matter how many cases you have open with us."

I shot her a grateful smile. She was such a big-hearted person, so truly good. "Thank you, Kate. That means so much to me. It could be the difference between me getting to adopt Lissy or just staying her foster mom."

"Don't you worry. This adoption's gonna go through. I know it." She rounded her desk and gave me a hard hug. "You two were made for each other."

Yes, we were. Even more so than Kate knew. Despite all my lies—both of commission and omission—I could see the hand of fate in this. Or maybe the Rebel Jesus. He was meting out justice in His own way. So far as I could tell, everyone came out a winner. Except for Bobbie.

And Alyssa.

I pushed that perilous thought away before it could swamp me with emotions. "Look," I said to Kate. "I just came in to bring my reports for tomorrow's meeting, then I have to run. Lissy's being evaluated by one of the state's psychologists as we speak, and I have to be back there by eleven. But I'll see you tomorrow."

"Great." Kate looked at me over her reading glasses. "You're never actually in the office that much anyway."

"Kate," I said in a warning tone. "I mean it. Just one case at a time now. Until she's really settled and going to school, I'm putting all my energy into Lissy. All of it."

I meant it too. I sat at one end of the conference table and made my phone calls. I scheduled two home visits, verified a court appearance, and copied several pertinent documents from files on Penelope Telford—thirteen, abused by two stepfathers, now removed from her mother's custody, just like poor Bethany—and Scott LeBlanc, a ten-year-old who refused to live with his mother and her series of lousy boyfriends. He kept running away, trying to find his father who, unfortunately, wasn't interested in raising his desperately needy son.

It was enough to depress a saint, and I was no saint. But my child was dead; these were alive. I could never set aside that fact. I know that makes me sound cold, unfeeling even. But it's just the opposite. Having lost a child of my own is what made me a first-rate CAJA. It helped me keep perspective. Because as bad as some of these individual cases were, at least these kids had a chance.

By eleven I sat in the waiting room outside Dr. Meg Cordell's office, thumbing through a copy of *Parent* magazine. I wasn't actually reading any of the articles. Just holding that particular magazine in my lap was a major accomplishment. I hadn't returned to my ob-gyn's office since Alyssa's death, because every table in her waiting room held copies of *Parent* or *Child* or *Family Life*. Like sly tormentors they lay there, entertaining and informing the other patients. But for me they rose up flaunting their pages of happy children and whole families like cobras spreading their hoods, threatening and dangerous, taunting me with my loss. So I'd quit going for my annual gynecological exam.

Yet here I sat in a cheerful cream-and-aqua child psychologist's office reading a parenting magazine. My hands didn't even tremble. Was this what was meant by moving on?

I closed the magazine—and closed my eyes. I didn't want to move on. I didn't want to forget Alyssa and how much I loved her and missed her. And yet, look at me. *Parent* magazine wasn't setting off an anxiety attack.

"Ms. Haines?"

My eyes snapped open and I tossed the poisonous magazine aside.

"You can go to the play corner now," Dr. Cordell told Lissy. "While I talk to your mom."

Lissy stared at me, and then stuck her thumb in her mouth. Always the thumb, reminding me that if not for my adamant need to have my daughter *not* suck her thumb, Alyssa might still be alive.

Bracing myself against the never-absent weight of my guilt, I turned away from Lissy and followed the doctor into her office. Once there she folded her hands on her desk and smiled. Neither of us spoke, and I had the unnerving sense she was reading my mind. That she *knew* what I was hiding. So I started humming "The Star-Spangled Banner" silently in my head to block my thoughts.

Dr. Cordell straightened in her chair. "Okay," she said as if she really had run into the roadblock in my mind. "Let's talk about Lissy and you." She patted a file on her desk. "Lissy is a bright child with no discernible learning problems. She can count to twenty and say the alphabet—normal for her age. Socially she's somewhat immature, not comfortable with either children or adults. That's not unexpected, given her history. With time, consistent guidance, and abundant affection, however, she should thrive."

But. She didn't say the word, but I heard it. *But.*

"But I'm concerned," she went on, "that you don't seem to

offer her a lot of affection."

"She seems uncomfortable with it." I shifted on the chair, suddenly feeling on the defensive. "Since we don't know exactly what her life was like, I hesitate to push myself on her too fast."

"Yes, I understand. But a smile, a pat on the shoulder. Little things like that are hardly pushing yourself on her, Diane. She needs to know you care for her, that you love her whether or not she's ready to return that emotion. Because eventually she will return it."

"Okay." I nodded earnestly, desperate for her to believe I could be the mother Lissy needed. Because I *did* want to be that mother. I wanted to be the best, most protective mother ever, and raise a happy, successful child. "I'll work on that. It's just that her home life was so messed up, and we don't know for sure if she was abused or just neglected."

"Actually, we're getting a better take on that. I've been in contact with Lissy's mother."

"Lissy's mother?" My heart lurched into overdrive, into a break-my-chest-wide-open thunder. She'd spoken to that drunken, child-murdering teenager turned child-neglecting junkie? Why? *Why?*

Then a solitary shaft of clarity pierced the furious panic that threatened to undo me. *Unclench your fists. Put on your CAJA face. Be the detached professional.*

Somehow I released my tautly held breath and sucked in a calmer one. "I – I wouldn't put much stock into anything Lissy's mother says. She's hardly likely to paint herself as a neglectful parent."

"I'm aware of that. But whatever she's done in the past, Lissy's mother now seems intent on making sure her daughter has the best life possible."

My fists tightened once more. Was she actually on Bobbie's side? "Lissy's so-called mother should have thought of that before she got arrested, before she put her child in this situation."

"True," Dr. Cordell conceded. "But considering her dire circumstances—ten years is a long time for a twenty-three-year-old to go to jail—she's thinking about what's best for Lissy."

I jutted out my chin, then caught myself before I said something I shouldn't. "Sorry," I muttered. "I'm probably overreacting, but I've see too many kids suffer at the hands of their parents to feel anything but contempt for those parents. Lissy deserves better."

"Yes. And I'm sure you'll provide that. But you need to know that Lissy's mother wrote a letter to Child Protective Services asking that Lissy *not* be entrusted to her mother or Lissy's uncle, or any other family member."

I shrugged. "So?" Denying those two was a no-brainer. "Besides," I went on, "she probably didn't do it for Lissy's benefit. It could just be her way of striking back at her own mother by denying her any money the state would offer to her for caring for Lissy."

"Perhaps. But I'm not so sure. Would you like to see her letter?"

I took the paper she handed me, a faxed copy of a hand-printed letter in a not very sophisticated handwriting.

To who it may concern,
    I am Roberta F. Davis, mother of Lissy Anne Davis. I am in prison and I won't be out until she is 14 and ...

I read in silence, willing myself to breathe in and out, to calm down and not reveal so much emotion. Afterward I read it again.

"She's giving up her parental rights," Dr. Cordell said. "She's removed the last obstacle to completing the adoption."

"That's ... good," I said, a smile forced onto my face. Inside though, a part of me seethed.

It was a stupid reaction. I should have been elated that I was getting what I wanted. But the truth is, I didn't want Bobbie to agree to this. I wanted her to *oppose* the adoption, to fight it tooth and nail even. Because I knew she'd fail. The courts would rule in the best interest of the child, and the best interest of Lissy was to not float for ten years in foster care, not when a responsible adult was willing to adopt her. The only question mark in this whole deal was whether my connection to Lissy's mother would be discovered, and with every passing day, every favorable report, that fear was slowly easing.

But my need to have Bobbie suffer was not passing. I wasn't adopting Lissy out of vengeance. My beef was not with a neglected little girl. In fact, I had come to adore the child. She was thawing something inside me I thought never could be unfrozen again. But that didn't change my feelings toward the woman who'd so casually killed Alyssa. In my head they were two vastly different issues. I wanted to protect Lissy. But I also needed to punish Bobbie. And that need perversely continued to grow. With every milestone I couldn't celebrate with my child—shopping for her first bra, consoling her through her first heartbreak—just seeing her smile every morning across the breakfast table ... Alyssa would be almost twelve by now, nearly a teenager. How could my need for vengeance on Bobbie Davis ever do anything but grow?

I handed the letter back to Dr. Cordell. "That's good," I repeated, my voice carefully blank.

"Yes," she agreed, sliding the letter back into Lissy's file. Then once more she folded her hands and studied me with her disturbingly astute gaze. "So. All the obstacles are settled. The final piece of this puzzle is you."

My heart stuttered to a stop. "You have doubts about my suitability?"

"Not doubts," she answered. "Concerns."

"Because I can't do a victory dance and shout hurray when some lousy parent finally expresses real concern for her child?" I tried hard to hide any hint of animosity. Or fear.

"It's not that. Given the work you do, your cynicism is totally understandable."

"Oh. Well. Is it the touchy-feely thing? You think I'm not warm and loving enough?"

"I'm not saying you're not a warm, loving person, Diane. But motherhood doesn't always come naturally. Lissy's not a helpless infant; she's a troubled four-year-old."

"Yes, and I deal with children like her all the time." That's what I said. But inside my head I was jumping up and down in anger. *Motherhood does come naturally to me. It does!*

She smiled. "I know about your work with CAJA. The reports about you are consistently glowing. But the traits that make you a great CAJA aren't necessarily the same traits that will make you a great mother."

"What do you mean?" I leaned forward, needing her to approve of me, to know what a good mother I could be. "I love children. How can you doubt that?"

"I don't doubt it. You love children, otherwise you wouldn't do the work you do. But once those children are situated and your involvement in their lives ends, how do you feel?"

I sat back in my chair, stifling a shudder. "I never forget them. Never. And I never stop wondering about them. Worrying about them. Loving them."

"I can see that. But that kind of love, a love that knows it has to eventually detach from a child, it's different from the kind of love a parent feels for her child, whether her child is natural born or adopted." She stared at me, but kindly. "I sense that you're holding back on Lissy, not giving fully of yourself just yet. It's probably a holdover from the detachment you need to be a good CAJA, and we'll work on that. But I believe you'll get there." Then she smiled. "I know you will."

In the midst of fighting my need to defend myself, I suddenly stopped. Was she saying that she was giving me the final stamp of approval? That, despite her qualms, she was approving the adoption? I stared at her. Her smile said yes, and for once when I smiled at her it was sincerely, full of relief and joy. I thanked her and listened to her final instructions—about her continuing to see Lissy and me for the first six months, and longer if needed.

But all along a small part of me wondered if she was right. Could I ever love Lissy as much as I'd loved Alyssa? Did I even want to? Or had my ability to love without restraint died in that car along with my baby? Had it died when my marriage died, and my mother died? And had I kept it dead by only dealing with children I could never fully love?

I knew I would be good to Lissy, do all the things good parents do. And I thought I loved her. But did I *fully* love her? And if I couldn't, if it was only a partial kind of love, would Lissy feel the lack? Would she believe that her terrible first mother, for whom she'd probably been an accident, had loved her better than her second mother? After all, even though I meant to do whatever it took to raise her into a healthy, happy young woman, I would always hate her mother. Always. Would that hatred cast a shadow over the love I felt for Lissy? Could she grow up to be healthy and happy with that pall over us? The truth was, I wasn't entirely healthy or happy myself, so how could I expect her ever to be?

On the other hand, even though what I was doing was legally wrong, it was still a hell of a lot better than leaving Lissy adrift in the foster care system.

Hating the tug-of-war in my head, I pressed my fingertips against my temples.

"I'll fax my report in this afternoon," Dr. Cordell went on. "You should hear from them within two weeks or so. And then ... " She smiled at me. "Then you and Lissy can officially start your lives together as mother and daughter."

My hands froze at my temples. *Mother and daughter.*

I don't know why those words made me cry. I hadn't cried in so long, neither for sorrow or happiness. Not even when I packed away all my mementos of Alyssa. I'd held it all in. But these tears were different, neither for sorrow or happiness. I took the tissue the doctor offered and sobbed into it, a confusing storm of relief and fear and all the other mixed-up emotions I'd felt since I'd first discovered Lissy.

It had taken almost eight months to go from CAJA to foster mother to adoptive mother. Not such a long time. But it felt like forever, getting to this moment. Now that I was actually here, I realized how momentous it was. I was turning a corner in my life. *Another* corner. I'd been a mother for six years, if you counted those wonderful months of anticipation during my pregnancy. Then for the past seven years I'd been childless.

But I was childless no more.

I left the doctor's office and went into the waiting room. Lissy had a rag doll on her lap and was pretending to read her a story. She looked up at my entrance and started to put her thumb in her mouth. But she stopped and her little brow creased with worry.

"Are you sad?" she asked.

I guess my tears were more evident than I thought. Wordless, I just nodded.

She studied me a long time. "Sometimes I'm sad too." She paused. Then she added, "Do you miss your mommy?"

I couldn't help it; I started to cry again. I *did* miss my mother. Almost as much as I missed Alyssa.

That's when Lissy got up, crossed over to me, and hugged me around the waist. "It's okay to cry," she said against my khaki slacks. "I miss my mommy too. Dr. Cordell said it's okay to cry if I want to. So it's okay for you too."

Overwhelmed by her sweetly innocent gesture, I dropped to my knees and pulled her into my arms. She wasn't Alyssa. She would never be my Alyssa. But she was a wonderful little girl and I adored her. And best of all, she was all mine.

CHAPTER THREE

BLOCK-C INCIDENT REPORT
9/12/96

Prisoner Davis C 3-0092 has been admitted to the health clinic with a knife wound to her left forearm. Fourteen stitches were administered. Davis and Prisoner Leonard C2-3111 have a well-documented, ongoing feud, however Davis refused to implicate Leonard in this attack which apparently occurred in the kitchen. As a precaution both prisoners have been placed in Block F solitary and will be reassigned to different jobs.

OFFICE OF CHILD PROTECTIVE SERVICES
OCTOBER 10, 1996

To Who it May Concern:
    The only reason I have not signed the final papers so Lissy can be adopted is because I don't want my mom or Ken's brother Hal Davis to adopt her. I'm not trying to mess things up or change my mind. I just need some paper that's legal and everything that says she CAN'T be adopted by them. Because they don't really want her. They just want

that monthly check. Plus, my mom was NOT a good mother to me or to her first two kids who was taken away from her even before I was born. And Hal is just a sick pervert. So as soon as you give me a paper that says they CANNOT adopt her, then I will sign everything.

    Respectfully,
    Bobbie Davis
    LA C3-0092

DIANE

That day was a turning point for me, and for Lissy too, as if my tears had turned a key in the lock on her emotions. It might have been Dr. Cordell. Maybe she and Lissy had made some special headway. But I knew it had more to do with my honest emotions. Up to now I'd kept everything contained, just like Dr. Cordell said. Not just my lie, but the rest of my feelings too, the good as well as the bad. And that's what I'd gotten back from Lissy: contained emotions.

But today she laughed like a four-year-old is supposed to laugh. And when she fell in the McDonald's play spot and scraped the heel of her hand, she ran to me crying. I hugged her and rocked her in my arms, and kissed her boo-boo and made it all better. I was better too. I was a mom again. My reason for being had been restored, and the whole world gleamed sharper, warmer, golden.

After she ran back to play with a little boy on the jungle gym, I cried again, but not such a huge, weeping flood. I just sat there dabbing at the slow leak of tears that I couldn't seem to stop.

Lissy fell asleep in the car seat on the way home, and I carried her to bed. Shoes off, teddy tucked beside her, and a crocheted afghan draped over her.

That became a pattern for us: McDonald's for lunch, playtime, and then a nap. We both gained weight. French fries will do that to you. She needed the extra pounds; I could have done without them. But what I couldn't do without was watching Lissy bloom. That's the only way to describe it. She was still a cautious child, wary of new people and situations. But given time and encouragement she warmed up to them. And as she bloomed so, it seemed, did I.

On Halloween she wanted to be a fairy princess, complete

with wings, a tiara, and a star-topped wand. By then it had become a habit, me denying her nothing. Trick-or-treating with her running ahead, then retreating to grasp my hand and lean on me for reassurance, was wonderful. Bittersweet, to be sure. But I let myself relax and enjoy it all. To enjoy her.

That's why she bounced around the house that night on a sugar high, and woke up the next morning with a stomachache. I gave her Pepto-Bismol and crackers, but nothing helped. So no nursery school for her. Which presented me with a dilemma. It was All Saints' Day, the traditional day in Catholic New Orleans to visit the graves of our loved ones. I'd planned to visit the family tomb where Alyssa and my parents were buried while Lissy was in school, only I couldn't go now, and it felt so wrong, like a betrayal of a sacred trust.

While Lissy napped, I pulled out a photo album of Alyssa and me. It was the only memento of her I'd allowed myself to keep in the house, in the bottom of a box on the top shelf of my closet. Her birthday, the anniversary of her death, and All Saints' Day were sacrosanct, days I always visited her grave. I went other times too. But those three were necessary parts of my mourning ritual. I had to go. I *had* to, especially this first year after I'd brought Lissy into my life. What would Alyssa think if I abandoned those rituals now? That I loved Lissy more? That she'd taken over the spot in my heart that Alyssa had always owned?

I traced the outline of her face, the line of her arm hooked so casually around my neck. I'd already put everything else I had of her into storage. Too many questions to answer if Lissy discovered them. Now I was abandoning her grave site?

No. I slid the picture back into its slot. I had to go to the cemetery. I'd just have to take Lissy with me. I wouldn't mention Alyssa though. Lissy knew my mother and father were in heaven, but since she couldn't read, she wouldn't understand the third name or the dates.

By two-thirty Lissy felt better. I was a nervous wreck. I always visited the grave alone. This spring on Alyssa's birthday I'd almost run into Jim. He must have driven in from the Mississippi Gulf Coast, and was standing at the tomb when I turned into the cemetery. Fortunately his back had been to me. I don't know why I say "fortunately". All I know is that I didn't want to see him. He was the only person in the world who shared in the total devastation of Alyssa's death. But even he hadn't truly understood. If he had, he never would have abandoned me when I so obviously still needed him. So I'd ducked back into my car and waited until he left before reentering the cemetery.

But Jim wasn't Catholic, so he wouldn't be here on All Saints' Day. Lissy would though, and it filled me with a nauseating confusion. I grabbed my purse anyway, herded her to the car, and buckled her in. But the whole time guilt pressed down on me. Guilt. My ever-present companion. Usually it only raised its brooding face when I enjoyed Lissy too much, or hugged her too long. I worried that Alyssa wouldn't understand. But today was worse. Would Alyssa feel that I was betraying her by bringing Lissy with me? Would my mother approve of what I'd done to make Lissy my own? My father had died before Alyssa was born. But after the accident when I finally left the hospital and visited her at the family tomb, I'd prayed to him, entrusting her to his care. Would he approve of my deception now? Would any of them understand—or forgive—my growing attachment to this new child? Roberta Fenner's child?

Lissy was quiet until we turned into the cemetery. "Look. There's Jesus," she said, pointing to a statue of Jesus and the children on a pedestal in the middle of a round reflecting pond.

Jesus. As soon as she said his name I felt better. The Rebel Jesus would approve of me having Lissy. That meant Alyssa and my parents would too.

I smiled at Lissy as I unbuckled her car seat. "That's right. That's Jesus. You know about him?" I'd never brought him up or taken her to church, so anything she knew about him had to come from her former life. Or more likely, nursery school. I didn't picture Bobbie telling her about Jesus.

"He takes care of dead people," she said as we got out of the car. "I came to see him before."

"Here?" I blurted out. "You came here before?"

Her eyes got big at my sharp tone, and she flinched away from me. Then she stuck her thumb in her mouth.

I could have kicked myself. I crouched in front of her and forced a smile. "I'm sorry, honey. I sounded mad just now, didn't I? But I'm not mad, especially not at you. It's just that ... it makes me sad to come here."

She nodded. "You miss your mommy," she said past her thumb.

I nodded back. "Yes. I do. And my daddy."

She pulled her thumb out and stared at me with her serious hazel eyes. "You can cry if you want to. My mommy always cried when we came here."

As if she'd slapped me, I reared back, nearly toppling over in the process. She'd come here with her mother? But why? Surely not to visit Alyssa's grave. A wave of nausea surged up my throat, and I fought the urge to retch. Once more Lissy's eyes got huge, and the thumb went back in her mouth.

I shouldn't have brought her here. I should have waited and come another day. Because I didn't want to know that the woman who killed my child came here. She had no right to defile Alyssa's grave that way. No right at all!

At the same time, though, some sick part of me wanted to know more. I never asked Lissy about her mother or her previous life. As much as I wanted to know every sordid detail, I wanted even more for Lissy to forget every moment of her first few years. If Bobbie ever did find her, twenty, thirty, even fifty years from now, I didn't want Lissy to remember *anything* about her birth mother. It would be my last jab at the woman, and I would relish it even from my grave.

I suspected that Dr. Cordell had talked to Lissy about her previous life. But those conversations would end soon enough. After that I would make sure any memories of her birth mother faded forever from Lissy's mind.

But today the urge to know more about Lissy's mother was too strong. I took Lissy's hand, and started down the gravel path. "Did you come here a lot with your ... " I almost choked on the words, "With your first mommy?"

"I don't know," she answered in a hesitant voice.

I stopped and turned. Then I pulled her into a hug. "It's okay, Lissy. I'm glad you came here before. It's very pretty, isn't it?"

"Uh-huh. Like a park," she said. "There are rabbits."

"There are? Wow. I've never seen any rabbits here. You must have very good eyes."

"Not real ones." She grinned. "Pretend ones. Standing by the door."

"Oh. You mean statues of rabbits?"

She nodded. "You want to see them?"

"You know where they are?"

"Uh-huh." But she looked uncertain as she glanced around the grounds. "That way. No. Over there."

Maybe Lissy and her mother hadn't been to Alyssa's tomb. Maybe a relative of theirs was buried here. Her father had died two years ago.

Holding my hand, she led me down a path that paralleled the path to my family tomb. "Are you sure of the way?" I asked as she paused and looked around.

Then she pulled free of my hand. "There they are!" She sprinted down the gravel walk, her sand-blond hair streaming behind her.

That's when this massive attack of déjà vu struck me dumb. It froze me mid-stride and set my heart thundering. Alyssa had only come with me once to this cemetery, to visit my father's grave on the fifth anniversary of his death. It had been a beautiful balmy day, and she'd run up and down the paths, just like Lissy was doing.

"Slow down," I tried to say now. But it came out cracked and low. Somehow I pushed myself forward. She was Lissy, not Alyssa. Yet today they seemed to blur into one child, one moment that crossed the gap of eight years and made them the same.

Then she turned to me with a smile—Lissy's smile, not Alyssa's—and I jerked back to the present. Thank God.

"See! I told you. Three rabbits." She grinned up at me, her eyes sparkling green in the autumn light. "Flopsy, Mopsy, and Peter. That's the names me and Mommy gave them."

"You are so smart," I said despite my lingering shakiness. I watched her go from one concrete rabbit to the next, petting their ears and repeating their names.

"Flopsy, Mopsy, and Peter Cotton-tail." She looked up at me. "They're in a book, you know."

"Yes. I know." So she *had* been to this cemetery.

"Mommy used to read it to me." She hesitated and then went on. "I like Peter the best."

"You do? How come?"

"Well, 'cause he's the most fun. And he's very, very brave."

"Yes. But sometimes he's bad. He doesn't always listen to his mother."

She shifted her teddy from her left arm to her right. "Yes. But sometimes mommies are bad too."

What? I squatted down and stared into her now serious eyes. "Oh, really? Who told you that?"

She tucked her chin down and averted her face. "I don't know."

"It's okay, baby. You can tell me. I need to know because ... because I'll never do anything bad. I'll only do good things for you. And I'll always protect you," I added fiercely. "From everything. So tell me," I went on. "Who told you that mommies sometimes do bad things? Dr. Cordell?"

I waited, and after a few moments she peered cautiously up at me. "Mommy told me. On the phone, after the police took her to the jail."

"I see." Given her track record of doing "bad things", how else could Bobbie explain to her little girl what was happening? "You don't have to worry, Lissy." I told her. "That will never happen to me. I promise."

She didn't look entirely convinced. I knew, though, that only time could prove me right. Only time would allow her to trust that I would not disappear on her like her own mother had. "Come on," I said. "Let's walk around and see if there are any other rabbits for Flopsy, Mopsy, and Peter Cotton-tail to play with."

She grinned at that. "There aren't any other rabbits, Diane." I hadn't asked her to call me Mom, and she hadn't seemed inclined to do it on her own.

"Are you sure?"

"Uh-huh. But we can go see the lily girl."

"The lily girl?" I should have known. I should have known that irises are often mistaken for lilies. But as Lissy tugged me around the back of the tomb with the rabbits and guided me through the narrow passage between two other three-tiered, whitewashed tombs, I didn't make the connection. Not until we came around the corner and I was abruptly face-to-face with my own family tomb with its granite panels etched with irises.

The lily girl. Alyssa.

Every visit to my daughter's final resting place had been devastating. But this time, with Lissy's warm baby hand gripping mine even as the cold etched letters of Alyssa's name confronted me, I completely shut down. The world tilted sideways—granite tombs, dark moss-laden oaks, the crushed-shell paths. I couldn't breathe. I couldn't think or talk or even stand up. My legs crumpled and I fell hard to my knees.

Alyssa. My baby that no other child could ever replace.

Oh, God! How could you be so cruel?

On all fours I reached toward the tomb, toward that awful date. August 16, 1989.

Then I heard crying. A child's crying.

When I'd collapsed I'd knocked Lissy over.

It took every bit of willpower I had to turn my back on Alyssa and reach out to Lissy. Lissy, not Alyssa.

I'm not too clear on how I got through the next few minutes. How we got out of the cemetery. How I got us home. What I most remember is that the minute we reached the apartment I ran to the bathroom and threw up. Not just my lunch and my breakfast. I threw up everything down to the last dregs of bile and stomach acids. My stomach rebelled for all the parts of me that had held it in so well. I puked until I was too weak to stand

and had to kneel over the toilet, my arms shaking and my face feverish with tears.

Beyond the door I could hear Lissy's terrified sobbing. I'd just promised her I wouldn't disappear, yet here I was, sounding like I was dying.

Somehow I dragged myself to the bathtub and turned on the water. I washed my face and rinsed my mouth. "I'm all right, Lissy," I croaked the words out. "I'm all right." But she wasn't. I struggled to my feet. Then clutching the doorknob for support, I pulled open the bathroom door.

Lissy lay curled on her side right outside the door, sobbing in absolute terror. "Baby. Baby, it's okay." I scooped her up, then slid down the wall, holding her trembling body tight against mine. "Don't be scared, Lissy. Everything's okay."

If she could have burrowed beneath my skin I think she would have. Her skinny arms clung to my neck and she wrapped her legs around my waist. We sat like that, my arms pressing her to me as we both rocked and cried.

"Mommy … " I heard her muffled cry into the front of my blouse and I tried not to let my heart break. Of course she would cry for her mother. She was just a baby. It hurt, though, to hold this terrified little girl while she cried for her mother.

But wasn't that what I was doing? Crying for my real child? Wanting the one I couldn't have more than I wanted the one in my arms right now?

"Mommy," I heard her say again. Then she raised her tear-streaked face and stared up at me through wet, spiky lashes. "Are you my mommy now?" A sob caught in her throat. "Really, really my mommy?"

I nodded because I couldn't speak. Yes, I wanted to say. Yes, I really am.

I felt her shudder of relief. Then she buried her head back in my chest. "Can I call you Mommy now?"

Her words were indistinct, barely a whisper. But I heard her loud and clear. *Can I call you Mommy?*

"I'm your mommy now," I said once I found my voice. I kissed the top of her head and breathed in her warm scent, baby shampoo, Play-Doh, and sweaty little girl. A sudden surge of gratitude rushed through me, gratitude for her warm weight against me, for her presence in my lonely life. For her need to be comforted by me. Me.

"Oh, Lissy. My sweet, sweet Lissy. I'm your mommy now, and you're my little girl. For always."

CHAPTER FOUR

G.E.D. APPLICATION
3/21/1997

Name/# Bobbie Davis LA C3-0092
Educational History: completed 10th grade, Slidell H.S. 2.1 GPA; Some GED classes in Mississippi Juvenile Facility

MARCH 29, 1997
ST. ANNA'S WOMEN'S PRISON

Dear Lissy,

    Even though the adoption people told me I can't write to you, I decided to do it anyhow. I kind of like it because it helps me to think about how you are growing up and changing while I'm in here. I try to picture in my head what you must look like now. Like if your hair has got long or if your new mom cut it cute and short. You would look pretty both ways. You are almost five. Such a big girl. I hope you will like big school and learn alot. I am going to start going to school too. It's something to do and it makes the warden happy to see that you are trying to improve yourself. That's there favorite thing to talk about, how we can improve ourselves.

Like being in jail is an improvment over anything!

Anyway, if I get my GED, then I might study how to be a nurse or a secertary or a chef. I haven't decided yet.

It's very boring in here. After you finish your work, you can watch TV if you haven't got in any trouble. But there's always trouble. I become a real good fighter. Real good. When I get out I might learn karate or Kung Fu or something like that.

I hope your new mom gives you martial arts lessons. It's good for a woman to be strong so nobody can take advantage of you.

Your birthday is coming and at 9:14 in the morning I will sing Happy Birthday to You because that is exactly the time that you were born. I hope you will think of me at 9:14 too. But I know you probly won't.

Love, Your Mom
(Bobbie Davis LA C3-0092)

DIANE

We stayed in New Orleans for six more months. Although I lived in daily fear of Dr. Cordell uncovering my lies and reporting me to Child Protective Services, a part of me regretted ending our sessions with her. She was so good for Lissy. Plus, she made me more aware of myself as a mother—what I did right and what I did wrong. Our talks centered around my relationship with Lissy, but so many of the issues resonated with my past experiences mothering Alyssa.

Some things I knew already—like not pressuring Lissy to quit sucking her thumb. But other lapses in judgment I could only now see: letting Alyssa sleep with Jim and me; arguing with him about parenting issues in front of her; always jumping in so that she never had to deal with frustration or disappointment.

"She's learning coping skills," Dr. Cordell explained when I worried about Lissy's moody times, her obsessive thumb-sucking sessions, and her shyness. "She's learning self-soothing and how to take care of herself."

I knew that from CAJA, and it made sense for kids who didn't have any other choice. But I didn't want my child to *have* to self-soothe or take care of herself. That was my job, and I wanted to do it. After all, she was barely five, the same age as Alyssa when she died.

Only I couldn't bring that up. I couldn't argue that a parent could never be too careful, too diligent, too observant when it came to the safety of her child. You could do all the right stuff and yet still, in an instant, disaster could claim your life. *Her* life.

So I didn't argue with Dr. Cordell. I buried my feelings, swallowed my opinions, and guarded every word so that I wouldn't accidentally reveal that, yes, I'd once had a child, and yes, I knew Lissy's mother, much better than I ever wanted to. I couldn't risk giving myself away. Because I refused to let anyone take Lissy away from me. I'd lost one child. I would not lose this one.

If Dr. Cordell sensed my emotional restraint she seldom pushed too hard or probed too deep. When she did, I always steered the conversation back to Lissy, and for the most part she let me get away with it. Until our final mandated session.

I'd been considering continuing on with our sessions— or should I say, Lissy's sessions. They'd done her a world of good, and I had no real reason to end them. But that particular morning I'd received a shock. It shouldn't have surprised me, that brief notice on the wedding announcements page. Jim was a man who needed to be married, who needed a woman to take care of, both financially and emotionally. That's what had finally driven us apart. I couldn't accept the comfort he offered me when he started to heal. I resented him healing, and I resented him expecting me to do the same.

Now he'd found someone else to accept what he had to offer. Krista Elizabeth Carter. Lucky girl. She was getting a really good man. Not that I wanted him back. We'd had a good marriage, a good family life. But that had ended, and we could never get it back. Overcome with emotions too confusing to sort out, I'd touched the small, grainy photo of him and his new wife, wished him well, and made myself turn the page to read *Garfield* and *The Far Side*.

But now with Dr. Cordell doing her gentle but relentless probing, I felt shaky and vulnerable all over again. I shifted in the leather armchair, struggling against the urge to tell her about Jim and Alyssa—how Lissy's mother had wrecked everything, but that I was making things right. As right as I could.

And yet I knew I couldn't take that chance no matter how painful my need to tell someone. Anyone.

"Lissy told me she loves you," Dr. Cordell said with a smile. "Has she said that to you?"

"No. But she calls me Mommy all the time now."

"How do you feel about that?"

I smiled, all caution melting away. "I love it when she calls me Mommy." It was true. That simple little word in her sweet little voice, always shocked me with its power. It inflated my heart—my whole self—with an almost giddy sense of well-being. How empty my life had been before Lissy filled it once again with life and laughter. And love.

"Does she ever bring up her birth mother?"

My smile faded. "No."

She studied me a long, nerve-wracking moment. "Do you bring her up?"

I worked hard to keep my hands relaxed and to not cross and recross my legs. "We've been over this before. You think I should keep her birth mother alive for Lissy. I disagree."

She gave me a wry grin. "I figured it was worth one last effort. So, what now? Will I be seeing you and Lissy any further?"

"Of course." I knew it was a lie even as I made another appointment on my way out. Things were changing again. Jim was getting married, and I had this compulsive urge to tell Dr. Cordell the whole truth. Jim had moved on; it was time for me to do the same.

Computers are great. Within an hour I found an apartment in Jackson, Mississippi, one in a good school district, since Lissy was starting kindergarten in September. The following Wednesday I turned in my last CAJA file.

"What do you mean, moving?" Kate asked. "Like, out of town?"

"Out of state."

"But why? You and Lissy have finally settled in, and now you're moving?"

"I got this great job." It was scary how adept I'd become at lying. I stared at her without flinching. "Managing my uncle's dental office."

"Oh, lord. Are we going to miss you." She planted her fists on her hips. "I was hoping you'd take over a bigger load once Lissy started school."

"I warned you, Kate. I told you I wasn't staying for long. But I am going to miss you. All of you."

It was true. CAJA and the people I'd worked with were the only reason I hadn't lost my mind. They'd given me a place to go and something to do. Something positive. So, yes, I would miss CAJA terribly. Especially Kate.

"Well." She let out a heavy sigh. "It's probably for the best. Being around family will be good for you both. I didn't realize you had an uncle in—Where did you say you're going?"

"Birmingham," I lied again. But I couldn't very well say, "Someplace were Lissy's birth mom will never look for us."

"Birmingham. That's not so far. Let's keep in touch, okay? I go through there all the time on my way to see my dad in Atlanta. Maybe I can stop to visit."

"That would be great," I said as I gave her a final hug goodbye. But it was never going to happen.

By Friday what little we were taking was packed. I'd ordered a bedroom set from Sears to be delivered to our new place on Monday. I had the trunk packed with kitchen and bathroom stuff, and the backseat packed with clothes, toys, and Lissy's car seat. The front seat held three big plastic containers of papers I didn't want to part with. And my few photos of Alyssa.

"I never went on a vacation before," Lissy said.

"You'll like it," I told her as I helped her into her seat. "There's a swimming pool and a park to ride your bike in."

"I don't have a bike, silly."

She laughed when I tickled her tummy. "But maybe you're going to get one, silly," I said in reply. "What color do you want?"

I expected her to say pink or purple. She was such a girly girl. But she surprised me.

"Maybe ... a green one."

"Green? Why green?"

Her sweet little brow furrowed. "Because it's maybe time for a change. I got lots of pink stuff and purple stuff. Now I want some green stuff."

"Then green it is." I planted a kiss on the top of her head, then snapped her seat belt closed. "Once we get there we'll go find you a green bike."

The move was wonderful for both of us. It was just Lissy and me now. No shadow of state supervision. No threat of her being yanked out of my home. Since we knew no one else, we turned more than ever to each other. Not that there had been a lot of people in our lives before. But Lissy'd had her preschool and I'd had CAJA. And we'd both had Dr. Cordell. Now we had only each other.

We lived simply that summer. She got a green bike. I bought a yellow one. We got library cards and roller skates, and planted an herb garden on our balcony. Our lives in the small apartment complex were uncomplicated and satisfying: bike to the library for story time in the mornings; afternoons I taught Lissy how to read, and rewarded her hard work with swimming lessons in the courtyard pool. We played board games, learned to decoupage and crochet, took naps, and watched every Disney movie ever made.

Lissy blossomed and I think, maybe I did too. I slept better than I had in years. My face quit breaking out; I stuck to my exercise routine; and I started cooking again. And every move I made included Lissy, my precious little shadow.

The second Saturday in August we got up early to go to some garage sales. At the third stop we hit a bonanza. A woman with seven-year-old twin girls was moving. Lissy took one look at the pile of little girls' clothing and dove right in.

"What a cutie." The woman handed me my change. "First grade?"

"Kindergarten."

"Where's she going to school?"

"Hammet Elementary."

"Oh, you'll love it there." She squatted down in front of Lissy. "You're going to have so much fun in kindergarten."

Lissy immediately stepped back from the woman, wrapped one arm around my leg, and stuck her thumb in her mouth. She wasn't as cautious as she used to be, but it still took her a while to warm up to strangers.

"Ooh, you'll have to give up that thumb before school starts. You don't want the other kids making fun of you, do you?"

Lissy's arm tightened around my thigh. I stiffened, then put a protective arm around her shoulder. "We try not to make a big issue about thumb-sucking."

Still smiling, the woman glanced up at me. "You might not make a big issue out of it, but trust me, the kids at school will."

"Thanks for your unsolicited advice," I bit out, when what I wanted was to slap the smug, big-mouthed bitch. How dare she make an issue out of something my child obviously still needed to do?

"Good grief," she exclaimed. "I only meant—"

"Yes, I know what you meant!" I snatched the bag of clothes from her, then spun around and steered Lissy back to the car.

"What's her problem?" I heard her say to the several other staring shoppers.

What *was* my problem?

My hands shook as I fastened Lissy in her car seat. My whole body vibrated with outrage at the woman's offhand comment. And yet I knew I had overreacted. Badly. When that woman criticized Lissy my maternal urges had leaped into overdrive and I'd immediately gone on the attack. Yes, her thumb-sucking would eventually cause problems for Lissy. But that woman had no business pointing it out. Especially not in front of her.

"I don't like that lady," Lissy said as I climbed into the front seat.

"Me neither." I twisted around to look at her. "But I like you. I love you."

She grinned. "I love you too." She stuck her thumb back in her mouth for a moment, then pulled it out. "Nobody likes a thumb-sucker."

It came out *thumb-thucker*, which was cute. But a five-year-old worrying about what people think of her is not cute.

"Lots of kids suck their thumbs. I did." *Alyssa did.*

"But what if I'm the only one at kindergarten who sucks her thumb? What if all the other kids call me a baby?"

"Then … " *We won't go to that school anymore.* That's what I wanted to say. That's how violent my need to protect her had become. Fortunately I caught myself. "Everything will be just fine." I reached back and squeezed her knee. "Plus, kindergarten will be so much fun, you'll probably forget to suck your thumb. You know, if you want, you can just save your thumb for when you're at home. How about that?"

I could tell she wasn't convinced, but she didn't say anything until we got home. "Do I hafta go to big school?"

For a moment I considered it. A lot of people homeschooled their kids. Why not me? Look how much she'd learned this summer. I could teach her and protect her, be her teacher *and* her mother. I hadn't been diligent enough to protect Alyssa. But I would be with Lissy. Except that I knew Lissy needed to be around other kids. I'd seen her at playgrounds, at the library and the pool. Her eyes followed the other children but she was too shy to join in their games, even when they made overtures to her. She was okay one-on-one, but groups of children intimidated her. If she was ever to get over that shyness, she had to be around people other than just me. That meant school. The thought of letting her go out into the world terrified me. And yet for her sake I had to do it. So I shoved down my fears and cupped her face in my hands. "You have to go to school, sweetheart. All children do. I promise you'll have even more fun than you had at nursery school."

She peered doubtfully at me from beneath her pale lashes. "You promise?"

"I promise. Plus you'll have lots of friends, maybe even a best friend. Won't that be nice?"

That perked her up and she nodded.

"I have a good idea," I went on, trying to cheer her further. "How about after lunch we ride bikes over to your new school?"

We ate and she took a nap while I washed our garage sale purchases. That woman had been thoughtlessly frank, but she did have great taste in children's clothing. As I folded the yellow cotton sundress, the denim shorts, and the pink gingham camp-style shirt, I thought about this new life I'd created. It was time to introduce the last part of my plan to distance Lissy from her old life. When the adoption papers had been finalized I'd had another document prepared. Lissy Davis's name had been legally changed for several months now. I'd registered her at school as Lisa Haines. It was time now to introduce her to the change. I got my chance as we circled the fenced school playground on our bikes.

"Mommy, look! A big jungle gym. Oh look, Mommy, look! That one looks like a big red spiderweb!"

"It sure does. Do you think you can climb that high?"

"Yep." She nodded, making her braided pigtails bounce beneath her green-and-yellow helmet. "I'm a very good climber. Can we go climb on it now?" she asked when we stopped by the gate.

"Not today, baby. It's locked. See? But when you start school, you and your friends will play here every day."

She looked at me with shining eyes. "I think I'm gonna like this school, Mommy."

"Good. I have another surprise for you too, sweetheart. Now that you're going to big-girl school, I think it's time for you to have a big-girl name. You know how you used to call me Diane, but now you call me Mommy? And we both like that better, don't we?"

When she nodded I went on. "So, I think now that you can ride a big bike and are going to big school that we should change your name from Lissy Davis to Lisa Haines." I smiled at her, nervously awaiting her response.

She got a little pucker between her eyes, and at first I thought she was going to object. Then she said, "What about Anne? Lissy *Anne* Davis?"

"You can keep the Anne. Lisa Anne Haines, big five-year-old kindergarten girl. What do you think? Lisa," I added.

She giggled. "Like Miss Lisa at the nursery school. She was nice and she played the piano for us."

"But you're even nicer, and one day if you want, you can take piano lessons and learn to play the piano too."

Again she giggled. "Okay. I can be like Miss Lisa."

"I bet Miss Lisa doesn't ride a bike as good as you," I said. "Let's go!" And off we went, laughing and pedaling along the sidewalk beneath a canopy of spreading oaks and towering sycamores. Squirrels scampered, blue jays scolded and bees zoomed from oleanders to ixora to roses. Life was good, and everything had worked out even better than I had planned.

That night, though, after supper when I let Lissy—Lisa— watch a little television before bed, she sat up, pointing at the screen. "Her name is Bobbie," she said, referring to an animated butterfly. "Bobbie, just like my first mommy."

From contentment to sudden tension, the mention of Bobbie soured my mood. I reached for the remote control. If only I could switch Bobbie off as easily as switching off the TV, to make Lisa forget she'd ever existed. Only she hadn't forgotten. Suppressing my frustration, I seized on the opportunity to steer Lisa further away from her unhappy past with her biological mother. "Her real name isn't Bobbie. That's just a nickname. Bobbie Butterfly's name is really Barbara Butterfly. But Bobbie is what everybody calls her."

Lisa looked over at me, so trusting it made my lie turn bitter on my tongue. "My first mommy was really named Barbara?"

I swallowed hard. "I think so."

"Barbara Davis?"

"I suppose. You had her last name when she was your mommy. But that doesn't matter anymore. You have my last name now. And anyway, it doesn't do any good to think about all that. Oh, look," I added in a more animated voice. "That spider is trying to catch the butterfly in its web."

We watched until Lisa fell asleep and Bobbie Butterfly escaped. But I sat there a long while thinking about the web I'd built and the tenuous strings holding it together. I was determined that Roberta would never find her child. I doubted she'd even try to locate her, but just in case ... At the same time it was equally important to me that Lisa never look for her mother. It wasn't enough for Lisa *not* to be able to find her mother. I didn't want Lisa to *want* to find her. That was the only revenge I could wreak on Bobbie, so that was the revenge I wanted. The truth is, it terrified me to imagine everything I'd built coming undone, of me ever losing Lisa. I loved her and she loved me. She was so embedded in my life, she *was* my life now. I couldn't imagine going on without her.

Terror and love. Those were the emotions that drove me. And the more I loved Lisa, the worse my terror of losing her. It fueled disturbing dreams of lost children and empty graveyards and huge, threatening pickup trucks. It made me get an unlisted phone number and caller ID, and to move to a second apartment in Jackson—this time without leaving a forwarding address. Bobbie Davis would never find us. Neither would anyone from the adoption service.

Thank God my marriage and divorce records were in Florida, and that I'd returned to my maiden name and then moved first to New Orleans and now here. Hopefully it would be harder for anyone to trace my connection to Lisa's birth mother and Alyssa's death at her hands. With any luck no one would ever discover my lies or find Lisa and me. Terror and love—they were my enemies and my allies.

But the one emotion I never felt anymore was guilt. What I'd done was good for Lisa. No one who saw her now, happy and healthy and brimming with life, could deny that. I'd covered my tracks well and would continue to do so. She was five. I only had thirteen more years to protect her from the system.

As for Bobbie Davis, by the time she left prison, Lisa and I would be long gone from here. Even if she searched for Lisa—Lissy—she would never find her. I'd make certain of that.

CHAPTER FIVE

THE TIMES-PICAYUNE MAY 7, 1999

PRISON GUARD QUESTIONED ABOUT INMATE PREGNANCIES

Vernon Oldham, a prison guard at St. Anna's Prison has been fired and may face charges regarding the impregnation of two inmates in the all-women's facility. One of the inmates, identified by relatives as Katherine Leonard, 32, is already six months pregnant while the other, Roberta Davis, 26, was in her first trimester. The situation was revealed when Leonard attacked Davis over what is being called a lovers' triangle. Davis miscarried after the fight. She is recovering in the prison infirmary. Leonard has been removed to another Louisiana facility.

JUNE 21, 1999
ST. ANNA'S PRISON

Dear Lissy,

    It is my birthday today. I am 27 years old, but I don't get cake or presents or anything like that. But tonight at supper my friends Sonya, Oretha, and Mae sung happy birthday to me. Mae gave me her dessert because she has diabetes and is trying to lose weight so she won't have to take insulin every day. I'm studying to be a nurse now and I work in the health clinic. I was sick a couple of months ago, and this is NOT a good place to be sick in. That's when I decided to study nursing. At least it's something to do. They're teaching me how to give shots and everything. That's how I met Mae. She's pretty cool. A lot of the women are. But there are some you have to just stay away from. Same thing with the guards. Specially the men.

The only good thing about when I was sick was that I got a lot of time to think. I see how the dumb things I did got me into trouble. My own stupid choices are what got me stuck in here, and they made me let you down.

I hate this place. I have been here ever since I was 23, but it seems like forever till I get out. I bet you are good at math. If you subtract 23 years from 27 years you will know how long I have been away in jail. And if you subtract that number from 10, you will know how long until I can leave here and maybe find you again. I think about you alot and I miss you more now than in the begining. Sometimes I wonder if you even remember me. I hope you do.

Love from your Mom

P.S. The answer to the math problem is 6 years until I can leave. (It's Really 6-1/2 but I don't think you have learned fractions yet.)

P.P.S. Work hard in school. If I had studied more and stayed in school I probly never would of gotten in trouble and gone to jail.

DIANE

I missed visiting Alyssa's grave in New Orleans. Two years went by and I didn't go for her birthday, for the anniversary of her death, or for All Saints' Day. But I never stopped thinking about her. Time moved on, but even as each anniversary was marked and passed, as Lisa became older than Alyssa ever had a chance to be, my fear never entirely vanished. In some ways it intensified, because my whole plan was working so well. We were so happy together. Surely at the moment I least expected it, the other shoe would drop. Someone would discover something in Lisa's file and connect her to me through her mother and Alyssa, and they would come looking for us.

But no. My trail was too muddy. Even if no one discovered my lies, though, couldn't the universe exact its own justice for me not keeping Alyssa safe? Maybe take Lisa away from me? Or hurt her somehow?

Crazy thoughts, I know, but I couldn't completely douse my fears. So I became obsessive about her safety. I drove a Volvo, safest car on the road; we had a state-of-the-art security system; she swam like a fish, knew not to talk to strangers, and how to stop, drop, and roll. I got her a thorough physical every year. I supervised her every move, even school outings. It was my job to keep her safe, and I lived and breathed it every single day—but in a good way. I was a good mom. Everybody said so, especially the other moms from Lisa's class.

One thing I couldn't do, however, was to let go of Alyssa. So to commemorate Alyssa's birthday I always did something with Lisa and her classmates, something Alyssa would have enjoyed too. One year I took Lisa's entire class to Davis Planetarium. The next year I planned an outing to the Jackson Zoological Park. One of the other room mothers, Vera Landers, couldn't get over it.

"It's hard enough planning a birthday party for this many kids, and you're doing this for no reason at all?"

I just shrugged and smiled. "We started the tradition in kindergarten, planning an outing during the spring for her classmates. Lisa loves doing it. Now she won't let me stop."

Vera laughed. "You're a braver soul than I am. But then, she's an only child, isn't she?"

"Yes." I turned away on the pretext of herding three wayward boys back to our group at the camel exhibit. But inside I ached. Lisa appeared to be an only child, but she wasn't. I missed Alyssa and I always would. Usually I could keep that heartache locked away, my private hurt to nurse. But having to pretend she'd never existed and that today was just a day for these other people's kids, gouged holes in my soul.

"We'd love to have Lisa over sometime," Vera continued. "Does she like to skate? There's a great skate park near us that my kids love."

I managed a smile. "We haven't tackled skating yet."

She laughed. "I know. Skinned knees. Scraped elbows."

Twisted ankles. Broken arms. Concussions. I stiffened. "A skate park sounds a little too rough and tumble for her."

"And that is what helmets, knee pads, and wrist guards are for. Tracy and her brother love it."

"I don't know." That's when Lisa ran up, cheeks flushed, pigtails flying. "Mommy, the sun bear has two cubs. Twins! Come see them."

She grabbed my hand and I let her tug me forward. Vera was a nice woman and Tracy was a sweet child. But no way was my Lisa ready for skates.

As we laughed over the cubs' antics, I leaned over and hugged Lisa. I loved her every bit as much as I loved Alyssa.

But it was a fiercer kind of love, shadowed always by the fear of losing her. With Alyssa I had taken so much for granted. Good health, a happy family, a great future. Then in an instant I'd lost everything.

I didn't trust in anything anymore, only my own, eternal vigilance. But even vigilance has its downside. I was so careful with every aspect of Lisa's life, so much more so than with Alyssa's. It took all my time, all my energy, though I was happy to do it. It's all I wanted to do. But why hadn't I done that for Alyssa? Why hadn't I recognized all the pitfalls that surrounded us?

I'd loved Alyssa so much, but it almost seemed that I loved Lisa more. I never visited Alyssa's grave; never wore the locket with her picture; never spoke of her to anyone at all. I was too afraid someone would ask questions and then maybe figure everything out. So I kept Alyssa buried even as I tried to keep her alive in my heart. But it was a precarious juggling act.

I watched Lisa now, running to the ostrich exhibit, hand in hand with her best friend Amy. *I love you both, Alyssa. My love for her is love for you too.* I closed my eyes and worked to bring Alyssa's face to mind. It's all for you, I silently prayed. *I don't have you to love anymore, so I love her twice as much, for the both of you.* I meant to protect her twice as well. Ten times as well.

The next year on Alyssa's birthday I planned a camping trip for Lisa and three friends. I was in the kitchen packing the ice chest when the phone rang. "Hello, Diane?"

I'd been divorced from Jim for almost ten years. I hadn't spoken to him in four. Yet I immediately knew his voice. The slow Southern cadence, the familiar masculine timbre. I responded as I always had, with unaccountable joy.

"Jim!"

"Thank God," he exclaimed. "When did you move to Jackson?"

And that fast I plummeted from joy to fear. If he could find me, then anyone could. But how had he done it? And why? I answered him with brutal honesty. "I moved here when I heard you were getting remarried."

I heard the swift intake of his breath, and for a wonderful, terrible moment we were one again, Jim and I, breathing in sync. Then he exhaled and we separated, came apart into the two people we'd become since the accident. Jim Leftwich, divorcer of his terminally sad wife, remarried now with no business calling Diane Haines who'd finally—*finally*—begun to live again.

"What do you want, Jim?"

"Just ... just to know you're okay and—"

"I am," I cut in. I clenched the phone until my hand cramped. I needed to hang up, but I couldn't.

"You know what today is?" he asked, his voice low and shaky.

"No. I've forgotten," I snapped, furious and desolate at the same time. "Of course I know." Just the sound of his voice—the one person who knew and understood—and all my miserable emotions boiled up and overflowed, scalding everything in their path. "What do you want?" I repeated, but my voice had lost its bite.

"I didn't mean to hurt you, Di." Outside I heard Lisa laughing with her friends. On the phone Jim sounded like he was crying.

"I know." I sighed and rubbed my eyes. "I know. But you did hurt me." I edged into the bathroom and closed the door. "The divorce. Your remarriage. This call. I'm trying to get on with my life, Jim. Can't you let me do that?"

"That's all I want too," he said, openly weeping. "I want to get past all the pain. But I can't."

I wanted to say something flip like, Why don't you talk to your new wife about it instead of calling your ex? But I was way past being flip. "Do you think I've gotten past it? No. Never. But ... " Again I sighed. "This is our life. This is what we have to work with." Then because some part of me hadn't entirely forgiven him, I added, "How's married life treating you?"

"Don't, Diane." I heard the tinkle of ice in a glass and the muffled sound of swallowing. Was he drinking? Was he drunk?

I started to ask, then didn't. It wasn't my business. He'd always been a social drinker, but after Alyssa ... After Alyssa we'd both drunk way too much. I'd used a lot of sleeping pills too. I didn't drink anymore because it dredged up too much sorrow. Maybe it dredged up Jim's sorrow too.

"Fine. So. How did you find me?" I asked, deciding to be practical. If I was going to evade Bobbie, I needed to know where I was falling short.

"Internet directory," he said.

"But ... I have an unlisted number."

"There are ways around that, Diane."

"What do you mean? What ways?"

"What does it matter? I found your number and—Wait a minute. Is it *me* you're trying to avoid? Do you hate me that much? Damn it, Diane, I was depressed too. It wasn't all about you—"

"It's not you, Jim. Everything isn't always about you either."

"But you said you moved because I got married."

So I had. "I was planning to move anyway. Seeing your wedding announcement just pushed me into action."

We were both quiet a long moment. Again came the tinkle of ice. "I miss our talks," he murmured.

So do I. But what I said was, "It was only twice a year." Alyssa's birthday and the anniversary of her death.

"I know. But it meant a lot to me. I miss you," he added. "I miss our family. Our Alyssa."

Our Alyssa. That's who she'd been to us. *Our* Alyssa. To hear those familiar words in his familiar voice was my undoing. Sorrow rose in a mighty wave, blinding me with tears, strangling me with memories.

"I know," I whispered back, in sync with him once more. "I know."

Then the back door slammed, I heard Lisa and her friends, and I forced myself to shove those old sorrows brutally back into the past. "Look, Jim. Thanks for calling but … " I steeled myself. "Don't call me anymore. Okay?"

"But why? Look, I understand that you were mad, but—"

"No. You don't understand anything." *And you don't need to.* ""You have a new life now, and so do I. We can't undo the past—"

"I know that—"

"—and I don't want to relive it."

"Can't I even inquire about how you're doing? Whether you're happy? If you've remarried?"

"I'm fine; I'm as happy as I can be; and I'm not married. Anything else?"

I was hurting him and I knew he thought it was because of the divorce and his new wife. But the truth was that I was okay with that. Finally okay with it. He could do whatever he wanted now that I had Lisa.

But Jim could never know about Lisa. No one from my old

life could. And if that meant being cruel and driving him away, then so be it.

"No," he said after a long pause. "Nothing else."

I counted his breaths. One, two, three. Then, "Good-bye, Diane. Have a nice life." And he hung up.

I pressed the phone tighter against my ear. "Good-bye, Jim." My throat ached with unshed tears. "Have a nice life."

I hung up the phone, then erased his number from the caller ID. Jim was gone for good from my life. But his call had undone any feelings of safety—of invisibility—that I'd cultivated. If he'd found me, anyone could. I would have to do something. Maybe get another phone number. But this time no land line that a tech-savvy guy—or girl—could track down. This time I'd get a cell phone.

"Mom?" Lisa called from the hall. "Tracy's here. Would you unlock the car so we can put our stuff in the trunk?"

"Okay." I grabbed a tissue, wiped my eyes, then blew my nose. We were going camping to celebrate Alyssa's birthday, even if I was the only one who knew it. Alyssa's life might have been short, but it had been sweet. She hadn't wanted for anything, especially love. I hope that had been enough.

I stuffed a rain poncho into my backpack, grabbed my visor, and went into the kitchen. Lisa was counting out bottles of water.

"Three each per day, right Mom?"

"That's right." I resisted the urge to smother her in a hug. "How many is that?" I asked as Tracy, Marigny, and Amy crowded around the table with her.

"Four people times three bottles of water." Her brow furrowed in concentration. "That equals twelve bottles of water a day. Times three days, right? Thirty-six bottles," she said with a grin of triumph.

"What about me? Don't I get any water?"

"Oh, yeah." She laughed. "Okay. Five people times three bottles."

"Fifteen," Marigny put in.

"Times three days is—"

"Forty-five," they all crowed together.

"Right," I said. "And since these bottles come in packs of twenty-four?"

"We need two packs," Lisa said. "Okay, Tracy and Marigny, you take that one to the car. Me and Amy will take this one."

"Amy and I," I said.

"Amy and I," she dutifully repeated as she and Amy lugged the case of water to the car.

I stared after her, amazed at the child she'd become. She was smarter and more resilient than I'd expected all those years ago. She'd thrived and I felt a great sense of pride in that. And thankfulness. I had a lot to be thankful for: Lisa; the years I'd had with Alyssa, short though they were.

And Jim?

Despite everything I was thankful for Jim too. For a few perfect years I'd known love in every way that matters. Parents, husband, child. I'd had it all. Then I'd lost them all. Now I had another child, and that had to be enough.

As we piled into the car, stashing bedrolls and backpacks, and buckling up, I tried to let go of the panic Jim's call had roused in me, and concentrate instead on the love buried deep within his feelings of guilt. It's what Alyssa would want.

But an edge of fear remained the entire drive to New Goshen Springs. It remained as I watched them throw bread from the boat dock to the ducks and fish, as they foraged for wood, as they edged too near the fire with their marshmallows on sticks.

And from that fear a reluctant conviction grew. It was time to move, to find us a new place to live, a place with good schools, a warm climate, and no connection to Jim or anyone else that knew us. Lisa would hate it; I wasn't too keen on the idea myself. We'd built a happy, comfortable life in Jackson.

But we could do that again, somewhere else. We had to. Because if Jim had found me, so could the adoption people—and so could Bobbie.

.....

"You'll like this school," I told Lisa for probably the twentieth time that morning. We'd left Jackson just two weeks ago, a much more difficult transition than the last move. "It's a wonderful school," I went on. "You'll love it."

Lisa didn't seem to believe me any better now than she had the first time I'd said it. It had killed me to rip her away from the home and community she'd come to love. She'd flourished during our years in Jackson, both of us had. The move was even harder for her to understand because I couldn't explain it to her. Why? She'd asked me so many times. Why do we have to move?

At least she wasn't crying anymore. She had a strong sense of pride, my Lisa. She might cry at home or in the car driving over. But in front of other kids? No way. She'd seen how "crybabies" were teased, and she refused to go there. But just because she wasn't crying didn't mean she wasn't heartbroken.

"I want my old school. With my old friends," she muttered. The same thing she'd been saying since I sprang this move on her in mid-July.

"I know this is hard, Lisa, but you'll make new friends. And you'll like them just as much." I reached for her hand as we walked into the schoolyard, but she sidestepped the gesture and sidled away from me. And when we arrived at room 115, her new fourth grade class, she wouldn't hug me either.

In the hall opposite us a teary-eyed little girl clung to her mother. Lisa glared at them. "Crybaby," she muttered.

"Maybe she just needs a friend," I countered. "Somebody like you." Lisa worked her jaw back and forth. I could almost see her anger at me warring with her otherwise compassionate nature.

"Do you want me to go in with you?" I asked.

"No." She was only nine, yet it came out a sullen, teenaged "no". I was in unfamiliar territory and it scared me. Would Alyssa have reacted like this? Or was Lisa taking after her mother, and heading for trouble? How could I know? Alyssa never had a chance to be a teenager—or even a nine-year-old.

Nor would you have needed to yank her out of her school and community.

I shook my head, refusing to compare the two girls. I hated that Lisa was hurting. But it was for her own good. I had no other choice.

"Well. I guess I'll go now." I hesitated. "I'll meet you at the front gate when school's out. Okay?"

She just shrugged, and again I saw the teenager she soon would be: strong-willed and petulant, but smart and kind, if the glances she kept shooting at the other girl were any indication.

"Bye," I said, and forced myself to leave. But I caught her quick glance at me and the silently worded, "Bye."

At the end of the hall I couldn't help myself. I stopped and peered back at her. Children shouted and laughed and darted through the crowded passageway. Parents waved good-bye, some with relieved smiles, others with expressions of regret. That's when I saw Lisa cross the hall and stop before the weeping little girl and her worried mother. I don't know who said what. But as I looked on, the mother hugged her child, then transferred her daughter's hand to Lisa's.

And as two mothers watched with trepidation and hope, two little girls walked hand in hand into their new classroom.

I smiled and felt a huge weight of guilt lift from my shoulders. Seeing my smile, the other mother came up to me and said, "Are you Lisa's mother?"

My heart seemed to swell in my chest. Proudly I nodded. "I am."

CHAPTER SIX

BLOCK C INCIDENT REPORT
9/11/01

The entire C Block is under lockdown after the television set in the dayroom was smashed. Although emotions were running high as inmates watched the aftermath of the attack on the World Trade Center in New York, it wasn't until after the second building collapse that an inmate-unknown-threw a folding chair at the television. Nearly a dozen inmates started to fight while the others scattered. Seven inmates were sent to Block F solitary. Suggest all cell blocks be kept on lockdown as emotions are running high among guards as well as inmates.

DEC. 24, 2001
ST. ANNA'S PRISON

Dear Lissy,

I am really down today. It's always harder during the holidays, especially Christmas. But today I found out that my mother died last month. That's how long it took for anyone to remember to tell me. It's like I don't exist anymore, not to you and not to anybody else. And now my mother is dead.

I don't know why that bothers me so much. It's not like she ever was a very good mother to me or to her other two daughters. You didn't know you had two aunts, did you? Well, you do, my half-sisters. I never knew them because they were taken away from her before I was even born. That's how bad a mother she was. And that's why I wanted somebody else to adopt you. She wanted to adopt you, but I said no. She didn't really want you. She just wanted the money the state would give her to take care of you.

She never knew nothing about how to be a good parent. I think she loved her kids, even though we was just accidents. But I *know* she loved you. When you was a little bitty baby she liked to give you your bottle and then rock you and burp you. She said you were the prettiest baby she ever saw. And she was right. But she was the wrong person to raise you. So that's why you had to be adopted by somebody else.

Maybe if she was a better mother to me, I would of learned how to be a better mother to you. But I never did learn, so it's better that you have the good mom you have now.

I hope you don't forget, though, that you *do* have another mom who loves you, and you used to have a grandmother who loved you too. So to help you remember, I decided to draw you a family tree. It will show all the people you are related to. At least all the ones I know about. I checked out a book from the library to show me how to do it. (Yes, there is a library in prison.)

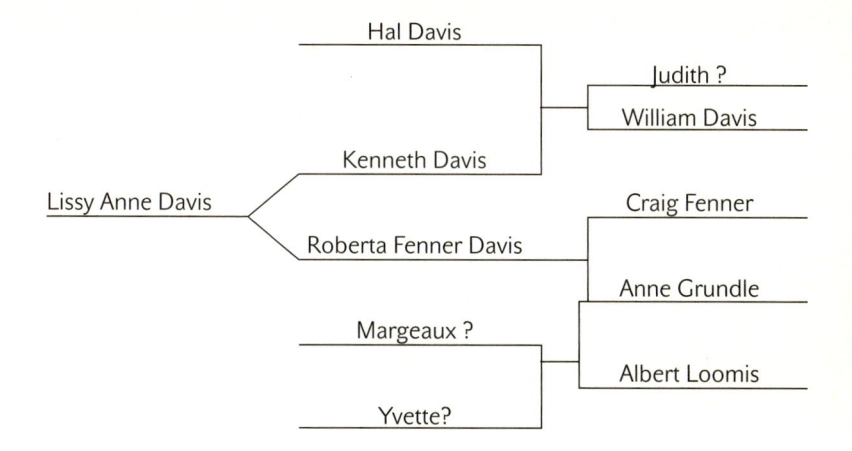

```
                    Hal Davis
                   ┌─────────┐
                   │         │   Judith ?
                   │         ├──────────────
                   │         │   William Davis
                   │
                   │ Kenneth Davis
Lissy Anne Davis ──┤                  Craig Fenner
                   │                 ┌──────────────
                   │ Roberta Fenner Davis
                   │                 │  Anne Grundle
                   │
                   │ Margeaux ?
                   │         ┌──────────────
                   │         │   Albert Loomis
                   │ Yvette? │
                   └─────────┘
```

I don't know my half-sisters' last names. Maybe they are still Loomis, maybe not. But they are your aunts, and your father's brother is your uncle. But I don't recommend you ever look for Hal. He was a real lowlife and he's probably worse now. Your dad was never as bad as him. If Hal hadn't turned your dad onto drugs maybe Ken would still be alive. Maybe the three of us would still be together like a real family.

But it doesn't do any good to imagine what might have happened. What is, is. That's one thing I learned in this place. Also, that it's up to us to make our own future. We can't hang around waiting for the right man to make our lives turn out right. That's what my mother did and it never happened. That's how I started off too. But I know better now. Men are losers, and they make a woman's life harder than it already is. It's weird, because prison has made me alot smarter and way stronger than I used to be.

Still, it makes me sad to think my mother is dead. She never got the life she wanted. But maybe I'll have a second chance to have a good life. And you have the best chance of all. You're nearly ten years old. I know you're smart because even when you was three you knew how to count and say your ABC's and sing almost every song that come on the radio.

Wow. This letter is getting really long. I think it's because, even though I'll be 30 next year, it's weird to think that now I'm a orphan. I'm totally alone in the world. Totally. It feels sad and makes me really heavy in the chest. I hope you never feel that way, or if you did, that you stopped feeling that way after you was adopted.

And I especially hope you always know that even though I wasn't around, I always loved you as best I could. You're the very best thing I ever did, Lissy. And the second best thing I ever did was to let you be adopted.

Merry Christmas with love, Mom

DIANE

On Lisa's tenth birthday she had a sleepover with her three new best friends. Fourth grade had been a rousing success—except for the boys. She hated them. Most of the fourth grade girls hated them too. And the boys pretty much felt the same way. Gross, noisy, and stupid were the most commonly exchanged barbs.

They were all so adorable. I gave them a year, maybe two, for their opinions to change—a change I wasn't exactly looking forward too. Meanwhile the girls painted their nails, tried on makeup, and played with their hair to impress each other and their preteen, heartthrob, poster boys: Justin Timberlake, the Hansons, and Lil' Romeo. Just as I'd hated Madonna's influence on Alyssa, I now hated the Britney Spears look Lisa tried to emulate.

But this was a party, and my job was simple: keep the lemonade, pizza, and popcorn flowing. Around two AM. after both versions of *The Parent Trap*, the noise level from Lisa's room finally dissipated. I tiptoed from my bedroom to turn off the television, switch off the lights, and pick up any leftover food that might draw roaches.

In Lisa's room her friends Muriel and Hope lay on the floor sound asleep in a tangle of sleeping bags. I expected to find Lisa and Kim knocked out on the living room couch. Instead I discovered them on the couch facing each other, propped up with pillows, and embroiled in some deep preteen conversation.

"—she tells me everything," Kim said. "But she doesn't know—" Kim broke off when she saw me in the doorway.

Lisa's head jerked around. "Mom!" she exclaimed, an odd note in her voice.

What was going on? "Sorry," I said, trying not to look too curious. "Aren't you girls tired yet?"

Kim, a petite girl of Asian descent, obligingly rose from the couch. "Yes, ma'am. I'm really, really tired." But then she shot a quick glance at Lisa, a glance that obviously meant, "We'll finish this conversation later."

"Brush your teeth," I called after them, despite the alarm bells clanging in my head. Something was going on that they didn't want me to know about. Lisa had never been a secretive child, so why now? I lay awake half the night worrying. Surely it couldn't be drugs or anything illicit. They were too young. Then again, I'd been with CAJA long enough to know that ten *wasn't* too young. Still, I found it hard to believe. More likely it was about boys.

But Kim had said "she". *She* tells me everything. *She* doesn't know. Maybe her mother, or an older sister. Could they have been talking about sex? Was I lagging in my explanations to Lisa? I wasn't trying to hide the facts of life from her, but she hadn't shown much interest so far. At least not to me. But to her friends ...

Maybe it was time for me to take the initiative and have a heart-to-heart discussion with her.

By noon the next day the girls were gone, the house was back in order, and most of the dishes washed. After lunch Lisa fell asleep on the couch. She was a nine-hour-a-night kid and she'd had at most six hours last night. Around three she woke up, and that's when I made my move.

"Looks like the party was a success," I said, putting a plate of apple slices on the side table beside her.

She grinned, and her eyes sparkled like bright emeralds. "It was *sooo* much fun, Mom. I never stayed up so late in my whole life."

"Don't get used to it." I propped my feet up on the oak

coffee table. *Be nonchalant, Diane. Take it slow.* "I like your friends. Muriel's a little shy, though."

"Uh- huh." She reached for an apple, and then settled back. "Guess what?"

"What?"

"Kim's adopted."

My heart stuttered, then started up again. So that was what the secret conversation was about. I'd rather it had been about boys. "Adopted," I echoed, looking away from her, at the blank television screen. "I see."

"Yeah. And she has a sister that's adopted too."

I glanced sideways at her. Up till now I'd always been able to divert her from questions about her birth parents. I affected a bland tone. "Her parents must be really nice people to adopt two children."

"Yeah, they adopted two kids. But I'm not talking about her adopted sister. I'm talking about her *real* sister. She was put up for adoption too, by their *real* parents."

Real parents. Like jagged glass the words ripped into my heart. What did that make me, an unreal parent? A pretend parent? A fake? I knew what Lisa meant, but she had no way of knowing how insignificant those two words made me feel.

"Her real parents had two girls that they let be adopted because they wanted a boy," she went on, her brows drawn together in outrage. "That's so not fair. Anyway, that's why Kim has a sister she never even met."

I pulled my heels onto the edge of the sofa and wrapped my arms around my knees. "Here in America?" I managed to ask in a credible rendition of my normal voice.

"Yeah."

"How can she be so sure?"

"'Cause her mom found out—her adopted mom." She stared at me, the apple slice forgotten in her hand. "Do I have any sisters or brothers who are—"

"No."

Her eyes widened at my curt reply.

"Your mother only had one child," I went on, struggling to release my death grip on my knees. *Relax, Diane. Relax.*

"How do you know?"

"They told me that when I adopted you. She was very young when she had you and wasn't able to take care of you."

She chewed on her lower lip. "Did they tell you her name?"

"I told you that before, Lisa. Her name was Bobbie, which is short for Barbara. But it was a closed adoption. That means she doesn't know anything about us, and we don't know anything about her."

She mulled that over a long moment before brightening. "But you know she didn't have any other kids."

"Because if she did … " I flailed around for a logical reason. "I would have adopted them when I adopted you," I finished in a flash of brilliance.

"Oh." Lisa frowned and hugged a throw pillow to her chest. "Maybe she had more kids *after* me. Maybe I have a baby sister or brother."

There were times when Lisa's mother didn't cross my mind for days. Weeks, even. I neither hated nor feared her during those intervals. She was just … nothing. But I never deluded myself into believing she was truly gone. Like a malevolent spirit she hovered relentlessly in the background of our lives, waiting to strike. Like now.

I didn't like lying to my daughter—mine now, not Bobbie's.

And I hated Bobbie even more for forcing me to do it. But I feared her too. I hated her for Alyssa, for my divorce, for my mother's untimely death, and for the lies she made me tell. But more than that, I feared her, especially now that Lisa's curiosity was strengthening.

So I struck back at Bobbie the only way I knew how: by killing any hopes Lisa harbored for one day finding her. "No. She didn't have any more kids."

Lisa's face fell. "But ... but how do you know?"

Don't tell her. She's too young to hear this. But I steeled my heart and told her anyway. "Your mother is in jail, Lisa. In Alabama," I added, to muddy the waters just in case. "She did some terrible, terrible things. Not just once, but lots of times. That's why you were put up for adoption."

It was excruciating, watching the light fade from my little girl's eyes. I told myself it was for the best, that I couldn't hide it from her forever. But I felt mean, and small.

Her chin sank into the pillow she now held in a death grip. "What did she do?"

"She stole things." *Like Alyssa's life.* "She did drugs."

"Drugs?" Her eyes went round with horror.

Lisa knew about drugs. Her school brought in the D.A.R.E. program every year, and I'd made a point of expressing my opinion on the subject whenever the situation presented itself. Ten-year-olds all over America know that drugs are the demon, the downfall of kids, families, and societies. It's harder to convince them of that when they're fifteen, though, or eighteen. But Lisa was still ten and she reacted as I knew she would.

"Drugs," she repeated, shrinking back into the couch. "But why?"

I shook my head. "I don't know."

But I did know. Bobbie was the result of her bad upbringing. There'd been no CAJA around to intervene when she was a kid, nobody in her corner when her neglectful mother with her string of abusive boyfriends made life unbearable.

Bobbie never had a chance. As a *thinking* human being I understood that. But because she'd never had a chance, my Alyssa's chances had been cut short too. As a *feeling* human being—as a mother—I could never forgive Bobbie for that.

But Lisa was too young to understand. It was enough for her to know that she shouldn't idealize her birth mother.

I shifted nearer her on the couch, and pulled her into my arms. "I'm sorry you don't have any brothers or sisters, baby. I didn't have any either, and I always wanted one. But I was an only child, and so are you."

I felt her little nod against the curve of my arm.

"It's not so bad, though. You don't have to share your room, or babysit or change diapers when your mother is busy."

"I could do that," she said. "And I wouldn't mind, either." She tilted her head to look up at me. "You know, you could still have a baby."

I laughed. "I'm forty-one, sweetheart."

She straightened in my arms. "Timothy's mom is having a baby and she's even older than you."

Timothy from her class was one of seven children and it was all the talk that his parents were expecting number eight. In a Catholic school where every other family had no more than three children, they were naturally the stars. Sister Cecilia adored them, as did Father Franklin. "I'm pretty sure Timothy's mother is younger than I am," I said.

"Nuh-unh. Timothy said she's forty-four. Then Robert said his grandmother is forty-four, and we all laughed." Her fair brows knit together as she studied me. "You *could* have a baby if you wanted to."

"Hmm. Well, I guess we'll have to leave that in God's hands, won't we?"

"No, Mom. First you need a boyfriend."

Oops. I guess she and her friends *had* been talking about boys and sex and the mystery of making babies. "Yes, Lisa. I know. But I think a husband would be preferable to a boyfriend."

"Yeah. But first he has to *be* your boyfriend."

"But I don't have a boyfriend." *And I don't want one.*

"God helps those who help themselves. That's what Sister Cecilia says. If you go get a boyfriend, then God will help you get married and have a baby."

That was my Lisa, nothing if not practical. "Well, *if* I get a boyfriend, and *if* we get married, then maybe—*maybe*—that could happen."

"Yippee!" She started clapping her hands.

I laughed at her excitement. "That's a big maybe, Lisa. Don't get your hopes up. Now, don't you have homework to finish? Science and social studies, as I recall. And I'll test you on your spelling words after that."

"I can do it after dinner."

"No. Now. You know how I feel about leaving homework for the last minute. You were supposed to finish it *before* your friends came over," I added.

She pulled away from me, her mouth turned down in a pout. "Fine," she muttered as she headed to her room.

But it wasn't fine. Lisa hadn't brought up the subject of her adoption in years. Now she was friends with a girl who was putting all kinds of new ideas in her head.

Bad enough that Lisa was pushing me to marry and provide

her with a sibling—which was never going to happen. To marry someone you first had to fall in love, which I could never do again. Plus, marriage required trust, which required honesty, which would require me admitting I'd been married before, that I'd had a child, and that I'd schemed to get *this* child—none of which I was willing to do.

Far worse than that pipe dream, however, was Lisa's budding interest in her birth mother. Like a grim specter Bobbie still hovered over us. I might push her into the background for awhile, but she always lurked there, waiting for the right time to pounce, the right time to wreak havoc on my carefully created little family of two.

But let Bobbie pounce. And let Kim fill Lisa's head with foolish visions of a happy reunion with a wonderful birth mother. Bobbie still had four years left on her sentence. Meanwhile, I had Lisa. I had control of whom she spent time with, and if it came down to it, I also had the ability to move us again. Because I was not going to lose another child to that selfish junkie-convict, and nothing anyone did would change that.

. . . . .

Unfortunately only a week later Bobbie descended on us again.

"Kim's friend Peter is adopted too," Lisa told me when she came home from school on Monday. "He's in the fifth grade."

"That's nice," I murmured, deliberately not looking up from my computer screen. I'd been researching the adoption laws in Louisiana to see if there were any new loopholes that might help Bobbie search for Lisa. When Lisa arrived I switched over to her school's brand-new Web site. "Look," I said. "They posted the winners in the spelling bee, and there you are. First place for fourth and fifth grades—Lisa Haines."

"Let me see!" She crowded up next to me.

"See? Right there." I circled her shoulder with one arm, reveling in how easily she leaned against me.

"Cool. I beat Henry Sharp, and he's the smartest boy in fifth grade."

"But he's obviously no match for the smartest girl in fourth grade."

"Kim's the smartest girl in fourth grade," she countered. "I'm just the best speller."

"You're a lot smarter than Kim. You've just been slacking off lately."

"No, I haven't, " she countered, pulling away from me..

"What do you call a B on your social studies test?" When her shoulders sagged in concession, I nodded. "That's right, a B. But you'll do better next time. Meanwhile, how about a snack? Do you have much homework?"

She shrugged one shoulder. "A little. But Mom," she went on in a brighter voice. "This boy Peter, he says he's in an open adoption. That means he gets to know both his moms."

Stifling a curse, I glared at the computer screen. How was she finding these kids? What did they have, neon lights flashing on their foreheads saying "Ask me about my adoption?"

"She sends him birthday cards and presents," she went on, edging closer to me again. "And when he's thirteen they get to have a meeting."

"Huh." That was all I could manage. *Huh.* My heart pounded way too fast, shooting this hot surge of blood and fear through my brain, rendering me speechless. I was aware of one thing, though. As if she were here in the room with us, I felt Bobbie's tormenting presence. Her malignant essence.

I could feel Lisa watching me, but I just stared at the computer screen. She knew I wasn't receptive to this subject, yet still she brought it up. Why was it so important to her to know about her pathetic excuse for a parent? Wasn't it enough to have me love her and push her and make sure she grew up right?

"Mom?" she said in a plaintive voice. "Did you hear me?"

"I heard you. And I've heard of open adoptions too. But I'm betting Peter's mother isn't in jail." I turned to face her. "Am I right?"

She shifted from one leg to the other. "No," she admitted in a subdued tone. "She's in college studying to be a doctor."

"I see."

Silence stretched between us. I tried to focus on the computer and pulled up the Alexandria city Web site to search out sports programs within the recreation department. Lisa had shown a talent for soccer and volleyball. If I kept her involved in after-school sports, maybe she'd be too busy to worry about her birth mother.

I heard her sigh. "Is she gonna be in jail forever?"

"I don't know." *God, I hope so!* "But I know she'll be in jail until you're all grown up." Just a little white lie.

"That long?"

I steeled myself against the disappointed note in her voice. "Yes, that long. That's why I was able to adopt you. Someone had to raise you because your *real* mother obviously couldn't." Then, finally relenting, I reached out to her. "I know this makes you sad, baby. And I'm sorry your birth mom did bad things and had to go to jail. But I'm glad—very glad—that I got to adopt you. I love you, Lisa." I paused, then took a deep breath and plunged on. "I'm sure your birth mom loved you, in her own way. But she didn't take very good care of you. And then she went to jail. So someone else had to be your mom. And I'm that lucky someone."

Her arms snaked around my waist and she rested her head against my shoulder, and for a moment we were perfect together, like when she was five years old. "I love you, Mommy. I really, really do. It's just—I don't know. I can't help it but I'm curious about her. I wish I had a picture of her or something. She shouldn't have done those bad things. But she's still my birth mom and ... and I love her too. I mean, you love me even when I'm bad. Right? So can't I love her even if she used to be bad? I don't have a daddy, so can't I have two mommies?"

Like stakes into my heart her simple logic tore jagged wounds in my argument. How could I possibly oppose that logic? "Of course you can love her," I answered slowly with words that tasted like gall. "And I suppose she loves you as best she can. But there are no pictures of her, and there will be no letters." I pressed a kiss to the top of her head. "It would be better for everyone if you would just forget about her. I don't think you should talk to Kim and Peter about their adoptions anymore either. It upsets you too much."

She squeezed my waist. "Father Franklin says we can't expect to be happy all the time. Bad things happen to good people, and that's the test God gives us: to keep on being good even when it's hard."

I went to bed that night with those innocent words resonating in my head. In my soul. I hadn't thought about God in a long time. I sent Lisa to Catholic schools because I knew she needed more spiritual guidance than I could give her. Now she was giving that guidance to me. Maybe God did still exist despite my long denial of Him. If so, He'd given me quite a test when

He'd stripped me of everything I loved. Every*one*.

In the dim quiet of my bedroom I stared blankly at the ceiling. Had I passed His test? Had I continued to be good? Was that why He'd put Lisa in my path?

Yes, I told myself. And I believed I'd passed his test. I'd worked hard at raising Lisa, protecting her, nurturing her. We ate strictly organic, got our vitamins from healthy foods. She was an A student, played sports and the piano. Everyone said she was the perfect child, like that was a given, like she'd been born that way. No one understood that I had *made* that happen, that she could just as easily have turned out rotten, exactly like her mother.

I didn't regret a minute of my hard work, and I'd been relatively happy since I found Lisa, happy in a way I'd never expected to be again. And so had she. But what about my lies? My evasions? What about Bobbie's hovering threat to my happiness and Lisa's?

Maybe that was just more of the bad stuff that happened to good people, more of God's test. He hadn't been finished with me when He took Alyssa and the rest of my life away from me. He'd given me this chance with Lisa, but it wasn't a free ride.

"Okay," I muttered into the heavy silence of the room. All that meant was that I had to become even more careful than I already was. Even more vigilant. "I can do that."

I *could* do that. I would give Lisa as much of the truth as I dared. But maybe I would also go on the attack. In four years Bobbie Davis would be a free woman, assuming she hadn't done anything to prolong her sentence—didn't I wish! Between now and then, I needed to find out everything I could about her. Then I would do everything I could to avoid her.

CHAPTER SEVEN

NOTICE TO ALL INMATES
JANUARY 2, 2002

Some individuals used the attack on the World Trade Center as an excuse to riot and destroy prison property. Those inmates have been dealt with harshly. In addition, Warden Tricou has retired and Warden Pratt has taken over effective today. At present there are no rule changes. However, infractions of existing rules will result in more punitive penalties as follows:

- Fighting–30 days solitary plus 30 day loss of all privileges (TV, radio, phone, visitation)
- Theft–30 days solitary
- Striking a guard or other prison employee–60 days solitary plus 60 days loss of all privileges
- Dereliction of Duty–7 to 30 days solitary plus 30 day loss of privileges.
- Attempted Escape–60 days solitary plus a revisitation of original sentencing guidelines.

ST. ANNA'S WOMEN'S PRISON
FEB. 4, 2004

Dear Lissy,

Today is visiting day, just like every Sunday. I haven't had a visitor in so long. I don't even remember who the last person was. Not my mother. She never came here. Oh, it was my old friend Carla. She actually came to visit her aunt, but since I was here she visited me too.

Anyway, I never have any reason to go to the visiting room, but sometimes when I'm on duty in the clinic I see some of the people who come. Moms and dads—but mostly moms. Husbands and boyfriends. Kids.

Kids are the ones that get to me, because everyone of them, even if they're boys or black or don't look anything like you at all, they still remind me of you. One might have your hazel-colored eyes. Another laughs just like you used to. One little boy was so shy and he sucked his thumb the whole time, just like you would do when you were nervous.

You're such a big girl now that I guess you don't do that anymore. I hope your new parents didn't make you stop, that you just did it on your own. I knew this little girl once and her mom wanted her to stop sucking her thumb so bad.

I didn't exactly *know* her. But I think about her sometimes and how everything would have been so different if her mom had just let her stop when she was ready to stop. But it really wasn't the mom's fault.

Anyway, whenever visiting day comes, even though I know nobody's coming to see me, I still imagine what it would be like if one day you came. I don't really want you to come here, though. It's a terrible place, gray and hard and cold. And the people inside are that way too, the prisoners and especially the guards. It's like the concrete walls surround you and suck the life and heart and soul out of you. Sometimes I feel like I'm turning into a robot. I don't have any feelings left–except for when I write to you. Then I can remember how it feels to be a real person, connected to somebody else in the universe.

It seems like the longer I am in here, the more I miss you. At first I was just scared and angry all the time. Now I'm mostly lonely, especially for you. Sometimes I'm so lonely for you that it hurts, like somebody stabbed me in the chest. Like my heart is bleeding. I missed all your growing up years. Pretty soon you'll be a teenager. But I hope I won't miss all your teen years. When I get out of here the first thing I'm going to do is look for you. I may have messed up my life, but I need to be sure I didn't mess up yours.

Love, Mom

DIANE

To say I became motivated by Lisa's innocent inquiries about her birth mother was a serious understatement. Bobbie was six years into a ten-year sentence. I didn't know if she'd try to look for her child when she got out, but I wasn't taking any chances, especially given Lisa's newfound curiosity about the woman. No way would I let that lowlife anywhere near my child. Mine! I couldn't get my old life back—my old family—but I could damned well protect my new one. So I decided to educate myself. I took an online course in private investigation. I bought books on how to find people who don't want to be found and learned, conversely, how to become invisible in a society that was becoming more and more transparent. I got a private post office box for incoming mail, quit using credit cards, and only used checks for bills I couldn't pay in cash.

I still used my computer to go online, though I wondered if perhaps I should switch over to the library computer. Then again, my online account remained the same no matter which computer I used.

But the more I learned, the more anxious I became. By the time Bobbie Davis was released from jail, I wanted to be completely impossible to trace. Not that Bobbie would be looking for *me*. She'd be looking for her child, Lissy Davis. Only Lissy Davis was Lisa Haines now, and she went to private schools that kept their records private too. But on the remote chance that Bobbie ever connected her child to me, I wanted to be completely lost to the system.

I reminded myself that Bobbie wasn't all that smart. A high school dropout with a drug problem—would she even remember that she had a child, let alone figure out how to track her down? No, we were safe, Lisa and I. But still, I never let down my guard.

Then when Lisa was in sixth grade I heard about the perfect job, a part-time secretarial position in a small detective agency. Chris Evans's wife Pat was pregnant with their second child and couldn't work full time with him anymore. So I started two days a week, then moved up to three days. It was nice having the extra money. Lisa and I managed okay on the income from my rental units in New Orleans, but money was always tight. My salary, though modest, made a nice difference. The main benefit, though, was learning even more about how to find people—and how to stay unfound. I listened, I learned, and I applied everything I discovered into protecting Lisa and myself from Bobbie and anyone else who might ever come looking for us.

But there was another unexpected benefit to the job: being with people again. I hadn't realized how lonely I was for adult company. For years Lisa had been the sole focus of my life. When she was at school my life went on hold, waiting for her to come home. To fill that void, I'd become room mother and assistant soccer coach. I drove for field trips and attended every sporting event, play, talent show, and spelling bee. Although I met lots of other parents as well as all the school staff, our conversations always centered on our kids and the school.

Not until Chris stormed into the office on my third day, muttering about stupid judges who had no concept what the separation of church and state really meant, did I recognize just how much I'd missed intelligent adult conversation.

"But if our government is supposed to be blind when it comes to religion, how can you condone one defendant's religion's Ten Commandments posted on a courtroom and another defendant's religion not represented at all?" I asked.

"I agree with that in principle," Chris said. "Certainly it's not the government's place to spend money on a big crèche scene in front of city hall or a giant menorah in front of the courthouse. But if Mary Smith wants the Ten Commandments in her private office, what's wrong with that? What's next, no crucifix or Star of David jewelry? Why can't we apply logic to the problem and recognize that there are shades of gray in the situation, not just black and white, right and wrong?"

"Because there's always somebody ready to sue over every little thing. Besides, how comfortable would you be dealing with a bank teller whose face was covered up by a burka? It's a legitimate symbol of the Islamic faith, but no one likes the idea of masked faces in any bank."

He flung his newspaper down on his desk and hung up his jacket. "You have a daughter. What happens at her school? Do they let kids pray like before a sports activity, stuff like that?"

"Lisa goes to a Catholic school. They pray all the time. But if she went to public school and didn't pray there, that would be fine with me. Quite frankly, I don't want anyone guiding her religious upbringing but me or someone I choose. I certainly don't want some speaking-in-tongues or other sort of extremist telling her things I don't believe."

"But that's just it," Chris said. "We can have middle-of-the-road, nondenominational acknowledgement of God or Allah or your higher power in schools and government without it being some undercover way of converting people to specific religions."

"What about atheists? Do they get to raise their kids free of the religious convictions of everyone else who does believe in some form of God?"

It was a debate that could have no conclusion, not in such a pluralistic society as ours. Democracy is messy. That's what my father used to say when he and I argued politics. But I'd forgotten how invigorating that messy debate could be. Chris and Pat's views were a lot more conservative than mine, but I loved them just the same.

Life in Alexandria fell into a comfortable routine. I had my job, and Lisa thrived at school. We spent Easter and Thanksgiving with Chris and Pat and their extended family. At Christmas Chris closed his office for a week and they went to visit his parents. That's when I realized how alone we were. We surrounded ourselves with activities: Lisa's sports and school affairs, my job, the piano lessons we both were taking. We were this little island, Lisa and I, just as I'd planned, and it was safe. But a part of me knew that as much as we loved each other, it still wasn't the well-rounded family experience I wanted for her. I needed to let other people in.

I guess that's why in a weak moment, when Pat mentioned that her brother-in-law's brother was single and would I like to meet him, I impulsively said yes.

"You're going on a date? A real live date?" Lisa exclaimed when I told her.

"Yes, a real live date. You're acting like I said I was going to walk on coals or something." Only to myself would I admit that I wouldn't have been as terrified of the coals as I was of Stan Chilton.

I leaned nearer my dresser mirror, carefully applying first mascara, then eyeliner. Me, wearing eyeliner again. I'd had to buy a new tube since my unused ten-year-old stuff had turned to concrete. "If you don't want me to go, I won't," I told Lisa, even though I knew better than to give a kid that kind of power—or that kind of responsibility. But I was scared, and I guess I was looking for any reason to cancel the date.

"No. You can go. You should go." Lisa looked doubtful, though.

"It's nothing fancy. We're going to the art festival, then to have lunch at that little place across from the park." I closed one eye and with my shaking hand tried to paint a line above my eyelashes.

"Put it on thicker," Lisa instructed.

"Thicker?"

"Yeah. And some under the bottom lashes too."

"I'll look like a raccoon."

"No, you won't."

I did as she advised and then stared at my unrecognizable, charcoal-rimmed, full-lashed eyes. "A raccoon," I repeated, reaching for a tissue.

"Don't." Lisa grabbed my hand. "Put on your lipstick first. And some blush."

I stared at her. "Who are you? My daughter is only twelve and she doesn't know anything about eyeliner, lipstick, and blush."

"Mom!" she said, laughing. "I know I can't *wear* makeup—"

"That's right. You're way too young."

"Maybe. But when we have sleepovers, Kim and Muriel and I experiment with it."

"What?" Another reason to disapprove of Kim. Despite all my subtle efforts to sabotage their friendship, nothing had worked. Now it turned out they were practicing tarting themselves up at Kim's house?

"Here. This lipstick." Lisa thrust an ancient tube of azalea rose at me. I took it reluctantly. It was dry and didn't smooth on as easily as it once had. But it did the job.

"See?" Lisa said, her infectious smile in full bloom. "The lipstick makes the eye makeup look just fine."

I stared at the stranger in my mirror, a woman I used to know a long time ago, and swallowed a lump of confusing emotions.

Did I want to know her again? Maybe.

Dragging my eyes from my reflection, I managed a smile. "Okay. You're right, the lipstick helps. But that doesn't mean I like the fact that you're right."

"Mom!" She stretched the word into three syllables, laughing all the time.

"I want you to go back to being nine again, not almost a teenager." I grinned when I said the words, but I'd never meant anything more. Though I knew it was stupid, I dreaded Lisa growing up—growing away from me. It wasn't just the threat of Bobbie's reappearance that I feared. It was everything: high school and boyfriends, then college and marriage, and Lisa building a life of her own, without me at its center.

The quick sting of tears behind my lids warned me away from that line of thought. Like it or not, life only went forward, never back. I'd learned that lesson the hard way. But it didn't mean I liked it.

"So." I turned away from the mirror and headed for my closet. "I thought I'd wear these pants." A pair of tried-and-true khakis. "And this navy sweater set. What do you think?"

Her nose wrinkled.

"You don't like it?"

"It's too ... I don't know ... plain."

"What do you mean, plain?" But I knew. Even without her dramatic eye roll I knew.

"At least wear your white pants instead of the khakis. And wear sandals. And lots of jewelry."

"I'm not twenty-five, you know."

"Even old ladies wear jewelry, Mom. And you're not old," she added before I could protest.

It was strange having my preteen daughter dress me for a

date. But after I dropped her off at Kim's house, I admitted to myself that she was right. I kept looking at myself in the rearview mirror, impressed with how much better I looked. Younger and prettier. I even felt slimmer. I looked like a woman who actually had a life of her own beyond her daughter's.

It was scary territory, but still tempting.

I met Stan at the entrance to the art market, a monthly event that included dozens of vendors displaying jewelry, ceramics, paintings, and other crafts. Pat had told me he was tall with dark hair just beginning to gray at the temples. Forty-eight, three years divorced, with two kids in college, he was an electrical contractor who played drums for fun.

Me dating a drummer. When I was eighteen that had been my fondest desire. Now, as my glance met that of a nice-looking man who fit that description, I felt first panic, then an overwhelming urge to laugh. How could I be on a blind date at my age?

He smiled as he approached. "Diane Haines?"

"That's me."

Stan was a nice guy. We spent two hours in the park taking each other's measure. It's interesting how much you can tell about someone from the art they like. He liked realism; I liked whimsy. He thought plates were for eating off of; I thought they were perfectly plausible art objects. We both liked silver jewelry better than gold, though, and believed in supporting local artists.

I bought a pink-and-turquoise glass-bead necklace for Lisa, a money clip for Chris, and a bamboo wind chime for Pat's back porch.

He bought a pair of sock monkeys for their kids, and a tumbled glass pendant on a black silk cord for me.

"You don't have to do that," I protested. Jewelry on a first date seemed somehow inappropriate.

"It's only twenty dollars," he said. "So far you're a really cheap date."

I laughed. "You haven't seen how much I eat."

He ordered a club sandwich; I had a salad. I appreciated that he asked for iced tea instead of a beer. I had lemonade.

"I guess electricians must get shocked pretty often."

"It depends on how careful you are."

"Are you careful?"

He grinned. He had a nice smile and nice teeth. "I am now. A few sharp zaps and we all get more careful."

"Why is it you never hear of women electricians?"

"I know a few."

"I've never met one," I said.

"Have you met many male secretaries?"

"No. But that's different."

"Maybe once it was different. But I can tell you, a good electrician is a good electrician, male or female. A woman can make a decent living as an electrician." He tilted his head. "Are you interested?"

"I doubt Chris would appreciate you tempting me away from my job with him."

Our eyes held for a moment. "Am I tempting you?"

Thank goodness the waitress appeared and I didn't have to deal with the double entendre in his question. Was I tempted by the job? No. But the man?

Maybe. That's as far as I let myself go. If he asked me out again, I would accept, even though I didn't feel that instant physical attraction I'd felt with Jim.

Jim.

I was not comparing Stan to Jim. No way. Stan was attractive enough. He just didn't ignite any raging fires in me. Not that

I wanted him to. After all, I was a middle-aged woman, not an adventurous college kid.

But maybe I did want to feel that old familiar heat. Maybe I did want to find out if my libido was totally dead or just dormant. Unfortunately it probably would take more than a date or two to figure that out.

We shook hands when we parted. I thanked him for the necklace; he thanked me for a great afternoon. Then we walked to our respective cars and drove away. He hadn't tried to kiss me. He wasn't going to call. I frowned into my vanity mirror. My eye makeup was intact, but my lipstick had lost ground to the salad. What sane man wanted to date a raccoon?

"Did you have fun? Was he nice?" Lisa asked as soon as I arrived. Rita, Kim's mother, raised her brows expectantly. Lisa had obviously told them about my date.

"He was very nice," I said. "And we had a lovely time." Then I turned to Rita. "Thanks so much for having Lisa over."

"No problem. They practiced their spelling bee list and watched a video."

"Well, thanks again. You ready to go, Lisa?" I didn't like chitchatting with Kim's mother. She was a nice woman and evidently a wonderful parent to her two adopted children. But I didn't want our kids to be such good friends, and I sure didn't want to do the let's-compare-notes-about-our-adoptions thing. So I always kept things superficial.

I did that with a lot of people. The truth was, Chris and Pat were the closest friends I'd made in all the years since the accident. My boss was my best friend. Even I knew that was pathetic. I smiled over at Rita. Maybe I should try harder with her. Or with Stan.

But before I could act on that impulse, Lisa headed for the

door. She was in a hurry to get to the car, probably to pump me for details about my date. As we drove away, though, I felt bad that I didn't have much to tell her. The truth is, I'd discouraged Stan with the same aloof manner I used on everyone I met. I was never rude, but they picked up the signals anyway. The restrained smile; the stiff body language. I hadn't been quite as stiff with Stan. But I sure hadn't encouraged him.

"Did you like him?" Lisa leaned forward in the backseat to tap me on the shoulder. "I bet he liked you."

"He was nice, Lisa. Very nice."

"Was he, like, a stud?"

I burst out laughing. "A stud? I don't think any man my age can be called a stud. But he was good-looking, I guess. Tall, with nice hair."

"Did he make you laugh? That's what all the magazines say girls like the most: a boy who makes them laugh."

I concentrated on driving. Yes, he'd made me laugh. Several times. And it had felt good. But I was not discussing the details of my date with Lisa. We were mother and daughter, not high school pals.

"I wonder," I said. "Are you going to answer all my questions about the boys you date?"

"I don't date."

"Not yet. But it's just a matter of time. When you're seventeen and you come home and I'm waiting in the living room, how happy are you going to be if I start grilling you about your latest date?"

"Come on, Mom," she pleaded in that cajoling tone that never failed to work. "You know you're going to be curious. Just like I'm curious right now."

"The question isn't whether or not I'll be curious. The question is, will you answer my questions?" I met her laughing gaze in the rearview mirror. "Answer them honestly," I added.

Her mouth was open, ready with a quick retort. But instead she closed her mouth and looked away. Then she sat back, out of my line of vision. That fast from sunny child to sullen teen. I gave a mental shrug. I'd obviously made my point. But something in the abrupt way she caved in didn't sit right.

"I'll tell you this much," I said, sorry that I'd put the kibosh on our conversation. "Stan is a nice guy and a lot of fun. He bought me a necklace. Here." I passed the bag back to her. "It's really pretty. I bought Christmas gifts for Chris and Pat while we were at the art show."

I heard the rustle of the bag as she opened it. "It *is* pretty," she said. Then her face came back in line with the mirror. "Did you get anything for me?"

I waggled my eyebrows and grinned. "That's another question I'm not going to answer."

She attempted a smile—halfhearted at best—then once again subsided into the backseat.

The back of my neck prickled with alarm. What was going on? As we drove the last few blocks home I traced our conversation. Her mood had changed from teasing answers out of me to a full-fledged retreat when I'd said "answer them honestly".

Honestly.

Did that mean she knew she wouldn't be honest with me about her future dates? That seemed awfully calculating, given her age. But what if she wasn't being honest about something else? Something right now?

Once home she headed straight for her room. "You know

what?" I called after her. "I don't think I can hold onto your gift until Christmas. How about I give it to you now?"

"Now?" She spun around and barreled right back into the kitchen. "Okay. What is it?"

Relieved, I laughed. "Do you want me to tell you or do you want to open it yourself?"

"Open it. C'mon, Mom. Let me see."

We sat at the kitchen bar, my secretive little girl and me. She loved the bead necklace, as I knew she would. And I told her I would go out with Stan again if he asked me, but that I doubted he would.

"He'll ask you," she said with the indisputable confidence of youth. "You're pretty and smart, Mom. Did you make *him* laugh?"

"A few times." I decided not to probe into her sensitive territory even though she was probing into mine.

"Did you ... you know ... " She tucked her chin but peered up at me curiously. "Did you kiss him?"

"No."

"How come?" she asked, following me when I turned away and went to check the mail.

"I didn't want to. I wasn't ready to kiss him." I turned to face her, embarrassed at my shyness, but also wishing I could be totally honest with her about everything. That I'd once been in love and married. That I'd had a child, but had lost her. Only that had to remain off limits. Better to turn this into a life lesson for her. "Don't ever let a boy convince you to do anything you don't want to do, Lisa. You hear me? If you say no and he doesn't like it or never calls you again, all that means is that he wasn't the right guy for you. You understand?"

"Okay." She stared up at me, guileless once more.

"And if you ever need advice about boys, you can ask me. Anything," I added. "Or you can ask somebody else if you prefer. I won't mind."

She nodded. "You mean a grown-up." She hesitated. "Like Kim's mom or something?"

Kim's mom. "Sure," I said after a moment. "Although a school counselor would be fine too."

"Okay," she replied.

But as Lisa left to feed her fish and gather her laundry, I worried. Something was going on, something based, no doubt, at Kim's house. It had been a good while since Lisa had brought up anything about her adoption and her birth mother. But who knew? On the other hand, there were lots of other issues our preteens were heading toward. Though I dreaded the thought, I knew I needed to talk to Kim's mother. Because my daughter was hiding something, and I needed to know what.

I called that evening while Lisa was taking her bath. "Thanks for watching Lisa today," I said when Rita answered. "She always enjoys spending time with Kim."

"Think nothing of it. We love having her over."

"The thing is … " I trailed off, at a loss about how to begin.

"Is there a problem?" Rita asked.

"Not a problem. At least I hope not. The thing is, I need your advice. On the way home I got the feeling that Lisa was keeping something from me."

"What do you mean?"

"It could be something with boys or … " I hesitated. "I don't know."

"You don't mean alcohol or drugs, do you?" Her tone turned defensive.

"No. Not that. I mean, sure, I guess we need to brace ourselves for that eventually. But not yet. I'm sorry. I know this is vague, but I don't know. I just got this strange vibe from her."

"You don't have to explain. Sometimes we moms have nothing else to go on but our gut feelings. And as adoptive moms, we probably doubt those feelings more than most."

Adoptive moms. Maybe that *was* the secret.

"I wonder," I said. "You know, Lisa's always been fascinated by the fact that Kim knows who her mother is and that she has another sibling in America."

"Yes, I've noticed."

"And there's a boy at school who's part of an open adoption."

"Peter Vincent. I know his parents. We belong to the same Adoptions International support group."

A support group? Ugh. "Really?" I said, trying to sound interested.

"Yes. It's great. You ought to join, Diane. You'd be surprised how helpful it is to share your worries with other parents in the same situation. There's a Web site you could check out."

A Web site. All at once I felt a chill.

"Did Kim and Lisa spend time on the computer today?"

"Probably. Kim has our old computer in her bedroom. But I have a block on it," she added. "They can't get to any sites that are inappropriate for children. We're very careful about online stalkers and pedophiles." She paused. "Do you want me to check what they did? What sites they visited?"

"You mean ask Kim?"

She chuckled. "We have faith in Kim, but we're not stupid. Kids are impulsive and way too trusting. So we have a parent-overview program set up on our computer, and hooked up to hers too. I can check where she's been online without her knowing I'm checking. And I can block sites I don't like."

"That would be great," I said. But inside I was worried. What if Lisa was looking for her mother?

"You know," Rita went on. "They're just a year away from being teenagers. I don't know if regular parents obsess as much about their kids as we do, but I do know that adopted kids have more struggles than other kids. I mean, they're all a mixture of hormone-fueled bravado and insecurity, one minute laughing hysterically, the next in the throes of despair."

"Yeah. I remember being that kid myself."

"Me too. But with our kids, at the same time they're naturally growing away from us, they can get obsessed with finding their birth parents." She paused. "Listen, Diane, since you called me for advice, I'll give you some: Don't get too bent out of shape if that's what Lisa's doing—trying to find her birth mother. I know it hurts. It feels like she's abandoning you for this other person, this stranger who for whatever reason didn't have what it takes to raise a child. But try not to take it personally. It's not about you. It's not even entirely about the birth mother. It's just this need they have to know where they come from, who they are."

I nodded, knowing she was right. But my adoption of Lisa wasn't a normal adoption. If Lisa found her mother, the truth of my connection to Bobbie would come out, along with all my lies and evasions. The worst part, though, was that Lisa might doubt my reasons for adopting her. She might doubt my love for her, and that was a risk I refused to take. The last thing I wanted was to hurt my little girl—and that's all finding her birth mother could ever do.

"I hear you," I said to Rita, needing to end this conversation. "Then again, maybe it's not that at all."

"Maybe," she conceded. "But I'll check Kim's computer trail and let you know what I find. Okay?"

"Okay." I took a steadying breath. "Okay. And thanks. You've given me a lot to think about."

"Good. Check on the Web site I told you about. There are lots of other online support sites for adoptive parents too."

"I will," I promised. "Thanks again." After we hung up I just sat there, trying not to worry, but worrying all the same.

"Hey, Mom." Lisa's call came from the hall. "This week is spirit week. We're supposed to wear the school colors on Friday, but my grade decided we're wearing green and white all week."

I blinked and turned to look at her standing in the doorway to my bedroom. "Green and white all week. What about your uniforms?"

She wrinkled her nose. "We have to wear our uniforms every day except for Friday. But Kim bought two rolls of ribbons, one green and one white, and we're all going to wear ribbons in our hair each day."

"Good idea."

"Ponytails on Monday," she said, pulling her long hair back in one hand. "Pigtails on Tuesday." She mugged the style for me. "A French braid on Wednesday. Two braids on Thursday—even though Shelly's hair isn't really long enough for that. And on Friday we're wearing French twists."

Coming into my room, she finger-combed her hair back. Then she twisted it up onto the back of her head.

"How are you going to wear ribbons in a French twist?" I asked.

"We can tie the ribbons on the hair clip. But Kim's tying her ribbons on two chopsticks. Her hair is so long and thick, and she knows how to crisscross the chopsticks so her hair will stay up." Bending to peer into my dresser mirror, she picked up one of my hair clips and fastened her hair high up on the back of her head. A few long curls slipped down to coil around her face and one fell at the nape of her neck.

She had such pretty hair, dark gold streaked lighter here and there by the sun. Then she struck a pose in the mirror, her eyes twinkling green and gold in its reflection, and that's when a lightning bolt from the past struck me, searing me with the old pain, paralyzing me with the old grief.

Lisa looked just like her mother, like the smiling high school picture of Roberta Fenner that had run in the paper after Alyssa died. In the mellow light of my vanity lamp, with her hair up, her smile full of mischief, and her face less a child's and more a young woman's, she was the exact image of her mother.

I recoiled without thinking, lurching up from the bed toward the bathroom. Anything to avoid that image. "Time for bed." I choked the words out. "Is your homework done? Your backpack ready to go?"

"Yes and yes," she said, sighing. "But before I go to bed can I figure out what to wear on Friday. Please?"

"Fine." I braced myself on the door frame, still not looking at her. "Fifteen minutes till lights out. That's all."

"Okay." Oblivious to my near panic, she skipped out of my room. I peered anxiously after her as she went down the hall, watching as she removed the hair clip. Her long, wavy hair spilled down her back, and in a blink, with her pink shortie pajamas, her skinny legs and bare feet, she went back to being my little girl. My Lisa.

I took a slow, shaky breath, relieved beyond measure. For one awful moment there ...

A shudder ripped through me. How had I never anticipated the possibility of her looking like her mother?

I went into the bathroom, gripped both sides of the lavatory and breathed deep, trying to calm down. Finally I bent over and splashed cold water on my cheeks and eyes. Lisa looked just like her mother, and she might be searching for her too. I raised my head and stared at my stricken, middle-aged face. Lisa's birth mother was only a few short years away from freedom. That was something I couldn't change, just like I couldn't change the way Lisa looked like her. But I damn well could stymie her search for her pathetic excuse for a parent.

In the mirror my face hardened, along with my will. It if was the last thing I did, I would make sure the two of them never met.

CHAPTER EIGHT

ST. ANNA'S PRISON
APRIL 9, 2004

Dear Lissy,
Today you are 12. That is so amazing to me. Already 12. I wish I could give you a present so you would know I haven't ever forgotten you. I was watching this TV show today with my friends Sonya and Mae, and these guys were making up songs right on the stage. It was so funny and they were so good it gave me a idea. So I made up a song for you. Here are the words. You should sing them to the tune of When the Saints Go Marching In.

> Oh, when I first saw Lissy Anne
> Oh, when I first saw Lissy Anne
> I was so happy I was crying.
> Oh, when I first saw Lissy Anne.
>
> Oh, when I last saw Lissy Anne
> Oh, when I last saw Lissy Anne
> I was so sad I couldn't stop crying.
> Oh, when I last saw Lissy Anne.

Oh, when I next see Lissy Anne
Oh, when I next see Lissy Anne
I'll be so happy I'll start crying.
Oh, when I next see Lissy Anne.

I know it's not as good as the made up songs on that show. But it's my true feelings. Maybe I'll come up with a better one. If I do I'll write it down for you.

Love forever,
Your Mom

INCIDENT REPORT BLOCK C
APRIL 14, 2004

Prisoner Sonya Washington, LA C3-0714 was discovered in her cell at 06:07 hours during routine rounds with what appeared to be self-inflicted wounds to her wrists. Loss of blood was heavy and the best estimate is that she cut herself after the 2 AM rounds. Officer Leslie Hertz called for medical backup and the prisoner was rushed to the infirmary. Dr. Phelps arrived at 06:55 and pronounced Prisoner Washington dead.

INCIDENT REPORT BLOCK C
APRIL 16, 2004

Prisoner Davis LA C 3-0092 attacked Officer Leslie Hertz in the hall outside Latrine #2. Officer Hertz suffered a black eye and split lip. Prisoner Davis has been confined to Block F solitary.

DIANE

I realized that if I was going to thwart Lisa's attempts to find her mother via the Internet, I'd have to know more than she did about the medium. So I signed up for an online class. Computing: How to be Smarter than Your Smart Kids.

I'd gotten pretty good at using the Internet to track down people, thanks to my job with Chris. Phone records and credit card information were tricky because there were privacy issues that only certain law enforcement people had access to. But there were other sources: court records, police files, school records. It's scary how much information is out there about each of us. And as the online community grew—chat rooms, music sharing, personal Web sites—it was like people were advertising themselves, asking to be taken advantage of.

But not me. I closed all my credit card accounts. Then I formed a small corporation registered in the Cayman Islands, opened a bank account there and applied for just one credit card through it. I changed my phone and utility bills into the corporation's name, and everything else I paid for with cash.

I didn't know if Bobbie had access to computers or not. But I made damned sure that any trail on Diane Leftwich and Lissy Davis hit a dead end.

As for Lisa's online activities, I was right. According to Rita, Lisa and Kim had visited all sorts of adoption sites, many of them guides for tracing both your adopted child and your birth parents. There were other sites too, chat rooms and forums of adoptees. And there were the registers. Because of her age, she couldn't register without my consent. I wondered how long before she approached me about that. And how I would respond.

A more immediate problem occurred, however, when Stan called almost two weeks later and asked me out.

"A—a movie?" I stammered, trying to organize my thoughts to come up with a rational response—a negative response.

"That's right, a movie. You know, dark room, big screen, lots of popcorn? I'll feed you first too," he added.

"Um ... what night did you say?"

"Friday. But Saturday is fine too."

"Um ... " Yes, no. Yes, no. Why was I so frozen with indecision?

"If you don't want to go, Diane, just say so. But I could swear you had a nice time on our first date."

"I did. I really did." My knuckles had turned white from strangling the phone. "Okay," I blurted out. "That sounds great. Really great."

This short silence crackled between us and I thought for a minute that he'd decided to back out. Then he said, "Good. You know, another guy might take that as a bad sign—that obvious hesitation. But I'm going to take it as a positive, that you've weighed the pros and cons, and that you like me more than you fear the dating scene."

I laughed and knew at once that I'd made the right decision. "It's scary how clairvoyant you are. So, what movie do you have in mind?"

"Ah, the first test: chick flick versus action-adventure. Since this is just our second date, I was thinking chick flick."

"Good choice. You know, if you really want to make Brownie points, pick a foreign movie. Women *love* subtitles."

He groaned. "You're killing me here, Diane. But if that's what you want, I think *Amélie* is playing downtown."

Again I laughed, and it felt good. "The fact that you've even heard of *Amélie* gets you Brownie points. But you're in luck. I've already seen it. To tell the truth, anything short of hardcore horror will be fine."

We settled on a time and when I hung up I was still smiling. I liked him. How amazing was that? He was easygoing and funny, and if he didn't get me all hot and bothered, well, maybe we were too old for that. What mattered most was that I liked him and he liked me, a combination that hadn't occurred since Jim.

I don't know why, but having a date with Stan kept Jim on my mind. The meter reader walked like him; I heard a song he used to love; his birthday was coming up, his forty-fourth. So that night after Lisa was asleep, I tried to look him up online. I'd never done that before. A part of me was afraid it might help him find me again, though I know that was crazy. Besides, after our last conversation, why would he ever want to look for me again?

He was easy to find, still living on the Gulf Coast, working for a big accounting firm, married with two kids now. I knew resentment was a totally inappropriate reaction, yet that's what I felt. He had two kids now. Did he still think about Alyssa? Did he still love her and miss her and grieve for her like I did?

I turned off the computer without shutting it down properly and went into the bathroom. But I didn't cry. Alyssa had been dead fifteen years. Jim and I had been divorced for thirteen. I'd been Lisa's mother more than eight years, and now I was dating. We had both moved on with our lives like we were supposed to, and I wasn't sorry about that. But I'd always be sorry about Alyssa. And the death of our family.

That night I dreamed about making love. I didn't know who the man was at first. Then he became part Jim, part Stan. In the dream I didn't reach an orgasm. But when I woke up I felt restless and uneasy and, I suppose, a little bit horny.

Maybe that was a good thing, because I hadn't felt that way since before Alyssa's death. I wasn't certain I wanted to feel it now, though, not with my date with Stan coming up. Because even if

I was horny as hell, I was not ready to make love to him. Not to anyone, but especially not to someone I might actually like.

Illogical, I know. Because the flip side was that maybe I wouldn't mind having sex with someone I *didn't* like. The only sense I could make of it was that sex with a stranger would come with no strings attached, no emotions involved, and no threat of emotional pain.

Was that what I'd been doing with my paralyzed libido all these years? Avoiding pain?

The next day I had my hair cut, gave myself a facial, and made an appointment for a manicure.

"I like it," Lisa said of my newly layered, shoulder skimming, swingy style. "It makes you look younger."

"I like it too. She wanted to color it, but I said no."

"Ooh." Lisa's eyes got big. "You could try auburn, or maybe chocolate brown. Or have streaks put in!"

"I don't think so. When I color my hair, it'll only be to cover the gray."

"You don't have gray hair, Mom."

"Sure I do. See?" I pointed out a spot above my right temple that used to be just five or six wiry gray strands but had expanded significantly in the last year.

"Oh, yeah." Her brow wrinkled. "But you don't really notice them."

"Eventually you will, sweetheart. It's just a matter of time."

She sat back on her heels and just stared at me. "How come you're all of a sudden worried about getting old? How old are you anyway?"

"Almost forty-four—and that's between you and me, you hear?"

She giggled. "Don't worry. I won't tell. Besides, with your new haircut you look nearly as young as Miss Oliver." Her new favorite teacher. "And she just had her thirtieth birthday." Then Lisa's brow wrinkled in thought. "Are you going on another date with that Stan guy?"

I leaned toward her, nodding. "I am. This Friday we're going to a movie."

"Cool. Can I spend the night at Kim's?"

I straightened a bit. Kim. Always Kim. "I suppose so. But I want your homework done before you go—all of it."

She rolled her eyes. "But I have the whole weekend to do it."

"There's no reason to procrastinate. You'll be glad once it's done. And neatly, you hear? Your report for science was so messy. You could see every place you erased something."

"It's my report," she muttered. "Not yours."

I raised my brows. "What was that?"

"Fine!" She plopped down on the couch, the epitome of a pouty kid.

"I suggest you watch that attitude," I warned, then immediately regretted it. I'd had my hair done and was having a nice chat with my daughter, and then that fast I'd slipped into drill-sergeant mode and ruined the moment.

I sat down in a chair opposite her. "Look, Lisa. You know you'll be glad once your homework is done, so let's not fight about it." When she only shrugged, I leaned toward her. "Maybe you can help me pick out something to wear on my date. You did such a good job last time."

She pursed her lips, then lifted her mutinous gaze to mine. "Okay," she said, and I watched her stormy emotions fade away. "But if you keep on dating him I think I should get to meet him." She paused, then blurted out, "Are you going to marry him?"

I jerked upright. "Of course not." I said the words reflexively, because I couldn't imagine myself ever marrying again.

Her head tilted to one side and her brow wrinkled in confusion. "You don't ever want to get married? Never in your whole life?"

I flailed around in my head, looking for a way out of the hole I'd just dug. "Don't you think I'm kind of old to be getting married?"

"Mr. Tidwell got married over Christmas vacation." He was their PE teacher. "And he's really old."

"No, he's not. He just has prematurely gray hair."

She looked doubtful. "Well, he really ought to dye it. But seriously, Mom, why are you going on another date with Stan if you don't want to ever get married?"

"Can't I just have a little fun?"

"Well, yeah." Then her eyes got big and her mouth went round. "Oh," she said, stretching it out like she all of a sudden understood something.

I frowned. "What does that mean, *oh*?"

She looked away and her hair partially hid her face. "It's okay. I know grown-ups do it."

Do it?

It.

Oh, my God. She meant sex!

"Lisa, what are you saying? You think I'm going out with Stan just to—" I broke off, unable to make myself say the word.

"I'm not stupid, Mom!" When she looked up her face was pink with embarrassment. "I know all about … it."

"You don't know anything. Sex is only for people who love each other." *Thank goodness I'd cleared that up in my mind.* "I don't care what you read or see on TV or hear from your friends. Some people may have sex without love. Most boys pressure their girlfriends to do it. But you'll be much happier if you hold out for love. Believe me, honey. I know what I'm talking about."

She stared down at her hands long enough that I wondered how this conversation had segued from my new haircut to sex. When she looked up I braced myself. "So, were you ever in love before? You know, enough to ... you know."

Oh, no. For years I'd evaded the subject of my past. My marriage. It was to avoid the treacherous path that led to my divorce, Alyssa's death, and Lisa's mother as the catalyst for it all. But now I was trapped.

I took a deep breath. "Okay, Lisa. Since you're asking me these questions, I think maybe you're old enough to hear the answers." I hesitated a moment, then plunged on. "The truth is, I was once in love like that. And ... I got married."

For about five seconds she digested what I'd said. Then came a barrage of questions. "You were married? When? What happened to him? Did he die?"

"We got divorced."

Again she momentarily was silenced. "Divorced? But why?" Then she went pale. "Because of me? Because you wanted to adopt me and he didn't?"

"No." I grabbed her hands and stared fiercely into her eyes. "Jim and I were divorced years before I found you. You weren't even born yet. That's why I never told you, because it was so long ago and it had nothing to do with you. Anyway," I said, releasing her hands. "Getting back to my date with Stan. Just because I'm going out on another date with him doesn't mean—"

"But Mom. Why did you get divorced? Didn't you love him anymore?"

How could I explain something that I didn't fully understand myself? I took the coward's way out. "Jim divorced me, baby. I guess he just didn't want to be married anymore." *At least not to me. Not without Alyssa.*

Without warning she flung herself at me and wound her arms around my neck. "He must've been an idiot," she muttered. "A stupid, mean idiot. You're the best mom in the whole wide world, and I bet you were the best wife too."

"Maybe." My arms wrapped around her as I reveled in her loyalty and love. "The thing is, it was a long time ago. Now I'm so used to not being married that I just don't think I could do it again. But that's not the point. The point is that love is the most important part in any relationship, whether it's between a woman and a man or a grown-up and their child."

Her arms squeezed me even tighter. "Even a mom and her adopted child?"

"You better believe it," I murmured against the sudden press of tears. It was terrifying how much I loved Lisa. More than I'd ever thought possible. More than was probably healthy. But what really scared me was that I couldn't remember loving Alyssa this much. I know I must have. But it was hard to remember that exact feeling. My grief over losing her sometimes loomed bigger than my actual life with her. And when my feelings for Lisa welled up like this ...

I extricated my neck from her grasp. "Now," I said, flicking the end of her nose. "No more talking about Stan and marriage in the same sentence. Okay?"

She tilted her head and grinned. "Okay. But can I ask one thing?"

Uh-oh. I braced myself again. "What?"

"Well. Like, how long did it take before you knew you wanted to get married? You know, to that guy, Jim?"

To Jim. How strange to hear his name on her lips. "I don't know. A long time. Almost three years." *Including the time we lived together before we got married.*

"Three years?" she exclaimed.

"That's right. That's why all this talk about Stan and me is silly. This is just our second date. We're barely friends yet."

"Okay," she said, stretching the word out. "But if you *do* fall in love with him, don't keep it a secret from me. Okay?"

"Okay."

"Because people who love each other aren't supposed to keep secrets."

I gave her a teasing grin. "None at all?" I asked, hoping to divert her and move on to a less touchy subject.

But she didn't bite. "You know what I mean, Mom. Big secrets. Like you being married a long time ago."

Or about another child I loved long before you came along.

"Okay," I agreed with her. But as guilt raised its prickly head I realized that one day I would have to tell her about Alyssa. She deserved the truth.

But not until she was an adult herself, preferably with a child of her own whom she loved beyond life itself. Because that's the only way she would ever understand why I'd done what I did. And why I'd maintained the lie so long.

CHAPTER NINE

INCIDENT REPORT BLOCK C
4/23/04

During an unscheduled contraband search Officer Leslie Hertz discovered a handmade knife and a stash of metal strips made from flattened tin cans hidden in a hollowed out bed leg of Inmate Davis LA C3-0092. Inmate Davis was transferred to Block F Solitary.

ST. ANNA'S PRISON
MAY 27, 2004

Dear Lissy,

    I am trying so hard to be a model prisoner but it's getting harder and harder. It's like when you get close to getting out, the guards can't stand it and they start looking for reasons to hold you back. Not all of them. But some. Especially this one. She's a class A bitch with a real mean streak who doesn't give a shit about us. But she'll get hers one day. I'm sure of it.

    I know I don't usually use bad words in my letters to you but there's no other way to describe her. Besides, by the time you ever read this, you'll be old enough to not mind a curse word or two from your old mom. But don't go using words like that all the time. They mark you as a certain kind of person and attract the wrong kind of friends. Sometimes, though, you just have to call them like you see them.

Anyway, I guess I'm just having one of my down days. I hope you're doing OK though. Pretty soon you'll be a teenager and then you'll start having all kinds of crazy feelings and wild impulses and probably lots of temptations too. But I hope you'll listen to your other Mom's advice and not do anything bad, especially drugs, drinking and sex. My life would be so different if I'd followed that advice.

Be safe. I love you. Your Mom.

ST. ANNA'S PRISON
JUNE 2, 2004

Dear Lissy,

I been sick lately, sick in the body, but mostly sick in my soul. Sometimes I don't know if I can make it, if I'll ever get out of here. My friend Sonya, she used to get depressed a lot. But I would cheer her up, try to make her laugh. We would count the days till we could leave and we would imagine all the things we would do once we got out. Like get a place together and get jobs and buy sexy clothes and cool shoes and go out dancing till dawn, breaking men's hearts but not trusting one word they said.

I never had a sister (Margeaux and Yvette don't count) But Sonya was like a sister. We just clicked, you know? I hope you have a sister by now. And maybe cousins. And lots and lots of friends. Lots.

Anyway, the reason I am sick in my soul is because Sonya died. She just couldn't take it anymore and I didn't even know how bad she was feeling! She never let on. I was just yakking and yakking, bitching about this and that and everything that's horrible around here. The food, the guards, the lousy soap and no air conditioning. She didn't say much, but I think maybe I got her even more depressed than usual. And now she's dead. And the worst part is that it doesn't matter, not to anybody around here except for me.

When the guard found her, she was like, "Hey, what's wrong with her?" "Hey, wake up." "Oh, look, blood." "What should I do? Scratch my ass or scratch my head?"

That guard could have saved her only she wasted precious time scratching her fucking ass! Finally she called for first aid but she could have let me in to do CPR and try to save Sonya's life. Only she wouldn't. She just stood there ignoring my screams, waiting for the other guards and the doctor, and she let Sonya die.

I know I should just forget about it. It's been nearly two months. But I can't forget. Even if I'm watching TV or working or whatever to stay busy, when I lay down at night I can't forget. I never cried so much as I cry now. Even in the beginning when I was so scared and always having to fight somebody off, I didn't cry as much then as I cry now. Even though I know crying doesn't help. It doesn't help anything. It doesn't make you feel better. It doesn't do shit. The only thing that helps is getting even.

So that's what I do. In whatever little way I and Sonya's other friends can do, we get even. That's one lesson I've learned here, Lissy. Always be true to your friends.

Always.

Love, Mom

INCIDENT REPORT BLOCK C
6/14/2004

During a routine escort to the infirmary Officer Leslie Hertz collapsed and went into convulsions. Three witnesses confirmed she was not attacked and she had no external injuries except for a split chin from where she hit the floor. By the time Dr. Phelps arrived Hertz was not breathing. CPR was administered and she revived. She was rushed to Our Lady of the Lake Hospital in Baton Rouge where initial tests indicate she may have brain damage due to the seizure or from oxygen deprivation after the seizure. A preliminary investigation has uncovered no obvious reason for her collapse. She has no known history of seizure disorders.

ST. ANNA'S WOMEN'S PRISON
JULY 2, 2004

Dear Lissy,

The closer it gets to when I can leave this place, the longer that time seems to stretch away from me. Today is 500 days exactly till the end of my term at St. Anna's. Compared to the 3153 days I already served, that shouldn't seem so long. But it does. It feels like forever. It feels like for every day that goes by I slip back two more days. I'm not the only one who feels that way. In group a lot of us talk about it. Our group leader says it's because we're afraid of being free. Most of us laugh hysterically at that idea. We're all real big on what we're going to do first. Go for a walk. Go to the beauty parlor. Go swimming. What I want is to go out to the country, somewhere so far out I can't see any buildings or hear any cars or music or anything. Just me by myself with Mother Nature.

The next thing we talk about is all the big plans we have for our lives. I'm an LPN now and when I get out I can finish the classes to be an RN. They can make good money and I plan to make lots of it. Sonya and I were going to get an apartment together and jobs together. We had it all worked out.

But now when I lay down at night quiet in my cell, I know our group leader is right. I'm scared to death of freedom. I didn't do so good with it the first time around. What if I screw up again? What if I mess up before I find you? Once I'm out it will be just me on my own with nobody to back me up. No family any more. No friends. You're all I have, you know? But you don't know, do you? Because even though I wrote all these letters, you've never read them. I've saved them though, every single one. Once I write them I put them in this box and it's pretty full. Even though I can't send them to you, it makes me feel better just to write them. I'm never going to throw them away. After I'm out and start looking for you I'm going to keep everything I learn about finding you in the box too. And in case I never find you, I'm going to put a letter on top of the box asking whoever finds it to try and find you. Even if you're a really old lady when you get these letters I'll be happy, no matter where I end up after I die, up above or down below.

I know when I get out of prison that I will have paid my debt to society. But I worry that maybe God won't be satisfied. I did worse things in my life than what I got arrested for. Things I don't think any amount of jail time can make up for. When you hurt people down to their souls I don't think you can ever undo the damage. You have to find other ways to seek forgiveness, other people to help since you can't help them. So much of the bad stuff I did was passed down to me from my mother and probably her mother too. I was in the middle of passing all that bad stuff on to you when I finally got arrested.

It's probably hard for you to understand, but even though I hated every second in this hellhole, one good thing came out of it: I couldn't pass all that bad stuff on to you. I broke the cycle when I gave you up. So now you can only get good stuff from your new mom. When I get really down, thinking about just ending it all, like Sonya did, I tell myself that my time here was for the best, and when I get out I'll be a much better person than I would have been. Maybe when I find you, I might actually be somebody you could be proud of. I ought to be able to get a job pretty quick after I get out, so I hope I won't have any reason to slip back into my old ways. I'll probably live in a transition house first, then once I save up I'll get a place of my own.

But the whole time I'm going to school and working, I'll still be looking for you, Lissy. I don't know how I'll find you, I just know I won't ever stop looking.

Love forever,
Your Mom

DIANE

To my surprise, I liked Stan. I mean, *really* liked him. He made me laugh and he didn't rush me in the romance department. But after our seventh date I knew we were approaching that moment of decision. We'd gone to an old-fashioned USO dance at the American Legion Hall and danced all night to big-band music. If anyone thinks dancing isn't one of the greatest forms of foreplay, take it from me, they are *sooo* wrong. If Lisa hadn't been at home with her friends Kim and Muriel spending the night, I definitely would have invited Stan in.

But the girls were almost thirteen and old enough to stay alone, and it was getting harder and harder to say no to their eager requests, especially since both other mothers approved and none of us was more than a phone call away. It couldn't be safer, I reassured myself. And maybe I'd agreed because subconsciously I'd been protecting myself from Stan, from the possibility of us actually having sex.

Three hours of dancing, first blood-pumping swing, then slow, sexy cheek to cheek, had me seriously hot for the man. After a frustrating make-out session in his car though, we regretfully said good night. Then I came inside, checked on the girls, took a long, cold shower, and went to bed.

It didn't work, though. I lay in my empty queen-sized bed thinking about Stan, and thinking about sex. It had been thirteen years since my divorce. Thirteen years since I'd had *any* form of sex. Probably more like fourteen.

I know that sounds insane. But after Alyssa died I was frozen inside, all my emotions encased in the hard, bitter ice of my pain. All these years I hadn't once felt any desire for sex. None. Not until Stan Chilton came along.

So what did that mean? Was I falling in love with him? Or

was he just my rebound man, albeit a decade late? Then again, did it really matter? We were both adults and ready to move to the next level of our relationship. More than ready.

But what if I didn't measure up to his expectations?

I lay in the dark considering my not-so-perky breasts, my not-so-firm thighs, and my not-so-flat belly. But it wasn't those imperfections that worried me most. He knew how old I was; surely he knew that in the end gravity always won.

No, my biggest worry was the actual sex. It had been so long. What if I'd forgotten how to do it? Not the mechanics of what part went where. But what if I didn't have an orgasm? He would be disappointed—so would I—and it would be embarrassing.

I groaned and flung one arm over my eyes. Use it or lose it. I'd read that in some women's magazine. What if I'd already lost it? Just thinking about it gave me the jitters and made me sweat. It was too hot beneath the covers, so I kicked them off. But still I felt overheated, from the inside out. And I was hyperaware of every inch of my skin—of the soft cotton gown hiked up above my thighs, of the rumpled sheets tangled at my ankles. Of the rise of dampness between my legs.

I felt guilty when my hand slid down over my belly. Crazy, I know. But guilty all the same. Closing my eyes, I pressed the heel of my hand down into the soft spot just above my pubic bone, pushing hard against the pressure brewing deep inside me.

Oh, damn. What was I doing?

Just do it. Just do it!

So I did. I'd never masturbated much. I met Jim too early to have perfected my method, and after he and I got together, I didn't need to perfect it. But I needed to now, if only to make sure everything down there still worked.

I pushed every thought aside except for bringing the itchy heat inside me up to the surface. To stroke and probe and finally—finally!—reclaim a part of me I thought I'd lost. Maybe that's why, after the stunning release of all that pent-up frustration, I burst into tears. I turned my face into my pillow and wept guilty tears of relief.

How insane was that? Guilt that I was abandoning one more emblem of my mourning, the frozen state I'd kept myself in since my life fell apart. Yet at the same time I felt such relief to know I wasn't entirely frozen. That I was still a woman with a woman's core that seethed with needs all her own.

But it still didn't feel right. It didn't feel like me.

"You're just out of practice," I muttered to my old, frozen self. I'd relearned how to love a child. Why couldn't I relearn to love myself?

I laughed out loud at such a pop-psychology notion. And yet I knew it was true. Learning to be fully human again was painful even now, all these long years after my heart had gone dormant. With shaky hands I tugged my nightgown down past my hips. Then I sat up and swung my legs over the side of the bed.

Okay. I hadn't forgotten how to have an orgasm. That was good. But it begged the larger question: If I was finally relearning how to love myself, did that mean my next step would be learning how to love a man? Not just physical love, because I knew now I could do that. But could I love *him*? Could I commit my heart to another man, whether it was Stan or some future fellow? Could I trust another man as much as I'd once trusted Jim? Most of all, could I reveal all my hopes and dreams to him, as well as my scars and sins?

Maybe, I told myself as I rose from the bed and headed to the bathroom. Maybe I could do all those things with the right man at the right time. But one thing I knew: There was no one I would ever trust with the truth about Lisa's mother, Alyssa's death, and the tortured connection I'd forged between us all.

·····

I felt heavy the next morning in that weary, yet cleansed way you sometimes feel after you've had a huge fight with someone you love, then cried and patched things up. In a way I guess that's what I'd done last night: had this huge emotional scene with myself. Now in the light of a new day I felt better, so much better that I decided I'd call Stan and invite him over for dinner next weekend.

Dinner.

I smiled at my rumpled appearance in the mirror as I brushed my teeth. I'd make him a wonderful dinner. Then I'd offer myself for dessert. A sweet shiver of anticipation shot through me, a tiny reminder of my successful experiment last night. The truth was, I could hardly wait.

"You slut," I murmured to my idiotically grinning reflection. And between now and next weekend maybe I'd practice just a little more so that I'd be sure to have the orgasm thing down pat.

Lisa and I had a lazy Sunday after her friends went home, just the two of us with leftover pizza and an old Tracy and Hepburn movie on PBS. "You want something to drink?" I asked as I rose from the couch.

She shook her head.

I looked at her, small and pale against the navy blue couch. "Are you feeling all right?"

She shrugged one shoulder. "My stomach hurts a little. And ... I don't know. I just feel kinda weird. Like, tingly." She wiggled her fingers in the air.

"What time did you three get to bed?"

"I don't know. Not that late." She shifted on the couch, pulling the lap blanket higher around her shoulders. "I fell asleep way before they did."

"Maybe you're catching something," I said. "Let me feel your head."

If she had a fever it wasn't much of one. But as the day wore on it became obvious that she was sick. She slept four hours on the couch and could barely sit up between her nap and dinnertime, she was that weak. She only nibbled at dinner, saying she wasn't hungry. I checked her forehead before I went to bed, with the same results. If she had a fever it was slight. I decided she probably had a mild case of food poisoning. With any luck it would pass through her system and by tomorrow she'd feel just fine.

Come morning, however, I ditched the food poisoning theory, at least the "mild" part of it. She was weak as a kitten, and I had to help her walk to the bathroom. I called Chris to let him know I'd be late to work. Then I called her pediatrician, helped Lisa dress, and took her in.

I didn't have much experience with sick kids. Alyssa had seemed immune to all the childhood illnesses—stomach aches, ear aches, and colds—and up till now, Lisa had been similarly fortunate. I attributed it to a healthy diet, a spotlessly clean house, and rigorously enforced regular hand-washing. Lots of vegetables and plenty of soap would prevent most of the illnesses in the world.

But no matter the cause, Lisa was sick now, and it was terrible. I wanted so badly to take that pain away from her, to take it on myself. It wasn't like my bright, lovely daughter to be lethargic and whiney. I told myself not to worry; whatever she had, Dr. Whalen would figure it out, prescribe something, and within a few days she'd be right as rain. But after he examined her, did a throat culture, took blood—twice—and then called his partner in, I was sweating fear.

"We'd like to admit Lisa to the hospital," he told me in the hall outside the examining room. "Just as a precaution."

There's a reason behind the cliché "my blood ran cold". Because that's exactly how I felt, instantly cold down to my bones. "The hospital? Why? What's wrong with her?"

"We're not exactly sure. She presents with flulike symptoms, but it's not flu season. Her white blood count is high, so we know there's some sort of infection. But her lungs sound clear, and her symptoms don't fit with food poisoning. Especially the tingling sensations. We need to run a few more tests to isolate the problem, and it'll be easier to do that if we admit her."

More tests turned into two days of using my poor baby as a pincushion. As her tingly sensations turned into numbness, and the tests ruled out migraines or a stroke, I became absolutely frantic and unable to sleep. Meanwhile she slept almost constantly. I only left her side once, to run home for clothes and toiletries and a few other necessities. Otherwise I remained at her side. But all those times between tests while she slept, my mind churned. What was wrong with Lisa? Where had she been? What terrible disease could she have been exposed to?

And then, chipping away at the edges of my consciousness was another fear, one I did not want to face. Could it be something genetic? One of the first things I'd done was give the hospital her medical history. But how complete could it be when all I knew of her family history was their predilection for drugs, alcohol, and selfishness?

Then came a crisis when her breathing became so labored they rushed her to ICU.

"You can't go in there," one of the floral-clad nurses said as I tried to follow Lisa's bed into ICU.

I wrenched my arm from her grasp. "I have to. I have to!"

"Sorry." Another nurse blocked the way. "Wait here and we'll keep you posted."

"But she needs me!" I started to cry. "Is she going to die?" When she didn't answer, I began to hyperventilate. She caught me as my worst fears closed in, dark, ugly, smothering. I was going to lose Lisa like I'd lost Alyssa.

"Sit here." She pushed me into a chair. "Put your head between your knees. Come on." Her hands bent me over. "Now breathe. Breathe!"

I gasped once, twice as I caught my breath and got my panic under control.

"Your daughter's in good hands," the nurse said. "The doctors are with her and they'll figure this out. Meanwhile you have to do your part."

I raised my head and stared desperately at her. "What? What can I do?"

She looked at me, this no-nonsense woman whose eyes nonetheless were filled with compassion. "Three things," she said. "You pray, you eat something, and you call someone to be here with you."

Pray? I was way out of practice with prayer. Besides, I wasn't sure I actually trusted God to help me or Lisa.

But maybe the Rebel Jesus would help me.

So I prayed to Jesus. I sat in the fluorescent-lit ICU waiting room and prayed. I ate the energy bar somebody handed me, and drank a bottle of water someone else gave me. After an eternity one of the doctors came out to tell me the crisis was past but that they were keeping Lisa in intensive care. "We've got her breathing under control. But we've decided to consult with specialists at Tulane University Hospital in New Orleans."

Specialists from New Orleans? "Don't you know what she has?"

He grimaced. "We've eliminated several things but we still don't know for sure. We think it might be some sort of peripheral nerve disorder."

A peripheral nerve disorder? *Oh, God!* "Could she … " I swallowed hard. "Is it ever fatal?"

He stared at me a long moment. "We hope not," he finally said.

We hope not! My knees went week and I sat down hard on the arm of the vinyl couch.

"Listen," he said. "I'm not trying to scare you, but we're trying to cover all bases. The other thing," he said, rubbing the back of his neck with one hand, "is that it could be congenital. We need to know everything we can about your daughter but her medical history is pretty thin. Her chart says she was adopted?"

He paused, and in that pause I knew what he wanted.

"Her father's dead," I blurted out.

"What about her mother?"

I shook my head, unable to respond. No way was I contacting *her.* No way!

"Do you know who she is?" he pressed.

I looked away.

"Look, Mrs. Haines. I know this adoption business can be tricky. But if you love that little girl, you'll do anything it takes to help us." He grabbed my arm, hard. "Are you listening?" His eyes bored into mine.

"Yes." I nearly choked on the word. "I'm listening."

"Good. So. Do you know who her birth mother is?"

I nodded, hating what he was making me do, but knowing in my heart that he was right. "I can find her."

"Okay. And be quick about it." Then he was gone.

I sat there in that cold waiting room, breathing hard as I contemplated doing the very last thing I ever thought I would do. Contact Roberta Fenner. The very idea made me gag, made me want to throw up what little I'd eaten since Lisa had become sick.

Roberta Fenner. Bobbie Davis. Convict. Junkie. Child murderer. And yet she might hold the only key to Lisa's recovery.

I had to do it. There was no other way. But before I made myself call the prison, I called Jim. I needed to talk to someone else first, and he was the only person I could think of, the only person who would understand my utter terror.

He had a new number and a new address. And when a woman answered with a sleepy voice, I remembered he also had a new wife. Panicked, I snapped my phone closed without speaking. How could I—his ex-wife—turn to him now? He didn't even know about Lisa, and I didn't want him to. But who *could* I call?

Stan? No. Chris or Pat? Maybe. But they had their own family to worry about and a business to run. What about Kim's mother? She would understand my terror. Or would she? She was so open with Kim about her adoption. Besides, she didn't know about my history with Bobbie. Nobody did.

And nobody ever could. I had to do this on my own.

"Oh, God," I begged in a broken voice. "Oh, God." *Please don't let her die.*

This time I sank to my knees, bent over the cold, plastic seats in the ICU waiting room, and prayed—to God, to Jesus, to Mary, and every other saint I'd ever heard about. But no matter the object of my prayers, the answer remained the same: I had to contact Bobbie Davis or someone else in her family and get a full medical history. That was the only way I could help the doctors help Lisa.

Resolved, I dried my eyes and struggled to my feet. Leaving the hospital, I drove straight to the office and logged onto the Web. It didn't take long to discover that Bobbie's mother, Lisa's grandmother, had died. Also that her uncle Hal was in jail for nearly killing a man in a bar fight. I stared at the newspaper article about him, fighting the urge to put my fist through the computer screen. What was wrong with these people? Were they all insane?

That's when I knew I was backed into a corner. I had to contact the prison where Bobbie was still incarcerated. To hell with hiding Lisa from her. I'd worry about that later. Right now I needed the prison's medical staff to do a complete history on Bobbie. I needed to know what was wrong with my baby, because she had to get well. She had to!

I could not cope if anything bad happened to my Lisa.

PART TWO

BOBBIE
OCTOBER 2004

CHAPTER TEN

OCT. 25, 2004

Dear Diary,

Kim and Muriel and I had *soooo* much fun last night. Mom actually let us stay home alone while she went on a date with Stan. Of course, she left a whole list of rules. But the minute she left we called Jake Evans, Muriel's boyfriend, and we checked out all these chatrooms too. Kim knows about this new thing called MySpace where everybody has like their own website but it's kinda like a giant chatroom too. But her mom won't let her join it till she's sixteen, and I *know* my mom would never let me do that.

She looked really nice when she left to meet Stan, really happy too. So far I haven't met him, but she obviously likes him a lot, so pretty soon she'll have to introduce us. It's so weird. Usually she's so serious and strict but yesterday she was practically giddy, like a kid, not a mom.

Anyway, she let us girls stay alone for the very first time, mostly because all three of us already took babysitting classes, and because we're almost thirteen. And because Muriel's mom convinced her we would be fine and that she would be home and we could call her if we needed to.

Kim brought the first two Harry Potter movies with her and we tried to watch them one after another. Except that I fell asleep. I was *soooo* tired.

They just left a little while ago and I'm like ready for another nap. My stomach's kind of icky. I guess maybe I had too much popcorn, pizza, nachos, and M&M's last night. And now my fingers feel all tingly. It's kinda hard to hold the pen.

I guess I'll finish this later
—Lisa

BOBBIE

Ten years is a long time. Especially if you're locked up in the same grim place with the same grim routine and the same grim faces around you. I used a 1996 calendar over and over to mark off my days in prison. So what if it's 1997 or 1998? Every year has twelve months, fifty-two weeks, 365 days. As far as leap year went, I knew there would be three extra days during my stay at St. Anna's Prison for Women. Three more days on top of the other 3650 I had to serve.

I don't remember much about the first year. I worked in the laundry, forced down my three squares, and lived for the one hour a day out in the yard. I went to meetings when told to and tried to avoid the butch gangs. That was about it. Oh, and I cried a lot. But only when I was alone—or in a meeting. You couldn't cry in front of the other inmates. No way. It marked you as a sissy, as a pushover who could be bullied, robbed, and worse.

The only exception was when the social worker was leading your inner motivation meeting, or the AA person was leading an AA meeting, or the minister was leading a prayer group. In fact it was good to cry then. A smart move. It made them feel like you were getting in touch with your feelings, like you were making progress. They'd write that down in your chart, that you were working hard on yourself and really making headway. Cry in the meetings, do your job, and keep your nose clean. The inmates all understood that kind of crying, and most everybody did it. That's what earned you good time and sped up the date of your release.

Only that didn't work for people convicted under the three strikes laws. People like me. I had to serve the whole 3653 days of my term. Every single minute.

But for the most part I fell into the routine anyway. The first year I did it in a fog, this gray confusion of dark cells, paralyzing fear, and an oppressive dread of the future. Only a few moments pierced that clammy fog, vivid nightmare moments I couldn't pretend weren't real: My arrest in November when I tried to escape but was too loaded to outrun a cop twice my age and three times my weight; the one and only visit when Mom brought Lissy to see me in jail and she cried the whole time; the letter from Child Protective Services saying Lissy was going into foster care; and finally my trial in March where I was convicted in a proceeding that took three hours max. The jury went out an hour and a half and came back before supper time with a decision. I bet they never thought about me again after that. They just went home to their families, maybe stopped to buy some Popeyes on the way, while I was handcuffed and shuffled back to the black hole of jail. Within a week I was shipped off to my new home, a deeper, blacker hole that in my soul I believed I would never get out of again.

I had credit for the seventy-three days I'd already served, and that reduced my sentence to 3580 days. But it still felt like forever, the rest of my life. I would be thirty-three when I got out, practically middle-aged, and my baby would be almost fourteen.

Lissy. She's the only light left in my life, the one feeble ray of hope I clung to in that first awful year, and all the endless ones that followed. At the same time she was the cause of my worst pain.

No, that's not true. *I* was the cause of my own pain. But she was the source of my misery, the reason for my shame, my guilt and my deep self-hatred. If not for her I could have endured those 3653 days better. I learned how to fight. I learned how to stand up to anybody, even when I was scared shitless. It was either face them down or become everybody's whipping boy—or their personal whore. So I got tough and I made a few enemies—inmates and guards. And I spent my share of time in solitary.

But I never got tough when it came to Lissy. Was she okay? Would she remember me? Ten years from now would she even want to see her ex-con mother?

It was even worse when the letters I sent her started coming back. Once she was officially adopted, she wasn't a part of the state's foster system anymore. That meant Child Protective Services quit tracking her.

I tried not to panic, but as the letters mounted up it was hard. After I went to jail she'd been put in foster care. Although I knew that was better than her being raised by my mother and her series of pervert boyfriends, I'd been so scared for my innocent baby girl. I guess there had to be *some* good foster families, but I never heard of any. All I'd heard were horror stories: kids who'd rather live in the streets than stay in the system; kids who'd been nothing more than slave labor and a monthly check for their foster families. Lissy's dad had been in foster care from the time he was eleven until he ran away at sixteen. And look how he'd turned out, even worse than me.

No, Ken wasn't worse than me. He might have been a junkie and a thief, and he sometimes could be so mean. But at least he'd married me two weeks before Lissy was born. That had been really important to me, and he'd finally agreed. The other good thing about Ken was that he'd never killed anyone, especially not a little kid. That was *my* particular sin.

Still, I hoped and prayed that the family who'd taken in Lissy until she was adopted had been a good one. Maybe they'd been decent people. But how could I ever be sure? That's why I agreed to let Lissy be adopted. Even though I wouldn't have any control over who was going to raise my little girl, I figured people who actually adopt other people's children must really, really want them. So Lissy went into the foster care system and less than a year later she was adopted. Sometimes I imagined her with her new parents: A pretty, middle-aged woman, plump and smiling, who baked brownies and sewed pretty dresses for my Lissy, a graying man who gave her piggyback rides and sang her to sleep at night. People who'd been waiting for a child like her all their lives and were so happy to have her now. Lissy deserved parents like that. Every child did.

Then that grim fog would come over me and I'd get really down, remembering the little girl whose life I'd stolen. For years I'd tried to forget her. Drugs were a big help. When you're loaded all the time, all you ever think about is where your next fix is coming from. But in jail—sober—I couldn't escape her. She was relentless, like a movie loop playing over and over in my mind. Alyssa Leftwich, sweet and innocent. Six years old, with her whole life ahead of her—and dead because of me. Her parents had looked like good people—until I wrecked their lives. I didn't mind God punishing me for what I'd done to her. I deserved everything I got, and more. But it got really bad when I lost the baby.

I wasn't trying to get pregnant. I was just bored. And Vernon Oldham wasn't half-bad to look at. But he was fucking everyone he could, and Katherine Leonard didn't like it one bit. She wanted him all for herself. Like that was ever going to happen. I didn't even know I was pregnant when she attacked me. But when I started to bleed so bad, and then the doctor said I lost a baby ...

It shook me so bad. Worse than I ever expected. I'd killed another child, just as unconsciously as I'd killed Alyssa Leftwich. How many ways was God going to punish me? First guilt over Alyssa; then losing Lissy; next losing a baby. Was he a boy or a girl? I'll never know. But my biggest fear was that God might punish me through Lissy, by giving her to someone who would be mean to her.

Could he be that awful to an innocent child?

He had already been cruel to Alyssa. Why wouldn't he do something like that to Lissy?

I talked to the prison chaplain about it once, and he told me it was just the opposite, that God was showing me his forgiveness. That Alyssa and my poor unborn baby were with God in heaven. And he said that by letting Lissy go to a good family, I was preventing her from falling into the same bad kind of life I'd lived.

I clung to that idea, that God was forgiving me, because I didn't know any way to be sorrier for my past than I already was. I knew Diane and Jim Leftwich would never forgive me. Why should they? If the situation had been reversed I'd never forgive them. As it was, I'd lost my daughter, and my little baby too. Only I had no one to blame but myself. And the only way I could show God how sorry I felt was to live a better life. To use my time in jail wisely. To get smarter, not just in schoolwork, but in making life decisions too.

That's why I never stopped writing to Lissy. One of the teachers who came to the prison encouraged me to keep on with the letters. She said it was good practice for me and would make my writing skills better for when I got out and started looking for a job. Plus, if I ever found her I could give the letters to her and she would see that I'd never stopped loving her.

Miss Gardner. That was the teacher's name. She was really smart and sometimes she led the AA meetings too. She knew where it was at. She was the one who convinced me to get my G.E.D. and then to get in one of the job training programs the prison offered: secretary/accounting, nursing/med tech, or culinary arts. Even after she quit teaching here I kept on going to school to improve myself. That's how I became a licensed practical nurse and got my job working in the prison health clinic.

Now I'm trying to see if they'll let me take some online nursing classes from one of the nursing schools so that when I'm out—one year, three months, four days—I'll be closer to becoming a registered nurse. RN's make a lot more money than LPN's. Of course, ex-cons can't get registered in some states. But since I wasn't tied to anybody or anyplace—except Lissy—I figured I could move to wherever I could get licensed. Besides, that's years away.

I was putting a blood-pressure cuff on the oldest prisoner at St. Anna's—Louella Starnes, seventy-six years old—when my boss stuck her head into the exam room. "When you're done here, come see me."

That was Dr. Phelps for you, abrupt to the point of rudeness. I used to think she was afraid of us prisoners, like we were gonna jump her skinny-ass bones or something. But in time I figured out that she was one of the good ones, one of those doctors who really goes the extra mile for us, the dregs of society. She demands a lot from me and the others who work with her. But she explains everything she does, which really teaches us so much. She's not a soft, touchy-feely person, but she's always fair.

So when she blurted out "come see me"—not a request, no please or thank you—I just shrugged it off. She was either giving me something new to do, or else going to chew me out for doing something wrong—and then teach me how to do it right.

"So how'm I doin'?" Louella asked as I slowly released the pressure on the cuff.

"A little high. But better than last time. If you just cut out the salt and butter, Doc could probably lower the dosage of your pressure medicine."

"Hunh." She pulled her sleeve down, and then looked up at me. "Think she'd give me a few Xanax? I been kinda nervous lately. Have a hard time sleeping."

Once a week she came in and she always asked the same question. I shrugged. "I'll mention it to her."

She didn't argue her case. We both knew the answer. But once a junkie, always a junkie, at least most of the time. Not me though. I'd been clean every day of my sentence and now that I had a marketable skill, I was determined not to blow it. I'd been down that dead-end road. In a way I was lucky to have been slapped down when I was still young. I had nowhere to go but up. And I still had the time to do it. I planned on being one of the success stories coming out of this place.

Any time my attitude took a nosedive, or the gray fog moved in to smother me, I forced myself to look at Louella and all the other inmates in here who would never change. I did not want to be like them, just like I did not want to be like my mother. I wanted to be like Miss Gardner or Dr. Phelps. I wanted to do good things with my life, to help people who really needed somebody to believe in them. I'd broken the cycle of being like my mother. I wanted to start a new cycle instead.

"What's up?" I asked Dr. Phelps once the guard took Louella away.

"Sit down," she said, looking at me with this odd, really serious expression. She's not big on smiling, but I'd learned to read her moods. Today, though, I couldn't tell what was going on with her.

After I sat opposite her desk, she folded her hands together over the smooth oak surface. "I received a request to do a complete medical history on you."

"What? Why?" Then I frowned. "If this is about those online nursing classes, I don't see that it's any of their business. I might be in jail, but that doesn't mean I don't have a right to privacy." We prisoners are real big on preserving what few rights we still possess.

Dr. Phelps shook her head. She looked tired, or maybe just stressed. "It's not about that. It's about—" She took a breath. "It's about your daughter."

The world stopped.

Everything—the squeeze and release of my heart, the in and out of my lungs, the electrical impulses between my brain cells. They all came to a jarring halt.

"My daughter? Lissy?" I think I said those words. But maybe I only thought them. Because suddenly I felt faint, like I was far, far away from this room. Like I was watching a TV show. I wanted to stand up to see if it was real or not, but I couldn't move. *My daughter? Lissy?* I'd never spoken to Dr. Phelps about Lissy. So what was she talking about?

"... she's sick in the hospital. ICU, in fact. And they're having a difficult time pinpointing the problem."

I started to shake. First inside, then my hands and my legs and even my jaw. "Was she ... was she in a car wreck?" That was my ever-present guilt talking. But it would only be fair, that God would kill my baby in a car like I'd killed little Alyssa Leftwich.

"No, not an accident. She's come down with something her doctors haven't yet been able to diagnose. They're contacting family in case there's a genetic component."

It wasn't a car wreck. Thank God. *Thank you, God.* Then I realized: ICU. And now they were consulting *me*? My solitary moment of relief shredded to dust and once more it hurt to breathe. "Is she ... is she going to be all right?"

Doc's dark-brown eyes held with mine. But though I saw compassion in them, she remained as blunt as ever. "I'm assuming the situation is serious if they're contacting us. From what they told me, she was adopted when you first came here and there's been no contact since."

"Those were the rules," I choked the words out. "No contact, though I tried. I write her letters. I don't send them, but I still write them."

She nodded. "You were right to let her be adopted, Bobbie. Now, let's do that history."

"Okay. Whatever they want, I'll do it." I slid forward to the front edge of the hard-bottomed chair. "Did they tell you anything? Like how long she's been sick? What the symptoms are? What hospital she's in?"

Dr. Phelps shook her head. "I got a phone call from the warden relaying the request. I don't know any more than I just told you."

"Okay." I pressed my lips together and slid back in the chair. "Okay." But it wasn't okay. Not hardly. I was terrified. My baby, my sweet innocent Lissy was sick, and here I sat, stuck in prison, no use to her at all. So what if I'd got my G.E.D., become an LPN, and was studying to be an RN? Big fucking deal!

I'd failed my child in every way a parent could. Giving her up hadn't been a generous act. I'd had no other real choice. If I'd really loved her I would have given her up the day she was born, let some good family have her instead of subjecting her to nearly four years of my fumbling, failing attempts at motherhood.

"This isn't your fault," Dr. Phelps said. "And it's probably not her new family's fault either. Children get sick all the time, Bobbie."

Maybe. But not every child had a mother who'd killed

someone else's child. The world had a way of handing out justice that wasn't always fair. People did it all the time. God did it too. If He didn't, every child would live a perfect life. But none of them did. Especially mine.

I took a shaky breath. Then I sat up straighter and turned to face her. "What do you need to know?"

As little as I knew about my family's medical history, I knew even less about Ken's side of Lissy's family tree.

"I guess that's it, then," Doc said when we'd gone through the whole form. "All we know is that your mother had diabetes and emphysema. Your father's mother died in childbirth. No known evidence of heart disease or hypertension. Addiction disorders on both sides, but you're in perfect health now. And as a child you had chicken pox."

"And I had a lot of earaches," I added. "Until I was in school. So did Lissy until she was three."

"Any other illnesses or viruses she had as a baby?"

I closed my eyes, trying so hard to remember something—anything—from my few years with Lissy that might help her now. The problem was, I'd been so depressed and so overwhelmed back then. And so stoned. As much as I'd loved my new baby, that happiness had only deepened my guilt for stealing the life of the Leftwiches' little girl. Then Ken had OD'd, and so much of the rest of it became a blur.

I remember thinking then that his death was God punishing me for Alyssa Leftwich. Then after I was arrested I thought having to give up Lissy was my punishment. Even my miscarriage five years ago had still felt like God's cold hand of justice. Not that I'd wanted to get pregnant by that prick guard. I'd just wanted somebody to cut me a little slack. Still, I'd been devastated when I lost the baby.

But I saw now that those had just been warm-up acts for the main event. My baby, not even thirteen years old, was fighting for her life. Her doctors were so desperate they had turned to me for help. Me, the queen of fuckups.

I don't remember the rest of that day. I returned to my cell and lay there in some kind of stupor. Nobody made me get up and go back to work, or to the yard for exercise, or even to dinner. A tray of food appeared—probably Doc's doing. I know the guards didn't give a damn. But I couldn't eat. All I could do was think about my baby. And pray for her.

Trouble was, I wasn't any good at praying. For the most part I go back and forth about God. My prayers are mainly apologies for everything I've done. I never ask Him for anything, because I don't feel like I have the right. Like He would punish me if I even tried. He's a God of vengeance. All you have to do is look at a sick or abused kid to know He's got a mean streak. So I prayed to Jesus instead. It's not logical but what in life is? I prayed to Jesus and to his mother Mary, and to Ken and to my mom. Even to the little unborn baby I'd lost three years into my sentence. *If you're somewhere out there, you have to help her. Please help my Lissy.*

The next morning I was a wreck, still too nervous to eat. When I got to the clinic I barged into Dr. Phelps's office. "Have you heard anything?"

She raised her gaze from her computer screen, but she didn't look angry at my departure from procedure. "No, nothing." She pushed away from her desk. "Don't get your hopes up, Bobbie. When I spoke to the warden she said the best she could do was inform you if ... if things didn't go well."

Didn't go well?

"You mean they'll tell me if she dies?" I'd been holding the gray fog back—barely. But now it descended thick and terrifying until I could hardly breathe. "What if ... what if she never walks again? Or goes into a persistent vegetative state? Or goes blind? Or turns out—"

"I don't know. I just don't know."

I stared around the plain room with its off-white cinder-block walls and fixed metal cabinets. I had to do something or I would explode. I looked down at Doc. "I have to talk to the warden."

She nodded. "I figured you'd say that. You know the drill."

I knew it all right. I'd only had to put in for an appointment with the warden once and that was to get into the online RN program. At the time I'd been super nervous about facing her because I'd had more than my share of run-ins, both with prisoners and guards. Pretty young blondes are a popular item in a women's prison—only I'd refused to be that kind of popular, and I have my share of scars to show for it. I'd spent enough time in solitary for fighting that I practically had my own room there. Added to that, everyone knew Warden Pratt liked having people beg and grovel for favors. But that's what I'd done to get in the program. Yes, ma'am; no ma'am; thank you, ma'am.

This request was so much more important though. If I had to grovel and beg on my belly to find out how Lissy was doing, I'd do it, and with a smile on my face too.

Doc slid a request form across the desk. "I picked one up for you."

Without warning, embarrassing tears stung my eyes. It's a lot easier to control my emotions when people treat me like shit, or at least like they don't care one way or another. I have a couple of friends here, though my best friend of all died. We watch each other's backs, and maybe sometimes we reveal parts of our true selves. But never to people like Doc or the guards. Or the warden.

That's why Doc's unexpected kindness was so hard to deal with. I shuddered the tears down, nodded my thanks, and took the paper. She nodded back, then patted a short stack of patient files on her desk. "When you're done with that, these charts need filing. We have six appointments this morning, and don't forget inventory."

I worked hard. It was easier than worrying and waiting. Three days went by before I met with the warden. She was a strange bird. I mean, what kind of person grows up thinking, I want to be a prison guard when I grow up, and maybe rise through the ranks to become warden?

On the flip side, what kid grows up thinking, One day I want to go to jail, preferably for a really long time? Maybe Warden Pratt had started off with an entirely different goal. Or maybe she'd had no particular direction. Maybe she'd just drifted here. Like me.

She was working at her desk when I walked in. She didn't ask me to sit, didn't even look up from the open file in front of her. She just answered the question she didn't give me time to ask. "Your daughter is still in the hospital, but is no longer in intensive care. That's a good thing. Beyond that I can tell you nothing. She's legally someone else's child. Not yours."

I knew that. Yet hearing her say it so callously made me crazy. "Yeah, it's a good thing if she's on the road to recovery," I snapped back at her. "But it's not a good thing if she's in a rehab ward or in a hospice program. Just because she's out of ICU doesn't mean she's doing fine!"

When her head jerked up I realized I was shouting, and that my hands had knotted into fists. "This is all very touching, Inmate Davis," she drawled, staring at me with steel-cold eyes.

"But I've never seen any indication that you cared where your child was." She gave me a thin, mocking smile. "Why so maternal all of a sudden?"

Forget groveling. What I wanted was to leap across her shiny, obsessively neat desk and strangle that smug smile right off her ugly face. She looked like somebody's plump, pink-cheeked grandmother, but her deliberate nonchalance regarding *my* child—and my feelings for her—said otherwise. "Why would I—why would *any* of us—ever reveal our true feelings to *you*?" I spat the words out, not disguising my utter contempt for her.

When her brows lifted in surprise at my nerve it only stoked my rage. I strode up to her desk. "I pity any child of yours." I sneered the words, venting all the poisonous emotions I had bottled inside me for too long. "What did you do when they screwed up, lock them in a closet? Put them on bread and water rations, or deny them the sight of sunlight? Or maybe—"

Before I could finish my tirade I was yanked off my feet, my arms practically dislocated. She must have had a buzzer under her desk, because she hadn't moved or said a word. She didn't say a word as they dragged me away either, which only multiplied my fury.

"You stupid bitch!" I screamed. "Heartless cunt!"

"Shut the fuck up," one of the matrons said with a sharp elbow to my ribs.

But I couldn't shut up. I'd tried to be a model prisoner. For eight and a half fucking years. Three thousand fucking days! And what did I get? Not even the courtesy of knowing if my child was on the mend. She was alive. That's all they would tell me.

Well, it wasn't enough. It would never be enough.

CHAPTER ELEVEN

MAY 31, 2005

Dear Kim,
 I still can't believe we're really moving away from you and all my friends and our whole life in Alexandria !!! Right now we're in the car–mile marker 219. I'm sitting in the backseat like a prisoner. I refuse to sit up front with Mom. I hate her!!. Why is she being so mean? I keep asking her why we have to move. WHY? Correction: I *kept* asking her why right until she locked the apartment door and returned the key to the apartment manager's office. Since then I haven't said anything to her. And I'm not going to. She's always been like paranoid and all, way stricter than anybody else's mom. But now it's like she's gone crazy. And she's making me crazy too. Like it wasn't bad enough it took four months for me to get better from that stupid Guillain-Barre syndrome. You know how hard I worked at physical therapy to make my nerves and muscles work right again. I caught up with school and everything, and now nobody can tell I ever was sick. But how does she reward me? By making us more someplace where I won't know anybody!

She keeps looking at me in the rearview mirror, but I refuse to look back at her. Why is she being such a witch? We don't *have* to move. She just *wants* to. Just like every other time she gets this insane idea and we have to move. First we lived in Slidell then Jackson then Alexandria and now Hot Springs. Why?

I asked her if it was because of Stan. Did they have a big fight or something? She didn't say anything so I thought maybe they did. But I answered the phone one day when he called and I asked him what did they fight about and he said they didn't have a fight. So then I asked her again why we were leaving. She didn't want to answer, but I refused to let her off the hook. Finally she says I'm bored here. We need a better place. Like, where would be better than Alexandria except for maybe Beverly Hills or Hawaii or someplace cool like that? But no, we're going to stupid Arkansas. I swear, if I knew where my real mom was, I'd run away and live with her instead.

Uh oh, we're pulling off the highway. Gotta go. As soon as we get set up I'll e-mail you.

Best Friends 4Ever, Lisa

BOBBIE

After my run-in with the warden I lost my school privileges and my cushy job in the health clinic. Three weeks in solitary feels like three years. No window, no arc of the sun or the moon to mark the passage of time. In the winter it's too cold. In the summer it's sweltering hot. The only diversions are the guards—two were chatty, the other four weren't—and the one hour of exercise.

I've learned how to be alone here. You have to learn, otherwise you'll go crazy. Like Sonya.

I tried hard not to think about Sonya or Lissy, but there were always with me. As was the guilt I felt over them. I'd let them both down, big-time. Meanwhile, here I sat, as useless as ever. At least Sonya's struggles were over. But my poor Lissy ….

There were no sharps in my cell except for my nails and teeth. So I bit myself. On the inside of my arms, once a day to mark the passage of time, I bit myself until I drew blood. It hurt like hell, but it felt good too. The red, welling blood proved that I was alive. The unnatural stabbing shaft of self-inflicted pain reminded me that I was still a feeling person, still a part of the human race. And the lingering sting when my own sweat found the raw wounds and burned with unexpected fire drove home what I already knew: There were consequences in life. For everything.

The chaplain visited once a week and talked about bad ripples and good ripples. All the ripples I'd created so far were bad ones. But she told me I could create good ripples if I worked at it.

I wanted to believe her. When I lay there sweating, with my raw, chewed-up flesh burning from the excess salt in my own body, I visualized Lissy and prayed to Sonya and vowed to one day be a person who puts out good ripples. And I vowed to toe the line for the rest of my time and make it out of here without another single day being added to my sentence.

Once my stint in solitary was over they put me in housekeeping and laundry, alternating one week at a time. I didn't set foot in the health clinic for three months until I got a huge splinter in my palm. When I came in, the nurse, Candida, frowned at me.

"What you doin' here?"

I held out my hand. "Splinter."

She shrugged one shoulder. "I can take care of that. You don't need to see the doc."

"Oh, you're an RN these days?"

"Fuck you," she muttered.

"You wish." I signed in, then sat down and just ignored her. The thing is, I knew where her attitude was coming from. When I got yanked out of the clinic, she moved up with better shifts and the perception of more seniority. Now here I was waiting to see Doc, and Candida was afraid I was trying to move back in on what was her turf now.

I'd had plenty of time to think about my boneheaded run-in with the warden. Yeah, I'd been freaked out about Lissy. I'd been exhausted from worry and lack of sleep, and frustrated by the impenetrable wall of silence that kept me away from any news about my baby. But even so, lunging at the warden had been stupid. Did I really think threatening her would make her change her mind and fill me in on all the details of Lissy's illness? The bitch had let me into her office, knowing I'd end up in solitary. I found out from Mae that the guards had a betting pool going that day on how long it would take before I exploded and they would be buzzed in to drag me away. And like the stupid, impulsive fool I'd always been, I played right into their hands.

I know the guards hate me. Most of them hate all the prisoners, but some of them hate me even more because of that bitch guard, Leslie Hertz. They suspect I had something to do with her nearly dying, but they can't figure out how. And they never will. They're too stupid to suspect that a con like me could figure out how to poison a big, tough guard. All it took was a peek into her med records and the slow accumulation of drops of the one medicine she was allergic to. Then I made a point to irritate her one day. It wasn't hard. Of course when she patted me down she kept the candy bar she found on me. Malt balls, her favorite.

She didn't die like Sonya did, but she almost did. And she never came back to work here.

But the guards hadn't forgotten, even though they never could pin it on me. Soon, though, they wouldn't have me around anymore to torture. Meanwhile, no more stupid knee-jerk reactions for me. I had to smarten up if I was ever going to make it, and not just book smarts. People smarts.

Still, it sometimes felt like I was being eaten alive with fear and grief. And guilt. It never went away, that smothering swamp of emotions. Instead it grew in me like some voracious cancer. I'd gotten it under control after about a year here, and had been maintaining for a long time, like I was in remission. Then Sonya died and Dr. Phelps did that medical history on me, and bam! I went straight to stage four.

But it was not going to kill me. No way. My only solace as I slogged away in the ungodly heat of the laundry house or slopped soapy bleach water in the latrines was that after dinner I could cross one more day off my term. One day closer to freedom and the real start of my search for my baby.

Any hesitation I had about looking for her, about how my reappearance might disrupt her life or confuse her, had vanished. And with every load of dirty bed linens, towels, and prison threads, my determination to find her grew and swelled and morphed into this monster need, this Godzilla mom who would trample anything in her path to find her baby.

It took six months for me to earn back my school privileges, and another three to get a job transfer. But I didn't go back to the health clinic. This time I was smart. I acted like I wanted the health clinic. But it was my second choice that I really wanted. I acted disappointed when I was reassigned to the library, but inside I was ecstatic. Why? The computers. I wanted access to the Internet, and to get that I needed two things: a computer, and somebody's password.

You can learn a lot in prison if you're motivated. To survive you have to notice everything about everybody. Who's most likely to go off on you for no reason; who's a snitch; who's rock solid; who's about to snap. And who, especially among the guards, staff, and trusties, could be sweet-talked or bribed into looking the other way.

Toolie Fastbender was one of that last group. Word had it that she was the widow of the former warden of a big men's prison. He'd died young, without enough time in the system to earn a pension. She had some kind of disability, agoraphobia, I think. So somebody had given her a job here and a little cottage right outside the prison gates to live in. She knew me from my high school and nursing classes held in the library, but she was still wary of me at first.

"Shelve these books, then wipe down all the shelves—and the tops of the books too—starting at the top. Use two separate rags," she told me. "Put Pledge on the one you use on the shelves. But don't get Pledge on the books. Be very, very careful not to get Pledge on the books."

"Yes, ma'am. I'll be careful," I said. And I meant it. I would "yes, ma'am" her to death, and be the most attentive and thorough library aide she'd ever had, if that's what it took to earn her trust. No Pledge on any books during my shifts. I arrived early, stayed late, and always saved my desserts for her.

"I never did have much of a sweet tooth," I told her the first time I brought her my Friday brownie. Monday was chocolate chip cookies, Sunday was cake with icing. The other days were either Jell-O or pudding.

She stared at the brownie I put on her desk, all folded up in a napkin. It wasn't true, of course. I love chocolate desserts as much as anyone. But I love Lissy more. Toolie had a serious sweet tooth, though. I'd figured that out right away, one of those little facts you notice and store away for future use. Yeah, she wanted that brownie all right.

She peered up at me, then back at the brownie. "Well. If you're sure."

It only took six weeks. That's six brownies, four chocolate chip cookies—I slipped up and ate two of the cookies—and six slices of cake. I was meticulous with the dusting and the Pledge, and never sloppy with the re-shelving. I also lined up the spines of the books, keeping them no more than one inch from the face of the shelves. Plus I asked her advice about books to check out, then discussed them with her after I read them.

I guess she figured a hardworking, meticulous bookworm couldn't be all bad. Because one day she asked me if I knew how to type.

"Sure do. I'm not that fast, though."

"But you understand how to use Microsoft Word, right?"

"The basic parts. Is there something you want me to do?"

She made a face, like she was debating if she should ask me or not, and stared at the computer screen on her desk. "Are you any good at math?"

"It was my best subject when I was a kid," I lied, trying not to reveal my excitement. Whatever she wanted me to do, I would learn how to do it. Anything to get access to her computer.

"Okay," she said on a large gust of breath. "Pull that chair over here."

It turns out that Toolie was terrible with numbers, and the new inventory program Warden Pratt had converted the whole prison to was way over her head. But it wasn't just inventory. We only had about seven thousand books in the library, and twenty-two magazine subscriptions, so it wasn't that hard to keep track of things. Plus our budget for new purchases was a pitiful two thousand dollars a year. The main thing the warden wanted was to track who read what. What kind of books were most popular and why? Very Big-Brother-is-watching-you. It was a huge violation of privacy—I'd read articles in the local paper and in *Time* magazine about that issue after 9/11, when the government wanted to know who was reading what, the Bill of Rights be damned. But what was an invasion of privacy for regular folks was just another day behind bars for inmates.

So I took over that task for Toolie. While I read the user's guide and slowly figured out how to set up spreadsheets and how to input each title as it was checked out, Toolie shelved and dusted and carefully applied her Pledge. And when I finished that project, I broached another.

"I've read about Amazon.com," I said. "How they sell used books as well as new ones. I bet if we shopped around for used books in good shape, we could buy a lot more books for the library. You know, stretch the budget."

"Really?" she said.

"Yeah. I mean, you'd have to go online." I gazed guilelessly at her.

"Online," she repeated. "I don't know."

"I'll help you. I mean, it can't be that hard. You already use e-mail." I knew she used e-mail, but only to respond to the warden's e-mails. Everything else having to do with the computer she left to me. But even though I didn't know how to use e-mail or Google, or anything else online, I'd been reading every article I could get on the subject so that when the moment came, I'd be prepared. "Did they give you a password to use?" I asked. The cursor blinked expectantly.

"Um, yes." She pulled a drawer open and rummaged around in it. "Here." She handed me a printed form that had assigned her the password *Library1*.

After a few false starts we were on the Worldwide Web and had found Amazon. I tried to hide my exhilaration but it was hard. I was online! That meant I had the whole of the Internet at my command to find Lissy.

But I made the whole online process seem more complicated than it was to Toolie. "Be careful of the control button. If you hit it at the same time as other certain buttons, the computer might do all these other things you don't expect. You can really mess stuff up. At least that's what the tutorial said," I added.

"The tutorial?"

"That's the instructional portion for the various programs on the computer that tells you how things work."

She nodded. Then she asked, "How do you find the tutorial?"

"Well, you have to know where to look. It's in different locations depending on the program you're using and the application you plan."

With every deliberately vague answer I gave, she leaned farther and farther away from the computer screen. "Oh," she said. "I see. Well, I sure am glad you understand this stuff, Bobbie."

That's how I came to be the library's unofficial computer geek. Once I got the system set up, it only took me fifteen minutes or so a day to keep library business current. Most of the rest of my shift I spent online, supposedly shopping for the best bargains on books. But I also helped Toolie shop for shoes online. She wore an eleven wide, and was hard to fit. I helped her use an online bridal registry to buy a gift for her nephew who was getting married, and I even burned a CD of her favorite Roy Orbison songs as a gift from me to her.

In return, she left me alone with the computer.

We both knew it was against the rules for me to go online with her password. But she kept quiet and I kept quiet, and all in all everything was perfect.

Except that I couldn't find anything about Lissy anywhere. Not when I Googled her and not on any site I could think of. Juvenile case records were closed, as were files in the office of child support. I found a record of Lissy's birth, Ken's death, and my arrest. But nowhere else was any record of Lissy Anne Davis listed. So I started searching for just Lissy. There were thousands. Then I got the bright idea to search census records.

I found myself, but no Lissy. I had her after one census, but lost her before the next.

That's when I started to get really depressed. It was like she'd never existed. I mean there were thousands of Lissy's. Lissy Callahan, who was cut from the U.S. Olympic trials because of steroid use. Lissy Thompson, who was arrested for hoarding seventy-nine cats and thirty-two dogs plus various exotic birds and two ferrets. Lissy French who was marrying Daniel Listz so she could be Lissy Listz.

I spent every minute of my time in the library, and as many of those minutes as I could on Toolie's computer. I neglected my nursing class and got a D, which meant I'd have to retake that course. But I didn't care. I needed to find my Lissy, or at least some lead to point me in the right direction.

And as the weeks and months ticked down, and the day of my release neared, I began to panic. I was desperate to leave this place, yes. But then what? Where would I begin my search in earnest?

"I bought you a going-away gift," Toolie said three days before my scheduled release. "Something to make your new home more ... well, homey."

It was a crocheted tissue-box cover with a pair of matching crocheted hot plates, the kind crocheted around bottle tops.

"Yellow and green," I said. "My favorite colors." I looked up at her, unaccountably moved.

"Yes. I know," she said, self-consciously smiling. "And I know something else," she added. "Pull the first tissue out."

Perplexed, I did as she asked. On the corner of the tissue I saw something written. I smiled, expecting some sentimental something about how she would miss me and good luck on my new life. She really had been nicer to me than anyone else in this place. But my smile faded when I read the words *Siobhan Gullihay, Tulane University Hospital, New Orleans.*

"What's this?" I asked. "A job lead?" She shook her head, then folded her arms like she was cradling a baby.

A baby. My heart lurched so hard it hurt. "Lissy?"

I hadn't meant to say the name out loud. But Toolie nodded. "That's all I know," she said. "It's probably where she was treated when she was sick."

I could hardly hear her, the blood beat so loud in my ears. "But—but—"

"But how did I know?" She grinned. "I don't like computers,

Bobbie. But I'm not a hopeless idiot. The new deputy warden asked me why I was using census records and other government agencies. Of course I knew it had to be you. But I told her I was working on my family tree. I figured, though, that you were looking for someone specific, and since I knew about your run-in with the warden about your little girl being sick, well ... " She shrugged. "I checked your file one day and saw a telephone message from a Dr. Siobhan Gullihay. Kind of a strange name. So I made a few calls."

I'd never touched Toolie Fastbender. It was strictly forbidden for any inmate to touch staff or guards. But not today. I grabbed her and hugged her, and after a slight gasp of surprise, she hugged me right back.

"Okay," she said when we pulled apart. "Now flush that tissue and get back to work, you hear? I've only got you for a few more hours, and I want that last order ready to go before you leave."

"Yes, ma'am," I replied.

Yes, ma'am! I had a direction now, a starting point. I was thirty-three, nearing the halfway point in my life. In three days I would get the chance to start anew, and I was not going to blow it.

And I was never going to forget the people who had helped me either. There were plenty of people in this place that I hated, and more people like them out in the world too. But Miss Gardner, Dr. Phelps, and Toolie Fastbender had stepped up. Despite working in this grim outpost of humanity, they'd done more for me than my own mother had. If I ever got the chance to help someone or guide them like they'd done for me, I promised myself I wouldn't forget to do it. Because if I was going to live a good, straight-arrow kind of life, I had to remember to do good whenever I could.

CHAPTER TWELVE

From: Lisa
To: Kim
Re: boring Arkansas

It took a whole year but I finally have something good to say about living in Arkansas. Actually, two. First, I got my own online account. My paranoid Mom has all the parental checks on it. Of course. She's so afraid I'm gonna look at some site I shouldn't be looking at. But I'll eventually figure out how to get around them.

Second, after last year was so boring and the closest Catholic high school is like 20 miles away, I staged a walkout. I told my mom I wasn't going there next year, and if she tried to make me, I would do something to get kicked out. She was *soooo* mad! But I won. No more uniforms! I wanted to go to the regular public high school, but she wouldn't go for that. I don't know why she's so insanely anti public schools. But then she's insane about lots of stuff. Anyway, I'm going to this magnet school that has a special focus on art and music so there's lots of cool kids. Especially boys.

So what's new in the old 'hood?

From: Kim
To: Lisa
Re: new school

Wow. I can't believe you pulled it off. Would you really have gotten yourself kicked out of school? I guess you're a lot braver than me. Everything around here is the same except for you being gone. Muriel finally got her period. She is so relieved. But now she hates it, just like we all do. School starts next week. I am so jealous you don't have to wear uniforms. Yesterday we bought mine. Mom would only pay for my initials on one of the blouses. I'll be such a geek without initials! So I'm saving money from babysitting to put initials on the other four.

Guess what? My real sister and I started e-mailing and we talked on the telephone three times, and Mom and Dad said in August we can take a vacation to Oregon where she lives. I am so excited!

Did you meet any cute boys yet? I think Larry Crestor likes me because he always splashes me at the pool. Muriel says hi.

From: Lisa
To: Kim
Re: sister

That's really cool, meeting your real sister. Your mom and dad are so much cooler then my mom. She told me I don't have any brothers or sisters, but who knows if that's true? But one day I'll find my real mom. I've already started looking though I haven't got too far.

I met this cool girl Nikki at the Pic-n-Pac down the street. She goes to Lincoln Arts School too, but 10th grade. She told me the kids dress really artsy and like if I don't want to be labeled a Major Loser on the first day I better watch what I wear. She told me about this cool shop called X-Top but my mom freaked when we went there. Everything is like black and bare midriff and really like sexy. All she let me buy was a pair of jeans and a belt. But I saw this tank top I loved, so I gave Nikki the $$ to buy it for me. You'd really like Nikki. She is so cool. Not like anybody I ever met before.

And hell yes, I would've gotten myself kicked out of that Catholic school. With all their stupid rules, it would've been a breeze.

From: Nikki
To: Lisa
Re: Got it!

Meet me at the PNP tomorrow after dinner.

From: Lisa
To: Nikki
Re: Parents!!!

My mom wants to meet your mom before I can hang out with you. I know that's gross, but she's CRAZY.

From: Nikki
To: Lisa
Re: Crazy moms

They're all crazy. Just tell her to call my mom on her cell 555-1101. Once you're 16 we won't have to worry about this bullshit. BTW, tell your mom you need a cell. Everybody at LAHS has one.

Instant Message from Lisa to Nikki: Meet me at the PnP first so I can change my shirt before the bus comes.

From: Lisa
To: Kim
Re: LAHS

My new school is so much cooler than my old school. The kids are really different. They wear cool clothes and we have cool art projects and it's so laid back–and no Friday mass or morning prayers. I met this cool guy Brett. I know you would like him because he's half Malaysian. But he's not adopted like us. Anyway, it would be just perfect if you were here too. But you're not.

BOBBIE

Life outside turned out to be so much harder than I expected. Don't get me wrong. I was drunk with happiness to walk away from St. Anna's. I had $212.75 in my pocket, two changes of clothes in a tote bag, a standard-issue bag of toiletries, and a piece of paper saying I could stay two weeks for free in a halfway house while I looked for a job.

But when I climbed into the van that took me to the bus station, and we pulled out onto the two-lane highway, I got real queasy. Everything was flying by so fast—trees, houses, the other cars. I kept my face pressed to the window, trying to take it all in and not miss a thing. I saw a pasture with four cows and one horse. I saw the Emmanuel Baptist Church and Crazy Eights Barroom. I saw two kids crawfishing in a ditch. I hadn't thought about crawfishing once while I was in jail.

We passed a fruit and vegetable stand, and a high school with a football field in the back, and I felt dizzy with the world going by so big and fast.

"Sit back," the driver said. "Look straight ahead." Then she handed me a plastic bag. "Whatever you do, don't barf on the seat."

I managed to hold on until we reached the Greyhound station. But the minute my feet touched free ground I threw up, over and over until I was weak and shaking and thought I would pass out.

The driver handed me a paper towel through the window. "You okay?"

I nodded even though I wasn't. I wiped my mouth and tried to spit out the nasty taste. Then I stuffed the paper towel into the barf bag and knotted it closed.

The driver put the van in gear. "They have your ticket inside on the St. Anna's account. Good luck." Then she was gone, and

I stood there in the gravel parking lot, as scared and lonely as I'd ever been in prison. Even though the breeze was warm and soft, I felt cold and clammy. I smelled fried chicken cooking, and my stomach did a gurgling flip-flop. I was free, but I was scared to death of that freedom.

If I had a family to help me or a home to return to, it would've been easier. But I didn't have anyone. Not even a parole officer. That's because I'm not on parole. I'm straight-up free. I can live anywhere I want, cross state lines without reporting to anyone. But though I'm happy about that, it's scary. In some ways it's pathetic. I have this weird soundtrack running through my head. First comes that song from *Pinocchio*, "I Got No Strings on Me." Then comes that old Janis Joplin song about freedom being just another word for nothing else left to lose. That song is real popular with prisoners.

Anyway, those two songs summed me up pretty well: I got no strings on me, and nothing left to lose. But I did have something to gain, something to work for. That's why I'd decided on a halfway house in New Orleans. Since Hurricane Katrina the town was crawling with jobs.

Sure enough, I had no trouble getting one in a coffeehouse. With my first paycheck I started the legal process to change my name back to Fenner. I figured it would be a lot better to be Bobbie Fenner with only a juvie record than to be Bobbie Davis, convicted felon. With my second paycheck I bought a used computer and got an online account. No more sneaking around on library computers. And no partying either.

After a couple of months in the halfway house, I found a one-room apartment and got a job in a small clinic. By day I worked with AIDS patients. Two nights a week I took nursing classes, and the rest of the time I kept up my search for Lissy.

But dead end after dead end has a way of beating you down. The first dead end was Dr. Gullihay and Tulane University Hospital. Dr. Gullihay had left New Orleans after Hurricane Katrina, apparently returning to Europe. As for the hospital, a year after the storm it still hadn't entirely reopened, and there was no record of Lissy ever having been a patient there. Not that they were particularly forthcoming. But when I applied for a job there I nosed around. One of the clerks was only too happy to check into it for a crisp one-hundred dollar bill. But she found nothing.

Maybe Gullihay had seen her in an off-campus office or consulted independently about her, but the clerk couldn't find any paper trail on Lissy anywhere in their system. So if Lissy wasn't in New Orleans, why was I here? The problem was, I had no clue where to look next.

"Hey, girlfriend," Ivan said late one Friday afternoon. He was the boyfriend of one of our patients, and we'd become friends. "What're you doing tonight?"

"Me?" I shrugged. "Not much. I'm happy just to soak my feet, put them up, and watch something mindless on TV."

"Girl, how old *are* you? Sixty? Seventy? You *way* too young and *way* too hot to be staying in on a Friday night."

Laughing, I struck a pose and primped my hair. "Oh, yeah. I am one hot babe in my baggy scrubs and orthopedic shoes."

He rolled his eyes. "Don't give me that. Put on some makeup, girl. Some tight pants and high heels, and the men'll be throwin' money at you."

"Hey! What kind of girl do you think I am?"

He grinned. "You know what I mean. I hear you talk about work and about school but I don't hear nothin' 'bout a boyfriend. Or a girlfriend." He raised his perfectly plucked eyebrows expectantly.

Again I laughed. "I *used* to like men. Now I don't like anybody."

That's when he hooked his arm in mine. "Yeah, I figured you for a fag hag. So come out with me. Dack's not up for going out these days, but he gets jealous if I go out without him. But if *you* go with me, well, we'll both be happy."

So that's how I came to be at a raucous party at a mostly gay bar in the Quarter around midnight. I'd limited myself to two drinks and had turned down innumerable offers of weed and X and blow. I wasn't even tempted, which made me feel good about myself. All those AA and NA meetings had paid off.

But as I watched people pairing off—men and men, women and women, and some men and women too—I felt even more alone than ever. Ivan was having a blast, dancing with everyone and flirting like crazy, though he never crossed the line with anyone. Meanwhile I danced with Ivan a few times and with a pretty gay girl who was really pissed when she wanted to get cozy and I told her I was straight.

"Time for me to go home," I told Ivan as the house band's version of "Iko Iko" gave way to "Hey, Pocky Way". "I have work tomorrow, and so do you."

"Oh, all right," he said with an exaggerated pout. "Besides, Dack needs his rest, and if I know him, he's pacing the floor waiting for me. Just let me get something to go. Something exotic. Like me," he added with a wink.

I waited by the door, watching the Bourbon Street foot traffic wander by. It was colorful, loud, and yet surprisingly mellow. Some parts of New Orleans were still reeling after Katrina, but the older parts of town, the high and dry parts, were almost back to normal. Especially the French Quarter.

At one time all I'd wanted was to be grown up enough to hang out in bars on Bourbon Street or in dance clubs in Fat City and have a good time every night. Then reality had slapped me in the face. Several times.

Maybe it was the rum or else the hopelessness of my search for Lissy catching up with me. Or maybe it was the sweet coconut fragrance of the frothy drink Ivan thrust at me. "Take a sip. It's *soooo* good, like a tropical dessert."

It was delicious, but that sip only made me feel worse. I'd been drinking a coconut daiquiri the day I got in that car wreck. I guess that's why, as the cab dropped me off and I climbed the steps to my spartan studio apartment, I was overwhelmed with memories. Not of Lissy this time, my beloved child whom I so desperately wanted to find. But of Alyssa. Alyssa Marie Leftwich, the little girl I'd killed.

It had happened a lifetime ago. I'd been seventeen. Now I was thirty-four. But it was as real—as bitter—as ever. I was on this frustrating, endless search for my child. But Alyssa's parents didn't have even that much. They had no child to look for, no hope for a reunion ever. I'd stolen that dream from them.

Depressed by the liquor and weighted with guilt, once I got inside my tiny apartment I stripped off my jeans, tank top, and sandals and slipped on an oversized T-shirt. I didn't turn on any lights because I didn't want to see myself in the mirror. I didn't want to see the image of the person who'd killed a child and spent only eight months in juvenile detention for it.

"No more drinking for you," I muttered as I turned on my thirteen-inch television. While I knew I'd never forget Alyssa Leftwich, I didn't need any additional reasons to remember her either. And drinking alcohol did that to me. It made me maudlin and sad.

I lay in the dark, watching the muted images flitting across the television screen. Someone got shot. Someone fell but got up and ran. Who cared? Who cared about the fictional dramas of a few overpaid actors who were too beautiful to be real? There was too much drama around me already. The daily struggles of our patients. The endless struggles of so many folks to rebuild their lives in their ruined city. Some were still trying just to get back home. And then there were the quiet struggles everyone grappled with: guilt, depression, addiction, hopelessness.

I'd had all those since that fateful day when I'd jacked my mother's latest boyfriend's truck for a joyride and ended up killing a little girl. Everything since then had happened because of that day. Me meeting Ken at a bar. Having a baby. Naming her Lissy. Even Ken's overdose. If he'd had a different kind of girlfriend, someone who wasn't all about getting blotto every night, he might never have pushed himself so far.

Tortured by my demons, I flipped on the light and turned off the TV. Then I sat in front of my computer and began my nightly routine, my nightly search. But this time I didn't search for Lissy Anne Davis. This time I searched for Alyssa Marie Leftwich, and for her parents, James and Diane Leftwich.

By dawn I felt even worse, and it wasn't because my back ached, my eyes burned, and my right wrist had all the indications for carpal tunnel syndrome. That I could deal with. That I deserved. What weighed on me—what ripped a jagged hole in my chest and threatened to suffocate me with its ugly darkness—was guilt. Not just the old guilt about ending a child's life before it had barely begun. This was a new guilt piled on top of the old one, a new realization that our mistakes—my mistakes—live on and on in new, ever morphing forms. My bad ripples were even worse than I knew. For not only had I killed James and Diane Leftwich's child. It turns out I'd killed their marriage too, because he was married to someone different now.

I stared at a picture of Jim Leftwich pulled up from a newspaper article. He was a partner in a CPA firm, and the 2004 winner of their service award for his work with the Head Start program in Mobile. In the photo he stood between Head Start's national administrator and their local chairman. If his name hadn't been printed there I would never have recognized him. He was gray now and no longer wore a beard. He was also thinner, almost gaunt.

But it wasn't just the outward changes. In the picture he was smiling. I'd only seen the man three times. Once in the emergency room, before he knew who I was. Once at the juvenile court hearing. And once when he and his wife showed up to oppose my release from the juvenile detention facility. He hadn't smiled any of those times. Neither had his wife.

I'd tried not to look at them. It had been too painful, like swallowing splinters of glass. But even so, I'd been morbidly drawn to them. My eyes wouldn't turn away from their haggard faces, and I'd never understood why.

But now as I looked at the man whose child I'd killed, whose marriage I'd obviously wrecked, I saw his kind expression and the laugh lines beside his eyes. That's when I understood that my morbid fascination had everything to do with the power I'd wielded over him and his devastated wife. Without knowing it even existed, I'd carelessly used that power to destroy their lives forever.

Borrow a car, drink too much, and bam! I'd done it without once considering how fast a speeding car could veer from joyride to murder weapon.

Back then I hadn't understood such power. I'd been sick with remorse, desperate for my apology to make things all right. Making things right, though, was a power I did not possess.

My power was to wreck things, not fix them. Hadn't I done the same with Ken, recognized his addictions and yet ignored them? And then with Lissy ... Who'd taught her to count? Not me. The lady in the next trailer had done that. And who'd taught her the ABC song? My mother or maybe my friend Carla. I couldn't remember, but she hadn't learned it from me.

The Leftwiches had been perfect parents to their child, while I'd ignored my responsibilities and taken my baby entirely for granted.

Swallowing hard, I closed my eyes against Jim Leftwich's smiling face. But it was too late. His image had burned itself into my brain, into my memory bank. He was happy now, remarried with two kids, and successful in his career. But I knew he still loved and missed his first child.

Did he still love and miss his first wife? Did he stay in touch with her? Was she okay?

Opening my eyes, I rubbed the soft scars on the inside of my right arm, then forged on. So far as Google could tell me, Diane Leftwich had pretty much dropped off the map. The divorce papers were the last reference I found to her. Prior to that there wasn't much about her either. But after the divorce I found nothing. She'd probably moved to another state or maybe even another country. Maybe she'd remarried too. I hoped so, even though it would make my search more difficult. Given enough time, however, I still might find her.

But why did I want to?

Sighing, I said good-bye to Jim Leftwich's picture, and turned the computer off. Then I reached across the desk, pulled a tissue from Toolie's crocheted tissue-box cover and blew my nose. I didn't need to find Diane Leftwich. And yet, as I pushed myself away from the desk, turned on the coffeepot, popped three aspirin, and then turned on the shower, I knew I'd added another person to my search list. I did need to find Diane Leftwich because I needed to know that she'd built a new, satisfying life for herself. That she'd remarried and had more children. I needed to see a picture of her smiling.

Unlike my search for Lissy, though, I didn't want to ever meet Jim or Diane Leftwich.

Somehow I managed to get to work on time. And I managed to get through the day by drinking coffee pretty much nonstop. Diane hovered in the back of my mind though, and she haunted my dreams that night. And afterwards she was never far away. Never any farther away than Lissy.

CHAPTER THIRTEEN

From: Nikki
To: Lisa
Re: Brett has a car

    We're ditching school today at lunchtime. Brett's brother is out of town so he's letting Brett drive his car to school. We're heading up to Goat Springs to go swimming. Bring food.

From: Lisa
To: Nikki
Re: Brett has a car

    You mean skip school? What if we get caught?

Instant message to Lisa:

    Nikki: 1st of all, it's an art school. They expect us to do impulsive things. 2nd, it's May and they expect us to have spring fever.

Lisa: Not skip school, though.

Nikki: If they catch us–IF–we'll just get a warning. I skipped 5 times last year and only got caught once. My mom never found out a thing.

Lisa: I don't know. It would be just my luck that my mom would find out and ground me 4ever.

Nikki: A) she won't find out. B) she can't ground you anymore than she could make you stay in your old school. And C) Brett really wants you to come.

Lisa: He does?

Nikki: Oh yeah. He and I have been friends since 3rd grade. We're like brother and sister, and he tells me everything. He's had a few crushes on a couple of girls, but never like this. He told me you remind him of Estelle in that Edgar Degas painting on page 97 of our art history book. You know how he is about Degas. He said even though you don't look anything like her, you have this tragic beauty about you just like her. Like you're innocent and world-weary all at the same time.

Lisa: Wow. That is so sweet. He really said that?

Nikki: Absolutely. So, are you in or not?

BOBBIE

On the one-year anniversary of my release from jail I sat at my little kitchen table with a yellow pad, a cupcake, and a pint of Captain Morgan rum. The rum was my birthday present to myself, and I intended to make good use of it. But as depressed as I was about my life—or should I say, the lack thereof—I remembered enough from AA to feel guilty about my plan. So I decided to be methodical about it. Weigh the pros and cons. Thus the yellow pad.

I drew a line straight down the middle of the page. On the left side I wrote *loneliness*. After staring at the letters a long while, on the other side of the line I wrote *education*. I was lonely, but I was educated. I'd made no real friends, but next month I'd finish the last two courses I needed to be an RN. Whoop-dee-doo. Since I couldn't get a job as an RN in Louisiana unless I got an expungement on my record, it seemed almost pointless.

To the left side I wrote *sad*, then *depressed*, plus *frustrated* and *guilty*. On the right I listed *healthy*, *free*, *can afford mascara*, and *hair grown out*.

A pattern was beginning to emerge. All the external markers were good. On the inside, though, I was a wreck, and no amount of shiny hair and clear skin could offset that. Hopelessness had set in big-time. So I wrote *hopeless* on the left. Opposite that I wrote *350-thread count, 100% Egyptian cotton sheets that no one else has ever slept on.*

Captain Morgan was obviously winning.

Then I wrote *helpless* because that's how I felt these days. Nothing I could do with my freedom or my education or my obsessive use of every new hair-care product that came out on the market seemed to have any impact on how I felt inside. I was hopeless and helpless, and everything in my life conspired to keep me there.

I put down the pen, grabbed the rum, and tore off the paper seal. I wasn't an extravagant person and I lived in a quasi-dump. But my job did pay enough for a couple of luxuries like drinking the best rum and sleeping on the best sheets. What the hell good was any of it, though, if the one thing I wanted in life stayed so far out of my reach?

I twisted off the top of the rum and immediately breathed in that sweet, tropical scent. Two or three good pulls—no glass needed since I wasn't sharing it with anyone—and I'd be well on my way to feeling better. Another shot or two beyond that and I'd be totally wasted. No unhappy memories for me. No bad dreams. No hopes dashed on the sharp rocks of my helplessness.

"So poetic tonight," I muttered. "'Hopes dashed on the sharp rocks of helplessness'."

I took a sip, just a taste, and wrinkled my nose. It was strong. Was I strong?

Apparently not. On the left side of the paper I added *weak*, and then *stupid, cowardly*, and *selfish*.

Why cowardly? Because I was taking the easy route of drinking my troubles away?

Maybe. But the truth went deeper than that. I was a coward because I'd avoided the one painful task I knew I had to deal with. Time and again I'd talked myself out of it. I'd found Jim Leftwich online and reassured myself that he was happy once more, that making amends to him, like the ninth step says, wouldn't help him but instead would probably hurt him.

But what about Diane? I couldn't locate her. Was she happy? And even if she was, could either of them ever be completely happy? Maybe letting them vent their rage at me might not initially seem a kindness. But in the long run, venting that poisonous rage on the target who deserved it might be therapeutic.

If I was brave enough to face them.

I took a last sip of rum. My hands trembled at the thought of actually facing either of them. But maybe that was what I needed too. Maybe God or the universe or whoever was in charge was waiting for me to grow a backbone and really face up to what I'd done before he/she/it would let me find my own child.

I stared at the two lists on the tablet. Maybe I wasn't as helpless as I wanted to believe. After all, I'd gotten even with the bitch who let Sonya die. Maybe it was time for me to even up the other side of the scale, the side where I was the one who deserved punishment.

It wasn't easy to pour all that rum down the kitchen drain. Afterward I ate my anniversary cupcake. Then I folded up the piece of paper and tucked it into my sock drawer. I was starting my second year of freedom. I'd accomplished a lot, but it was all outside stuff. This year I would work on the inside. I would find Jim Leftwich, express my sorrow and regret to him, and accept whatever he threw back at me. I would also continue my search for Lissy. And for Diane.

And who knew? Maybe Jim would tell me where Diane was.

Ha. Fat chance he'd help me with anything. Still, easy or not, my search for the Leftwiches needed to become as important to me as my search for Lissy. Because I was positive now that in the realm of good and evil, of right and wrong, of God and the devil, the two searches must surely be connected.

· · · · ·

In May I qualified for a week's vacation so I put in for it. Meanwhile I shopped for a car. At a small used car lot on Canal Street one of the salesmen strolled up to me as I checked out a pale green SUV.

"That's a nice vehicle there, ma'am. Nine years old but with less than ninety thousand miles on it. Mostly driven back and forth to work by a librarian."

"Why'd she sell it?" I asked, looking away as his avid gaze raked over me. What a creep. I focused on the vehicle, a Chevy Tahoe that looked spacious enough to stretch out in if I had to sleep in it—which I would have to do if I bought it because there would be no money left over for a motel room on my trip to Alabama to find Jim Leftwich.

"I heard the former owner went into a nursing home," he answered.

What a crock. Stifling my skepticism, I glanced at him. "A nursing home?"

That's when his mouth gaped open and his fleshy eyelids lifted higher over his rheumy eyes. "Bobbie?" he said.

I stiffened.

"Bobbie Davis," he went on, no question in his voice this time. "Ken's wife. Right?"

I took a step backward, my alarm system on full alert. Anyone who knew Ken or me way back when *had* to be bad news. "Do I know you?"

"Yeah, you know me." He smirked, his hand pointed to his chest. "I'm Hal. Ken's brother."

Hal. A shudder ripped through me. The pervert who'd wanted custody of Lissy.

"C'mon, Bobbie. I know it's been awhile, but you couldn't've forgotten your one true love's only brother."

I should have denied it. I should have said, "Sorry, mac, but that's the lamest come-on I ever heard." But I was too shocked by his unexpected reappearance in my life, by the thirty years of damage the last ten years had wreaked on him, and by my instinctive revulsion.

"Hal." Bile rose in my throat. "I figured you'd be dead by now."

He laughed, showing a mouth of yellowing teeth that needed major dental work. "Yeah, well I guess Ken's death and a little visit to Angola Prison straightened me out. I quit the hard stuff, I don't know, four years ago. Five. Something like that. What about you? Where you been?"

Where had I been? Didn't he remember me going to jail? And how he tried to get custody of Lissy?

Apparently not. I shook my head. "Out of town," I managed to say.

"Right. So." I jumped when he slapped his meaty hand down on the hood of the SUV. "Wanna test drive this baby?"

And get in a car with him? No way. I made a doubtful face. "I don't think so. I need something that gets better mileage."

"Well, then. We got a Corolla in the back. It just came in. Why don't we take a look?"

"Actually, I don't think I want a used car. I'm leaning toward a new one." It was lie, but it was the only way I could think of to get away from him.

"Aw, Bobbie. Don't do that. A new car is a big waste of money. It's like throwing away five thousand clams the minute you drive off the lot. But if you want something newer than this, I've got a nice Oldsmobile. Only three years old with less than thirty thousand miles. All highway too."

"No thanks," I muttered as I turned away and headed toward the streetcar stop two blocks down.

"Wait up, Bobbie. I can make you a good deal. For old times' sake, you know?"

"No thanks."

I thought he'd gotten the message, that I'd escaped with little damage. But as I reached the corner he called out, "Hey, didn't you and Ken have a kid together? I'd sure like to see my little niece sometime!"

That's when I started running. Stupid, I know. He wasn't chasing me, and even if he'd tried to, he didn't look healthy enough to make the block. But still I ran—from the man and his fetid aura, and from the putrid nightmare of the life I used to live. I ran past the first streetcar stop and down to the second. Then I held onto the metal-and-glass shelter like I couldn't stand up on my own. And all the while I gasped for breath, futilely fighting down my panic.

He didn't even remember that I'd gone to jail, that he'd tried to get custody of Lissy. He probably didn't even remember her name.

Thank God.

I took a roundabout route home. Don't ask me why. Hal would not come looking for me. By tomorrow I doubted he'd even remember seeing me—that's how fried his brain probably was. Still, I was taking no chances. I'd severed all connections with my old life, and I wanted to keep it that way.

But after a long, hot shower where I scrubbed myself practically raw, I knew that wasn't true. Some parts of my past I could put behind me forever. But other parts waited still to be dredged up. I realized then that my search for Lissy would never succeed until I'd first dealt with my past.

That's why the next day I bought a seven-year-old Hyundai with 87,000 miles on it. That's why I bought a sleeping bag, a small ice chest, and two flashlights.

Next week I was driving to Alabama to find Jim Leftwich, to dredge up the worst part of my life and hopefully make some sort of amends, and to get a line on his ex-wife. Once I found Diane Leftwich and discovered how she was doing—good, bad, or somewhere in the middle—and let her vent her anger and sorrow and whatever other emotions she needed to throw at me, then maybe I'd be able to move forward in my search for Lissy.

And maybe God or the universe—my higher power—would finally let me find her.

CHAPTER FOURTEEN

ACCOUNT OF LISA HAINES: SEARCH

State of Louisiana
Department of Vital Records
Live births, 1992

March: Carmalita Marie Ybarzybal to Angel Faust / Thomas Paul Ybarzybal

Melissa Elaine Youngblood to Hannah Smythe Youngblood / Jeremy James Youngblood

Anthony Joseph Ziblich to Lynda Fields Ziblich / Vincent Joseph Ziblich

April: Kinsey Alyce Aberdeen to Katrina Johnson Aberdeen / David Charles Aberdeen

Emory Francine Adams to Elaine Florence Adams

Damian Micah Austinto ...

From: Lisa
To: Nikki
Re: the mommy hunt

Do you know how many kids are born in Louisiana in just one month? Thousands. I'm going blind looking for women named Barbara who had a baby in 1992. So far I've found three, but one had a boy, so I'm down to two.

From: Nikki
To: Lisa
Re: the mommy hunt

Then wait till you're eighteen and register at a site for adopted kids. You'll probably find out she's already registered and waiting for you to find her.

From: Lisa
To: Nikki
Re: the mommy hunt

I don't want to wait 3 more years, and my mom will never ok it, so what choice do I have?

From: Lisa
To: Nikki
Re: BETRAYAL!!!

I can NOT believe you told Carrie that my mom was in jail!!! She thought you meant my adopted mom and now she's told everybody!!! Then I had to tell her it was my birth mom, which made Carrie feel horrible (which she deserved to feel). So now she's telling everybody that she got it wrong. But everybody still knows my birth mother is a criminal. So then Annalise lost her wallet while we were in gym class, and everybody starts looking at me. Like all of a sudden I went from everybody's pal to everybody's public enemy #1. Fuck! How'm I supposed to ever show my face at school again!!

From: Nikki
To: Lisa
Re: Sorry!

I didn't come right out and say Lisa's mom's a jailbird or anything lame like that. We were out smoking behind the sculpture building and I had that book *Dead Man Walking* and she told me about this other book she read by this death row guy and then, I don't know. It just kind of slipped out. I didn't know she would like shout it out to the world. I'm really sorry. And I already told Carrie not to talk to me ever again until she makes everything okay with you.

From: Lisa
To: Nikki
Re: Are you for real?

How can she EVER make things right with me? Is she going to erase everybody's memories? I don't think so. So now everyone will always think I'm Miss Light Fingers.

From: Snake
To: Lisa
Re: Jailbird parents

Just wanted to say that I get what you're going through. Been there with my own dad and it's a bummer. If you need to vent, let me know.

From: Lisa
To: Nikki
Re: Omigod!

You'll never guess who just e-mailed me!

BOBBIE

Jim Leftwich lived in a pretty neighborhood. It was an older subdivision with lots of trees—huge live oaks, towering pines, and spreading red maples. I'd become obsessed with trees in the last year. Maybe because I hadn't seen too many in the previous ten years. Anyway, Jim Leftwich's neighborhood was green and shady, a lovely, serene place. Exactly how I picture the perfect place to raise a family. He drove a navy blue Camry and his wife, a petite, curvy woman with gorgeous chestnut-colored hair and a great wardrobe, drove a gold Chrysler minivan. They had two children, about five and nine, and if I'd been a casting agent, I would have hired them for any commercial that called for the perfect, all-American family. Tall dad, smiling mom, energetic son and darling daughter.

They even had a dog, a cute mutt with floppy ears.

I knew all this because I spent three days watching them.

All right, three days *spying* on them—on him, mainly—trying to work up the courage to call him. How do you start that sort of conversation?

Hey there, remember me? I'm the girl who killed your daughter and nearly killed your wife. Your first wife, that is. Oh, and by the way. Did I have anything to do with your divorce? And then finish up with a sincere, *I'm so sorry for your loss*?

Every time I imagined facing him I got this awful urge to throw up. Yet I knew I couldn't leave without facing him.

On Thursday my chance came. The previous days he'd left the house before his wife and children. But today they left earlier than usual. I gripped the steering wheel until my knuckles hurt, waiting for him to leave, wishing he would come outside so I would *have* to do what I'd come here to do.

When it became obvious he wasn't going anywhere soon, I

forced my fingers to release the molded plastic steering wheel. One by one they unwrapped from it. Open the door; climb out. Lock the door, then walk to the house. 2819 Elm Street. Did elms even grow this far south?

I didn't know. It wasn't important.

The door had a brass knocker in the shape of a pineapple. The symbol of welcome, or so I'd learned from some decorating magazine I used to read in jail.

I used the doorbell instead.

When he swung the door open I took an involuntary step backward, overcome with nauseating panic. I couldn't do this. Why had I ever thought I could?

"Can I help you?" he asked. His voice was pleasant. His brows lifted as he waited for my response. "Miss?"

I sucked in a painful breath. "Um. You probably don't remember me," I began. Just five little words, but saying them left me gulping for air.

After a moment he shook his head. "I'm afraid not. Want to give me a hint?" he added with a half-smile.

I swallowed hard. "We never actually met. But ... I'm Bobbie. I mean, I'm Roberta Fenner."

I don't think it registered at first, because his expression didn't change. His mouth still curved up a little more on one side than the other; his eyes still creased at the corners with well-worn smile lines.

Then he went pale. His skin turned the color of ashes and the friendly light in his eyes turned to horror. Perversely, it was his revulsion that spurred me on. "I know I'm the last person you expected, but I wanted to tell you, face-to-face—"

"No!"

I fell back a step at his roar of rage. "I'm sorry," I said. I lifted a hand toward him, then let it fall. "I'm sorry."

"No," he muttered, this time through clenched teeth. "I don't want to hear your pathetic apology."

He didn't slam the door in my face, though, so I went on. "I've never forgotten her. I know I took her life, and wrecked your marriage. And I know I can't undo any of it."

"Why are you here?" He gripped the door frame, one white-knuckled hand on each side, as if he needed the support.

I shook my head. "I needed ... I don't know. To tell you face-to-face how sorry I am."

His nostrils flared with every one of his labored breaths. "I don't give a damn how sorry you are."

"I know." I pressed my lips together and tried hard not to flinch away from his bitterness. His pain. Finally I nodded. "Okay. I'm leaving."

"Have you killed anyone else lately?"

I stiffened. His words hit like barbs, flaying the flesh of my soul. He wanted to see me bleed, and I guess part of me wanted to let him. "No," I answered. "No one else." I'd tried to kill the prison guard who'd let Sonya die, but unfortunately she'd lived. Did that count? And what about Ken? Would he still be alive if I'd straightened out sooner? If I hadn't been so filled with self-loathing for what I'd done to Alyssa Leftwich and participated so eagerly in his mind-numbing drug orgies?

Jim Leftwich's eyes were fixed on me now, like laser points ferreting out my flaws, my weaknesses. "What have you done with your life?"

I didn't want to tell him. I didn't want him to think even worse of me than he already did. But I had to be honest, with this man above all others. "I—I went downhill. You know, after the accident."

"Downhill from baby killer?" he said with such scorn it was like an ice pick to my heart.

"I—I buried my grief in drugs. I had a child and got married, but—I couldn't keep it together. I went to jail."

"For what? Certainly not for Alyssa's death."

"Drugs. But I'm out now, and I've turned my life around."

He made a sound of disgust. "Yeah. Right."

"That's why I came here. And why I want to find your wife. Your first wife, Diane—"

"No!" He barked the word out before I could finish. "No. You leave her alone."

"I don't want to hurt her. I just want—"

"To make yourself feel better? Twist the knife in her and call it making amends?" He was screaming now.

Across the street a mail carrier paused to stare at us, and suddenly this felt like an awful mistake. I backed away from him, whispering, "I'm sorry. I'm sorry." He didn't want to hear it, but I needed to say it.

"Stay away from Diane!" His furious words pelted me as I climbed into my car, words fueled by years and years of pent-up rage. "You hear me, bitch? Don't you go anywhere near her! Because if you do—"

I slammed the door, then clenched my eyes closed and pressed my hands over my ears. Why had I come here? Why, why, why? Yes, I'd given him a chance to vent his rage at me, and though I hated it, I knew I deserved it. But what good had it really done for him?

Then something crashed against the side window. I flung myself across the passenger seat.

"Get the fuck out of here!" Clutching a brick, Jim Leftwich drew back his arm and struck the window again. The glass cracked, but it didn't shatter. But though it protected me from physical harm, it couldn't shield me from the hatred he spewed, the hatred I deserved. And it catapulted me back to that nightmarish day, when he'd arrived at the accident scene. I'd been on a stretcher by then, dazed, still drunk. But not drunk enough to blot out the image of him wielding a golf club on the truck I'd been driving. The one I'd just used to kill his baby girl.

Somehow I got the car started. All the while he pounded the windows on the driver's side until I peeled out and sped away. I didn't drive far, though. I couldn't. I was shaking too hard, crying so much I couldn't see. And the last thing I wanted was to get in a wreck. So I took the first right turn and pulled over a few blocks down. Then I just sat there, clinging to the steering wheel and crying.

It was horrible, even worse than the day of the accident, because that day I'd been drunk. Today I was stone-cold sober, unable to avoid the consequences of what I'd done. All I could do was huddle there, crying for Jim and his lost wife and dead child. Especially for Alyssa. Deep in my soul I knew I would cry for her forever. This sorrow could never, never end. Which only made me cry harder.

Until someone tapped on the window.

"No!" I screamed, covering my head and flinching away.

But it wasn't Jim Leftwich following me with his brick and his righteous anger. It was the mail carrier who'd seen our confrontation.

"You okay, miss?" He bent down to peer through the shattered window. "Do you need me to call the police?"

"No." That was the last thing I needed. "No," I repeated, swiping at my face with my sleeve. "No. It's ... all right."

"It sure doesn't look all right. Your car." He grimaced at the damage.

"It's all right. We have ... history," I said. "Bad history." Then because I didn't want him to blame Jim, I faced the mail carrier full on. "It's all my fault. He's a good man. But I ... " I shook my head. "A long time ago I did a terrible thing."

He hesitated a minute. Then with a shrug he turned away and continued on his route. I watched him go, his left shoulder hunched against the weight of his leather satchel. How many personal dramas had he witnessed along the many miles of his delivery route? Domestic tragedies. Neighborhood feuds. Family disputes. How many lives had he eavesdropped on as he delivered legal notices, sympathy cards, and Dear John letters?

Did he enjoy it, his own personal reality show? Or did he turn away from all the ugliness and try to put it out of his head in the evening with reruns of *The Andy Griffith Show* or *Sanford and Son*?

I watched him go up the steps of a pretty yellow house with foxtail ferns and red begonias in two window boxes. Did he ever deliver good news? Birth announcements? Scholarship awards? How many years did it take to look at an envelope and recognize the difference between good news and bad?

Or did he even care?

I found a napkin in the glove compartment and blew my nose. But for a long time I couldn't move. What now? Was this was a sign that I should abandon my search for Diane Leftwich?

That night I parked my car into a rest stop along I-10. I tried to sleep but it was hard. I lay in the flattened cargo area on my sleeping bag and flinched every time a car door slammed or a voice pierced the dark silence. It was only truckers who needed a nap, or traveling families who needed a bathroom break. But what I heard was bricks striking my window, and a terrible voice tortured by grief and pain, warning me to stay away.

Stay away from me! Stay away from Diane!

And another voice too, a woman I didn't know telling me to stay away from Lissy. But how could I do that? It had been almost three years since I'd learned how sick Lissy was. There was no way I could stop until I knew what had happened. No way until I knew she was all right.

Eventually I must have slept, because I dreamed about trucks and golf clubs and a peaceful cemetery with statues of rabbits and a tomb with lilies engraved on it. I woke up with a massive headache and a crick in my neck, feeling like I'd been beat up or something. But when I saw a sign for McDonald's and turned in for breakfast, I knew what I had to do. I needed to go to Alyssa Leftwich's grave.

I hadn't visited her grave once since my release, rationalizing, I guess, that it hadn't done me any good in the past. Why would it help me now? And yet I felt this compulsion to go.

As I headed west, past the site of my teenage tragedy and back to Louisiana, I tried not to think about the shattered car windows. They could be fixed. What I'd done all those years ago, that could never be fixed. I reminded myself, though, that I didn't expect it to be fixed. What I was searching for was forgiveness.

Not Jim Leftwich's forgiveness. I didn't deserve that. Nor Diane Leftwich's either. How could anyone forgive such an act? But if I was ever going to get on with my life, I had to find a way to forgive myself, to accept my guilt as just punishment, and find the will to live my life in a different way. I knew, though, that I never would have changed my ways if not for the mistakes I'd made and for the ten years I'd been give to make some sense of them.

I'd seen Jim Leftwich and accepted his anger. I was on my way to visit Alyssa's grave. Maybe then I'd discover a way to locate Diane.

And after that, Lissy.

CHAPTER FIFTEEN

From: Lisa
To: Nikki
Re: skool

I don't think you should drop out. I mean, this year already started off so cool. The new block schedule will give us a lot longer time in the art electives. I'm taking Photography and Sculpture 1st qtr, then Rendering and Video 2nd qtr.

From: Nikki
To: Lisa
Re: R, R & 'R suck!!

If I could just take art I'd stay. But the minute I find a job I'm outta there.

Instant message to Nikki:

Lisa: What does Brett think of you dropping out?

Nikki: Brett is too depressed about you to think about his oldest friend

Lisa: stop with the guilt trip, ok? Brett is a cool guy, but he was my 1st ever BF and nobody stays with their 1st BF. You didn't. I can't help it if I'm in love with Snake. He's just so cool. So different.

Nikki: yeah, he's cool, and you're so not his 1st girlfriend, and you won't be his last.

Lisa: So? For now I like him and he likes me. And anyway, it could last. We have this really special bond between us.

Nikki: yeah, yeah, I know, moms and dads in jail. But Lisa, he's the kind of guy who'll probably end up in jail too.

Lisa: He did NOT tag the principal's car. He told me he didn't, and nobody could prove he did.

Nikki: whatever. Who do you think I buy my weed from? Who do you think supplies kegs for those parties in Goat Springs?

Lisa: In social studies they call that entrepreneurship.

Nikki: in court they call it a felony.

Lisa: I thought you liked him. And anyway, since when did you get so uptight?

Nikki: I do like him. He's really cool, and I'm not being uptight, just practical. You're just way too naive for a guy like Snake.

Lisa: I'm not naive. And I don't care what you say about him. Just like you don't care what I say about you dropping out of school.

Nikki: apples and oranges. I'm planning my future. If you're not careful, you could be ruining yours.

Lisa: I am not! Gotta go. Bye

Instant message to Snake:

Lisa: How about we join the Green Club? They have cool field trips to the mountains.

Snake: Sure. Whatever. Too bad there's not a gun club at good old Lincoln.

Lisa: A gun club? I thought you were against hunting.

Snake: I don't mean animals. People. One day we're gonna be over run, either by Mexicans or the Chinese or even other Americans. We have to be ready to defend our turf. Didn't you see that movie when a meteor hits the planet and floods the whole east coast? Where do you think people will go? Here to our mountains. It would make all those Katrina evacuees that invaded here look like nothing.

Lisa: Just b/c there's a movie about it doesn't mean it will happen. Besides, if there was a disaster in Arkansas, wouldn't we want other people to help us?

Snake: You're too nice, Lisa. Too soft-hearted. The world's a hard place and we have to be hard too if we're gonna survive.

Lisa: something very weird just happened.

Snake: weird how?

Lisa: The mail came, and since I'm waiting for my new subscription to Rolling Stone I looked through the mail and there's this letter to my Mom.

Snake: You read your mom's mail? You must be bored.

Lisa: I didn't read it. I just looked at who it was from.

Snake: and ... ?

Lisa: I think maybe it's from her ex-husband.

BOBBIE

The trip to see Jim Leftwich turned out to be momentous, though it didn't feel that way at the time. What I felt after I left him and drove back to New Orleans, straight to his daughter's grave, was guilt piled on guilt. How long was I going to torture his poor family?

At Alyssa's grave I couldn't do anything but cry. I brought lilies, pure and white but still not as beautiful as she must have been. Lilies for the lily girl, as Lissy had called her.

Alyssa and Lissy. That they were bound together in my emotions went without saying. When I cried for one, I cried for the other. And that day I cried to the point of collapse. Two women, one obviously the other's mother, tried to console me, but just looking at them together made me feel worse. They still had each other, mother and child. But I was alone. And because of me, maybe Diane Leftwich was alone too. I hoped she wasn't, but I would never know for sure until I found her.

After the two women left the cemetery, one of the groundskeepers came to check on me. But I didn't want his help. I didn't want anybody's help. I wanted to kneel there, hunched over and crying, until I had no more tears to cry, until I was drained dry with no more guilt and no more sorrow.

The truth is, for the first time in my life, I really wanted to die. It wasn't that melodramatic I-wish-I-were-dead thing like when I was a teenager and first went to juvenile jail. This was an honest to God, I wish I had never been born, the world would be a better place without me, I can't bear this pain any more urge to die.

When it began to rain on me and on the lily girl's gray, granite tomb, it felt like tears falling from heaven, like a sign that maybe I *should* kill myself. Just drive to the top of one of the bridges over the Mississippi River, stop my car, and jump.

Drenched with tears and rain, I somehow staggered back to my car, drove to the first Circle K I saw, and bought a pint of vodka. Then two things happened in quick succession.

The first was a billboard for Alcoholics Anonymous. Right there alongside I-10 as you head into downtown New Orleans, a sign for AA with a 1-800 number. I looked at the bottle in the paper bag on the passenger seat. I planned to park somewhere, take four or five big slugs, and when it began to hit me, head up onto the bridge before I could chicken out.

That's when I saw the second sign. It was one of those big canvas banners slung beneath several windows on a building beside an elevated portion of the interstate. It said: *Make a Difference in Someone's Life. Become a Nurse.* Underneath it was a phone number for some nursing school.

Maybe I was just looking for a reason to change my mind. Or maybe it was a God thing, like they used to say in the AA meetings in prison. I tried to ignore the two signs, but I couldn't. I felt like God was talking directly to me, telling me that I still had work to do to make up for my past. People to help.

In the plus and minus columns of life I was still too heavy on the minus side.

That brought on even more guilt. I was a complete failure as a human being. But who was I to argue with God? I took the very next exit and then pulled into the first parking lot I came to—a neighborhood pediatrics clinic. Another sign?

It took a few calls, but I eventually found an AA meeting at a place called the Avenue Club. I got directions and drove straight there, even though the next meeting was an hour away. Where else could I go in my screwed-up state? And as I drove down Canal Street, farther and farther from high ground, I saw the lingering marks of Hurricane Katrina. Houses still empty two years later. Nice renovations side by side with the haunting scars of people's lives torn up by the roots.

I paused at a stop sign to watch a trio of little girls jumping rope in front of an abandoned corner store. New life blooming in the midst of so much death and destruction. Wasn't that a mirror of my own life? The tragedy of Alyssa's death had brought me to my knees, to the bottom I had to experience before my own resurrection could begin. Prison had given me an education and new direction, a chance to blossom. How could I let either Alyssa or Lissy down?

At the Avenue Club I sat through three straight meetings, listening hard to what others had to say. Finally, near the end of the third meeting I raised my hand.

"Hi. I'm Bobbie and I'm an alcoholic." And as I recounted my sins, as I exposed the ugliest part of myself to this room of total strangers, I knew that the vodka in my car and the bridge over the Mississippi were not the right answer for me. I didn't know what the right answer was. But if I kept trying, if I just kept doing the next right thing, eventually I might figure it out.

. . . . .

I returned to my job and my one-room apartment exhausted, feeling like I'd been through a hurricane of my own. Battered and sore, I nonetheless felt as if my soul had somehow been revived. But I worried about Jim Leftwich. And I prayed for him every night. Maybe my visit, as wrenching and painful as it had been for him, would in the long run help him. I wasn't sure how it could. I only hoped God had a plan better than I did.

Two weeks later Ivan's boyfriend Dack died. I went to the funeral, listening to the minister and Dack's many friends speak.

" … he had a hard upbringing as a kid. But because a neighbor lady stepped in to help him when he was only nine, he found that second chance so many kids don't get. And as we all know, Dack did not waste that second chance. He was active in dozens of good causes across our city, investing his time, talents, and treasures well. That's why in lieu of flowers he asked for donations to CAJA, to the STAIR literacy program, and to the NO-AIDS Task Force."

CAJA.

Like a lightbulb switched on in a black room, the acronym flashed sudden hope into my heart. CAJA. Of course! Lissy had been assigned a CAJA representative before she even went into foster care. Even though CAJA's involvement probably ended when she was adopted, maybe CAJA could steer my search for her in the right direction.

"Thank you, Dack," I whispered as Ivan held up the beautiful Newcomb pottery vase that now held Dack's ashes. I'd learned all about Newcomb pottery and the other Craftsman arts from Dack. He'd remained a collector until the very end and had picked out this particular piece to function as his urn. Now Dack was gone, and some new patient would take his place in my case files. But I would never forget him, because he was sending me in this new direction.

The only bad thing was that I had to lie to go there.

The next day I called CAJA and volunteered my computer skills. Thank God I'd changed my name back to Fenner. A really thorough background check might still connect me to Bobbie Davis. But since I wasn't asking to work directly with children, I hoped they wouldn't do as in-depth a check. I knew Bobbie Davis, the jailbird, would be politely turned away. Luckily Bobbie Fenner's offer to volunteer was accepted.

It was hard work. Not the actual typing and data input. That was easy. The hard part was reading the files and looking at the pictures of so many misused children. Some were smiling. Others look terrified. And just like during visiting days in prison, every one of them reminded me of Lissy.

"Can you spare a couple of hours this weekend?" my CAJA supervisor asked me one Thursday evening.

I looked up from the computer. "I work eight-to-eight on Saturday. But I have some time on Sunday. What do you need?"

Grinning, he shook his head. "Dinah told me you'd say yes. What's up with you, Bobbie? Don't you have a boyfriend? Something to do other than work all week and volunteer here?"

"Apparently not," I joked right back. No way was I going there. "What about you? You spend a lot more time here than I do."

He shrugged. "Before my wife died, Sundays were for church and family. Now, well, I figure helping kids is God's work, so working on Sundays has become my church and family."

I nodded, impressed even more by the man. Ethan was a rotund little guy with thinning hair and not much of a chin. He looked like a dim-witted slob. But his dull exterior hid a brilliant mind, a tenacious work ethic, and a soul as honest and pure as a child's. In the month-and-a-half I'd volunteered here I'd been awed by his dedication to so many other people's children. "What time should I get here?" I asked.

"Whenever you can. I'll be here about nine. What I want to do is transfer our closed files out of the file cabinets and into storage boxes. But we have to keep everything very clear and mark all the boxes so that if we ever need to reference an old file, it'll be easy to find."

"What do we do with them then?"

"We have a donated storage unit a few miles from here where we keep all our closed files. We've just been too busy and too shorthanded since Katrina to bring another batch out there."

A storage unit with closed files in it. Omigod! I hadn't found anything about Lissy in the computer records because her case predated the current operating system. And so far the only hard files I'd found dating back to 1996 were those that were still active. Hard to believe that some poor kids needed a court-appointed special advocate for that long.

Now, though, I knew where the old closed files were stashed. Surely Lissy's file would be among them.

Averting my gaze, I reached for a candy from the jar I kept filled on the desk. The last thing I needed was for Ethan to see my excitement. "Yeah," I said, unwrapping a mint. "We sure can use the space. Some of those file drawers are almost too tight to get files in and out. I'll be here at nine, then. Okay?"

That gave me two endless days and three unbearable nights to wait for my first real chance to get a lead on Lissy. You'd think I could have relaxed but no way. It was like gas poured on a fire, out of control. As soon as I got home I turned on my computer and started hunting. State agency Web sites were no use so I searched school sites. Lissy should be in tenth grade but there are close to a thousand public and private high schools in Louisiana, most every one of them with a Web site. And there was no guarantee Lissy was still *in* Louisiana. Even if she'd been adopted by a family from Louisiana, after Katrina a lot of people hadn't come back.

But nothing could deter me. I hunched over the computer until almost two, grabbed a few hours of sleep, and then put in a full day at the clinic—only to do the same thing on Saturday. Even then, Sunday at nine I was outside the CAJA office waiting for Ethan.

I couldn't work fast enough. Sort the files, box and label. Sort the files, box and label. How many Office Depot file-storage boxes did we have to fill before we could load them up and head for the storage unit?

A little after noon Ethan heaved another box on top of two stacked ones at the end of a row of three-high file boxes. He rubbed the small of his back. "Damn. I'm going to pay for this tomorrow. Big- time."

"Maybe," I said as I slid another file box toward the dozen or so we'd filled. "But look at all the file space we've freed up."

He grunted agreement. "You know, I think maybe we ought to save the actual transfer of these files for another day. Maybe Sid can help me when he comes in Tuesday."

"No!" I blurted out. Then I repeated more calmly, "No. After all this work, don't you want to finish up? Just tough it out and get it done?"

He shot me an exasperated look. "My back is fifty-seven years old and it's telling me 'enough'."

"Well, my back is only thirty-five and it's good for another hour at least. How about you take a break while I load up my SUV?"

He shook his head. "I can't let you do all the lifting."

"Yes, you can," I insisted. No way was I missing a chance to snoop in old CAJA files. "Think of it this way. I won't have to go to the gym tonight."

Again he shook his head, but I could tell he was wavering.

"Besides," I added. "Won't it be nice to come in tomorrow with this whole project complete? No files stacked in the aisles. Hey, and we can pick up something to eat on the way there. I don't know about you, but I'm starving." Then not giving him an alternative, I picked up a box and started for the door.

We filled my car and his. Then we locked up the office and headed to the storage facility. While he stopped for take-out, I followed his directions to the Self-Serve Store-All, unit 151. The door was a plain, white, roll-up garage door. No windows. Only one big padlock between me and something—anything—that might lead me to my baby girl.

I don't pray a lot, though I do believe in God. I can't think of Him as a man, though, or for that matter, a woman. I know we were supposedly made in His image, but I don't think that means two eyes, a nose, and ten fingers. I think it means something deeper, the part of us that makes us know right from wrong and good from evil. It's the part that gives us a conscience and makes us strive to be noble. God doesn't have a face for me, but He or She is very real. I feel His presence every day. But today I felt it stronger than ever. He'd led me here. I knew it.

So I stood there in the glaring sunlight reflecting off the pale concrete and the white metal doors, and I prayed. *Help me find her. Please help me find her, just to be sure she's okay, that she's healthy and happy.*

And if she wasn't?

I couldn't think about that. One day at a time, that was my plan. One day at a time. But today was one very important day.

"Okay, one grilled chicken sandwich," Ethan said.

Startled, I stiffened, then slowly turned toward him, my smile firmly in place. "Great. Do you want to eat first or unload the cars?"

"Eat."

I nodded, fighting to control my disappointment. Then I had an idea. "Could we at least open up the door so we can sit in the shade?"

"Sure, though I doubt there's much room to sit." Still, he dug in his pocket for a key not on his regular key chain. It was a small gold key on a purple plastic- coil bracelet. Easy to find in his desk at work, I hoped. And easy to duplicate.

As he unlocked the door and rolled it up, I held my breath. I swear I could feel Lissy there, her essence bursting free from its cardboard and manila confines. Then the cool air from the storage unit rushed out and I faced the mountain of file boxes already stored there. How many children did it represent? How many dysfunctional families?

I started to cry, hot silent tears.

"I know," Ethan muttered. "I had the same reaction the first time I came here." He patted my shoulder. "What do you say we unload the file boxes first and take our lunch someplace else to eat?"

I nodded. That was all I could manage. We worked in silence, moving the file boxes as a team. Inside they were stacked four tall with narrow aisles between the rows in case someone needed to find something in one of them. I noted some of the dates. 1998. 1999.

It was dark in the rear of the unit and I didn't turn on the light. But I knew—I *knew*—that I would find 1996 somewhere back there. All I had to do was steal that key and copy it. Then I could come back and search for Lissy's file in private.

By the time we finished, food was the last thing on my mind. But Ethan wanted to eat and it was his treat. So I followed him to a neighborhood play spot where we sat on a metal bench beneath a towering magnolia tree and ate.

"What made you pick CAJA to volunteer for?" he asked.

I shrugged. "I could have used a CAJA person back when I was a kid."

"Yeah. Me too. So, when are you going to take the plunge and decide to take CAJA training?"

"Me? No way."

"Why not? I think you'd be good at it."

"What's the matter, you don't like my office skills?" I asked, trying to deflect his questions from me to him. No way could I ever be some kid's CAJA. Not with my record.

"You're great in the office," he said. "But it's easy to find a good secretary. A good CAJA, though. That's trickier."

"Yeah. Plus they need to stick around for years, judging by some of those files. The thing is, I don't know how long I'll be here."

"What's the matter, you don't like your job at the clinic?"

"No, I like it. A lot. But ... New Orleans is a hard place to live in right now."

"Yeah, it is."

"Plus, it's hard watching your patients die. It's not as bad as it was years ago. HIV isn't necessarily a death sentence any more. But still."

"Yeah." He took a long sip from his soft drink. "I hear nurses burn out all the time. A lot of CAJAs do too."

"But not you."

He pursed his lips. "Nine years and counting."

We were quiet a long while. Then I asked, "Do you ever think about them, the kids you worked with years ago?"

"Are you kidding? All the time. Every single one of them. I pray for them every night and wonder how their lives turned out."

"Did you ever try to find any of them? You know, track them down later to check on them?"

"That's against policy," he said. "Once their situations are settled by the courts and CAJA's involvement is no longer needed we're not supposed to interfere in their lives. But ... " He hesitated. Then with a wry half-smile he went on. "Yeah. I've checked on a few of them. Most of them," he added with a shrug.

A blue minivan pulled up, and three little kids tumbled free into the playground, running, shouting, laughing while their mother pulled out a folding chaise lounge and settled it in the shade of a live oak. Ethan and I watched them play, a boy and two little girls. And as their mother spoke in pleasant tones, always saying "please" and "thank you" to them and expecting the same back, offering hugs and smiles and whoops of encouragement, I wondered if I could ever have been as good a mother as that. Certainly not when I was twenty-three. That's for sure. But now?

I like to think I could be.

Of course, Lissy wasn't a rambunctious preschooler any more. Could I be a good parent to a teenaged girl?

Very deliberately I shut the door on that line of thinking. My goal wasn't to reclaim Lissy. I knew I couldn't take her away from her new family. The fact is, I would be a complete stranger to her. She might not even remember me.

I just wanted to know that she was all right, and to give her the box of letters I'd written to her over the years. I hoped then that she would know how much I loved her. That I never once stopped loving her.

I watched the littlest girl climb the slide and sit down on the top. "Look, Mommy! Look what I can do!" Then down she slid, hair flying, squealing for joy while her mother laughed and applauded.

God, I hoped Lissy's adopted mother was as good to her as this woman was to her children.

And even though I was thirty-five years old, with ten years of prison under my belt, I couldn't help wishing my own mother had been that good to me.

CHAPTER SIXTEEN

MYSPACE: LISA LOST AND FOUND

SEPTEMBER 20, 2007

The question of the day is: when does silence become a lie? If there are sins of omission and of commission, can't silence be a sin of omission, a lie simply because it hides the truth? My mom has always been secretive and kind of paranoid about other people knowing our personal business. But it's getting worse, and now I know she's hiding something from me. At first I was so pissed. She got this letter, I'm pretty sure it's from her ex-husband b/c I saw the return address. I waited to see if she would tell me about it. I even asked her if there was any mail for me, just to give her a chance to mention his letter. But she didn't say anything. I don't see what the big deal is. She hasn't been married to him since before I was born.

SEPTEMBER 21, 2007

So I asked her. I just came out and asked her about this guy Jim's letter while we were driving to the big mall across town. We were going to get me some school clothes and stuff. I timed it perfectly so that she couldn't get out of answering me. But all she said was that her ex must have been drunk and depressed when he wrote it, and that she didn't want to talk about it. But I wouldn't let it go. So I asked her why they got divorced, and was he trying to get back together with her. She said no. She said it, like ten times. No, no, no, no, no. Like that.

So then I asked how he even knew where we lived. Because we aren't in the phonebook. She just shook her head and said we might have to move again. I started to argue. I'm in the middle of high school and I'm NOT moving again! But then she started crying. My mom never cries. I mean, like maybe 2 or 3 times in my whole life did I ever see her cry. That's when I got this bad feeling, like maybe he was abusive or something. Like maybe she escaped from this really bad marriage and that's why we moved so much, to stay away from him. I didn't argue with her after that. I wanted to ask her to just tell me. I'm old enough to hear the truth. But I couldn't stand seeing her cry. So we drove to the mall and she bought me, like, twice as much stuff as I thought she would. She didn't even argue about all the black and red stuff, and the new Docks, and that's so NOT like her. Then I noticed how all the other people paid with credit cards or debit cards. But she pulled out $50 bills. A huge wad of them. My whole life she only used cash or sometimes checks, and I suddenly realized that was another way a woman would try to hide from a man. But I didn't say anything, and now I'm wondering what I should do. Even though we fight all the time, I love my mom and I hate that this Jim guy has her so scared.

At the same time, I don't want to move.

SEPTEMBER 22, 2007

    Today I called this 1-800 # for a domestic abuse hotline. It was weird, because I couldn't tell them much. The lady was really nice though, and she suggested I give the # to my mom, that maybe my mom will call them if she knows that I already have. She also said that what this Jim guy is doing is called stalking and it's illegal if the woman files a restraining order. Then they could throw his ass in jail.

SEPTEMBER 23, 2007

    I gave my mother the hotline # and she started to laugh. Then she started to cry. I never saw her so crazy and emotional like that. I mean, she's always been crazy obsessive, and crazy strict, and crazy weird. But she's never been crazy emotional. Finally she chilled enough to tell me that Jim is not a stalker and that he never hurt her or threatened her in their whole marriage or afterwards. Then she said that Jim just makes her remember the saddest time of her life and that it's depressing. That's why she doesn't want to be friends again, like he wants to. She said she just wants to forget that whole part of her life because she's happy now and she wants to stay that way.
    I was like majorly relieved, and I guess I understand how she feels. But I'm like just the opposite of her. The saddest time of my life was when I got put in foster care and never got to see my birth mom again. Even though it was 11 years ago, I still remember how scared I was. I can't hardly remember my real mom, but I still remember how scared I was to lose her.

After my new mom adopted me I slowly learned how to be happy again because she was a good mom—until we moved the last time. But now I'm glad we moved here b/c I never would have met Snake. Anyway, just b/c I'm happy now that doesn't mean I don't want to know all about those early years and about my birth mom and her family, and maybe my dad's family too. Only I can't talk to my adopted mom about that because she would totally freak out. So I guess we're exact opposites.

But maybe we're also the same. Because we've both been keeping secrets from each other. That's the only reason I decided to let the subject of her ex drop. I think there's a lot more stuff about him she's not telling me. I mean, all this moving and avoiding everything in her past is way extreme. But since I don't want her knowing about me and Snake, or about my online search for my birth mom, I guess maybe I have to cut her some slack about her secrets too.

. . . . .

From: Lisa
To: Snake
Re: Where are you?

Did I do something wrong? Are you mad at me? You haven't been at school and I left you like 100 messages. Only you never answered any of them. What's wrong? I love you 4ever.

From: Snake
To: Lisa
Re: (no subject)

My mom flipped out Sunday AM. She was drunk and took some pills and I had to call an ambulance. She's ok now but she said it's my dad's fault. He's getting out of jail sometime this month and she has a restraining order against him but she's like all freaked that he's coming to get even with her. I don't know who's more fucked up, him or her.

INSTANT MESSAGE TO SNAKE

Lisa: That's like so not right. It's like you're the grown up and they're the rotten kids.

Snake: Tell me about it. You know she's bad-mouthed him so long that I always just believed her. But I was only 8 when he went to jail. Maybe he's not as bad as she says. I'm thinking I need to find out about him for myself. Maybe you should too, I mean about your birth mom.

Lisa: Yeah, I think you're right. Maybe she's getting out of jail soon too.

Snake: How about we meet up? I'm big time stressed and need to mellow out.

BOBBIE

After two evenings volunteering at CAJA with no chance to search Ethan's desk for the storage-unit key, I called in sick at my regular job and just showed up during the CAJA day shift.

"Hey. What are you doing here?" Ethan asked.

I shrugged and scanned the busy front office, trying to hide my dismay at the number of people there. "I figured I'd drop by since there was a mix-up in the scheduling of the shifts at work and I got an unexpected day off. I thought you might need some help, but it looks like you've got a full staff and then some."

He laughed. "Yeah. Well, it's not usually this crowded. But we're having a quarterly review, so a lot of the caseworkers are here. Actually," he went on. "Your timing couldn't be better. While Susan takes minutes at the meeting, could you man her desk in the front office?"

While everyone else was in the conference room? I resisted the urge to jump for joy. "Sure. Fine. Whatever you need."

A half hour later I had the front office all to myself, including Ethan's partially walled-off corner cubicle. No interruptions, he'd told me. No phone calls unless it was a life-or-death emergency.

That suited me just fine. I sat down and started to enter data into one of the old files. Once I pressed print, I went over to the office printer, perched on a scarred wooden table right next to Ethan's cubby. I shot a quick glance around the room. Then taking a deep breath, I ducked into his office.

I'd already decided that if I were caught I'd say I was looking for staples for the heavy-duty stapler.

But I wasn't caught. Though I sweated out what felt like a half-hour search, it took less than two minutes to find the purple coil with the key on it. It was in the left-side middle drawer way in the back inside a gray, metal, card-file box.

For a moment I was almost afraid to touch it. That little piece of brass metal was so much more than merely a padlock key. With one simple turn that key held the power to unlock my past—and maybe my future too. Because *if* it led to Lissy, and *if* she wanted a relationship with her birth mother, then everything I'd gone through—losing her, going to jail, and this long search to find her—would be worth it. Finally, finally worth it.

I snatched up the key and pressed it against my chest. Then with a silent, "Thank you, God," I slipped the key into my pocket, closed the drawer, and then collected the finished work from the printer and went back to work. I put in nine straight hours that day. Guilty atonement, I guess, for what I was doing. I didn't leave until Ethan did. Then I went straight to a hardware store and had a copy of the key made.

The next evening was my regular volunteer time. The minute Ethan popped into the men's room I ducked into his office, replaced the original key, and was out again. Five seconds flat. But my heart raced like I'd just stolen the Hope diamond.

Why was replacing the key just as scary as stealing it? I don't know. All I knew was that I was not cut out for a life of crime. How had I ever had the guts to pull off some of my youthful stunts? Shoplifting. Drug buys. Joyriding in stolen cars.

I suppressed a shudder and focused on my friend the printer. Open the paper-supply door. Tear open a new ream of paper. Fan the pages—top, bottom, both sides. Add paper to the supply basket.

Life is like a copy machine. Take care of the little details, anticipate problems and head them off, and slowly, eventually all the big jobs get done. I hadn't lived my life that way for the first twenty-three years. I'd drifted on the currents of life, battered by this storm and that, only looking for one thing: temporary shelter from my pain, whether it came in a bottle, a pill, or the arms of the wrong guy. But I wasn't that person any more. Thanks to ten long years with nothing to do but think and focus on myself as I struggled to survive, I'd learned how to live a different way: think ahead; plan out your route.

It had gotten me this far. I was educated and my boss considered me a good employee.

And if I still had the soul of a thief, I consoled myself with the reminder that the theft of this key wasn't meant to do anyone any harm.

On my first day off I drove by the CAJA office, saw Ethan's car in the side lot, and kept going. He was hard at work with no reason to go out to the storage unit. It was time. I had two flashlights with me, plus a notebook and pen, and a bottle of water. When I reached the Store-All I parked my car around back. Just in case Ethan should drive by. Then with my heart working like a jackhammer, I approached the roll-up door, inserted the key in the padlock—and I was in.

I turned on the top light, and then closed the door. No need to draw attention to a gaping opening. I hoped to be in and out real fast, but you could never tell. With flashlight in hand I scanned down the tall stacks of file boxes. Most boxes held ten or twelve case files. But some held only four or five, the thick, unhappy records of too many innocent childhoods forever ruined. As I scanned the dates on the boxes—1998, 1997, 1996—I prayed that Lissy's file was one of the thin ones, one with a happy ending.

There were three 1996 file boxes. Thank God for Ethan's careful labeling. I found Lissy's file in the second box. Clutching the manila file to my chest, I sank to my knees on the floor. It was thin. Very thin.

In the weak light from the bare, overhead bulb, I opened my daughter's CAJA file. On the left side were three stapled pictures of Lissy. That's when I began to cry. I'd had only two pictures of Lissy to stare at these long, long years. That's all. Whatever pictures my mother might have had were gone, lost after she died, I guess, when her landlord cleaned out her trailer.

But now there were these three photographs that I'd never seen. My little girl, so somber and sad in the first one. I recognized the shirt she wore, a pink-and-lavender striped T-shirt with three heart-shaped buttons on each shoulder. Her hair was like I remembered, though it looked stringy, as if it needed to be washed.

I flipped it over. It was dated three weeks after my arrest. She must have still been with my mother.

In the next picture her bangs had been trimmed, her hair was shiny and combed, and she wore an outfit I didn't recognize, a pair of blue corduroy pants and a yellow knit shirt with a pair of sad-eyed puppies printed on the front. I traced the outline of her dear, little face. She wasn't smiling, but her faced looked fuller, like she'd gained weight. Hadn't I fed her enough? Was I that awful of a mother?

In the third photo she was smiling, squinting against the sunshine. It looked like she was in a park. I could see a swing set in the background. She was holding someone's hand. You couldn't see the person, but it was a woman's hand. No rings, bracelet, or watch. No polish on her nails. Just a slender hand with neatly clipped nails. A nice woman's hand. Lissy wore a green-checked sundress with white buckled sandals and pink polish on her toenails. And she looked happy.

I turned over both pictures but couldn't read the dates because of my tears. My Lissy, happy with someone else. It was what I wanted. It was *all* I'd ever wanted for her. And yet ... it hurt to see her happiness. I hadn't put that smile on her face. It had taken someone else. A stranger.

I mopped my face dry as best I could, and then carefully peeled the photos from the file. I was keeping them. I hadn't planned to take anything from Lissy's file, only to jot down whatever pertinent names, dates, and addresses might aid my search. But I hadn't thought about photos.

I flipped them again. The puppy-shirt photo was dated the week I'd left to begin serving my ten-year sentence. By then she'd been in temporary foster care. The third picture was dated six months later. Could that woman's hand belong to Lissy's adopted mother?

I spread the photos out on top of the file box. Then I opened Lissy's file and began to read about her life. It took a lot longer than I expected, mainly because I cried so much. But as I read I slowly developed a sense of the life my Lissy had led.

She'd been removed from my mother's care a month after I was arrested, and put in a temporary foster home. CAJA had gotten involved six weeks later. I saw an initial evaluation: age, weight, height. Family situations: mother jailed; father deceased; maternal grandmother very likely unsuitable.

Once more the tears welled. How could I ever have been so stupid? So selfish? I'd put my innocent baby girl through so much turmoil and pain. After my own fractured childhood I should have known better.

"I'm sorry," I whispered to the three pictures. "I'm sorry."

I forced myself to go on. She'd been assigned a CAJA caseworker in March, a woman named Diane Haines. I saw her reports on the home visits to my mother and to Ken's brother Hal. She'd obviously seen straight through their bullshit, because she'd saved Lissy from her own family. Surely someone that caring and thorough would remember Lissy. Maybe she would tell me what happened to Lissy.

"Thank you, Diane Haines," I murmured. I studied Lissy's third picture and the hand she held so tight to. "Thank you for protecting her when I couldn't."

Then I found the letter I'd sent giving up my parental rights and giving permission for Lissy to be adopted. I remembered that day so clearly. By then I'd been sober three or four months, long enough for all my emotions to finally rise to the surface. I hadn't been able to hide, not from my sins or from the pain of doing for once what I knew was absolutely right. I'd had to let my child go. It had hurt to hold the pen, to put down every single word. But I'd had to write it.

I traced the letters. *To who it may concern.* Later I'd had to sign a bunch of forms to make it all legal. But this letter had been the hardest part.

Swallowing a lump of remembered emotions, I moved on. There were several reports from Diane Haines. Lissy was doing well, enrolled in a playgroup, sleeping better. A psychologist's report confirmed that Lissy was adjusting to her new life. Then in late April Diane Haines had become Lissy's foster mother. A month later she'd applied to adopt Lissy.

I reread that part twice. It was a lousy copy of an original form, exactly what I'd been hoping to find. Yet seeing it took me by surprise. Diane Haines, Lissy's CAJA caseworker and foster mother had become my baby's adopted mother.

My chest hurt and I thought I was going to pass out until I forced myself to breathe. This was it! I'd hoped to find the name of Lissy's caseworker as a lead to her foster mother and from there to her adopted family. I sure hadn't expected to find the name of her adopted mother in this file. But there it was in grainy black-and-white. The answer I sought. The path to finding Lissy.

I wrote down everything, even the name of the CAJA supervisor who'd sent such a glowing recommendation for Diane Haines to the adoption review panel. There was no confirmation in Lissy's file that Diane Haines had ever been approved as Lissy's adopted parent, but no other names appeared in her place. A general note about Lissy's adoption was noted, and six months later her CAJA file was officially closed.

I sat there on the dusty floor, utterly spent of emotion, with the closed file on my lap and the three photos laid out on top of the file box. I was blown away. My Lissy had been adopted by her CAJA caseworker. The first person who'd taken on Lissy's case had fallen in love with her and had taken my forlorn baby girl into her heart and into her home. That's why Lissy's file was so thin. Thank God.

And thanks to this Diane Haines.

Overwhelmed with joy, with sorrow, with regret—so much regret—I slid Lissy's file back into place. Then I stacked the files precisely as they'd been before, gathered up my precious photos, turned out the light, and left. I didn't drive home, I floated. I'd done it. After all these months going down one dead-end road after another, I'd finally found the missing link to Lissy. All I had to do now was find Diane Haines and I would find my daughter.

The minute I unlocked my apartment door, I turned on my computer and Googled Diane Haines. There weren't that many listings, only two references to her as a CAJA caseworker. So I started digging: real estate records, tax files, census records. I found her in the 1970 census, ten-year-old daughter of John and Lillian Haines, residing in the Third Ward of New Orleans. The Third Ward. That wasn't far from where I lived now. Since I knew her age and whereabouts, I started searching state marriage records, and then engagement and marriage announcements in newspapers.

It was 3:13 AM when I found what I was looking for.

3:13 AM when I discovered that Diane Marie Haines had gotten married on a beach in Florida on July 1, 1983.

3:13 AM when my euphoria turned to shock, because Diane Haines had married James Sterling Leftwich.

3:13 AM when my shock turned to horror and then overwhelming panic when I understood that Diane Haines Leftwich was the mother of Alyssa Leftwich, whom I had killed.

And now she had my child.

CHAPTER SEVENTEEN

From: Lisa
To: Nikki
Re: Bobbie = Roberta

I can't believe you knew Bobbie Altford's real name was Roberta and you never told me.

Instant Message to Lisa:

Nikki: What's the big deal? Just because she won the Octoberfest art show doesn't mean she's so great. I heard she's a real slut. That's probably how she won.

Lisa: I don't give a damn who won the art show! Or if she's a slut. Half the girls at school are sluts. The point is that I knew Bobbie was short for Barbara. But I didn't know it was short for Roberta.

Nikki: No duh! Robert/Bobby, Roberta/Bobbie?

Lisa: Ha ha. The thing is, I never knew anyone named Roberta before.

Nikki: It is kind of old-fashioned. So, you think maybe your real mom could be named Roberta?

Lisa: Maybe. I can't find a Barbara Davis anywhere who's the right age or lived in the right place. But maybe I can find a Roberta Davis.

Nikki: Cool. You go, girl. BTW, I got those birth control pills you wanted, and some Lion King band-aids.

Lisa: Good. Bring them tomorrow.

Nikki: Cool. Does Snake know about the pills?

Lisa: Yes. He hates condoms and I was afraid to get pregnant, so he told me to get the pills. He'll be really glad.

Nikki: Yeah. I bet.

Lisa: What do you and Steve use?

Nikki: Who says we need to use anything?

Lisa: Are you saying you're not doing it?

Nikki: Wouldn't you like to know.

From: Lisa
To: Snake
Re: Advice needed

I think I have a new lead on my birth mother's real name but all of a sudden I'm all freaked. What if she turns out to be a major loser? I mean, I guess anyone who goes to jail for that long has to be some kind of loser. I still want to know about her, but I'm getting cold feet.

From: Snake
To: Lisa
Re: loser parents

I get what you're going through. When I was ten my mom told me my dad was a crackhead who robbed two pharmacies and a vet's office, plus shot some other dealer on the street. It made me sick inside. I'm half him, you know? That's when I started cutting. The thing is my mom's no prize either. I guess she tries. But she parties too much and she's always changing jobs and changing boyfriends. Plus she's always broke. That's why I sell weed, for groceries and shoes and shit like that. Anyway, she hates my dad just like she hates all her exes even though a couple of them were pretty cool. So I'm thinking maybe my dad isn't so bad. I talked to him twice since he got out and he said as soon as he has some bucks and his parole officer okays it, he's gonna look me up. I think you should just find your mom, Lisa. Good, bad, or otherwise. If you don't, you'll always wonder.

From: Lisa
To: Snake
Re: loser parents

You're right. I don't know why I'm being such a wuss about her. Okay, I'm gonna Google her. I'll let you know how it goes. See you tomorrow.

Instant message from Snake:

Snake: Why wait until tomorrow? I'm at the Coffee Beanery. Can you sneak out and meet me?

Lisa: I don't know. My mom's still up.

Snake: So what's she gonna do about it?

Lisa: Freak out, that's what. Yell. Ground me.

Snake: So? If you sneak out tonight, you'll sneak out if she grounds you. What's she gonna do? Call the cops?

Lisa: You're right. Okay, just let me do this search first. I'll I.M. you when I'm done.

GOOGLE SEARCH

Key Words: Roberta Davis/arrest
Five listings found:
Slidell Newspaper–Local woman arrested 12/24/95
Slidell Newspaper–Prescription Ring Larger than Suspected 12/28/95
Times Picayune–Children of the Drug Trade 2/17/96
Slidell Newspaper–Big Day in Drug Court 2/20/96
Slidell Newspaper–Photo Lineup of Local Drug Trade 3/11/96

Instant message to Snake:

Lisa: Found photo of my mother!

BOBBIE

It was as if Diane Haines had dropped off the face of the earth. No phone listings; no address; no census records. I found all the newspaper articles about her and her husband and the car accident, when she was still Diane Leftwich. Though it didn't help anything, I read every word in every article again, including several letters to the editor calling for me to be imprisoned forever. I read them and wept, reliving all my own guilt and anguish, and understanding finally the horrible pain the Leftwiches had felt.

But I found nothing dated after the time she adopted Lissy.

I knew Diane existed somewhere. After all, Lissy had been sick enough to go to the hospital just three years ago. But I couldn't find out where they'd been then or where they were now, and it chilled me to my soul. How could anyone disappear in this age of computer everything?

Unless it was deliberate.

I sat back in my beat-up desk chair. Of course. If Diane had adopted my child, it had to be under false pretenses. The powers that be would never have given my child to Diane if they'd known the ugly connection between us. That meant she'd lied to get Lissy.

So contact the state adoption people.

If it hadn't been an hour before dawn, I might have done just that. But state offices wouldn't open for almost four more hours. So I kept on with my search. But this time I widened my search to Lissy Haines, in the hope that Diane Haines hadn't remarried. And that's when I unearthed my first nugget of hope. In October 2004 Lisa Haines, a seventh-grader in Alexandria, Louisiana, had represented her school at the parish spelling bee and had come in second place.

Lisa Haines. In the spring of 2004 my Lissy would have been in seventh grade.

I felt the blood rushing in my veins, the sound audible in my ears. Could this Lisa Haines be my Lissy?

I went immediately to her school's Web site. It wasn't much help. While the site posted an events schedule, lunch options, campus photos, and other general information, there was very little about the student body. And none of the photos had any students' names attached.

But that was okay, because I'd already decided to go to Alexandria. I had a strong feeling about this Lisa Haines. Forget the adoption board. Even if they sympathized with my situation and checked on Lissy, at this late date they weren't likely to yank her out of the only home she'd ever known. Not unless there was some serious abuse going on. And even I doubted that. Lissy was smart enough to win a spelling bee, and Diane cared enough about Lissy's health to risk contacting the prison for help.

No, there was probably no blatant abuse. But did Diane love Lissy? Did Lissy have *anyone* who loved her? I couldn't risk the answer being no; that's why I had to find her. Me, not the adoption people.

At eight o'clock sharp I called her school and made an appointment to visit. "I'm moving to Alexandria soon. A job change," I lied to the pleasant woman on the other end of the phone line. "My daughter is entering seventh grade, and since I'll be in town this week looking at houses, I thought I'd visit a couple of schools as well."

"Of course. Tell me what days you'll be in town. Then I'll check with the vice principal to see when she's available. She's the one who leads school tours," she added.

"Great," I said, breathless with the possibilities looming before me. "Great. I'm arriving tomorrow." If I couldn't get the day off on such short notice, I'd quit. "Could she see me then?"

"No. That's an in-service training day. How about the day after that? She could see you anytime between eight-forty-five and eleven."

"I'll be there at eight-forty-five."

And that was it. In two days I'd be at Lissy's school. She wouldn't be there, of course. It was a kindergarten through eighth-grade elementary school and by now she must be a sophomore. But still ...

I'd be walking the halls she'd once walked, and visiting the gym and lunchroom and library she used to visit. And maybe there would be a yearbook with her picture in it. I picked up the triple picture frame that now held the three CAJA photographs of her. She'd been so young then. Now she was practically a woman. I'd missed all those years in-between. How I longed to see even a couple pictures of her growing-up years.

Don't ask me how I got through that day at work. Though I hadn't slept a minute, I was buzzed on adrenaline. Four cups of coffee didn't hurt either. I found somebody to work my shifts at the clinic for the next three days and called CAJA to let them know I'd be out of town for a while. Then I bought myself a soccer-mom outfit, gave myself a manicure, and polished my best shoes. I was Roberta Fenner, widowed with one daughter—all true. The lies were that I had accepted a teaching position in the nursing program at Louisiana College in Pineville, and that my seventh-grader needed a school with a strong academic record and a wide variety of extracurricular activities.

The next day I stopped at the Tanger Outlet Mall outside Baton Rouge and bought myself a day planner. I wanted to look like the kind of parent the vice principal would want to woo—the kind of parent I wish I could have been, but suspected I never would have been. Not way back then. It had taken ten years of prison to wake me up. I couldn't undo any of that, my mistakes or the years of atonement. But I could make sure Lissy had gotten the life she deserved.

I found a Holiday Inn in Alexandria, ate a nervous dinner at Applebee's, and then tried to watch television. But it was a waste of time. Instead I drove by the school—three times. Back at the motel I took three Tylenol PM. Even then I didn't doze off until almost two. My wake-up call came at six-thirty. I struggled to make my hair behave, and put on just the right amount of makeup. Then I donned my new beige linen slacks with an apple-green twin set.

I stared at myself in the mirrored closet doors. That neat, classically dressed woman could be a nursing instructor. She also could be the very particular mother of an extremely bright seventh-grader. She looked both smart and self-sufficient. Whether I was either smart or self-sufficient, however, was a crapshoot. I sure wasn't anything else I professed to be.

"It's a Catholic school," I told my chic reflection. "They need every tuition check they can get." As long as they believed I wanted a good Catholic environment for my child—and that I could afford it—they would do backflips to woo me.

I repeated that out loud at least five more times before I pulled into the parking lot of the two-story, red brick school building. But my armpits still felt sticky with sweat. Sitting in the front seat, I slipped a tissue under my brand-new sweater set and mopped away any evidence of my panic. It was showtime. If I pulled off my part I might actually leave this building with a photograph of my daughter at twelve. If nothing else came of this charade, that photo would make it all worthwhile.

It's funny how an elementary school looks so different from

an adult perspective. I walked in through a pair of doors and up the five marble steps to the wood-floored main lobby. Opposite me was a glassed-in office with a hall stretching away on either side. The floors were worn but polished. Two bulletin boards flanked the office windows. One sported a cheery welcome-back message complete with photos of smiling teachers and a map of the school. The other one had a dozen or more group pictures of kids in action: the chorus performing on a stage; the soccer team making a score; the Green Club picking up litter along some bayou, and a trio of altar helpers serving Mass with a short, pudgy priest.

That's when it hit me. I was lying to the Catholic Church.

I'd done a lot of bad things and told a lot of lies to get this close to Lissy. So far, though, I'd avoided lying to any priests or nuns.

But I shrugged that thought off. As lies went, this one wasn't a bad one. It certainly wouldn't hurt anyone. So I took a deep breath, conscious of that distinctive elementary-school smell—books, paste, and floor polish—and crossed the hall to the office.

I expected a nun to give me the tour, so when a cheery-faced middle-aged woman wearing makeup, jewelry, and a wedding ring introduced herself as Colleen McCall, I felt this enormous sense of relief. I wouldn't have to lie to a nun.

"We'll have to be very quiet in the classrooms," she instructed as we headed to the second floor. "Middle-school children are actually more easily distracted than the younger ones, so if you'll save any questions until we return to the hall."

"Certainly." The questions I really had could only be answered in the library, so I steeled myself to endure the rest of the tour. But as we peeked into the science lab where eight groups of three kids each experimented with the properties of acid versus alkaline substance, and observed a math relay race on a trio of blackboards, I got sucked into the whole scene. These kids, so bright and shiny in their navy-and-white uniforms, brought tears to my eyes. They weren't Lissy, but they could have been. Eager to learn. Bursting with energy. They had their whole lives ahead of them, and all these good adults backing them up, teachers and parents.

As I walked those halls, pretending to fit in, I realized that I'd give the world to actually belong here. To be a real mother to a real girl who needed me to check her homework at night and wash her uniforms on the weekends. To send cupcakes on her birthday, and agree to drive for field trips. Such simple tasks for most people. For some parents they might even be an aggravation. But I'd do anything for that chance, that simple, ordinary sort of life.

I followed Mrs. McCall down to the lunchroom where the smell of spaghetti and chocolate chip cookies only made me more enamored of the place. And more depressed by all I'd missed. I could have been a good mother and had all this with my child. But I'd blown it. Even if I found Lissy—*when* I found her—it would still be too late.

Too late to have it with Lissy. But I could have it with another child.

That's the first time I considered having another baby. Even though I miscarried in prison, that didn't mean I couldn't get pregnant and have another child—and another chance. But was I really up to the challenge? Having a baby was one thing. Could I be a good mother 24-7?

"Just out of curiosity," I asked as we finally headed toward the library. "Do you give a tuition break to additional children in the same family?"

"Oh, yes," she answered. "Ten percent for a second child. Fifteen percent for any others. But I understood you just have the one daughter."

"Yes. Just the one. But I'd like more. Of course, I'd need a husband first," I added.

"Yes," she added, rather primly. "That's always a good idea."

What an idiot I was! Why had I said that? This was a Catholic school and now she probably thought I was divorced. Since the pope didn't approve of divorces, I doubt he approved of second marriages.

"I'm a widow," I blurted out. "Lissy's dad died when she was two." At least that was true.

"I'm so sorry," Mrs. McCall said, and I could tell she meant it.

More brownie points for me. "Oh. This is very nice," I exclaimed as we entered the library. Kid-sized chairs, miniature computer stations, and bookshelves only four feet high stretched across a spacious room painted in shades of peach and cream. In one corner the carpet was laid out with a seating pattern curving around a storyteller's chair. The walls were decorated with pictures of authors alongside covers of their books. Toolie would have loved it.

In one aisle a librarian shelved books, while a group of older kids worked at the several computer stations. Another group used laptops at the tables.

"May I just browse the shelves a bit?" I whispered to Mrs. McCall.

She glanced at her watch, then gave me a smile. "Certainly. Take your time. But I'll have to leave you here, all right? Duty calls. Before you leave, however, check in at the office. I'll answer any other questions you might have, and give you an application package."

"That would be great." *It would be perfect.*

She introduced me to the librarian, a sunny-faced woman about my age, and then left. "I'll just browse," I told the librarian. "Don't stop your work on account of me."

Of course, I wasn't browsing at all. I passed up the fiction section, scanned nonfiction, and then proceeded to the reference area. I was on a mission, but I found no yearbooks.

"We're relying more and more on online reference sources," Ms. Clarke said, startling me as I crouched in front of the two sets of children's encyclopedias. "That's why this area seems so skimpy."

"But I guess that's good," I replied. "Right? What about yearbooks?" I went on. "Are they all on video these days?"

She laughed. "They're heading that way. But we still have the old-fashioned kind too. Would you like to see them?"

"Great." *Better than great!* "That will give me a clearer idea of the extracurricular activities you offer."

She showed me to a shelf just behind the main desk. "Help yourself."

"Thanks." I smiled at her, and set my purse down on a table. "I'll just thumb through a couple of them." *The 2004–2005 yearbook in particular.*

I swear my fingers tingled when I picked up the blue spiral-bound yearbook. Lissy was in here—or rather, Lisa Haines. I glanced furtively around. Ms. Clarke was bent over a computer helping a pair of ponytailed girls. No one else was paying any attention to me either, not to my suddenly damp brow or to my massively quivering hands. I shook so hard I could barely turn the pages, and when I found the seventh-graders, I think I stopped breathing.

But then I saw her. I recognized her one-inch photograph

before I even found her name on the right edge of the page. Like a shining light in the dark, her face leaped out at me. It was her. My child.

I bent nearer the page before I realized that I knew her because she looked so much like I had at that age. Still sweet. Still innocent.

"Lissy." I breathed her name out loud. Then her face blurred and I felt the burn of tears. "Lissy," I whispered, wiping my eyes so that no tears could mar her picture.

Behind me a boy laughed. I heard the librarian's softly worded instruction and the indeterminate murmurs of other students. But here it was just Lissy and me, with her shoulder-length hair and side-swept bangs. Her teeth looked too big for her sweet, heart-shaped face, and it reminded me of how I'd felt at her age, like some toothy cartoon character.

I don't remember growing into my smile. But sometime around tenth grade those teeth had morphed from being my worst feature into my best. The girl with the sunbeam smile. That's what Ken had called me.

By then, though, my smile had become a tool, a way to manipulate guys to get what I wanted—presents, money, drugs.

I shuddered and closed my eyes, praying Lissy never needed to use her smile that way. I made myself search the book for more pictures, and sure enough I found her three more times. In the chorus, on the seventh-grade volleyball team, and at the parish spelling bee.

The last one showed her the best. Skinny and flat-chested. Slow to develop, just like I'd been. She looked adorable in her school uniform, and she was smiling this huge, victorious smile, holding a trophy in front of her.

My baby was beautiful, smart, and happy. Everything I'd

ever wanted her to be. Once more I closed my eyes. This time, though, I struggled with a whole different emotion: doubt. Why was I really trying to find her? How could me showing up out of the blue possibly help her when she already had every thing she needed? Everything I'd ever dreamed of for her?

When I opened my eyes, however, I had my answer. The date of the yearbook, 2004-2005, stared back at me. When these pictures were taken she'd been more than beautiful, smart, and happy. She'd been healthy. These pictures were all taken before she got sick.

I found the yearbook for the following year, searching for her eighth-grade self. But she wasn't in it and I shivered with fear. What did that mean? Was she too ill for school? God forbid, had she died?

No. She hadn't died. If she had died, Dr. Phelps would have told me.

But what if no one had told her? Or what if Lissy had lingered, only to die after I'd left prison?

I put that yearbook back onto the shelf and forced myself to reopen the one with her pictures. If she'd died I would know it. Somehow I would have sensed it.

Maybe.

Shaking off the beginnings of panic, I scanned the room. The copy machine stood in the far corner, right next to the librarian's desk. I needed to copy these pictures, but how could I explain that to the librarian? She'd think I was some sort of sick pervert.

That's when a buzzer sounded. At once the room erupted in activity. Books slammed shut, chairs pushed back, backpacks were hefted onto shoulders as the students headed for the door. The librarian stood there, bidding them each good-bye. That she knew every single child's name seemed so perfect. Why had

Diane Haines taken Lissy away from all this?

But I knew why. To hide her from me. That had to be the reason. I only hoped the next school she'd picked for Lissy had been this wonderful.

From across the room Ms. Clarke called to me. "Do you need any help? Because I'm going to run to the staff lounge before the next group arrives. Okay? I'll be back in two shakes."

Two shakes. That's all it took for me to make copies of Lissy's pictures. Lisa Haines's pictures.

Afterward I stopped at the office, thanked Mrs. McCall, took the application package, and told her with absolute sincerity that her school was the most wonderful school I'd ever been to.

And as I drove away I thanked God for giving Lissy the few brief years she'd had here. But as successful as my visit had been, I knew it was just one step along the path. I didn't have a clue where Diane had fled with Lissy, but it occurred to me that I knew one person who might.

CHAPTER EIGHTEEN

From: Lisa
To: Snake
Re: tonight

It's supposed to rain, so I don't know if I want to go out tonight. Can you get a car?

From: Snake
To: Lisa
Re: tonight

I wish. Vic's wheels are in the shop. But what's a little rain. Afraid you'll melt? Besides, you have to come. I just found out something very interesting about your mom.

From: Lisa
To: Snake
Re: tonight

What? Did you find out what prison she's in?

From: Snake
To: Lisa
Re: tonight

>Not that mom. Diane.

Instant Message to Snake:

>**Lisa:** Why are you checking up on Diane?

>**Snake:** I was bored. Anyway, it's seriously weird.

>**Lisa:** So tell me.

>**Snake:** Sorry, you'll have to come over.

>**Lisa:** You're a jackass, you know?

BOBBIE

I knew Jim Leftwich wouldn't talk to me again. But I had a plan. If I showed up asking for Diane Haines's whereabouts, he would freak out, scream at me, and slam the door in my face. Assuming he didn't kill me with a brick or some other handy weapon.

But what would he do after that?

He'd probably call Diane.

That meant he had to have her phone number written down somewhere, or else entered into his cell phone directory. All I had to do was get into his house and check his phone records.

I drove straight from Alexandria to Mobile, pausing only fifteen minutes at my apartment in New Orleans to change clothes, gas up, and make three peanut butter sandwiches. I was running low on money and missing work didn't help. Besides, I didn't want to stop anywhere to eat. I wanted to get to Jim Leftwich and see what I could learn.

He reacted exactly as I expected.

"I told you to stay away from here. Stay away!"

"I'm sorry. I'm sorry," I kept repeating. But I remained there on his front porch. I couldn't leave. I'd driven all day to get here and every second, every minute of the trip I'd told myself there was no other way. I had to make sure Lissy was okay, and if that meant I had to torture poor Jim Leftwich again, then that's what I had to do. I didn't want to hurt him, but I didn't see any way to avoid it. "Just tell me where Diane is," I pleaded. "Just do that and I swear I'll never bother you again."

"Leave or I'll call the police," he vowed, his voice low, his eyes bulging red with hatred.

Inside my heart bled for him, but outside I held firm. "I need to find Diane. To try to make amends." I didn't know if he knew about Lissy being with Diane, but I sure wasn't going to alert him—and thereby Diane—that I knew the situation. "I need to make amends to her," I repeated. "Please—"

"Jim?" I heard a woman's voice. His wife. "Who's at the door?"

He didn't respond to her. Instead he stepped onto the porch and pulled the door shut. Then he grabbed an umbrella out of an old milk bucket beside the door and pointed it at me like a bayonet.

"Get off my property," he snarled. "Get off!"

This time I stepped back. Everything was working just as I'd planned. After this he'd definitely call Diane to warn her about me. But instead of rejoicing, I felt sick. I was breaking this man's heart all over again, and breaking mine too.

"Just give me her phone number," I pleaded, backing away with my hands raised to ward him off. "So I can call her." *So I don't have to break into your house to find it.*

"I'll kill you first!"

When he charged across the porch I realized he meant it. I stumbled backward. Then I turned and ran.

That's when his wife burst through the door. "Jim! Jim! What's happening?"

Like a douse of ice water her cry chilled his murderous intent. He halted at the base of the porch steps, umbrella still poised. I stopped halfway down the walkway. Our eyes held, his filled with hatred and rage, mine with sorrow and regret.

"Jim? Who is this woman?" His wife came up beside him, her arms crossed tight against her chest. "Who are you?" she demanded, glaring at me. "What do you want?"

"Diane," I said. "I want Diane."

"Well, you can't have her," he muttered.

Her scowl shifted from me to him. "For God's sake, Jim. If that's all she wants, then tell her. Tell her!"

I could swear he flinched at her words, that he recoiled from them as if from pain. "No." He shook his head, glaring all the while at me. "I don't know where she is. But even if I did, you're the last person I'd tell."

He meant it. His new wife didn't understand why. But I did. So I took three more steps backward before turning and walking unsteadily away.

Behind me I heard her low, hissing voice. "What is it with you and that woman?"

I didn't know if she meant me or Diane. In either case, he didn't answer. When I reached the street I crossed it. Then I veered right, heading for my car, which I'd parked out of sight around the block. When I reached the corner, though, I paused and turned to see if he was still there. He was. His wife had gone inside, but he stood there, umbrella still gripped tight, his eyes narrowed, following my every step.

Not until I rounded a yew hedge and no longer felt the awful weight of his stare did I take a full breath. "Okay," I muttered to myself. I'd set the pendulum in motion. Soon I'd see how far it would swing.

Once in my car I changed clothes, pulled my hair into a bun, and mashed on a baseball cap. Then I drove around the block and positioned my car as far away as I could while still able to see Jim Leftwich's house.

After about ten minutes I saw a little boy come out with a medium-sized dog on a leash. He walked the dog down the street toward a neighborhood park, and fifteen minutes later he came back. The sun was setting, and deep shade colored the front of their house. Outside lights came on, probably on an automatic timer. Inside a light flipped on upstairs while others followed suit downstairs.

Were they having a normal family dinner after that ugly, emotional scene? Did his wife understand his rage? Or was she impatient with it? They had two children together. Did she see his protection of Diane and his lingering love for Alyssa as a betrayal of all they had? If I were her, how would I feel?

The answer to that was easy. I'd be jealous and I'd be afraid. I'd worry that he would always love his first wife and child more, that I'd never be able to fill the void their loss had left. And eventually I'd grow angry with him. I'd want more from him, proof of his love, and that would push him even farther away.

My eyes stung and blurred, and I had to wipe them dry. I was wrecking Jim's new family as surely as I had wrecked his first one. Maybe no one would die this time, but could their family survive the resurrection of his first tragedy?

God, I hoped so.

I slept in my car and woke up when the newspaper deliveryman went by. He steered with his right hand and tossed with his left, operating with careful precision and incredible aim. When he threw a paper into Jim's yard, it landed at the base of the steps, the same spot where Jim had stood glaring at me as I left.

A few minutes later Jim came out in a green robe over dark blue pajama pants. Figuring he wouldn't leave for a while, I cranked up the car, found a Burger King, ordered coffee and breakfast, and cleaned up in the restroom. By the time I returned, the Leftwich neighborhood was coming alive. The first wave was joggers and dog walkers. Then came kids leaving for school.

Jim had two, the boy I'd seen yesterday and a younger girl. A pair of kids paused in front of their home and yelled, and right away Jim's children ran out. I watched them head down the street, the little girl dawdling while the others ran and danced and dodged ahead. They were just four ordinary kids from an ordinary neighborhood.

And yet, were they? What was ordinary, anyway? On the surface Jim Leftwich had everything: a good career, handsome home, and an ideal family. He'd had all that once before, though, and he'd lost it. I'd stolen it from him. How could that not color his enjoyment of what he had now? How could he not anticipate some calamity robbing him once more of everything he loved?

How could he ever feel ordinary?

Beyond that, wouldn't the simple act of loving anyone again—a wife, his children—make someone like him mourn his missing loved ones even more? Did Jim feel guilty every time he hugged his son or kissed his little girl? Or made love to his wife?

I knew I couldn't afford to think about all that. I was here for a reason, and that's what I needed to concentrate on. But even so, the sausage biscuit I'd started to eat turned into a hard rock in my stomach, a congealed threat. Breathing through my nose, I tried to relax, but it wasn't happening. Then Jim slammed out of the house, my body went on red alert, and I forgot about the sausage biscuit.

He yanked open his car door, jumped in, and slammed that door too. But then nothing. He just sat there, and again guilt and grief pushed my breakfast higher in my throat. I'd done this, poured salt in his terrible, never-healed wounds. I'd caused this grievous rift within his new family. While I couldn't quite make him out in his Camry, I could picture him sitting there, both hands on the wheel with his head bowed in an agony of emotions.

"I'm sorry," I whispered, mirroring the pose I imagined him in. "I'm sorry." I prayed for him too, for peace and love in his life, for him to forgive himself for moving on. And I prayed for him to forgive me someday, if only for the peace that forgiveness would provide him. Because I knew I didn't deserve it.

When I finally looked up he was backing his navy Toyota down the driveway. As he drove off, the front door of his house opened and I saw his wife step onto the porch. She waited there, her shoulders slumped, watching him drive away. Then she trudged to the carport, got in her own car and drove off in the opposite direction.

That left me and their house. And their dog.

With the remnants of my breakfast sandwich firmly in hand, I climbed out of my car and looked around. A pair of women strode by, pumping their elbows and moving with practiced determination. I nodded at them, then after a few stretches and careful glances up and down the street, I started jogging. As I approached the Leftwiches' house, the next-door neighbor backed down her driveway and pulled away. I paused and bent down to retie my shoe. Once she turned the corner I stood. Then I very carefully turned up Jim's driveway, entered the carport, and slipped through the passageway between the house and the storage shed at the back of the carport.

I paused at the gate and fished the food from my pocket. One whistle was all it took to bring the dog rushing to the gate.

"Hey there," I said when he began to bark. I squatted down and pushed a piece of sausage through the wood pickets. "Come on, sweetie. Come see what I have for you."

He didn't look too sure, until he got a whiff of fried pork. His nose began to twitch, and his tail started a nervous wagging.

"Come on." I tossed another bit of sausage at him. And that's all it took. Half a breakfast sandwich and he was my new best friend.

Once in the yard, I looked for the easiest access with the most protection from any nosy neighbors. I didn't want to break a window. But I would if I had to. Fortunately they didn't have an alarm system. I'd noticed that yesterday before I rang the doorbell. It was such a nice neighborhood that crime probably wasn't an issue.

So why was there a blinking alarm monitor next to the sliding patio doors?

I approached the monitor cautiously. Why did it blink to warn potential thieves it was on by the back door, and yet there was no sign by the front door?

Because it was a fake, I realized, one of those catalogue doodads that looked like an alarm but actually held a spare key to the house. It had a three-tumbler combination lock underneath it to protect the key, but the multi-tool I'd brought with me made short work of the housing. Jam it in, pry it up, and the sliding panel popped right off.

I entered through the kitchen door with Fido right on my heels. The first thing I did was find a bag of doggie treats. Then I began my search, keeping the cheerful fellow happy with Milk-Bones.

It was a nice house, spacious but not fancy. Comfortable. Signs of family life were everywhere: children's art on the fridge; a stack of library books on the breakfast room table. Dr. Seuss, *Charlotte's Web*, and a pair of Lemony Snicket stories.

Had Lissy ever read these stories? Had Diane brought her to story times at her local library?

Would I have brought her if I'd raised her?

The truth was, probably not.

I moved on, searching for a telephone and their personal telephone book. I found it in the kitchen at a built-in desk. But there was nothing under Haines, or any Dianes at all. Though disappointed, I wasn't really surprised. The new Mrs. Leftwich wouldn't want the first Mrs. Leftwich's number in her family phone book. So where else might it be besides in his cell phone directory?

Listed in his cell phone bills.

Jim Leftwich was a CPA, and though he probably paid all his bills online, it turned out that he kept meticulous records of those bills in a file cabinet in an upstairs bedroom-turned-study. He had a file for every category of bill: auto insurance, life insurance, medical, dental, credit cards, household product information, household repair receipts, and phone records—further divided into landlines and cellular. The bills were divided into years also, a separate expandable file for each year going back three years.

I could take lessons from him on organization—later. Right now I pulled out the phone records, spread them on the neat desk, and began my search with the bills that had arrived right after I'd first approached him. I figured if he was going to call her, that would have been the time.

But there were no clues, just long lines of phone numbers with no names attached. How could I ever figure out which number was Diane's? As I studied the bill, though, I realized that many of the numbers appeared frequently. Some daily. Those wouldn't be Diane's. So I would narrow them down to the infrequent numbers dialed since I visited Jim, and then call every single one of them.

But as I waited for his desktop copy machine to warm up, I realized that reaching Diane on the phone wouldn't help me because it wouldn't tell me where she was. A 713 area code might indicate the Houston area, but she could actually be living in Florida, or Illinois. Or Alaska. I had to look deeper, find some clue to her actual address.

The rest of Jim's files were just as carefully organized as his bills. But though I found his children's school records, his investment files, his wife's mother's investment files, and their tax records going back seven years, I found nothing about his life prior to his second marriage.

Fighting panic, I stood in the middle of the room and turned in a slow circle. He had to have something in here. He wasn't the kind of man to just wipe the slate clean, throw away the remnants of his former life when something better came along.

Or was he? He'd divorced Diane at a time when she was probably still wallowing in despair. Why would he want to keep a paper trail of that? And yet his anger when I'd show up at his house both times, and especially his protectiveness toward his first wife, weren't the reactions of someone who'd totally moved on. No. Somewhere he had everything neatly organized and stored away. His first marriage certificate. Alyssa's birth records. Her immunization records. The newspaper accounts of her death. His divorce papers and old letters. They were all here, somewhere in this room. I could feel them.

I began my search with his desk. Every drawer, every cubby in the desk hutch. Then on to a trunk beneath the window. But it held old yearbooks and family photo albums—his current family. On to the closet where I found two sets of golf clubs, a tennis racket, the trophy he'd received for his volunteer work with Head Start, and a turquoise-and-black ski suit. On the shelf about the hanging rod he had a collection of caps, a pair of golf shoes stored in the original box, and a small suitcase. I stared up at it, wondering if maybe it held the records I sought. As I reached for it, however, I saw in the dimness another shelf even higher up. And as my eyes slowly adjusted to the darkness of the upper closet, I made out the shadowy shape of a box.

I had to pull his rolling desk chair over and balance precariously on it to get the box down. But the minute I touched it, I knew this was it.

Behind me the dog whined, but I ignored him as I clutched the box against my chest. I sat down on the chair with the box on my lap, but for the longest time I couldn't open it. It felt wrong, like I was violating Jim Leftwich's most private thoughts and emotions.

Felt wrong? There was no question that it was wrong. I was about to stick my dirty hands into his most sacred and painful memories. Into the deep, unhealed wounds of his soul. My heart beat like a panicked bird in my chest, like it was trying to escape before I did such a despicable thing.

But there was no going back for me. Stopping now wouldn't undo the past. Besides, with any luck Jim would never know I was here. I'd been so careful, putting everything back exactly as it was. Once I looked into this box I would put it back too, aligned just so, with every file precisely as it had been. He would never know, and so it would never hurt him.

That's what I told myself as I unwound the straps at either end of the box. He would never know.

I tried to hurry, but it was almost impossible. No matter my justifications, I felt like a rogue archaeologist come to plunder the great pyramids under the guise of the greater good, greater knowledge of cultures lost. That's all I wanted to know, that Lissy was healthy and happy. But was that sufficient reason to torture Jim Leftwich? Even if he never suspected this final violation, did it make it less wrong?

"Oh, God," I breathed the words. "I don't know. I just don't know."

But I did know. I took a breath and began to sift through

Jim's carefully tucked-away memories of his long-ago life. I knew that I was going to do this, no matter how it might hurt him. He was an innocent victim, but Diane wasn't. Not anymore. Not since she adopted my child under false pretenses. And until I understood her motives for taking Lissy, Jim's feelings couldn't matter to me.

So I went through the files, one by one. Alyssa's birth announcement, her baptismal certificate, her medical records. An envelope filled with her flattened golden curls. I steeled myself to be the analytical archaeologist as I looked, then put things away and moved on. I wanted only one thing: an address for Diane Haines.

Then on a piece of graph paper tucked into an untitled manila folder, I found it.

Actually, I found four of them, and three different phone numbers. She'd lived in Slidell, then Jackson, Mississippi. I found the Alexandria address too. But the address I wanted had to be the last one: Daspit Hill, Arkansas.

I don't know how he'd found her, whether she kept in touch with him, or if he had resources I hadn't been able to tap. Diane was the single name on the paper. No reference to Lissy, and again I wondered if he knew about her.

But that didn't really matter. I knew about her, and now I knew where she was.

I jotted down the address though I didn't need to. It was burned into my brain. Daspit Hill, Arkansas.

Once I made copies of the phone bills, I repacked the box and slid it back onto its shelf. Time to leave. I turned off the copier, and then backed out of the room, reassuring myself that it looked just as it had when I'd arrived. Everything exactly as it had been. The dog waited in the hall, suspicious once more.

But when I gave him three Milk-Bones he calmed down. Then tucking the precious information into my pocket, I shooed the dog out the back door and exited behind him.

I'd done it.

Like a marathon racer I sucked in great gulps of air and tried to reorient myself. Then I saw the broken phony alarm monitor. I managed to tuck the key back in, but the housing was broken. Somehow I jammed it in place, but I knew they'd eventually discover it.

"So what?" I told myself. Let them think someone started to break in but was scared off by the dog. Let them search the house and find nothing gone. I didn't care what they thought because I was finished here. Jim Leftwich wouldn't have to deal with me anymore.

I only hoped that eventually he would recover the peace that I'd so rudely stolen from him. Again.

PART THREE

LISA
OCTOBER 2007

CHAPTER NINETEEN

Date: 10/22/07
From: JLeftwich
To: DH504
Re: Diane, this is important!

    I know I'm the last person you want to hear from. But you need to know that Roberta Fenner is looking for you. She goes by Bobbie Davis now and she's been in jail for awhile. She's come to my house twice, supposedly to "make amends" for murdering Alyssa. But I know how that 12-step crap works. She wants to feel better, to assuage her guilt at *our* expense. I chased her off both times. But she's still looking for you. She begged me to tell her where you are. I didn't, but I don't think she's giving up. I know you don't want to talk to me, but I had to warn you.

Date: 10/24/07
From: JLeftwich
To: DH504
Re: Urgent! Diane, please respond!

Date: 10/25/07
From: JLeftwich
To: DH504
Re: Please respond ASAP

Date: 10/26/07
From: MailerServer
To: JLeftwich
Re: Unable to deliver mail to DH504. Address closed.

LISA

I don't remember anything from before I was adopted. When I was a kid I never needed to know about my life before the adoption because I was so happy with the life I had with my new mom. I mean, like, I probably wasn't too happy at first. There's this picture of me on my fourth birthday. I'm sitting in front of this adorable little cake, French *doberge*, taller than it was wide and decorated with pale pink flowers, light-green leaves, and a spun-sugar bunny. I'm dressed in a cute pink dress with patterned smocking across the top and my hair is up in pigtails with matching grosgrain ribbons. My bangs are cut straight across, and way too short.

Maybe that's why I'm not smiling. Mom and I have never agreed on how long my bangs should be.

But seriously. I'm not smiling, probably because I'd only been knowing her for a week or two, and I guess I wasn't used to her yet. I got used to her, though. Now I don't remember ever *not* being used to her. That picture is the only reminder.

I really loved Diane when I was a kid, like she was my real mom. But now all we do is fight. She's always been strict, and a real nag about school stuff. But our last move was the final straw. I did not want to move away from Alexandria, but she wouldn't listen to a word I said. She *never* listens to me.

We've moved so many times. I went to, like, four elementary schools and two junior highs. Now I'm on my second high school, but this time *I* was the one to decide on the change. After spring break last year I refused to go back to my all-girls Catholic high school. Mom got *sooo* mad and I was *sooo* scared of what she might do. But I didn't back down and in the end, I won. She let me transfer to Lincoln Arts High School and now I really love it. I mean, as much as anyone *can* love school. The thing is, I finally have some friends—and a boyfriend. Snake is just, like, so cool. He's a junior and his real name is Steven Niles Kinsey. SNK. Snake.

Mom doesn't know about him though, and I have no intention of telling her either. He's not exactly the kind of guy moms like. But their daughters do.

So this morning when I'm trying to get ready for school and Mom casually mentions taking a vacation to Colorado—about how beautiful it was with the Rockies, the low humidity, and the aspen trees—my radar went on major alert. I'd wondered why the Halloween decorations she pulled out of the closet were still sitting on the dining-room table three days later. I should have known something was up. And now she was sliding a brochure for Estes Park across the breakfast bar to me? The time to go on vacation was in the summer, not two months after school started.

I picked up the brochure and without even looking at, it ripped it in half and flung it at her. "I'm not moving."

She usually flips out when I act out. But this time she just lifted up her eyebrows, real innocent-like. "Who said anything about moving?"

I just shook my head and bent down to lace my boots.

"Who said anything about moving?" she repeated. "Can't we take a trip to see the colors change without you thinking we're moving?"

"We have plenty of autumn leaves right here."

"But not aspens. They're like trees of gold. Entire hillsides bathed in gold."

Did she think I was stupid? Ignoring her, I laced the other boot, stood, and then shoved my arms into my hoodie.

She was frowning now. "What's the big deal about moving anyway? I heard the schools in Colorado are fantastic. We could—"

"I like it here"

"Oh, really? Judging from all your complaining last year I couldn't tell. I'm still waiting for an improvement in your grades. Come on, Lisa," she went on, switching from Sgt. Mom to Wheedling Mom. "You'd love Colorado. Hiking in the summer. Skiing in the winter."

"I can hike here."

"But not ski."

"I don't care! My friends are here."

"They'll still be your friends. My God, as much as you text message each other it would be like you were still here. Plus you'll make more friends–"

"It *won't* be the same!" I shouted. I pushed away from the bar. "I'm *not* going!"

She stood too, with that who's-the-mother-around-here look on her face. "Now see here, young lady."

"No!" Was she serious? I wasn't a kid anymore, and I wasn't moving anywhere. "What's wrong with you? You *used* to be nice. You *used* to care what I wanted. How I felt. But now ... now you're just a bitch!"

I'd never used that word with her and I expected her to flip out. The fact that she didn't only proved how serious she was about this move. But why? "Come on, Lisa." She spread her hands wide and tilted her head. "You know that's not true. I–"

"But it is! It *is* true. It took me over a year to get used to Arkansas. I was miserable, Mom. Miserable!"

"You like it now, though. You made friends."

"Yeah, finally. But I'm not going through that again." Glaring at her I slung my Pony Express bag onto my shoulder. "I'm not." Then I jerked open the back door, stalked out, and for good measure slammed it. Hard.

What was wrong with her? Even though it was too early for the school bus, I ran all the way to the stop, dodging two old ladies who walked their five dogs together, and the gay guy who jogged in a muscle shirt no matter how cold it got. Grown-ups were screwed up and stupid, and they didn't care *how* kids felt about anything.

Somebody honked at me, some jerk old enough to be my father. "How about a ride, sweetheart?"

"Jerk off, asshole!" I shot him the bird. Then I veered between two houses, cutting through their backyards. More evidence—as if I needed any—that so-called adults were all fucked up. I slowed down when I came out on the next street. My side was throbbing, so I stopped, fished my cell phone out of my bag, and pulled up Nikki's number. "C'mon, c'mon," I muttered when her voice message came on. I hung up then called Snake.

"Dude," he said in this sleepy voice. "Why so early?"

"I had a fight with my mom."

"So what else is new? I'm not even out of bed yet."

"Let's go to Goat Lake. Can you get a car?"

"No. Besides, it's too cold."

"Who cares? I need to get out of here, you know?"

I heard him yawn. "Yeah. But I have to check in with Ms. Drab at lunchtime." Mrs. Dabney was the school vice principal in charge of discipline. Snake was on her shit list for several reasons—smoking, fighting, and skipping class. She'd warned him that if he had any more unexcused absences she'd kick him out and let one of the kids on the waiting list for Lincoln Arts take his place. Even though he hates school, he knows the regular public schools are worse. I didn't want him kicked out either. But I did *not* want to go to school today.

"Get Nikki to cut with you," he suggested, sounding more awake now.

"And go where? Besides, she's not answering her phone."

He snorted. "So you called her first? I guess I know where I stand with you."

"That's not true!" I switched the phone to my other ear. "I know you sleep late, and she's on the bus with me."

"Whatever. Look, I gotta get goin'. If you don't skip, I'll see you at lunch, okay?"

"Fine." But it wasn't fine. I shoved my phone back into my bag, then looked around. If I took the school bus I'd see Nikki. But I didn't want to be on a bus full of stupid kids who lived with their stupid parents in their stupid houses. They didn't know what it was like not to know your real mother, never have a father, and live with a crazy woman who lied to you. They didn't know what it was like to know your real mom was a convict, a junkie thief, too stoned to take care of her own kid. I was half her and half my dad, who died when I was a baby. Probably a junkie too.

Sometimes I wish Diane had never told me the truth about my real mom. It would be easier to believe she'd been just some scared teenager who got pregnant and couldn't keep me. She wanted to; she even tried for a couple of years. But it was too hard so she gave me up so I could have a better life. That's how much she loved me.

Or maybe that she'd died in an accident, or got killed trying to help somebody else. I read this article once about this lady at the beach with her family and somebody else started to drown so she gave them her boogie board because she used to be a lifeguard. Only then she ended up drowning instead in one of those riptides. I would rather have a good, brave mother like that who died, instead of the junkie, jailbird mom I got.

When I think about how she flaked out on me, and then how Diane stepped up and raised me like I was her own kid, it kind of makes me ashamed of how bitchy I can be. One thing I know for sure: Mom Diane loves me. Even when she does things that hurt me, I know she's not *trying* to hurt me. She's just seriously out of touch with reality.

Like moving to Colorado. As if! And that whole explanation about her ex-husband not stalking her? I don't buy into that either. There's a reason we moved so much and never used credit cards and didn't have a landline at home. If she wasn't avoiding him, then it must be someone else, because the way we lived didn't make sense.

I started for the bus stop out of habit. But before any of the other kids got there I split and headed over to the Walgreens. My boyfriend and my best friend had bailed on me, so screw them. There was no reason I couldn't skip school by myself. I hung out in the magazine aisle for a while, reading *Seventeen* and *Cosmo* and *People* until the manager came by and said, "Aren't you supposed to be in school?"

I slapped *Cosmo* on top of a stack of *Better Homes and Gardens* and said, "Whoa, I totally forgot!" and left. But not for school. I wasn't going to answer my phone or any text messages. My mom was being a selfish bitch. Snake was all worried about making Ms. Drab happy, and Nikki couldn't be bothered to answer her phone when her best friend called? Well, screw them all. Let them wonder for a change how come *I* wasn't available when *they* called.

I ended up at the public library, back in the nonfiction stacks on the second floor. I got online and checked all my e-mail, but I didn't open anything. Instead I went to Snake's MySpace page, then Nikki's, then mine. Then I just started jumping from page to page, like the free-association writing we did in English, only this was free-association Web surfing, no destination in mind, just moving around, depending on what name or subject or even word caught my eye.

Did you know there's something called white slavery? These pirates steal young girls off sailboats in the Caribbean. And pigs are smarter than dogs or chimpanzees. And kids who are home-schooled on average do better their freshman year of college than regular kids. Also, the worst-paying jobs are the ones that help people, like teachers and ministers. And artists too.

The best-paying jobs are the ones that screw people over, like lawyers and big-business jerks.

Anyway, by two o'clock I was pissed off and hungry and ready to go somewhere, anywhere but home.

It was raining so I sat on the library steps and decided to check my text messages. Three from Nikki; one from Snake. I opened his first.

Big newz, it said. Huge.

"Yeah, right," I muttered. Nikki's were more predictable. Where R U? I'm bored. Txt me and R U mad at me?

"No duh." I flipped back to Snake's. Big newz. Huge. Probably he'd sweet-talked Ms. Drab, and now she was his new best friend. I wanted to ignore him, but I couldn't help myself. What newz? I texted, then closed my phone. I was bored. By now the school might have called mom about me skipping. Or maybe not, since she hadn't called me or anything. I got up and went back inside. I needed something to read, something not about real life. Nikki had showed me these books of her mom's, all about vampires and blood and hot sex. Other ones were set in the olden days, but still with lots of sex. Her mom had tons of them, and that's what I was in the mood for.

I'd seen lots of sexy movies. I mean, that's how Nikki and I figured out how to do everything right. I didn't like watching them with Snake around, though. It was embarrassing. But when I read the parts Nikki marked in her mom's book, I was like, "Wow." It was a lot better even than the movies, like you really felt what the girl was feeling, and like you understood how much she loved the hero, even if she couldn't tell him.

So I went to the fiction section and found a whole shelf of paperback romances. I had just picked three—*Dance with the Devil*, *Thief of Hearts*, and *The Troublemaker*—when my phone rang. It was Snake. I didn't answer, though; I was still mad.

At the front desk the lady held her hand out. "May I see your library card?"

"I don't have one."

"Okay." She reached down, got a form, and slid it to me. "Fill this out and you'll have one in two shakes."

I rolled my eyes. I should've just stuck the books in my book bag and taken them. When I looked at the form, though, and saw all the spaces for address and phone numbers, I realized that here was another way to piss off my mother. Fill out this form with all the personal information she always kept hidden. Forget using the post office box; I put our street address, apartment number and everything on that form. And I listed both our cell numbers. But the main thing I did was to put my whole name: Lisa Anne Davis Haines. Davis was my birth mother's name from the newspaper articles about when she got arrested and I got taken away from her. That meant it was my name too.

"Okey-dokey," the librarian said. "One library card for Lisa Anne. These are the books you want?" She looked at me over her glasses when she saw they were romance novels.

"I'm in eleventh grade," I lied. "I'm old enough."

"I expect you are," was all she said.

Three little blips of her scanner and I was on my way to the

Beanery, this coffeehouse downtown. The rain had stopped but it was wet and gray and it had gotten a lot colder. I pulled the hood up on my sweatshirt. A dreary day to match my pissed-off, dreary mood.

By the time I reached the Beanery my feet were soaked and I was frozen solid. But it was warm inside and smelled really good, like strong coffee and fresh muffins. I headed for our corner table. No Snake. Only two hippie-looking women talking about some art market, and a few other people, all sitting alone hunched over their laptops.

Add one more to that number. I plopped down at the table, flipped my laptop open, and logged on. Thirteen new messages. None from Snake. Where was he? School had been out for almost an hour. I checked my phone. Two calls from my mom. She knew I'd skipped school.

"You know the rules," the first message began. *"You skip school, you get grounded."*

The second one said, *"Call me. Now."*

No way. From now on I was done with her rules. Totally done. So what if she didn't like it? What could she do about it anyway? Send me back to my real mom? Like that would ever happen. I called Snake to tell him about my new declaration of independence, but the call went straight to voice mail.

"Screw you," I muttered, snapping the phone closed. "All of you." I went to the counter and ordered a humongous brownie and a mug of hot chocolate with extra whipped cream. When I got back to the table I had an e-mail from Snake.

Though I wanted to be mad at him for ditching me today, what I really felt was relief. Even though he wasn't with me, just seeing his name on my screen gave me goose bumps. The thing is, Snake is like the hottest guy in eleventh grade. He's tall and his eyes are so blue they're like almost black. And he has long sideburns and just a little stubble on his chin. He's just the coolest guy at Lincoln Arts and he's *my* boyfriend. That's why I couldn't stay mad at him. I didn't even know *why* I was mad at him. This was really about my mom and her itch to move again.

If you're over your hissy fit meet me tonight, his message began. *I've got huge newz.*

What newz? I replied. *Tell me now.*

Nope. Sneak out after your mom's asleep and I'll show you then.

I shook my head and typed in: *I can't sneak out tonight. My mom's already mad at me for skipping school today.*

He didn't want to take no for an answer, but I wasn't in the mood for giving in to anybody today, even him. When he said he'd found out something weird about Diane, though, it pissed me off. I switched to instant message.

Lisa: Why are you checking up on my mom?

Snake: I was bored. Anyway, it's seriously weird.

Lisa: So tell me.

Snake: Sorry. You'll have to meet me tonight.

Lisa: You're being a jackass, you know.

Snake: Yeah, but you still dig me. Okay, I found her wedding announcement in some newspaper.

Lisa: So? I already know she was married. She told me.

Snake: Yeah, but did you know she had a kid before you? A little girl named Alyssa?

Lisa: What? No way. Are you sure?

Snake: Yeah. There's all these newspaper articles about them b/c they got in a car wreck and the kid died.

Lisa: Omigod! No. Are you sure? It's got to be a different Diane.

Snake: It's her. Married to Jim Leftwich, right? They're the right age and everything. It's her, Lisa.

Lisa: But she never said anything about that to me. Especially not about having a child that died. Why wouldn't she tell me this?

Snake: Who knows why parents do any of the stupid things they do? Whoa. I just found something else. Fuck. This is so screwed up.

"What could be weirder than my mother having a dead kid and never telling me about it?" I muttered as I typed my response. My adopted mother had a little girl named Alyssa that died? No way!

Then an old memory popped into my head: My name used to be Lissy. Lissy-Alyssa. An icy fingernail slid down my spine. Was that why Diane had adopted me, because my name was so close to her kid's name? Was that why she didn't want to see her ex-husband because of the car wreck?

Who was driving? I typed in. *Her or Jim?*

That's when my phone rang. It was Snake. "What?" I asked. "What's so weird? Who was driving? How could she not tell me these things?"

"Where are you?" he asked.

"At the Bean. What's going on, Snake?"

"Just sit tight. I'm coming over."

"Wait! What the fuck is going on? Tell me!" Three tables over the two hippie women looked up at me. But I didn't care. Snake was seriously weirding me out. "Tell me," I hissed into the phone.

He muttered something I didn't understand, then said, "Okay. Have it your way. How many people do you know named Roberta?"

"What?"

"Just answer the question. How many?"

I sank back in my chair. "Two. My real mom and Roberta at school. Why?"

"Because according to these articles from 1989, Diane Leftwich was driving her kid Alyssa back from some toy store when they were hit by a drunk teenager named Roberta Fenner."

For a moment I thought I'd heard wrong.

Then I thought, okay, three Robertas. So what?

But then this cold fog came over me, making me shiver, making my head hurt. *Roberta.* No way.

No way!

CHAPTER TWENTY

Dear Krista,

    I know you don't understand, and after our screaming battle this morning it's obvious you don't want to understand. I'm willing to go to marriage counseling; I'm willing to share every part of my life with you; I'm willing to be totally transparent about my involvement in Diane's life. But I'm not willing to forget she ever existed or promise to never contact her again. I can't erase a whole segment of my life, even for you.

    I love the life we've built. I love our kids. I love you. But I don't like you when you turn into an unreasonable shrew. You threatened me with divorce because I worry about my first wife? Have you ever considered that my worries for her are part of who I am, the person you loved and married? I don't abandon the people I love. Yes, I divorced Diane. At the time we were both so depressed and we were hurting each other more than helping. I still care for her, and she and I will always be connected because of the loss we shared. She's the only person who loved Alyssa as much as I did. Can't you understand?

    You don't have to be jealous of her. At the same time, I can't let that woman hurt her again. I just can't.

    Love, Jim

From: Krista
To: Jim
Re: Your note

I do want to understand. But when have you ever tried to understand how I feel? From the very beginning your ex-wife has hovered over us. I know that losing your little girl changed everything. You divorced but you're still tied to each other. But what about me? What about *our* kids? We can't be second place to her. You *have* to make us more important or you'll lose us too. Is that what you want? Do you want to be married to her again instead of me? Because that's how it feels. If you really love us best you'll give up this insane need to protect Diane from that awful Roberta woman. If she wants to apologize to Diane, then *let* her!

From: Jim
To: Krista
Re: (no subject)

I don't know if it's that you *can't* understand, or that you *won't*. Maybe I should be grateful that you can't understand how devastating the lost of a child is. I don't want you to ever understand that sort of endless, crushing pain. So that leaves only the other choice: that you refuse to understand.

Regardless, I have to warn Diane about Roberta. Unfortunately I have to go to Cincinnati to meet with two major clients. Or maybe it's fortunate. We could use a break from each other right now. I'll print out my itinerary once it's set.

GOOGLE ACCOUNT OF JLEFTWICH
Search: MAPQUEST
Enter: starting location:Mobile, AL
Destination: Daspit Hills, AR

LISA

I hunched over my laptop staring at the articles Snake had guided me to. Roberta Fenner. Could she be my mother? Was that possible?

But no. I wasn't even born at the time of that wreck. And Roberta Fenner was only seventeen. There weren't any pictures, so I couldn't compare this Roberta Fenner to the pictures of Bobbie Davis who got arrested six years later. None of this made sense. It was probably just a really weird coincidence.

And yet ... something didn't feel right.

I scowled at the screen, searching for more information about this Roberta Fenner person—where she was born, where she lived. Where she was now. But it was one series of dead ends after another.

"Anything?" Snake startled me with the question. I was so focused I'd blotted out everything, even him showing up.

I shook my head. "Nothing." Then like a big baby, I started to cry.

"Aw, man," Snake muttered under his breath, which only made me cry harder. My life was so fucked-up. Nobody understood me, not even him.

But maybe he did, because he dragged a chair next to mine, put his arm around me, and let me bawl like a baby against his shoulder. "Look," he said after my sobs finally turned into hiccups. "We can figure this out. There's got to be ways to either get a picture of this Roberta girl or find Bobbie Davis's marriage certificate."

So we started. Two computers are better than one. While I searched state marriage records in Mississippi where the articles said Roberta was from, Snake searched high school Web sites and reunion sites too, any place that might mention a Roberta

Fenner born around 1972 and graduated—assuming she did graduate—around 1990.

I got nowhere with wedding records in Mississippi, so then I started on Louisiana, since that's where I was adopted.

"Here's something," Snake said after what seemed like hours. "She might've gone to Slidell High. I found some guy through their alumni association. He graduated after she would have been there, but his sister is about the same age as your mom, so he's checking her yearbook. Yep, here it comes, a scan of Roberta Fenner's yearbook picture in her sophomore year."

I bolted around the table to peer at his screen.

"Holy shit," he said even before the page was fully up. "That one there. Yeah, it's Roberta Fenner." He glanced up at me. "She looks just like you."

She did look like me. It was totally whack. I stared at her, a pretty, smiling blond girl about my age. The picture was in black-and-white, one in a row of six, with five other rows on the same page. Girls, boys, white, black, Latino, and Asian. Yet her picture jumped out as if lit by a spotlight. You couldn't tell exactly what color her eyes were, but I knew. They were hazel, like mine.

Nothing else was clear though. Was she a jock or a nerd? An all-American cheerleader or one of the kids who smoked in the bathroom and skipped school whenever they could?

"She was drunk when she got in that wreck," I said out loud. That probably ruled out the Little Miss Sunshine persona.

"No, shit," Snake said. "Drunk as a skunk and driving a jacked truck."

I pulled my chair around and sat down, all the while staring at the smiling image of my birth mother at my age. She didn't look anything like the woman arrested six years later for drug possession. I hadn't wanted to be related to that woman. She'd look like a hunted animal, trapped and doomed with long, stringy hair and a face all haggard and thin. But here she was bright and smiling, like any other kid on picture day, her hair clean and washed, mascara and lipstick on, even if her mother had said no makeup till you're eighteen.

But in both versions she still looked like me. *I* looked like *her*.

Then it hit me, the ugliest part of this discovery: Roberta Fenner was my mother. Roberta Fenner had killed Diane Leftwich's little girl. And now Diane Haines Leftwich was *my* mother.

"So what was this?" Snake asked. "Some kinda twisted Louisiana justice? Like that thing from Shakespeare? I don't remember exactly. An eye for an eye and a tooth for a tooth?" He leaned back, tilting the chair onto its rear legs. "A baby for a baby?"

"That's from the Bible," I muttered. *Bonehead.*

"Yeah, whatever." He straightened and the chair legs hit the floor with a loud crack. "It makes sense, you know. It's understandable. She killed one kid, so she had to give up her own kid."

"No." I shook my head. "No!" I slammed his computer shut and mine too.

"Hey!" He grabbed his laptop and protected it in his arms. "Are you crazy?"

"What's fair about me not knowing the truth about any of this? What's fair about having one mom who kills a kid and another one who's lied to me my whole life?" I stared at him, all wild-eyed and shaking so hard on the inside I thought I might rattle apart. I wrapped my arms around my waist and began to rock forward and back. Forward and back. "And what about my name? I used to be Lissy. Lissy Davis. Was I named after Alyssa, a dead girl? That's, like, seriously fucked-up. This is so *not* fair!"

"Chill, Lisa. I only meant it was like, I don't know, twisted justice. It kinda makes sense that it went down that way."

"That it went *down* that way?" I yelled. People at the other tables were all staring at me, but I didn't care. My life was already screwed up. Now it was totally in the toilet. "She lied to me. My whole life has been one big fucking *lie*!"

I saw the manager headed my way. Probably to kick me out, but so fucking what? "I'm outta here," I muttered to Snake.

"Wait a minute, Lise."

"Miss, you'll have to calm down, otherwise—"

"I'm leaving!" I grabbed my bag and shoved my laptop inside. "See? Leaving. Now."

He crossed his arms and waited, like he wanted to be sure. Snake got up too. "C'mon. We'll go somewhere else and talk."

"Talk about what?"

He just grabbed my arm and steered me toward the door.

"Get your fucking hand off me," I muttered.

"Then quit acting all pissed at me. I'm not the problem, you know."

"No. You're just the idiot who thinks it's like some kinda twisted justice, man," I mocked his tone as I lurched through the door and turned down the wet sidewalk. It was dark and the streetlights made glowing circles of light in the cold, damp air. "So understandable that it went 'down' that way."

His face went dark with anger. "Dude! What's your problem?"

I spun around to face him. "Dude! I'm not a dude! I'm supposed to be your girlfriend and the worst thing that could happen to me *did* happen to me and all you can talk about is the twisted justice of it all. It doesn't feel like justice to *me*!"

It was too much. The dead kid. My lying mother. My

stupid boyfriend. I took off running, I didn't know to where. I heard Snake yelling after me, but I didn't stop. He just didn't understand. So I kept running until I didn't hear him anymore. Until I was out of breath and my side was killing me and I just couldn't run any farther.

"I hate you!" I screamed out at nothing. At everything. Across the street two guys were locking up the Auto Mart. I could hear them joking around, saying good night. It must be ten o'clock by now. The traffic light on the corner turned green and four cars and a school bus went by. A school bus this late? Then I remembered it was Friday. Football night.

I watched as it passed me by, full of band members. They'd done their halftime thing, cheering the team on to victory. Big fucking deal. All those goody two shoes band nerds. They didn't have a clue how totally fucked-up the world was. They were all going home to their moms and dads, their brothers and sisters and grandparents, aunts, and uncles. They had real families and they knew where they belonged. Not like me.

My teeth chattered and I clenched them to stop, but it didn't help. Who was I anyway? Because I felt like nobody, like this enigma, this kid with no identity, no place to belong. This split-personality Sybil. Good little Lisa with all the trappings of the loving home. But it was all a big fat lie 'cause my adopted mom was a crazy psycho, always on the run.

Then there was bad Lisa. No, bad *Lissy*, whose mother killed other people's little kids. Good Lisa and bad Lissy. Except that good Lisa was a lie, and bad Lissy was totally innocent.

I pounded the top of my head with one fist, wishing I could kill all the ugly thoughts in my head, squash them like a roach on a tile floor. It wasn't fair! What did I do to deserve baby-killer Roberta for one mother and lying Diane for the other?

I stared around me at the dreary night in Nowheresville, Arkansas. If only I had a car I would be out of here so fast.

"And go where?" I said to the dark, unconcerned night.

In my right front pocket my cell phone vibrated, but I ignored it. There was nobody I wanted to talk to. There was no place I wanted to go.

A distant crack of lightning lit the sky, followed by the slow roll of thunder tumbling down from the mountains. The rain started again and I began to shiver. No, to shake. But not from the damp cold. I was afraid. I'd never felt as alone as I did just then, or as scared.

Yes, you have.

A second wave of fear washed over me, but this time it was like déjà vu as I suddenly remembered this other time standing in the dark, in the rain. There were police cars, their blue- and-red lights turning and flashing, highlighting the rain on a trailer, the light hurting my eyes as I hid behind a cypress tree. I heard a woman cursing. "Stupid fucking girl. Stupid fucking girl." But it wasn't me she cursed. It was my mother, her daughter. "Stupid fucking girl."

Was that the night my mother had been arrested for drugs? I would've only been three or so. Did kids that little remember stuff? Especially bad stuff?

I hugged my arms around myself, trying to stop my shaking, but it didn't help. A cold drop of rain dribbled under my collar and down my neck, proving what I already knew: I couldn't change anything. Not my awful mothers, my stupid boyfriend, my selfish, so-called best friend, or the crappy weather.

Even my one chance at a grandmother had been a loser bitch who cursed her own kid. No wonder my mother had ended up in jail.

On impulse I dug in my bag until I felt the ice-cold handle of the box cutter. Strange how an inanimate object can crystallize your thought. Freeze them. Focus them. I carried the box cutter supposedly for art class, but I used it when I was stressed, when I couldn't smoke weed. A nick here. A shallow slice there. Quick, like the blink of an eye, and nobody would even notice. It's like letting helium out of a balloon: that high-pitched hiss of instant relief.

I slid the latch up, just one notch. I was shaking inside, vibrating like my guts and muscles were coming unglued from my skin and bones. But my hand was steady. I pushed up my left sleeve, then closing my eyes, I pressed the point of the blade into the fleshy area just below my elbow.

Sssssss.

I opened my eyes slowly as the shaking leaked out of me, along with the blood. It wasn't a lot of blood. But even in the dark I could see it welling, like black garnets against my pale skin. It welled up, then like a live thing, broke the surface tension of the drop and trickled down to my elbow, and then onto the street.

The traffic light turned over again, and I watched the next batch of cars go by. A minivan with a family; a Jeep Wrangler with a bunch of guys in it; a pickup truck with a couple sitting real close together.

That made me miss Snake. Sometimes he acted so stupid. How could he joke about my situation? But he still understood me better than anyone else. And he understood about the cutting. He had a long, snaky scar down one arm, and the raised welt of a carved fang above his left nipple. An art form a lot more personal than tattoos.

I hitched my hood over my wet head, and watching the

blood's slow leak, I pulled my phone out. Another call from my mother. From Diane. My throat got thick with emotion, but I swallowed it down. She was a lying bitch, and I didn't want to talk to her.

But what would I do if I ever got a call from my birth mom? From Roberta Fenner Davis?

Like that would ever happen.

A police car went by even as my phone vibrated again. It was Snake this time. I didn't answer. Let him wonder what happened to me. Let him worry and sweat it out. It served him right. But if I didn't call Diane soon she was gonna freak out. Not that I cared. But I didn't want her to call the cops and have them looking for me.

I dug out a Band-Aid from the stash in my bag and slapped it across my newest cut. Then I pulled down my sleeve, crossed the street to the recessed doorway of the auto-parts store and punched in Diane's number.

"Lisa!" she answered on the first ring, practically breaking my eardrum. "Where are you? Are you okay?"

Now *that* was an interesting question. But I doubted she wanted an honest answer. I stared at my arm, at the coagulating blood. "I'm fine," I said, my voice calm and normal. That's the magic of cutting. It lets all your putrid emotions out so you can act like everything is just peachy keen. "I went to the football game. I'll be home later."

"What do you mean, later? And since when do you not let me know where you are and who you're with?"

"Since now!" I said through clenched teeth. I was calm*er*, but not calm. After all, this was the woman who'd lied to me for twelve years now.

She gasped. "What is going on with you? Where are you—"

"I'll be home *later.*" Then I snapped my cell phone closed. *Take that, bitch.* I stared down at my sleek, silver phone, amazed at how easy it was to defy her. It immediately buzzed again. Her calling me back. I just shoved it down into my book bag and hitched it onto my other shoulder. I wasn't going home, maybe not until dawn. I needed to think about this, try to figure it out before I confronted Diane with what I knew. But where was I going?

I ended up at the all-night diner on Pin Oak Drive, the place where all the truckers and shift workers from the chicken plants go to fuel up on coffee and twenty-four-hour breakfasts. Besides the waitress, I was the only chick there. But it was warm and I could afford a plate of blueberry waffles with homemade maple syrup and lots of butter. Plus coffee refills were free.

When I saw two guys on their computers I realized the place had free wireless too. So after I took the edge off my hunger, I opened my laptop. What was I looking for now?

I set up a chart, listing what I knew about my life: when I was born; where; who my real mother was; when I was adopted. I made a whole timeline: when we moved, where I went to school. Mr. Daly from my ninth-grade study-skills class would have been so proud.

Everything I knew was true I printed in a blue font. True blue. Everything I wasn't certain of I did in red. I ended up with a nice chart all lined up and indented just so, but it had huge gaps in it. That's when I logged on. Time to fill in the gaps. It was a lot easier to find out things now that I had the right names and knew what to look for. I found out when my real mother was born and the name of my father. At least I hoped her husband was my father. I found out when he died and that my grandmother was dead too. And I figured out that my birth mom must have been sent to prison in Louisiana.

As for my adopted mother, once I started searching for her under all her guises, I was able to piece together a better picture of her life: where she'd lived, who her parents were, and what kind of life she had up till she got in that car wreck.

Then I Googled Alyssa Leftwich.

The articles in the newspaper didn't show a picture of her. But there was one on the obituary page. It was hard to look at her, to read about her life.

> Beloved daughter of Jim and Diane Leftwich. Five years old. Beloved granddaughter of Cynthia Haines and the late George Haines, and the late Harold and Louise Leftwich. A student at Torrence Elementary school, she will be much missed by teachers, students, and staff. Visitation Thursday from 7–9 and Friday from 9–11 with services to follow.

It was written so simply and everything, but it totally creeped me out, like I was living the life she was supposed to live. Like maybe I was supposed to be dead, not her. Except that kids aren't supposed to die. They're supposed to laugh and play and go to school, and grow up to have lives of their own.

Only that hardly ever happens anymore. Maybe in the olden days, but not now. Look at me and Snake and Nikki, not a normal family in the lot. And Alyssa, she'd been born into a normal family but it hadn't helped her any. She was still dead.

I stared at her face, fat cheeks, a big smile, and those little-bitty baby teeth. It was so unfair what happened to her. But though I felt sad for her, I felt jealous too. If she hadn't died, what would've happened to me? Why did Diane adopt me instead of some other kid? I wasn't born for like three years after that, so how did she even know about me? She must have been stalking my real mom, keeping tabs on her.

Then I had another creepy thought. What if I wasn't really adopted? What if she kidnapped me? Maybe that's why we moved so much and always had unlisted phone numbers and no credit cards. Not to avoid her ex-husband, but to hide out from my real mom.

"You need anything else, hon?"

Startled, I look up from the screen to find the waitress eyeing me. "No," I said. Then, "Wait. I'll have a ... a doughnut." I was almost out of money, but I figured I could afford that. I sure didn't want to go back out into the cold, rainy night.

She kept looking at me. "Does your mom know where you are?"

My heart started to race, but I gave her a totally fake grin. "'Course she does." I pulled out my cell phone. "We keep in touch."

"And she lets you stay out all night long? All by yourself?"

"I have a big school project and ... and it's too hard to study at home. We have a real big family and this really little house. A trailer, actually."

I could tell she wasn't buying it. "On a Friday night?" She shook her head disbelievingly. "No way. Call her now. I want to hear from her that she knows where you are." She held out her hand. "Call her and give me the phone."

I glared up at her, but she wasn't backing down. I didn't want to go back out in the weather, but I sure wasn't calling my mother. I decided to call the woman's bluff. "Why should I call her and wake her up. You're not my mom, so why don't you just get out of my face?"

She crossed her arms, not giving an inch. "I raised five teenagers, sugar, and I can smell a lie from a mile off. You call your mom right now or I'm reporting you as a runaway."

"Fine," I snapped, totally pissed off. I closed my computer, then flipped open my phone. While I acted like I was calling home, I glanced around. Only two other customers and no police in sight.

"It's ringing," I muttered to the bossy bitch, meanwhile sliding my laptop into my bag. "Mom, it's me," I said to the recording that answered my school's phone. "This waitress says you have to come get me. She's afraid I'm a runaway." I paused, then forced a laugh. "Yeah, I know."

"Let me talk to her," the woman said, extending her hand.

That's when I bolted. I pushed my chair against her, grabbed my bag and my sweatshirt and ran like hell. I heard her yell for me to stop, but once I was out the door she was history. It was colder than before, a wet, piercing-to-the-bone kind of cold, with a blustery wind to make it worse. But not cold enough to slow me down. I ran like the cops were already after me, darting down streets, twisting back, losing myself in neighborhoods I didn't know until my side ached and I couldn't catch my breath. I saw a gas station and crossed the street to squat down in the narrow space between two soda machines.

I was right back were I'd been earlier in the night. Cold, alone, and with no idea what to do. One thing I did know: I wasn't going home, at least not yet. Let Diane worry. Let her freak out and think the worst. She deserved to suffer after all the lies she'd told—and maybe worse.

But even if I went back home, I wasn't explaining myself. I was keeping my mouth shut until I found my real mom, until I knew if I was legally adopted or kidnapped or what. Something wasn't right in this whole mess. I'd been jerked around all my life. I deserved to know why.

CHAPTER TWENTY-ONE

From: Nikki
To: Lisa
Re: Mom on warpath!!

Where are you? Your mom called me like 100 times yesterday and now she just woke me up and it's only 5AM!! Jus 'cause you and your mom got in a fight is no reason to freak the rest of us out. Answer your phone b/c if you don't after 24 hours missing your mom can sic the cops on you.

From: Snake
To: Lisa
Re: sorry

If I knew you were so upset yesterday I wouldn't have joked about it. Call me.

From: Mom
To: Lisa
Re: You're scaring me!

I don't understand what's going on, why you're so upset. We don't have to move if you really don't want to. Please call me, Lisa, and let me know you're okay. I love you more than anything.

LISA

When the gas-station guy got there at six I had to leave. I found a coffeehouse that opened at six-thirty and used their bathroom to clean up. Then I bought a small coffee, took a table in a back corner, and checked my messages and e-mail. I was hungry again, I had a headache, and all I wanted was to lie down in my own bed and sleep for three days. But I knew Mom Diane was going to give me all kinds of grief. At least she was going to try.

But this time I was shooting her down before she got started. She could either get out of my face or the next time I wouldn't come home at all. That would shut her up. Because if she *had* kidnapped me she wouldn't be able to report me to the cops because then they might figure out her scam.

And if she *hadn't* kidnapped me?

I massaged my burning eyes and just sat there slumped in the corner, too tired to think straight. All I knew was that something didn't fit. Diane was definitely hiding something. She'd lied to me my whole life, even while she got on my case about always being honest, reassuring me that I could tell her everything, that she was my mother and she would love me no matter what I did.

Blah, blah, fucking blah.

Well, we'd see how much she loved me when I turned into a major bitch. And we'd see who would crack first.

I had a second cup of coffee—free refills—and when the caffeine finally kicked in I called Snake.

"Shit, Lisa. Where've you been all night?"

"Coffeehouses, diners. Where are you? Are you going to school today?"

"It's Saturday. I was sleeping."

"Oh, yeah." Saturday. "Can I come over?" I'd never been to his house before.

"You talked to your mom yet?"

"You mean Diane?"

"Yeah, Diane. Did you talk to her today?"

"Not yet. But I will. So, can I come over?"

"Why do you want to come over here? It's a dump."

"I don't want to go home and I need somewhere to sleep."

"I don't know, Lisa. My mom's home."

I squeezed my eyes shut and sighed. "Is she asleep?"

"Probably."

"Then what's the big deal? I know your address, Snake."

"Then you know this is a crappy neighborhood."

"I don't care. I just want to be with you."

After a long pause he said, "Fine," but in a tone that made it clear it wasn't fine at all.

"Where are you?"

"I'm not sure. Some place called Coffee Time near a big Walgreens and an IHOP."

"That's on the south side, down around the chicken plant." He gave me directions to the nearest bus line and told me which transfers to take.

"Don't get me lost," I said. "I'm down to my last two dollars."

"Hey. You're the one who got lost in the first place so quit bitchin'. Just tell the last bus driver to let you out at Eighteenth Avenue. I'll be waiting for you there."

"Fine," I muttered. Can you hate someone and still be desperate to see them, and at the same time want to make sure he doesn't see either one of those feelings? That was me, careening from one extreme to the other, and shaking apart with exhaustion from it all.

I nearly fell asleep on the first bus and again at the bus stop waiting for the second bus. There weren't very many people riding this early on a Saturday, but the buses still smelled like sweat and exhaust fumes. I stared at an ad for Consumer Credit Counseling, looking at the happy couple with the baby girl standing in front of a cute brick house with shutters and flowers and everything. They got their lives all straightened out with just one free phone call. I rolled my eyes. "Yeah, right."

"Eighteenth Avenue," the driver called. *Thank God.*

After sitting in the bus rocking along in that mind-numbing rhythm, I felt clumsy and slow as I clambered down. The sun was out and it wasn't as cold as before, but when I didn't see Snake I started to shiver all over again. Where was he?

The bus pulled off and I turned in a slow circle, scanning the intersection. An abandoned gas station. A scuzzy-looking bar. An overgrown lot and a convenience store, its windows papered over with ads for beer, cigarettes, and fried pork skins. Ugh! I'd never been in this part of town and I didn't want to be here now.

Then I saw Snake sitting on the curb beside the store. Forgetting I was ever mad at him, I darted across the street, and when he stood up I collapsed into his arms. I didn't want to cry but I couldn't help it.

"Shit, Lisa," he muttered. "If you're gonna be a hard-assed bitch, you better start acting like one."

"Shut up." I choked the words out against his sweatshirt. "I'm tired and hungry and I need to sleep. Where's your house?"

"Come on."

He took my bag and hiked it over his shoulder. Then we walked, his arm draped over my shoulders, my left arm tight around his waist. At that moment I would've followed him anywhere—that's how grateful I was—and done anything he asked. But not sex. Not now. I was too tired. I knew it was inevitable, but I hoped he could wait till after I slept.

He couldn't. We were barely in the door of the low-ceilinged apartment before he went for it.

The place stunk of cigarettes and greasy food—that was my first impression. But with the blinds closed and no lights on, my only impression was the low ceilings, too much furniture, and junk stacked everywhere.

"Mom's out," he whispered as he steered me though the room. I thought he meant out, like gone out. Then he pointed to the sofa, and as my eyes adjusted to the darkness, I saw her lumpy outline under a heavy brown blanket.

"That's your mom?" I asked as he urged me toward a door.

"Shh."

That's when she shifted to her side and let out a snort. She sounded so much like Wilbur the pig in *Charlotte's Web* that I started to laugh.

"Damn it, Lisa." He dragged me through the door and closed it. "I told you to be quiet."

"Sorry." But I couldn't help laughing again. I clapped one hand over my mouth and let out another muffled "sorry."

He tossed my bag onto a chair, but he laughed too. "She's drunk as a skunk. Again."

That killed my humor. As mad as I was at Diane, the one good thing I could say about her was that I'd never seen her drunk. Not even tipsy. Then again, she was so freaking tight-assed about everything, getting blitzed every now and then would probably do her a world of good.

"So." I looked around the room, dark except for the morning light filtering around the edges of the window shade. "This is your room?"

He shrugged and shoved his hands in his pockets. "We kind of share it since she mostly sleeps while I'm at school."

"Oh." I unzipped my jacket and wriggled out of it. The bed was made, but the rest of the room was pretty messy. Women's clothes hung in the open closet; jewelry and perfume bottles littered the dresser top. A pile of dirty clothes—Snake's—filled one corner and a pile of clean stuff covered a blue-painted chest. There was a cross hanging on the wall though, and a beige floral coverlet draped the bed.

I stared at the bed, nice and neat with an arrangement of throw pillows and everything. It looked out of place in this crowded, disorganized room. Had Snake made up the bed because I was coming? I glanced at him, grateful for his thoughtfulness. "That bed is like calling my name."

"Yeah." He grinned at me. "Mine too."

That's when I knew that we would have to have sex before he would let me sleep. "Okay." I gritted my teeth. If that's what it took. But I'd learned a couple of things in the last few months. When he was all hot and horny and I wasn't really in the mood, I could make him finish quicker just by talking and groaning and begging him to go faster—faster!—and telling him he was absolutely the sexiest, hottest man in the world and he was driving me crazy.

Sure enough, he was done in less than a minute. "Damn, that was good," he groaned as he rolled off of me. "So good."

"Yeah," I murmured, already almost asleep. "So good."

"Sorry it was so fast," he said, turning on his side to face me. "But I'll make it up to you."

"Not now," I muttered and turned my back to him. "I'm too tired."

I guess he got the message, because I don't remember anything after that. I woke up disoriented, lost, and panicked— until I saw Snake sitting by the window playing a handheld video game. He didn't notice I was awake. That's guys and video games for you. Video games are for fun. Girlfriends are just for sex. But I was relieved he didn't notice I was awake. I needed to figure this out, what to do next, where I should go. Eventually I would have to deal with my mom. With Diane. But not like before. Everything was different now, especially me. Two things I knew: One, I wasn't moving anywhere new; and two, I wasn't letting on about what I'd discovered about her and Alyssa. At least not yet.

Stuffing it under my hat would be majorly hard because I wanted so bad to jump down her throat. She was such a liar! But I needed to time it right, to know everything so I could catch her in every single one of her lies. Because I knew she would keep on lying just as long as she thought she could get away with it.

"Finally awake," Snake said from the window seat.

I closed my eyes. "Sort of." I lay there listening to the faint electronic beeps and sirens and snorts of whatever game he was playing. My stomach grumbled with hunger, and I needed the bathroom. I would've liked to stay in bed, just burrow down under the covers and stay dark and warm all day long. But I guess I couldn't. I rolled onto my side. "You got anything to eat?"

"Cereal. Maybe some milk. I don't know."

"Is your mom gone? What time is it anyway?"

"I dunno. Around one? She'll be getting up soon, so we gotta get goin'." I heard a final digital crescendo and he said, "Aw, shit." Then the game went dead, and he looked up at me. "Your mom has called you like a dozen times already."

"You checked my phone?" I pushed myself up onto my elbows, blinking to clear my crusty eyes.

"Hey, we got no secrets. Right?"

"Give me your phone, and I'll let you know."

He rolled his eyes. "I guess you woke up on the bitchy side of the bed. Again."

I closed my eyes and fell back onto the pillow. He was right. He'd taken me in this morning, even though I could tell he didn't want to, and here I was, first words out of my mouth, being a bitch.

"Sorry." I said it, but I didn't really feel sorry. All I wanted was food and to get out of here. I pushed back the covers and sat up. "Where's the bathroom?"

He poked his thumb toward a door draped with lingerie, and watched me as I crossed the room. I had on a long T-shirt—no underwear even—and it was embarrassing. I stooped to grab my jeans, then ran for the bathroom when I realized I'd just flashed him with my naked butt. But he was already tuned into another video game.

I was out in two minutes flat and shoved my shoes on—unlaced—then grabbed my book bag and coat. "Is it safe to leave through the front door?" I asked.

"Wait." He focused on the game and after a flurry of war sounds let out a whoop. "New personal best!" Then he tossed the game on the unmade bed and gave me that grin of his that always sucked me in. He has this way, with his dark, compelling eyes and smirky, sexy grin, of making you forget everything else except for him. That's how I know I love him. Because no matter how mad I get, if he just really focuses on me—just me—I can't stay mad.

"So," he said, "I'll reconnoiter the living room and make sure the coast is clear. You gather your gear, and we'll split this burg."

"What about breakfast?"

"You mean lunch?"

"Whatever. I'm starving."

"We'll find something. My treat."

His treat. I sighed, hugely relieved, since I was practically broke and I didn't see Mom—Diane—giving me any allowance in the near future.

"I need to get a job ," I told him once we'd made our escape.

"A job? Why?"

We crossed the street, running in front of a van that had to veer to avoid us. The driver gave us the finger even though on the side of the van it said *Unity Church: Give us a Try*. How ironic was that?

"I need my own money that my—that Diane can't control."

He shrugged. "There's always fast-food joints."

I looked at him sidelong. "You always have money—and not from Burger King either."

He laughed, that devil-may-care laugh that was so totally cool. "I don't think you want to sell weed, Lisa. You don't even like to smoke it."

"So? That only means I won't smoke up my profits."

"Yeah, but who you gonna sell to? The only people you know who smoke weed are the people I sell to. What, you gonna take over my territory? I don't think so." Then he gave me this crafty look. "Didn't you tell me your mom never uses credit cards or even checks, that she pays for everything with cash?"

"Yeah. So?"

"So where does she keep her stash?"

I stopped dead on the sidewalk. "Are you telling me to steal from my own mother?"

"No." His eyes glittered like a cat's. "I'm telling you to steal from Diane."

Same thing. That's what I wanted to say. She might not be my birth mother but she was still my mom. Except that it wasn't the same thing anymore. Diane was a liar and maybe even a kidnapper. If I did steal from her, what could she do about it? Yell, that's all. And if she yelled at me, I'd just split.

"Just a little here and there," Snake said. "She won't notice a missing twenty every few days."

"Maybe." I hitched my bag onto my other shoulder and started forward again. "But why stop at twenty?"

He laughed again. "Now that's what I'm talking about. The worst she can do is kick you out, only she doesn't sound like the type. So ... " He slung one arm across my shoulders. "Where do you want to eat?"

"Wherever you want." I didn't care about food though, not anymore. Because I knew now what I had to do, how to handle Diane and her lies and her lifelong insanity. Until I got all the answers about my background—and about my real mother, where she was now and how Diane came to have me—I was going to make her life hell. She thought I was bad now? Just wait. Lisa was an angel compared to Lissy, my first real self. Lissy was Roberta Fenner's kid, her look-alike, and a tough, street-smart kid who was sick of being jerked around. Yeah, Diane was in for a great big shock.

"Move over, goody-goody Lisa," I said under my breath. "'Cause here comes big, bad Lissy, and she's spoiling for a fight."

CHAPTER TWENTY-TWO

From: Lisa
To: Mom
Re: (no subject)

Quit calling so much. I'll come home when I'm ready.

From: Mom
To: Lisa
Re: (no subject)

Please call me, honey. Whatever the problem is, we can work it out. Where are you? I'll come pick you up if you want.

From: Lisa
To: Mom
Re: (no subject)

Forget the inquisition. All you need to know is that I'm not moving, I'm not answering any questions, and if you keep bugging me I won't be home any time soon.

LISA-LISSY

Diane didn't respond to my last e-mail. I stared at my in box and chewed on my left thumbnail. Did that mean she agreed to my terms?

Snake and I were camped out in the last booth of Hardy's Diner. He'd wolfed down the lumberjack's special: pancakes, eggs and grits, toast, fruit, and three kinds of meat. Meanwhile, as hungry as I was, the all-American breakfast platter had been way more than I could stomach. I shifted on the thinly padded bench seat waiting for a response from Diane while Snake finished off my plate, wiping it clean with the last triangle of toast.

"If you're gonna rule the roost, you've got to work it just right," he said between bites. "You don't want her kickin' you outta the house for good."

"Like she would ever do that."

"Famous last words," he said with a snort. "It happens to kids all the time. And you're not even her own flesh and blood."

"Shut up," I muttered.

He just shrugged and went on. "Besides, if she had the balls to kidnap you like you think she did, then she's capable of anything. Kidnapping is, like, a federal offense."

"Yeah. But this case is way different. Besides, I'm underage. If I get picked up and the cops plug me into the system, her whole scam could come undone. Plus, I think she really loves me. No, really," I said when he groaned and rolled his eyes. "Her own kid died."

"Get real, Lisa. No way is the killer's kid ever gonna fill that hole."

"Shut up!"

He just laughed. "But it's true, Lise. You know it is."

Clenching my teeth, I looked away from him. Sometimes

he was such a dickhead. Diane might have lied to me and who knows what else, but a part of me still wanted her to love me. Me, Lissy Davis. Again, I shifted on the bench seat and tried to sound calmer than I felt. "Lots of people have more than one kid and they love them all. Why can't she love more than one kid too?"

"Because of who you are. Of who your real mom is. Look, Lise." He pushed the plate aside and grabbed my hand. "I'm not trying to be an asshole. I'm just trying to look out for you. For my best girl. All I'm saying is that you have to do this right. Give her a way to remember that she loves you, then use that love as a tool to get what you want. Be her good little girl, then when she tries to order you around, skip school and don't come home at night. Stuff like that."

"Or ask her about my birth mom."

"Exactly." He grinned. "What's wrong with torturing her? It's not like she's been straight up with you or anything."

He was right. But later as I made my way home, scuffing my feet through the soggy leaves that had drifted into the dips and turns of the sidewalk, I knew the hardest part of dealing with Diane would be biting my tongue, holding back all my accusations, all my questions. I wanted to just let her have it, scream and rant and make her tell me the truth, no matter how awful and sordid it was. But how would I know if what she told me was true? She'd been lying to me for so long, did she even know the truth anymore?

That's why I had to just shut up and sit tight, until I found my real mom and knew her side of the truth. That's when I would finally confront Diane.

And after that?

I'd reached the corner of our block and I stood there, staring at our front door. After everything was out in the open, then ... I didn't know. It depended on my birth mom. And Diane.

I crossed the street, waving to Ben and Beau, the eleven-year-old twins who lived in the other half of our rented duplex. They had gotten skateboards for their birthday last week and spent every minute outside of school perfecting their technique. It was weird, because even though I wasn't even five years older than them, I couldn't remember *ever* being that carefree.

Because you never were.

They had a mom and a dad, a little sister, a dog and a cat. They had two sets of grandparents and all kinds of aunts and uncles and cousins. Sometimes when they had their whole family over, we couldn't even hear our TV because the laughing and talking from the other side of the wall was so loud.

The only family I had was Diane. Crazy Diane

And all she has is you.

For a second I felt guilty. Just a little. But then I saw her. She was standing in the front window staring out at me. She didn't wave. She didn't move at all, just watched me as I walked up to the house. I didn't want to look back at her, but I had to. Like Snake said, I had to stay in control of the situation and not give her the upper hand. That meant no yelling, no crying, and no big scenes. And especially no feeling guilty. I hadn't done anything wrong; it was all on her. So if she gave me any crap, I would just split. I know she cared that I was safe and that I went to school, so that's what I would hold over her head: my whereabouts, and skipping school.

But as I reached for the doorknob I could hardly breathe for all the mixed-up emotions twisting in my chest. Sometimes I hated her. But at almost the same time I wanted to go back to when I didn't know anything, when we just loved each other. Only it was too late to go back.

I took a deep breath and braced myself. This was going to be even harder than I thought.

"Lisa," she said, before I even shut the door. "Thank God—"

"Leave me alone," I snarled, finding sanctuary in anger. "Just leave me alone!" Then I ran up the stairs and slammed my bedroom door without once looking at her.

Coward. The accusation resounded in my head. *Stupid, spineless coward.* But I couldn't help it. I was so mad at her. And yet the minute I came in the house all I wanted was to throw myself into her arms and cry my heart out. Only if I did, I would've told her everything. And I knew I couldn't do that. Not yet. She'd lied to me for twelve years. She wasn't about to start telling me the truth at this late date, not until I totally backed her into a corner.

So even though I wanted to crawl into bed, throw the covers up over my head, and just sleep forever, I didn't. I stripped out of my clothes, pulled on some clean sweatpants and a faded red thermal shirt, and opened up my laptop. Where was Roberta Fenner Davis? That was what I needed to focus on. Where did she go to prison? For how long? And was she out by now?

Computers are so cool. But they're a pain too. There's so much info out there but you have to wade through so much junk to get to what you need. So I tackled the problem sideways. Since she was arrested in Louisiana, I decided to find out where all the women prisoners were sent to. Then I would get their phone numbers and just call them.

I started with the jail in New Orleans, the closest big jail to Slidell.

"We don't give out personal information about inmates without proper paperwork," the lady who answered the phone told me.

"But I think she finished her sentence by now."

"Then if she wanted to find you, I guess she would."

"But she doesn't know where I am. I was only four when she went to jail and we moved and—"

"How long ago was that?"

"Like 1995 or '96."

I heard her breathing on the phone, like she was considering helping me out. *Please, please, please.*

"Look," she said. "First off, everything is still a mess here since Katrina. Even the records that didn't get flooded, they either got moldy or lost or who knows what. And second of all, we don't keep inmates here for real long sentences. How long was she in for?"

"Ten years I think."

"Ten years? Huh. She was probably sent to St. Anna's then. With good time, though, she could've gotten out in three or four years. Unless she was a real badass."

Three or four years?

The woman on the phone must have realized how that threw me for a loop, because her voice got real soft and nice. "Look, kid. If she went inside in '96, she's probably been out since 2000 or so. And if she wanted to find you, she probably would have. Who do you live with?"

But I wasn't listening anymore. She'd been out of jail for maybe seven years? My birth mom had been out of jail since I was, like, eight years old, and in all this time she hadn't looked for me at all?

"Hey. You still there? Hey, kid—"

I hung up on her. I stared at my laptop, at the list of Louisiana prisons that held women, but nothing registered. No wonder she put me up for adoption; she didn't give a shit about me. She was out somewhere having a good old time, probably up to her old bad tricks. She sure wouldn't want a kid hanging around.

This time I did crawl under the covers and crushed a pillow over my head. I was so stupid, imagining how cool it would be to find her, how happy she'd be, how amazed at how I look and how good I'm doing in school. But it was just a stupid fantasy. My real mom probably never really wanted me. She probably hadn't even thought about me in years. I bet I was just an accident.

Which reminded me that Snake hadn't used any protection last night and I hadn't taken a birth control pill yesterday. And maybe not the day before either.

"Shit." I threw off the covers, found the pill pack, and sure enough I'd missed two days. So I took one pill, and then for good measure the other one too. I did *not* want to get pregnant. Snake would totally freak out.

Back in bed I pulled the covers up to my chin and just lay there. I didn't want to think, not about my real mom and how she abandoned me and not about Diane–

Diane. How Diane got to adopt me was still a mystery. No way could it be a coincidence. That meant she either kidnapped me, or my real mom gave me to her.

My head felt dizzy and light from that thought. But it made sense. Maybe my birth mom gave me to Diane to get a shorter sentence. And maybe the deal was that Roberta would never look for me. That was her main punishment, to lose her daughter forever. Which would mean she *wasn't* all bad. She stayed away to honor their agreement.

Like a shot I scrambled out of the bed flooded with energy and hope. That had to be it. It was the only explanation that made any sense. I ran down the stairs, ready to confront Diane, to make her tell the truth. But at the archway into the living room I stopped. It *might* be the truth; but it might not. And if it wasn't the truth, would Diane admit it? Or would she lie and say it was the truth in order to get out of telling me the *real* truth?

I turned back to the stairs, then stopped again, pressing the heels of my hands against my eyes. Everything was so totally screwed up! I didn't know what to think—what was up, what was down, what to believe, or how to get to the truth.

Then I heard Diane in the kitchen—the clink of a plate being removed from a cabinet, the sound of the fridge closing—and I darted back up the stairs. I wasn't ready to talk to her yet.

On the desk my laptop set, still open to the list of prisons for women. I sat down on the chair, folding one leg beneath me and stared at it. Maybe I should make some more calls, try to find out where she was and if she *had* been out since 2000.

First on my list was St. Anna's. "You have to make a Freedom of Information request," the receptionist said.

"How do I do that?"

"I don't know. Go online or something."

"Online with St. Anna's?"

"Yeah." She hesitated. "No. I'm not sure."

What an idiot. "Is there anybody there who *is* sure?"

I heard some voices in the background, then she said, "Hold on." After a long minute she came back on. "Are you with the press?"

"Yes." I said it without thinking. Then with my heart racing I took a deep breath and committed fully to the lie. "Is there a problem here, ma'am? And could I have your name. Spell it out completely, please."

She hesitated. "Hold on."

This time she must've put her hand on the receiver because I couldn't hear anything. Finally a new voice came on the phone. "May I help you, Miss ... "

"Miss Davis," I replied. "Lisa Davis with the *Alexandria Town Talk*." If I was going to lie I might as well do it on a grand scale. "I'm doing a story about the effects on children when their mothers are incarcerated."

When she didn't say anything I felt a wave of rising panic. But I fought it down. "May I have your name? For the record?"

After a long moment she said, "Toolie Fastbender. Are you looking for general information or something specific, like about a specific prisoner?"

"Um, I guess both." I slid off the chair and paced to the window, then to my dresser where I stared at my reflection in the mirror. Was she going to help me?

"And you said your name was Lisa Davis?"

"Uh-huh. With the *Alexandria Town Talk*."

"Oh. For a minute I thought you were somebody else. But your name is Lisa. Plus, she would be a lot younger than you."

The hair stood up on my arms. She knew something. She did! "Wait," I said, suddenly short of breath. "You know somebody with a name like mine? Like maybe Lissy Davis?"

"Why yes. I mean, I never knew *her*, but I knew her mother."

"Bobbie Davis? Roberta Fenner Davis who went to jail in 1996 when I was three and a half?" I was strangling the phone with two hands now, trying not to shout or cry, and failing on both counts.

She was quiet so long I thought she might have hung up. "Please, please, please," I begged. "I've been looking for her for so long."

Then she said it, the words I'd been waiting my whole life to hear. "She's looking for you too. She loved you and missed you and was desperate to find you."

I could barely hear her. I think she was whispering. But every single one of her words burned into my brain. My mother loved me. She missed me and wanted to find me. "Is she still there? I could come see her."

"Oh, no. She was released, what, maybe two years ago."

Two years, not seven. "Where did she go? How can I find her?"

"I don't know, hon. I haven't heard from her since she left. They seldom contact us, the former inmates. The only way we see them once they leave is if they get sent back. Or sometimes they might visit other inmates. You know, some of these women have a family history here, three or more generations. Grandmothers, then mothers, and then their—"

"Wait," I interrupted. "She never talked about where she wanted to go? Like back to Slidell or to Gulfport or maybe New Orleans?"

"No. Nothing specific. All I know for sure is she was trying to find you. Ever since that time you got so sick—"

"She knew about that?"

"You bet. The prison was contacted about a medical history of her and her family. Apparently your doctors didn't know what you had. What *did* you have?"

"Guillain-Barre syndrome," I answered automatically. But my head was reeling from everything this lady was saying. "Oh, my God!"

"Are you okay?"

"Yeah. Oh, man. This is so great!"

"No, I mean about that whatever you called it disease you had. Are you okay from that?"

"The Guillain-Barre? Yeah. Fine. I mean, it took a couple of months. It's this autoimmune thing with the nerves that affects the muscles. But I'm over it. What about my mom, though? She knew I was sick?"

"Oh, yes. But she never stopped worrying about you. That's because no one would ever tell her how things turned out for you, only that you didn't die from it. I think that's why she was so determined to find you, to make sure you were healthy. And happy."

I couldn't believe it. Everything I'd wanted to hear—that my mother loved me and worried about me and never once forgot me—was true. The knowledge filled me with a sense of well-being I'd never known before. She loved me and wanted only the best for me, her little girl, Lissy.

But there was still one huge, looming question. "Did she ever talk to you about Diane?"

"Diane?" She paused a long moment. "That name doesn't ring a bell. Diane who?"

A chill began to settle over me, cold and ominous. "She's my adopted mother. I thought maybe they knew each other."

"Oh, no," she said. "I'm pretty sure they didn't, otherwise Bobbie would've just called her to check on you. No," she repeated. "She never did know where you were or who you were with."

I twisted my head to face my bedroom door, the only thing standing between me and my adopted mother. "But … " I stopped and swallowed hard. "But Bobbie gave permission for me to be adopted, right?"

"Most likely," Toolie said. "Some of the inmates won't do it, even if they know they're gonna be here a long time. Others don't have any choice, especially if they've been convicted on child cruelty or neglect charges. The state takes their kids away from them. But I don't think your mom was in that group."

"So she *let* me be adopted?"

"I think so. But don't hold that against her, Lissy. She wanted the best for you. She wanted you to be raised up in a good family. That's the only reason she let you be adopted, because it was the best thing for you."

'Yes," I answered automatically, even as my mind spun with the implications. "I'm sure that was it."

My birth mother had always had my best interests at heart. But that couldn't necessarily be said about my adopted mother, could it?

CHAPTER TWENTY-THREE

ACCOUNT OF DITTODIANE: SEARCH

Key words: Roberta Davis/St. Anna's Prison
No matches found

Key words: Roberta Davis/Parole
No matches found

Key words: Bobbie Davis/St. Anna's Prison
No matches found

Key words: Roberta Fenner/2006
One listing found: State of LA, Parish of Orleans, 11/12/2006 Petitioner Roberta Fenner Davis' request to change her name to Roberta Fenner is hereby entered ...

Key words: Roberta Fenner/2007
No matches found

Key words: Bobbie Fenner/2007

Two listings found:
Times Picayune: AIDS Outpatient Clinic Reopens ... with the addition of LPN's Tim DeLorme and Bobbie Fenner as well as volunteers ...

Times Picayune: Jazz Funeral for Community Activist " ... Dack Landry did not let his illness rob him of his sense of humor or his sense of humanity," said nurse and friend Bobbie Fenner ...

From:Diane
To:Jim
Re:(no subject)

Do you know how to contact Roberta Fenner, because if she shows up ...

DELETE ABOVE MESSAGE

ACCOUNT OF DITTODIANE: SEARCH
Key words: Roberta Fenner/ATT
No matches found

Key words: Lissy Davis/foster care/Louisiana
No matches found

Key words: Lissy Davis/adoption/Louisiana
No matches found

Key words:Lissy Davis/Diane Haines
No matches found

ACCOUNT OF DITTODIANE
REVIEW OF PARENTAL CONTROLS:
  secondary account/Lisa Haines

10/1/2007 to date:no activity found

Account of DittoDiane: SEARCH

Key words: Lisa/Myspace/adoption
  11,419 matches found

LISA-LISSY

Toolie Fastbender said it was okay to call her again but not at work. That meant I had to wait all the way till five-thirty. I was, like, so antsy I was practically trippin'. It had started to rain again, a cold, nasty downpour I didn't want to venture back into. But no way could I stay trapped here the whole afternoon. Though she hadn't come up after me, I knew Diane was down there waiting to strike, straining to hear me and figure out how to shove me back into the box she'd always tried to keep me in. But I was out of the box now. I had been for a long time, only she hadn't known it.

She damn well knew it now.

Plopping onto the window seat, I slid up my sleeve, and then peeled back the Band-Aid over my newest slice. There's something weird about a cut so fresh the blood is still crusted on it. It's like one of those hyperbolic paraboloids in stupid geometry class. The moment of the cut is bursting with energy, most of it negative. Then comes the fast downward slope of relief. But later, especially the first Band-Aid change, it's all flat and low, like all the crazy emotions are gone. But they're not. Because soon enough you're either gonna build up to that bursting-with-emotions feeling again, or veer off to the side and slide down into darkness. A hyperbolic paraboloid.

I stared at the thin, reddish-black line that split the soft white flesh of my arm. What would Mr. Harding say if I posed *that* geometric hypothesis in class? Probably wet his pants then send me to the school counselor.

I pressed the Band-Aid back down, pushing harder than I needed to, until the cut split and blood seeped out around the Band-Aid again.

I had to get out of here. Now. I called Nikki, who answered

on the first ring. "Where have you been, girlfriend? What's goin' on with you?"

"Big stuff. Momentous."

"So give it up."

I peered through the slats of the window blinds. "Where are you?"

"Home watching some show on decorating. I was thinking about painting my room. Something dramatic, like black or purple. If I can talk my mom into it," she added.

"What does she have to do with it? It's your room."

"True. But I was hoping she'd spring for the paint."

"Buy it yourself," I said. "And paint it yourself too. Isn't that what parents want? For us to take the initiative?"

"You are so right." She laughed. "I should do it one day while she's at work. Then all she can do is freak out."

Freaking out parents. That sounded good. I switched the phone to my other ear and stared at the Band-Aid. "We ought to get tattoos." Now where did that come from? "Today."

"What? Are you crazy? That, like, hurts."

"So?"

"Needles digging into your flesh? Eeow! Besides, most places won't do it till you're eighteen." She paused and in the background I heard Slipknot playing. "What's goin' on, Lisa? These last few days you've been acting weird."

"Like I said, momentous stuff. Let's go somewhere. You got any money?"

"Yeah. Thirty bucks or so. Not enough for much of a tat," she added with a snort.

"Don't worry, I'll get some."

"Uh-oh. I smell big trouble with the parental unit. Am I right?"

"Yes. And no. I'll tell you when I see you. How 'bout we meet at Hank's Market once I get the cash. I'll call you right before I get there."

"Ten-four, good buddy," she said in this low, flat tone. Then she laughed. "I've been watching all these old black-and-white TV shows."

"Whatever." Shaking my head, I flipped the phone closed. Nikki was my best friend, but she could be such a flake. She was fun, but she was all on the surface, nothing deep about her. She didn't understand me like Snake did. Nobody did. For a moment I almost called him. But then I made myself wait. Right now I needed some money and to get out of here. I tore off my clothes and changed into my tightest jeans, a push-up bra I kept hidden under my mattress, and a blood-red sweater. I'd bought it at a thrift store, and it was too tight, with a V-neck that showed way too much cleavage. Exactly what I was in the mood for. Add my Docs, a heavy black chain necklace, and two leather wristbands, and my mirror reflected back a tough chick who was out for a good time—or maybe trouble.

"Watch out, world, here comes Bad Lissy," I muttered, sneering my lips as I said the words. "Watch out, Diane, you lying bitch."

Ready to face her, I slammed out of my room and down to the kitchen. I found a banana, a Dr Pepper, and a box of Wheat Thins and shoved them into a plastic bag. Then I stormed back up to my room, leaving the door open this time. I knew she was watching me. Even though I didn't look at her or acknowledge her presence at all, I'd felt her staring at me through the open door of the study.

I grabbed my book bag and my jacket, then stalked back downstairs. "I'm going out," I snarled as I shoved my arms into my jacket. "Give me my allowance."

When she didn't respond I whirled around and glared at her. I hated her so much, and I hated even more that she didn't have a clue why. *You lied to me about everything! Who I am. Why you adopted me. How you adopted me!* The bewildered look on her face only fired my anger hotter. How could she *not* get it? Her face was pale, like maybe she'd been crying, something she *never* did. But I didn't care. Not anymore.

"Lisa," she said, soft and pleading "What's wrong, sweetheart?"

What's wrong? I wanted to let her have it, just throw everything at her and watch her try to explain why she'd lied to me every single day of my life.

But I needed to wait. I needed to talk to Toolie first and find out everything I could about my real mom. Then I'd let Diane have it good. Besides, why not let her suffer a little longer?

"What's wrong," I said, hooking my bag onto my shoulder, "Is that there's nothing decent in this house to eat. I need money for food."

"I'll fix you whatever you—"

"No! I don't want to eat here. With *you*," I added, enjoying the way she recoiled from those two simple words.

"Now look, Lisa." She raked her hair back from her forehead. "You can't talk to me like that. I'm your mother and—"

"No!" I shouted at her. "No. You're *not* my mother! Not really. If you were, you'd listen to what I have to say. But you never do!" Then made brave by her misery, I charged into her bedroom, pulled open the bottom drawer of her armoire where she kept her supply of cash, and yanked out a yellow envelope.

"What do you think you're doing?" she cried from right behind me.

"Taking my allowance." I dumped the money on the bed, a

green flutter of twenties and fifties. Then I grabbed up a handful and turned to leave. But she stood in the doorway now, not a big physical obstacle, but a big emotional one, because she had her arms clasped around her waist and tears streamed down her face. Tears, from the woman who never cried.

"Please, baby," she pleaded, her voice trembling. "Please, Lisa."

I almost broke. Between my need to rage at her and my need to hear her explanation, my heart hurt so bad my chest felt like it had this monstrous hole in it, like I was leaking emotion all over the place. But the name, Lisa, on her lips plugged that hole. Lisa. Her name for me and the symbol of all the lies that lay between us. It turned my hurt back into rage, and the leaking hole in my chest concrete-hard with contempt.

I shoved past her, ignoring her gasp of shock and the thud of her elbow hitting the door frame, and barreled out of the house.

"It was easy," I told Nikki ten minutes later as we huddled next to the hot-dog warmer inside Hank's Market, counting the money I'd taken. A hundred sixty bucks.

But it hadn't been easy. As I'd huddled under the bus shelter, shoving the money into my pocket, trying to scroll down my cell phone directory through my tears so I could call Nikki, I'd known that my old life was over. I didn't want to cry over her; after all, she'd struck the first blow when she lied to me—when she kidnapped me or whatever she did to get me when I was only four. But I'd struck the mortal blow today. I'd run away; I'd stolen from her, cursed at her, and physically assaulted her. Not that it was much of an assault. But I'd been to all the personal-safety classes at school, so I knew all about inappropriate touching, sexual or otherwise. I'd pushed her, and she'd hit the door frame. Legally, that was assault.

The thing is, in all the time I'd been with her, Diane had never once hit me or spanked me or threatened me in any other way. I knew some parents did that, but not her. She browbeat me and nagged me, and demanded perfection in everything, even how I made my bed. But she never hit me. So pushing her against the door frame was huge. There would be no going back to our old life now. Not that I wanted to.

"So, what d'ya wanna do with it?" Nikki asked.

I heaved a sigh. "Get that tattoo." I had a couple of hours to kill until I could call Toolie Fastbender at home. Getting a tattoo should fill up most of that time. And maybe it would release the awful vibrating energy inside me. The needles would hurt, but that would be the best part.

"Where's Snake?" Nikki asked as we waited for the bus headed downtown. It was cold, a bitter, damp cold, even though the sun was finally out. We were the only people at the bus stop, the only people outside at all.

"Don't know. Home, I guess. Where's Tito?"

She just shrugged. "Don't know; don't care."

"What? I thought you two were, like, a couple."

She rolled her eyes. "So did I. So did Erin Marsh—think *they* were a couple, I mean. And so does Kate Sebring."

"Kate Sebring? You mean, Everybody-dates-Kate?"

"I mean Everybody-*makes*-Kate." She laughed, but it was forced. "That's what Snake says the guys all call her."

"You talked to Snake? Today?"

"He texted me last night."

"Why? I thought you two didn't get along."

She shrugged. "I like him all right. He's cool." She gave me a steady look. "I just don't want to see him break your heart."

I hiked my book bag higher on my shoulder. "He's not the one I'm worried about. I trust him—"

"You shouldn't." She turned away from me to peer up the street, like she was looking for the bus. "You shouldn't trust any guy. Ever."

"Just 'cause Tito's an asshole doesn't mean—"

"They're all assholes. Finally." She gestured with her chin. "The bus."

We dropped the subject of guys who couldn't be trusted, lulled by the warmth and the mesmerizing rhythm of the overheated bus. I closed my eyes but I couldn't totally escape. My arm hurt, and my chest, just like I really did have a hole in my heart. That's why it's called a broken heart, 'cause it really feels that way.

Could Snake ever hurt me as much as Diane had? No way. Absolutely no way.

If only I could be a little kid again, not knowing anything about anything, and blissfully happy in my ignorance. If I could've just fallen asleep and not dealt with any of it, and just ridden the bus all day, I would have. But Nikki nudged me when we reached Railroad Avenue, and two blocks later, on the wrong side of the tracks, literally, we got out.

The wind hit like a cold, wet slap in the face, and we both yanked up our hoods and burrowed down into our jackets. "Shit. It feels like January," Nikki muttered.

"It was never this cold—" Where? Alexandria and Jackson had both gotten pretty cold. But before that, when I was real little, in Slidell I guess, it had never gotten this cold. Probably because it was so close to the Gulf of Mexico. Where had I lived, though? Near the water? In an apartment complex? A nice little house? No. I remembered a trailer, that dark night when the police had come. A cramped, smelly trailer—

"You still want that tattoo?" Nikki broke into my thoughts. "There's two places to choose from."

I shivered, less from the cold and more from my dreary memories. "Yeah. Let's go for it. I'll pay for you to have one too."

"No way. I don't like the sight of blood. Especially my own. We should call Snake though."

"Why? What is it with you and Snake today?"

"Nothing. I just thought—God!" she exclaimed. "He's *your* boyfriend. Don't *you* want him here?"

I looked away without answering. I was doing it again, picking a fight with one person when I was pissed off at somebody else. "Forget it. I'm just ... I don't know. Must be getting my period." Then I saw it, Inksville, and I grabbed her arm. "I'm eighteen but I lost my driver's license, okay? No, my mom took it because I got wasted." I laughed. "Just following her example, of course."

"Is that what happened? Your perfect Donna Reed mother got drunk?"

"No! God, why are you so thick today? That's the story I'm giving the tattoo guy."

"I know that. Now who's being thick? I'm talking about why you're in such a bitchy mood."

"I'm not in a bitchy mood!"

She just raised her brows, crossed her arms, and stared at me like I was some sort of imbecile, which I guess I sort of was.

"Okay, okay. I'm in a bitchy mood. But not because my mom got drunk or anything."

"Then why? You are so not acting like your normal self, Lisa."

There it was again. Lisa.

"I'm changing my name to Lissy. I found out it was my name before I got adopted. Lissy Davis."

"Oh, so *that's* it. You're back on the mommy hunt."

"I never stopped."

"Find anything new? I mean, besides your real name?"

"No." I don't know why I lied. I just wasn't ready to tell her yet. "Look, can we go inside? My feet are like blocks of ice."

Inksville was a hole in the wall, a long, skinny room covered in tattoo designs, some printed on pattern sheets, others photographs of designs on different body parts. There was a crazy painted bench under the window, a counter with glass shelves with all kinds of other stuff for sale—weird cigarette lighters, oversized belt buckles, earrings and nose rings and every-other-body-part rings. Behind the counter were two ratty old chairs, a desk with a computer on it, and a lot of other equipment.

This huge bald-headed guy looked up at us, then back at his computer screen. He was playing some kind of car-wreck game, judging from the sound of the crashes. "What'll it be, ladies? You just window-shopping or am I gonna get to do some real art on somebody's tushie?" He looked up at us again with this smart-ass grin on his face. He was laughing at us, so sure we didn't have the nerve to go through with it. One more grown-up in a long line of grown-ups who thought they knew so much more than me, like they understood me so well. Only they didn't.

I pushed my hood back and tried to look older than I was. "I'm looking for something different. No hearts or dragons or barbed wire."

He cocked one eyebrow at me. "As you can see, we've got a lot more than that."

"Right."

"And you?" He was looking at Nikki now.

"Nope. Not today," she said, pushing her hood down too. Nikki looks older than me and she'd recently added a purple streak to her elderberry-ebony–dyed hair. She unbuttoned her jacket too, and I saw his eyes flick down to her chest. She'd grown a whole cup size since the spring and she was pretty damned proud of her girls. While he stood up and leaned on the counter to get a better look at her, I turned my back and studied the selection. Fairies, unicorns, American flags, and every sports emblem imaginable. Anchors, snarling dogs, and lots of Celtic and Chinese symbols. Snake would like those. But I wanted something else, something that said me, Lisa Haines who used to be Lissy Davis and now she doesn't know who she is. Up on the third row from the top a pit bull straining against a short leash caught my eye. That's how I felt. Sort of. Only I wasn't on a leash. It was more like a cage. I'd been in a cage all my life, but for a long time I didn't know it. I'd just been a kid, practically a baby when this all started.

I stared at a series of lady liberty designs without really seeing them. This whole mess that was my stupid life had been messed up even before I was born, starting when Diane's first kid was killed by my real mom. I was stuck into this cage way back then.

"Do you have any cage designs?" I asked without turning around.

"Cage? Yeah. Like a birdcage. T-13," he said. "Up on the wall over here, by the air conditioner."

I saw it, a neat round-topped birdcage, but it had blue bird in it. I shook my head.

"I can put anything you want in it. Words, a flower. A fairy, a heart. Anything."

"A baby?" I don't know where the words came from. But as soon as I said them I knew. I spun around. "I want that bird cage with a baby inside."

He wasn't smirking anymore. "Hey, if you're in that kind of trouble, girlie, I don't think getting a tattoo is a good idea."

"What do you mean, trouble?"

Nikki gasped. "Don't tell me you're pregnant?"

"What? No." I started to laugh. "No, I'm not pregnant. Omigod. The baby is me, Nikki. *Me.* The adopted kid kept in the dark and never told anything by my mom. Sometimes you're so damned thick."

"Sorry," she said with a sheepish shrug.

"How old are you?" the bald guy asked.

I dug in my pocket, pulled the whole 160 dollars out, and threw it on the counter. "Can you do a caged baby for that?"

His eyes flicked from me to the cash. "It depends on how big it is and where you want it."

"On your back," Nikki said. "Behind your shoulder. It would look really cool in the summer when you wear tank tops."

"But *I* wouldn't be able to see it."

"How about on your deltoid?" the bald guy suggested. "That's the rounded muscle at the top of your arm."

I rubbed my left hand over my upper right arm. "That would work."

That's how right around five-thirty, Toolie Fastbender's getting-off time, I came to be sitting at the Beanery, the center of everybody's attention. Nikki was all enthused about the sad-eyed baby in my three-inch birdcage. While I was under the needle she'd called Snake and he brought two of his posse, and by the time Toolie Fastbender should be getting home I was zooming high on so much caffeine my arm had quit hurting.

"I thought they had a no-tats rule at that school of yours," Snake's friend Dannyboy said.

"You hafta keep them hidden," Snake said. He was sitting close to me with his arm over my shoulder. It felt cool to be so obviously his in front of all his friends. I was feeling pretty good, strong and rebellious, like nobody could stop me anymore. But I still wanted to speak to Toolie.

"Look," I said to Snake while Dannyboy and Vic cleared the table for arm wrestling. "I gotta go. I have an important phone call to make."

"You want to go to my house? My mom's working tonight." He drew my hand under the table and rubbed it against his already hard dick. He was hot to screw the tattooed girl. No surprise there. But I had more important things to do.

Extricating my hand from his, I also shrugged off his arm. "Sorry, not tonight." I stood. "Ready to go, Nikki?"

"What?" She looked up from her spot between Dannyboy and Vic. "What's the rush?"

"She can't go," Dannyboy said, wrapping one arm around Nikki's neck. "She's my good-luck charm."

She gave me this helpless shrug. Normally that would have pissed me off. Your best friend isn't supposed to blow you off for a guy. But today I didn't care. I knew she needed to get back at Tito. Mainly, though, I wanted to be alone when I called Toolie. "Don't worry about it," I said. I slid out of the booth and then grabbed my jacket and bag.

She shot me a grateful grin. "I'll call you."

"That's cool."

"Hey," Snake said, following me. "Want a ride home?"

"You have a car?" It was nasty cold out there, and I wasn't looking forward to the wait at the bus stop.

"Vic does. Hey, Vic. Gimme your keys. I won't be long," he added when Vic frowned.

"That's what you said the last time."

"I'll make it worth your while," Snake threw back at him.

"Yeah?" That brightened Vic's swarthy face. "Fine." But I didn't want to be with Snake right now. Especially not alone in a car when he was horny. "Thanks, but no," I said even as Vic stood up to dig in his pocket. And before Snake could stop me I was gone, out the door and running down the darkening street before I even had both arms in my jacket.

I heard him yelling my name. "Lisa. Hey, Lisa!"

But I was Lissy now, Lissy Davis, and I didn't have to listen to anybody. I ran until my chest hurt from breathing frigid air so deep and hard, until I wasn't cold anymore, until I was almost halfway home and decided not to wait on the bus.

Eventually I got cold again and zipped up my jacket and started to jog just to stay warm. But I was pooping out. When I turned onto my street I was so glad to see my house. The light was on by the front door. It was on a photocell so it always came on at dark. But there were no lights on inside and my mom's car was gone. Was she out looking for me?

I hoped so. I hoped she was cold and scared shitless, looking everywhere she could think of. It served her right for being such a sanctimonious liar.

At the door I dropped my bag and dug in a side pocket for my key. That's when a car door slammed and I heard footsteps behind me. I spun around, not really scared, because Daspit Hill is a pretty safe place. But I wasn't stupid either. I'd been to two classes on safety for women and I knew a woman could never be too careful.

Sure enough, some guy was coming up the walk, someone I'd never seen before. Thank goodness my hand landed on my keys. I yanked them out and holding the keys like a weapon I pointed them at him.

"Get back!" I yelled real loud, just like I'd been taught. "Get away from me!"

He stopped cold and held his hands up. He even backed up

two steps. "Sorry," he said. "I didn't mean to scare you. I thought you were Diane."

"Well, I'm not." He didn't look scary, just some old guy. And he knew my mom's name.

He knew her name. The hair on the back of my neck suddenly prickled in alarm.

"I was looking for Diane Haines," he said. "Is this her house?"

"Who are you?"

He hesitated. "An old friend," he finally said, dropping his hands to his side.

I backed up to the door, not sure what to do. I wanted to get inside and lock him out. He wasn't threatening or anything like that. He had on nice gray slacks and leather shoes and a heavy all-weather car coat, like in a Neiman Marcus catalogue. But I'd never seen him before, and that freaked me out.

"My name is Jim," he went on. "Maybe she told you about me? I knew her … a long time ago."

I didn't hear anything else. Jim. Her ex-husband who she said wasn't a stalker. But maybe he was. Because he obviously hadn't called ahead to tell her he was coming.

My hand fumbled behind me to find the doorknob, but even with that reassurance my heart thundered. "I think you have the wrong house."

His brows pulled together in the middle. "But this is the right address."

"Maybe she lived here before we did. We just moved in when school started." Then I turned, shoved the key into the door, twisted it, pushed hard, and nearly fell inside. Spinning around, I slammed the door, turned the dead bolt and for good measure hooked the chain.

Then, holding my breath, I peered out at him through the peephole.

He stood there, just at the edge of the circle of light cast by the porch light, staring at the front door like he could see me through it. What was he doing here?

Then he stepped back, one long step like he was moving in slow motion. He shoved his hands in his pockets. I couldn't really make out his face anymore and that creeped me out. He had a body and no head. Should I call 911, tell the police this weird guy was stalking us?

No. Stalking her, not me. But still.

Then he turned around, and walked to a dark blue Camry parked under the streetlight across the way. When he drove away I finally remembered to breathe again. But was he really gone? I stood in the front hall a long time, caught between fear and curiosity. If he didn't buy my story about her not living here anymore he might come back.

But why? Did he want to get back together with her again? Or did he just happen to be in town and decide to drop by for a visit? Most people called first. Besides, how did he find us?

Unless Diane had called him.

Only I didn't think she had. Our whole lives I'd never met anybody from her past. Even her boss Chris and her only boyfriend, Stan—she'd dumped them when we moved to Arkansas and never looked back. I sucked in another long breath, then let it out. No, she didn't know her ex-husband was here.

So now I had to decide: Was I going to tell her about his little visit or not?

CHAPTER TWENTY-FOUR

ACCOUNT OF BOBBIE FENNER

Google Search: Daspit Hill High School/Lisa Haines
No matches found

Google Search: St. Louis Academy/Lisa Haines
No matches found

Google Search: Lincoln Arts High School/Lisa Haines
3 matches found:
Lincoln Arts News 3/4/07
Green Club Plans River Clean-up by Lisa Haines

Lincoln Arts News 4/16/07
MySpace/YouTube: Blogs and the Lincoln Arts Student by Lisa Haines

Lincoln Arts News 9/15/07
Letters to the Editor: Sports vs. Art and the Student Council Budget by Lisa Haines

From: JLeftwich
To: DittoDiane
Re: Roberta Fenner Davis

I know I hurt you and that you don't want to see me. I accept that. You probably think I'm stalking you, but I'm not. It's just that I have reason to believe that Roberta Fenner is in Daspit Hills. Know that I will NOT let that bitch hurt you again.

I went by your house earlier tonight to warn you but some teenage girl told me that wasn't your house anymore. Did you move again after I tried to contact you the last time? You don't have to keep changing your e-mail or moving, because I won't be contacting you again. My friend with high security-level clearances told me he can't help me anymore unless I tell him exactly what's going on. So this is it. I know I've hurt my new family with my obsession about protecting you from Roberta, especially since you don't want my protection. But it's almost over now. I'm letting you go, Diane. A part of me will always love you. And Alyssa. But even if I see you in town, I won't approach you unless you approach me first. (I hope you will.)

I'm staying at the Riverside Motel just till I settle a few things. But once I know you're totally safe from Roberta I'm going home. Thank you for all the wonderful years we had.

PS: If that was your house and your daughter, please tell her not to worry. I'm not here to bother you. That's the last thing I want to do. I hope she is your daughter. I hope you have a new family and that you're very happy. That's all I've ever wanted for you, so you don't have to worry about me bothering you anymore.

LISA-LISSY

I made myself some hot chocolate and heated a bowl of broccoli cheese soup. I couldn't take a shower because of my tattoo. So I washed up as much as I could, and stared into the mirror at the caged baby on my arm. It still hurt, this dull, throbbing hurt, but not like when he was zapping me with his electric-needle torture machine. That had felt good and bad at the same time. It hurt my skin, but it felt good in the pit of my stomach.

Nikki had freaked out, nauseous from the smell of burnt skin and ink. I was proud of myself for not wimping out, or even showing how much it hurt at the time. If I hadn't run so fast to get home and got my heart racing so hard since then, it wouldn't probably be hurting at all.

But it didn't matter if it hurt. In a weird way it felt good, sort of like throwing up when you eat too much. You don't want to throw up, but once you do you feel so much better.

It was a pretty tattoo, the cage black and curving, the baby just a little pinker than my skin, with a tuft of brown hair and sad eyes the same color as mine. She was naked and hunched over with her arms around her knees. But it wasn't like perverted or anything. It was an innocent little baby trapped in this cold cage of a life that she never chose.

"You're not bad, Lissy," I said to her. No child was born bad. Even the ones that went to jail, like my birth mom, they weren't born bad. They just grew up in bad families and—*Toolie!*

In all the excitement of my tattoo and running home to avoid sex with Snake, and then seeing that Jim guy, I'd forgotten all about Toolie Fastbender. Abandoning the bathroom mirror, I grabbed my book bag and dug out my phone. Then I planted myself cross-legged on my bed, scrolled down to her name, and pressed *talk*.

"Hi," I said when she answered. "It's me, Lissy Davis. Well, really, my name now is Lisa Haines."

"So should I call you Lissy or Lisa?" she asked.

"Lissy. Lissy is for the part of my life with my real mom. Lisa is for the part with my adopted mom."

"Okay. Lissy it is. How old are you anyway? Not old enough to work for the Alexandria newspaper." She chuckled, and in the back I could hear country music playing.

"No. I'm fifteen and a half."

"Is that where you live, Alexandria?"

"We used to. But we moved to Arkansas a couple of years ago."

"Arkansas? Why Arkansas?"

"I don't know. I mean, I like it here. It's really beautiful and I have friends and a boyfriend too. And I like my school, at least as much as you *can* like a school. But I don't know why we moved here."

After a short silence she said, "I'm guessing you're trying to find Bobbie—your mom. But I don't know too much about her except that she was a hard worker who did a real good job."

"How did you know her? Are you like a guard or something?"

"Oh no." She laughed, a soft, girlish giggle, and all of a sudden I pictured her, small and plump like somebody's grandmother. "I run the prison library. Your mother worked for me right up till she got released. But that was after you were sick," she added. "Before that she worked in the health clinic. She's an LPN, a nurse. She took classes while she was here and she did real good."

A nurse. I stared out the window without really seeing anything "So ... she could be working in a hospital or something."

"I guess. A hospital or a clinic. When she left she probably went to New Orleans. She had the name of the doctor who'd called about you from a hospital down there."

"A doctor in New Orleans? But we never lived in New Orleans. You're sure it was New Orleans?"

"Oh, yes. I found out that tidbit myself," she said, sounding kind of proud. "That was the year after Katrina, though. Everything was a mess down there, so I don't know if she ever found the man or if she found a job or even a place to live." She paused. "She probably found a job okay. Even if it was just clearing away debris or gutting houses."

"She never called you after that? Not even a Christmas card?"

"No, hon, and I didn't expect her to. Once our ladies go free, well, they want to forget they ever been here."

That made sense, but it would make finding her that much harder. "So, she's been out how long?"

"January 2006."

I thought back to that time. January 2006. I'd been in eighth grade, still furious about our move to Arkansas. Is that why we'd moved the previous summer, because Diane knew my mom was getting out of jail and she was trying to cover our trail? Had she been moving us around all those years not because of Jim, but because of my mom?

But then, why was Jim here?

"Have you tried to find her?" Toolie asked. Then she giggled. "Of course you have. That's why you said you were a reporter, right?"

"Yeah. And it was a pretty good idea, wasn't it?"

"Yes, it was. But what about Web sites that match adopted kids with their birth parents? Have you tried them?"

"You have to be eighteen. But I'm working on that."

"I guess your adopted mom isn't too happy about this."

"She doesn't know."

"You mean you haven't asked her for help? Why not?"

I fell backward on the bed and stared up at the patterns of stick-on glow-in-the-dark stars, planets, and comets I'd put on the ceiling. "'Cause I know how she is. She's always been ... evasive about that stuff."

"That's too bad," Toolie said in this nice, sincere voice. Once more I pictured her, this soft, grandmotherly person. I'd never had a grandmother. Most of the time I didn't think about the grandparents I never had. But all of a sudden I wanted a grandmother really, really bad.

I rolled onto my stomach. "Do you have kids?"

"What? No. Not me. I wanted some. At least one. But my husband and me didn't have any. And then he died."

"Oh. So no grandchildren either. Are you even old enough to be a grandmother?"

"Well, yes. I suppose I am."

"I don't have a grandmother." I just blurted it out. "Or a grandfather or a dad or any aunts or uncles or cousins. Nobody but me and my adopted mom."

"That's too bad, Lissy. I know how it feels not to have any close family."

"So who do you talk to?"

There was a long pause before she said, "Mostly to God. Who do you talk to?"

I sighed. "My friends mostly. But not about everything."

But maybe I could talk to *her*. I swallowed hard. Could I trust her, a grown-up? Sitting up, I stared out through the fogged-up window. "Can I tell you something, Toolie? Will you promise not to tell anyone—except for my real mom if she ever contacts you?"

"Why sure, hon. You want me to tell her your new name and your phone number? 'Cause of course I will."

"Yeah, that too. But there's more and ... and I don't know

what to think about it. It's just so ... so totally fucked- up," I blurted out.

"Excuse me?" she said, sharp and shrill. "What kind of language is that?"

"Sorry," I muttered. "I thought everybody in prison cursed."

"Yes, most of them do. But prisoners are hardly the role models a nice young lady follows."

My freshly inked arm began to throb.

"What makes you think I'm a nice young lady?"

"I don't know. You sounded nice, until you cursed," she said.

"I might be a juvenile delinquent." I rolled off the bed, suddenly angry with her and every other two-faced grown-up in the world. "I might be really horrible, a ... a serial killer in the making."

"You mean like your mother?"

"What? She's not a serial killer!"

"Oh, Lissy. Of course she's not. But she *was* a juvenile delinquent. She did some bad things in her life. She made some really bad decisions. But then she worked real hard to turn her life around. That's the point I'm trying to make. You might not be a nice young lady. I don't know. But you *could* be one," she added. "It's not too late. And I know—I *know*—it's what your mother would want for you."

In the silence that built between us I heard the lonely guitar and nasal twang of some man singing about his soul going where his mama always wanted it to go. It made me want to cry—and want my mother *so* bad. What made it worse was that I didn't know which mother I wanted more. The reliable one who had always given me, if not what I wanted, then at least what I needed? Or the absent one who looked like me and still loved me after all this time?

"So," Toolie said as I swiped at the stupid tears gathering in my eyes. "Are you a nice young lady or a juvenile delinquent? Or some place in-between?"

"I don't know." I gulped back a sob. "I got a tattoo today."

"Oh, dear."

"Yeah."

"Does your mother know?"

"You mean Diane? Not yet. She won't like it," I added before Toolie could ask.

"Huh. So I guess that's why you did it."

"No. I mean, I knew she would hate it. But I did it for myself. It's a little baby stuck in a cage."

"Oh, dear," she said again.

"Yeah. Oh, dear," I echoed. "I guess you don't need to be a shrink to figure that one out."

"No." She was silent again, but there was no country music playing any longer. "Well," she said. "Let's get back to before you said the F word. You wanted to tell me something."

"Oh, right. Okay. Um ... Remember you said that my real mom did some bad things in her life? Well, did you know that one of those things was that she got in a car wreck when she was like seventeen and it was her fault? And this little girl got killed?"

"I do know that. I'd forgotten about it, but today after you called I looked up her file and that was in it. That's not why she got sent to St. Anna's though. The negligent-homicide charge was a juvenile offense. Very sad, of course."

"Yeah, especially for the little girl's mom." *And dad.* It occurred to me suddenly that Jim had lost a child too. In my initial fear of him I'd forgotten about that.

"How did you find out about the car wreck?" Toolie asked.

"Her juvenile record was sealed."

"It was in the local newspapers back then. I Googled her."

"Oh, yeah, the Internet. You know, your mom got real good on computers before she left here."

"She did?"

"You bet. She was looking for you, of course. Everything she did that last year and a half was aimed at finding you when she got out."

I smiled, holding her words close to my heart. My real mom loved me and wanted me. If it weren't for Diane constantly moving us around she probably would've found me by now. I sat up straighter, bolstered by a renewed spurt of anger. "Okay. Here's the thing. I'm pretty good on the computer too, and I found out some seriously weird stuff. The lady whose little girl got killed in that car wreck with my mother?" I took a deep breath. "She's the one who adopted me."

Toolie didn't say anything for, like, a whole minute. Like she was processing what I said in her head. I got so antsy I jumped off my bed and paced from the door to the window and back. "Did you hear me?" I finally asked her. "Diane Haines is really—"

"I heard you," she said. "But how could that be? How did she find you? And anyway, I can't believe any adoption service would allow such a thing."

"No, duh. I don't know how she pulled it off, but there's no doubt who she is. I mean, her name was in the paper and everything."

"Oh, dear. That's astounding. But … has she been good to you, Lissy? I mean, she hasn't treated you bad or anything?"

"No. Not like abuse or anything like that. But she lied to me. She's been lying to me for my whole life."

"Yes." She paused. "My goodness, that's … "

"Suspicious," I said. "Very suspicious."

"I suppose so. What are you going to do? I'm guessing you only recently found this out. Have you told your mom—Diane—that you know?"

"Not yet."

"So ... why not? What are you waiting for?"

"I don't know. It's complicated."

"Yeah. I can see that."

I waited a heartbeat. Two. Three. Then, "What do *you* think I should do?"

"Me?"

"Yeah. I mean, if you had a grandchild, what would you tell her to do?"

"Well." She was quiet a long time. "I think I would try to get both sides of the story."

"That's what I'm *trying* to do. That's why I'm looking for my birth mom. And why I called *you*."

"Okay, okay. Then, well, I think you should just talk to her, to Diane."

I blew out a long breath. "Yeah. I guess. But she's gonna flip out."

"What do you mean, flip out? In a dangerous way?"

"No. She's crazy strict and has weird ideas and everything. But she's not dangerous or anything."

"So just talk to her. If it makes you too nervous, maybe you could have somebody there with you. Like a minister or a school counselor or something."

"I guess I could do that. But wait. It can't be anybody official. 'Cause if she did anything illegal, the counselor would have to, like, report her, wouldn't they?"

"Oh, dear. You could be right. Which means they could take

you away from her." She paused. "Maybe even send her to jail for lying and whatever she did to get you."

"Yeah. I thought about that. It would serve her right to go to jail. But ... Anyway, that's why I need somebody else to be there."

And that's when it came to me. The perfect person to be there when I confronted Diane with what I knew: Jim Leftwich.

CHAPTER TWENTY-FIVE

From: DittoDiane
To: JLeftwich
Re: Bobbie

How could Bobbie have found me here?

From: JLeftwich
To: DittoDiane
Re: Bobbie

Thank God you responded. I don't know how she did it, but I know she's tracking you down, supposedly to "make amends" for Alyssa. Can I call you on the phone?

From: DittoDiane
To: JLeftwich
Re: Bobbie

You have to ask? Don't you already have my #? You've found out everything else about me.

From: JLeftwich
To: DittoDiane
Re: Bobbie

You're very slippery, Diane, but yes, I do have your address and phone #. The point is, if I found you, Bobbie can too.

From: DittoDiane
To: JLeftwich
Re: Bobbie

If that woman ever shows up at my house, I'll deal with her. I don't need you to protect me.

From: JLeftwich
To: DittoDiane
Re: Bobbie

I know. But I need to stop Bobbie for my own sake. I'm doing this for me. And for Alyssa.

From: DittoDiane
To: JLeftwich
Re: Bobbie

What do you mean, stop her?

From: JLeftwich
To: DittoDiane
Re: Bobbie

It's just a figure of speech. BTW why didn't you tell me you had remarried and had a child?

From: DittoDiane
To: JLeftwich
Re: Bobbie

I didn't and I don't. Go home to your family, Jim. They need you. I don't.

LISA-LISSY

I didn't get to ask Toolie what she thought about me having Jim Leftwich there when I talked to my mom because that's when Diane decided to come home. I heard her car door slam, and I was pretty sure she wasn't going to cut me any more slack. So I said a quick good-bye to Toolie just before my mom burst into my bedroom.

"All right, Lisa. Enough is enough. There will be no more leaving the house without telling me where you're going, and no more not answering your cell phone when I call."

She looked terrible, worse than I ever saw her. Her hair was a dirty snarl; her eyes were puffy and red; and her face was dragged down and gray. She looked like an old-lady version of her real self, hanging on to the doorknob like she might fall down if she let go.

I'd done that to her—me—and I almost felt guilty about it. Except that she was scowling at me, totally pissed off and spoiling for a fight. The anger vibrated off her in waves. But I was pissed too, enough to want to piss her off even more. So I stood up from the bed real slow and lazy, and smiled at her. "I was out getting a tattoo. Wanna see it?"

She gasped. Her face went pale and she didn't take a breath for what seemed like five minutes. We stared at each other. I glared. Then she just sort of wilted. "Tell me you're lying," she finally said in this thin, shattered voice.

For one long terrible moment I felt awful. Mean, hateful. Vindictive. But the moment passed. She was a liar—a lifelong liar—and maybe even a kidnapper. All I'd done was get a lousy tattoo. What business was it of hers anyway?

"It's a baby trapped in a cage," I said. I started to pull the neckline of my T-shirt down over my shoulder but stopped when she took a step backward. "What's the big deal?" I was taunting her now, feeling strong and in control.

"Why ... why would you do such a thing?"

"For the same reason I cut myself!" I yanked up my left sleeve and thrust my arm out. "Because it *feels* good. It *feels* good to hurt. It calms me down!" I was breathing harder than her now, practically gasping for air. "You should try it some time," I finished, enjoying the horror that painted her face.

I turned my right shoulder back to her and tugged the neckline down. A few of the neckline stitches ripped and I felt the painful stretch of my newly scarred flesh. But who cared about an old T-shirt and a little bit of pain? "See?" Glaring hatred, I turned my shoulder toward her. "Isn't it pretty?"

She stared at my shoulder, her eyes wide, glistening with moisture as she worked her jaw back and forth, struggling for control. Before she could get there I went for the kill. "Oh, some guy came by to see you."

Her eyes jerked up to mine and she went, like, totally rigid. Her eyes had gotten huge, but in every other way she seemed to shrink, to get smaller—and older still.

I was winning. But it didn't feel as good as I thought it would. So I went for the jugular. "He said his name was Jim. Do you know him?"

She didn't answer. She didn't have to. We both knew who he was. But did *she* know that *I* knew? Did she remember that years ago she'd let it slip that her ex-husband's name was Jim?

If she'd just come clean right then and there, blurted out the whole pathetic story—who Jim was, about their little girl, and my mother, and me—then maybe I could've forgiven her, or at least cut her some slack. But instead her eyes got this remote look, hard and narrow. Like she was looking through me, not at me.

She straightened up and I could see her breathing, her chest going up and down, deep and heavy. She didn't look mad anymore, or sad. She didn't look scared either. It was like this ice-cold hardness fell down over her, almost like she turned into this different person that I never saw before.

It creeped me out, like in a horror movie when the crazy person finally goes ballistic. Only Diane didn't go ballistic, and that was even creepier. She just stood there, rigid and still. Then she blinked, and all of a sudden it was like she saw me again.

"You're grounded." She crossed her arms over her chest. "You're grounded until your grades improve. And your attitude."

I just laughed at her. "You can't ground me. We both know that doesn't work anymore."

Her eyes drilled into me, cold and determined enough to make me shiver. "Then I'll cancel your cell phone and your online service."

"You can't do that!"

"I can and I will if you pull any more stunts like staying out all night or that tattoo or that ... that cutting." Then she turned and stalked out of the room, like it wasn't even worth talking about.

I ran to the door and slammed it. "I hate you!" I screamed. Then I yanked open the door and screamed it again. "I *hate* you!"

But she was already in her bedroom with her door closed.

"I hate you!" I screamed once more for good measure, then slammed my door again. She could *not* take my phone and my computer access away from me. What had I done to deserve that? Didn't she know *anything* about raising kids! The punishment was supposed to fit the crime!

I grabbed my phone and started to call—who? Not Snake or

Nikki. They were my best friends, but at that moment I wanted my real mom. Or if not her, Toolie. But what could she do? She might know stuff about my real mom, but she didn't know how to find her. And what could she do about Diane or Jim and the weirdness going on between them?

I closed the phone, set it on my dresser, and tried to calm down enough to figure this mess out. The minute Diane realized Jim was in town, she'd turned into the ice queen. That's when it had quit being about me and my acting out, and turned into a Jim and Diane thing. He'd been invisible in our lives, and yet today it was almost like he was the key to everything.

Was it because he didn't know who I was and she didn't want him to find out and maybe blow the whistle on her? But why would he do that to her? He had as much reason to hate my real mom as Diane did.

Maybe he really *was* a stalker.

But I wasn't so sure of that anymore. Maybe he wasn't the reason we'd moved so much. After all, the last move came after I was sick, after Diane contacted the prison where my real mom was. She'd known all along where my mother was!

God, I wanted to kill her!

We'd moved all those times because of who my birth mother was, her gettin out of jail and all. And that's why Diane was all hot to move again, because she was afraid my real mom might be getting close to finding us. Only I wasn't moving, and Jim Leftwich was in town, and it was way past time to get everything out into the open.

But first I had to find Jim.

Not tonight, though. I'd spent one cold, awful night out on the streets. I didn't need another one. So I took a hot shower despite the tattoo—it felt so good—then zonked out the minute I crawled into bed. When I woke up it was still dark, and freezing cold in my room. Even under the covers with my warm breath to heat up the space, I was cold. Wasn't the heat on? Curled up tight and shivering, I debated jumping up, flipping the thermostat to 90 and leaping back under the covers. I dreaded the thought, but the alternative was freezing to death right where I lay.

Then a light switched on in the hall, and I immediately relaxed. Mom was up; she would fix the problem.

Sure enough I heard the muted whoosh of the central heat coming on. The light flipped off and I heard her soft footfall in the hall. She paused at my door, though. The knob turned; the latch clicked ever so faintly; and that's when I remembered everything that happened yesterday.

I tensed as she tiptoed into my room, and strained to hear. At the same time I tried to keep my breathing steady so she wouldn't know I was awake. She was checking up on me to see if I was still here.

When she opened my closet I had to stifle a gasp of outrage. What the hell? She was searching my room? I couldn't believe this! What about my privacy? And did she really think I was stupid enough to hide anything in my closet? My weed was taped to the bottom of my desktop above the drawer, and my blades were in my art kit.

Then she crossed the room toward the desk right beside the bed, and I held my breath—until I felt the soft weight of another blanket settle over me. She straightened it over my shoulders, then stood there a long moment, staring at me, I guess before she turned away.

It messes with your head when you zoom from super-pissed-off to mushy love and gratitude. As she crept from the room I started to cry. This was so totally fucked-up. I was still furious with her, but despite what I'd said to her, I didn't exactly hate her. I couldn't.

For a long time I lay there trying to figure out my next move. It got warm and toasty, and that made me want to just talk to Diane and ask her to tell me the truth. But would she ever tell me the whole truth? Besides, the whole Jim thing was too strange. He was here in Daspit Hill for a reason. Maybe it was the stars in alignment at last. My whole life had been so star-crossed, but this felt like the right time for straightening everything out. I could've fallen back asleep, but I made myself get up instead. I needed to find Jim and the only lead I had was the dark-blue Camry he'd been driving. I had to find it—and him—probably at one of the few motels in town before he gave up on finding Diane and left.

As quietly as possible I dressed. It hurt like crazy to move my shoulder, and the cut on my inner arm ached too. But I just gritted my teeth, found my gloves and a muffler, shoved my phone in my pocket and crept into the kitchen. I grabbed a banana, a breakfast bar, and then on impulse, the spare set of car keys from the junk drawer. There was no other way to get to all the motels, and anyway, with any luck I'd be back here with Jim before Diane even knew I was gone.

At the last minute I left her a note, after all, I didn't want her to report the car stolen and sic the cops on me.

> I borrowed the car but don't freak out. I'll bring it back soon. I promise.
> Lisa

I almost wrote *Lissy*. *Love, Lissy*. Wouldn't that mess with her head? But I didn't want to give everything away just yet.

Outside it was bitter cold, with frost on the grass and on the boxwoods that lined the driveway. I'd only driven three times before. Mom—Diane—wasn't in a big hurry to let me drive, and I'd had to beg really hard for her to teach me. I'd only driven on the weekends in the empty parking lot at the high school. And the roads sure hadn't been slick with frost and ice.

But I could do this.

I backed down the driveway. There was no traffic this early on a Sunday morning. The paper man had come by. Thick Sunday editions dotted the driveways as I inched down the street. Even on Clifford Road there were only a few cars, which was good because I knew I was driving way too slow. My heart was racing, but not the car. I passed the elementary school, heading for the Daspit Hills Inn. No blue Camry parked there. I turned around in their parking lot and pulled back up to the highway. Maybe I should call Nikki or Snake. Wouldn't they be impressed if I drove over to pick them up?

Only neither one of them answered their phones.

"Screw them," I muttered, tossing my phone onto the passenger seat. But I knew I shouldn't be mad. I wouldn't answer my phone this early on a weekend either.

Next stop was the Motel 6. No Camries there. Then the Red Roof Inn where I saw a dark-blue car, but it was a Chevrolet. I'm pretty sure he'd driven a Camry. But what if I was wrong? After all, it had been dark.

Still, I had to keep going. Three down, three to go, but now I had to get onto the main highway through town. I was driving like an old man, leaning forward with my hands clenched on the wheel by the time I left the Mountain View Motel. Traffic was busier on the highway and I was terrified of skidding on ice and being hit by an eighteen-wheeler. Just before the Riverside Motel driveway I was nearly rear-ended.

"Slow down!" I screamed as the truck driver zoomed by, laying on his horn. Who could drive with idiots like that everywhere?

"Please, please, please," I muttered as I lurched through the parking lot.

And then I saw it, a navy-blue Camry with an Alabama license plate. I'd found him!

Somehow I managed to park without scraping the giant SUVs on either side of me. Now what? I stared at the peach-colored two-story building. There must be a hundred rooms. How was I supposed to find him?

So I waited. I kept the car idling so I could run the heater and the radio. It was still cold, though, and I was hungry. I ate the banana and the breakfast bar, but I wanted something warm: grits and scrambled eggs, and hot chocolate and maple- syrup waffles.

There was an old picnic blanket in the backseat and I tented it over me. All I had to do was wait for him to come out, then take him to our house. Finally I would get to the truth about how Diane got me. But even that wouldn't help me find my birth mother. On the other hand, it wouldn't hurt.

I might have dozed off. I don't know. But I jerked wide awake when some guy rapped his keys against the car window. He squinted at me. "You okay?"

"Yeah. Sure." *Just scared out of my wits, you asshole!*

When he kept staring at me all curled up under the plaid picnic blanket I scowled at him. "I'm waiting for somebody."

He shook his head and pursed his lips. "A car running like that, you could die of carbon-monoxide poisoning."

I gave him a big, fake smile. "I'm fine." *Go away.*

He ambled away, still shaking his head, got into the Chevy

Suburban next to me, and pulled out of the lot. That's when I saw the green Hyundai parked three spaces over. A woman sat in the front seat very still. The engine was on—I saw the frosty white exhaust. It must be checkout time. Maybe Jim would come out soon. The small green SUV didn't leave, though.

I fiddled with the radio and found a Little Rock station that wasn't running a Sunday sermon. Avril sang her poser song. Casey Kasem would be on at ten. But still the woman in the green Hyundai sat there, like she was waiting for someone to come out.

Was she waiting, or was it a stakeout?

How weird was that, two of us staking out the same motel? Maybe she was a cop. Or the FBI.

On the radio Noodlehead's 'Shortnin' Bread' came on, his anthem against child abuse. Listening to the words made me think about how bad some kids had it. Even worse than me. I squinted at the woman in the car. Maybe she *was* an FBI agent, on a child-abuse case. Or kidnapping. Or even kiddie porn, like in the song.

Then she turned the engine off and got out of her car. She was bundled up in a gray parka with the hood pulled up. It was hard to tell how old she was, but not real old. She crossed the lot to a McDonald's next door that had opened. Good idea. I could get breakfast and get warm. As I followed her, I wondered why she didn't have a partner. On television the cops always have a partner.

Maybe she was a private eye. She didn't look like a private eye, but what did I know? And they did usually work alone. Maybe she was on a divorce case, taking pictures of some cheating husband. Or wife.

She headed to the bathroom, so I hurried and got a coffee and an Egg McMuffin, then slid into the corner booth next to the window and farthest away from the counter. That way I could keep a lookout for Jim, and that woman wouldn't see me watching her. When she came out of the bathroom she had her hood off. For one crazy moment I thought I knew her.

"Mom?" I squinted at her. Then when she scanned the dining room, I looked away, concentrating on my meal.

What an idiot! Just because she had blond hair and was maybe around the same age as my birth mother, that didn't make her my mom. I blew out a long, frustrated breath. I'd had too little sleep, and too much Toolie Fastbender. But I peered back at her, wishing she was my birth mother. If my real mom would just show up, it wouldn't matter about Jim anymore, or even Diane.

I sipped my coffee, too big a swallow that nearly scalded my tongue. "Damn." I pushed the cup away and dug into my McMuffin, but I couldn't look away from her. If only my mom could find me, all this confusion would be over with.

But deep inside, I knew that wasn't true. My birth mom hadn't gone to jail for nothing. And the Diane question was still there too. Besides, cop, detective, or whoever she was, she wasn't my mother. That was just wishful thinking.

I pried off the top of the coffee cup, held my cold hands around its toasty warmth, and blew on the creamy brown surface. If I had to drink coffee all day long, I was staying in here where it was warm until Jim finally came outside. My tattoo hurt like crazy and I wished I had brushed my teeth before I left.

A young couple came in, then a woman and three kids dressed for church. You could tell by their shoes. Three guys who looked like hunters in their camouflaged jackets. My coffee cooled. Somewhere along the way the cop lady must have left. I was almost to the last of my coffee, wondering how long I could sit here with an empty cup before anyone would notice. Then I saw him.

Jim Leftwich.

At least I thought it was him. He came out onto the second-floor balcony at the corner of the building. It was him all right. He had on the same forest-green coat as last night.

I slid out of the booth and started for the door. He wasn't getting away without answering a lot of questions.

But at the glass door I stopped. He was just standing there, like he was looking for something—or someone. Then he looked sharply to his left. I did too. A cab had pulled into the other end of the motel parking lot and, as I watched, a woman got out.

My mom. Diane!

CHAPTER TWENTY-SIX

From: DittoDiane
To: JLeftwich
Re: Bobbie

I've changed my mind. Tell me everything you know about Bobbie. I'd rather find her before she finds me.

From: JLeftwich
To: DittoDiane
Re: Bobbie

Don't worry. She won't be bothering you.

From: DittoDiane
To: JLeftwich
Re: Bobbie

What does that mean, don't worry? You've come all the way here to stop her from bothering me and now you're saying I don't need to worry?

THE THIEF'S ONLY CHILD

INSTANT MESSAGE TO DIANE:

Jim: She's scum, Diane. I told you, I won't let her hurt you again.

Diane: What does that mean?

Jim: It means she's a blight upon the earth. No one will miss her.

Diane: Jim, call me. OK? Don't do anything impulsive. Call me right now. 688-4688. Right now!

Diane: Please, Jim. Call me. Look. I need to tell you something. About the girl you saw the other day right outside my house. She's my daughter, and she's been acting out a lot lately. You showing up really upset her. Now she's missing and she's taken my car. She could be looking for you. And for Bobbie. (DELETE: And for Bobbie.) She thinks you're stalking me for a bad reason.

Jim: You told her I was stalking you?

Diane: Of course not! I told her just the opposite. But I don't think she believes me.

Jim: Don't worry about me. I'm going home just as soon as I deal with Bobbie.

Diane: You don't need to deal with her, okay? You said before that you've already seen her twice. Isn't that enough?

Look, can we get together? I need to see you before you go. Please, Jim, for Alyssa's sake. Please.

Jim: I still miss her so much, Diane. So damned much. I thought it would get easier, but ever since my two kids got to be older than Alyssa ever got to be, it's been even worse.

Diane: I know. It's hard and it's never going to end because we'll always love Alyssa. She'll always be our perfect little girl. But we can't get her back. Look, let's meet. Okay? Are you still at the Riverside Motel? Because I need to be with the one person who loved Alyssa as much as I did.

Jim: I'm still here. Room 227.

LISA-LISSY

I pressed my face up to the frosty plate-glass window. No way could Diane be here! But she was. How did she know where to find me? But then, when she just stood there looking up at Jim Leftwich, it hit me. She wasn't looking for me. She'd come here to meet him.

Good. Now I wouldn't have to drag him to our house to confront her about all her shit.

But it didn't feel good. It felt all wrong, like she was stabbing me in the back. Like the worst kind of betrayal. Didn't she care where I was, and if I was safe? Why was she here with him when she was supposed to be out looking for me?

Then an awful thought sucked the last bit of warmth from my soul. What if they were getting back together? What would happen to me then?

Like a robot going through the motions because that's what I was supposed to do, I pushed open the door. The wind hit me like a cold, wet slap. But I just zipped up my jacket. Diane had started up the stairs. Jim waited at the top. Pulling up my hood, I ducked and bobbed my way to the car and dove inside. But neither of them noticed me. On the balcony they just stood there. The sharp wind ruffled her hair. I saw him wipe a hand across his eyes. Was he crying?

Then he lurched forward and hugged her. And she hugged him back. Her arms went up and wrapped around him really tight. He'd divorced her and then stalked her, and now she was hugging him?

This was totally whack. I was supposed to surprise her by bringing him back to the house and making her tell the truth about how she got me, how she must have lied to get me. But now she was with him. They were together. Had he'd known about me all along?

I wiped my wet cheeks with my wrist, shivering in the frigid car. Through blurry eyes I watched them head around the corner, to his room, I guess. Now what? I sat in the car, no heat, no radio, trying to pull myself together. So what if he was here? Why should I give a damn? I sure as hell didn't need to cry about it. I knew what I needed to do: go up there, knock on the door, and do what I set out to do.

But I was too afraid.

That's when I decided to call Snake. He was good at parent stuff. It took four calls—hanging up when his voice mail came on and redialing—before he answered. "What the fuck—"

"Don't hang up! He's here and my mom went in a motel room with him!"

"What? Who? And why should I care? Damn it, Lisa, it's barely eight o'clock in the fucking morning!"

"Her ex. My mom's ex-husband is at the Riverside Motel and she just went in a room with him."

"So?"

"So? God, Snake! I'm, like, freakin' out here and all you can say is so? I thought you were my boyfriend."

"You're *always* freakin' out, Lisa. Every frickin' day you got something new to freak out about!"

People talk about guys beating up their girlfriends. I knew two girls at school whose boyfriends were mean that way. Snake wasn't like that though. That's why I knew he loved me. But what he just said, that hurt as bad as being slapped or hit or shoved into a wall. It felt like being slugged in the stomach and I couldn't catch my breath.

"Yeah," he said into my shocked silence. Then, "See ya," and he hung up.

I could hardly breathe. Somewhere a car horn sounded. An eighteen-wheeler ground its gears taking off from the traffic light on the highway. But in the frozen cab of my mother's Honda there was only an icy vacuum with no air left for me to breathe.

Was that it; he was dumping me? He didn't love me or care about me anymore?

My phone, so cold and light in my hand, felt like an enemy now. I tried to breathe, tried to think. But it was impossible. Then, like they were working all on their own, my fingers punched in memory, then edit. I scrolled down to Snake's number and punched in delete.

"Delete," I muttered out loud. "You are so out of here, you asshole." Then I gulped in air and it was like feeding the fire. "I hate you and I hope your dad is even worse than your mom said!"

A man walking past me to his own car paused and stared at me. I guess I was yelling, but so what? I snapped the phone shut and then worked at breathing, deep and slow so I could calm down and figure out what to do. My boyfriend was a jerk; my mom—my adopted mom—was a liar and a traitor, and my real mom was an ex-con, probably a junkie too. So now what? Did it even matter if I confronted Diane with her ex-husband Jim? I mean, what was the point?

Suddenly all I wanted was to be away from here, to just drive and drive ... to where? Maybe I could pick up Nikki. Snatching up my phone, I started to call her, then stopped. Across the parking lot a woman stood at the bottom of the motel stairs. That cop lady, if that's what she was, started up the steps, this slow, careful pace, like she was trying to walk real quiet or something.

I squinted through the foggy windshield. What was she doing, stalking Jim? Maybe she wasn't a cop or a private eye. Maybe she was a jealous wife planning to catch him cheating with his first wife. Omigod! Just like a Jerry Springer show, only there weren't any bodyguards to stop a fight if one broke out.

That's the only thing that got me out of the car. I didn't know why Diane was in a motel room with her ex-husband again, but I couldn't just sit here and let this woman beat her up.

Or worse.

Jumping from the car, I sprinted across the parking lot and ran up the stairs. I lost sight of her as I turned at the landing, and when I reached the second floor I didn't see her at all. Did she already know where Jim's room was? I peeked around a corner—no angry wife there, only another narrow balcony with half-a-dozen room doors. So I crept along, listening breathlessly at each door for angry voices or the sound of a fight. But all was quiet. Was his room further down, around the next corner? Maybe I should just start knocking.

A little kid about eight opened the first door. "Sorry, wrong room," I mumbled. The next two were empty I guess. At 217 a man answered wearing only a towel. "Sorry," I said lurching backward. "Wrong room."

He just grinned. "Are you sure?" And he dropped the towel.

Shocked and totally grossed out by his hairy, white belly hanging over his big purple dick, I bolted down the corridor. Were all guys such sick losers? I darted into an open breezeway with an elevator and three vending machines—then slammed into somebody.

"Sorry," I muttered, stumbling back from her.

"No problem," she said. "Are you okay?"

I was freezing; I was scared for my mom; and I was creeped

out by the man in 217. Other than that ... I shrugged "Yeah. Fine." Except that suddenly I wasn't. Every single hair on the back of my neck and my arms stood up, like I needed to be very careful, very aware. I turned to face her, still backing away, and nearly had a heart attack. It was the woman from the car! The cop or FBI agent—or Jim's wife

If she was his wife, though, she was a lot younger than I expected, considering how old *he* was. And prettier too.

She was smiling at me, not mad at all that I'd slammed into her. But then her smile started to fade. First from her eyes, then from her mouth. It was like slow motion, every nuance of her expression altering feature by feature, muscle by muscle. Pore by pore. At the same time something inside my chest began to swell, like I was filling up with knowledge and emotion, more than I could hold. And right then I knew. I knew!

"Mom?"

Her eyes got big and round, and it was her turn to stumble backward like I'd just whacked her with a baseball bat. She swallowed. I saw her throat working up and down. But she didn't say anything, and for one tiniest fraction of a second I wondered if I was wrong. Then she said, "Lissy?" and I was right. My mother—my birth mother, the one who carried me in her stomach for nine months—was here. When I least expected it and wasn't really looking for her, I'd run headlong into her.

Every emotion I ever felt in my whole screwed-up life seemed to bust out of me all at the same time. Joy and sorrow. Emptiness and feeling all filled up. Victory and this other aching, fearful dread. It was all just so ... weird. Too weird to deal with this fast.

"Are you following Jim?" I blurted out. Like *that* was the most important thing we had to talk about.

She nodded, wrapping her arms around herself. She looked

like she was about to cry. Considering how hard I'd been looking for her, it was crazy that I wasn't getting all weepy. Maybe I was just too stunned by everything.

I heard her suck in a harsh breath. "It's really you? My little Lissy?"

"My name is Lisa," I said feeling defensive all of a sudden. For some reason I felt wary of her. I mean, she looked like an ordinary person. But she'd spent ten years in jail for drugs. And she'd killed Diane and Jim's little girl—and named me after her. How sick was that? "Why are you following him?" My voice was belligerent, suspicious, and she seemed to retreat from it.

"To find you."

I shook my head. "That doesn't make any sense."

"But it does. And it worked. I used him to lead me to Diane and then to you. Only I didn't expect you to—" She shrugged one shoulder and tried to smile, but I could see she was trembling. She cleared her throat. "I didn't expect you to show up like this."

Everything was getting all muddy in my head. "Wait. You knew I was with Diane?" She'd *given* me to Diane?

That's when she went all steely-eyed, all stiff and cold-looking, how I always thought an ex-con would look. "I figured it out," she said. "How she lied to get you and then kept moving to hide her tracks." She stepped nearer, her arms were rigid at her sides; her hands had knotted up into fists. "Did she hurt you? Did she punish you for—"

"No. No! You're the one—" I broke off, filled with a twisted sort of hate toward her. Hate for how she screwed up my whole life, first by screwing up her life and going to jail, and then, even in jail, she was the reason we moved so much, why my whole life was this long struggle with different schools and different towns and different friends. Different everything. My chin started to tremble, but I clenched my teeth together really hard to make it stop. I hated her, but I loved her too. Just like with Diane.

"Why?" I barely got the word out. "Why did you—Why were you so—"

She shrank backward, getting smaller and not so sure of herself now. "Why did I go to jail?"

"'Cause you were a junkie, right?"

"Yes." She chewed her lower lip and nodded. "I was. But not anymore."

"And a really lousy mother." I bit the words out, wanting to hurt her.

She sucked in a shaky breath. "Yes. That too."

"So why are you here? 'Cause I'm not a kid anymore. We're, like, total strangers."

Again she nodded. "I just ... wanted to be sure you were okay."

"I am. No thanks to you," I added, feeling my power to hurt her. Snake was right. Kids do have power over their parents. They just have to know how to use it. "So. You've seen me and I'm obviously okay." I shoved my hands into my pockets. "So now I guess you can just go back to wherever you came from."

"New Orleans," she said after a moment. "That's where I've been living since I got out."

"Huh. That seems about right. You totally messed up your life, so now you live in a totally messed-up city."

She smiled at my lame insult, and in that smile I saw the girl from her yearbook picture, the one who looked like me. It gave me goose bumps. "You're right," she said. "It *is* the perfect place for me. Because just like me, New Orleans is on the way back. It's coming along, getting even better than before." She paused. "Healing."

Once again I caught a glimpse of tears in her eyes and it got to me. But I wasn't going there. "Whatever," I muttered. "So. When are you leaving?"

She swallowed hard. "I don't know." Her gaze flickered past me, then back. "I want to talk to Diane first."

I shrugged. "Fine." I turned to go, caught up in this tornado of hating her and still wanting to know everything about her.

"Wait. Wait, Lissy. Lisa."

"I can't," I said, glancing back at her. "I'm already in hot water with my mom." I said that on purpose, *my mom*, just to dig the knife in deeper. "I have to get home before she does."

"You mean she doesn't know you're here?"

I stuck my chin out. "I borrowed the car without asking her." I shot her a smug, knowing look. "I guess it must run in the family."

It was a low blow, and it hit her hard. Her shoulders sagged and she shoved her hands into her pockets. "Look, Lissy—Lisa. Don't make the same mistakes I made."

"Don't tell me what to do! You gave me up, remember? So you don't get to order me around."

"It wasn't an order. It was a plea."

"Whatever." I pulled out the car keys and jingled them in my hand. It was time to make my big exit, just walk out, head high, the winner in this, our first meeting. But if she left, would there be a second meeting? Did I even want one?

The truth was, I did. But not right away. I needed to talk to somebody about this first. Who, though? Not Snake or Nikki. They just didn't get it. And not Diane. She was too mixed up with Bobbie to ever see things clearly.

Then it came to me: Kim. She was adopted; she would understand better than anyone. *So call her.*

Fortified finally with something I could do, some source of help, I gave my birth mom a totally fake smile. "Well, gotta go. See ya."

I walked out to the balcony then turned right toward the stairs. But inside I was running as fast as I could, running away from Bobbie, running away from Diane too. Away from the totally screwed-up life they'd stuck me in. Only I refused to let her *see* my panic. So I sauntered to the stairs, took them one at a time, then strolled casually across the parking lot to the car, just in case she was watching.

After I was in the car, though, I could barely get the key into the ignition. My hand shook too much, and not because of the cold. I'd met my real-life mother when I was least expecting it. And now she was going to meet up with my adopted mom and her ex-husband. The two people who most hated her in the whole world.

Maybe I should hang around.

No. I started the car and pulled out, then hesitated at the highway and looked back at the motel. There was no sign of my real mom on the balcony. Had she already gone to Jim's room? Or maybe she'd chickened out. After finding me and not getting a lovey-dovey reunion, maybe she was all bummed out and confused about what to do now.

Was she disappointed in me?

A car right behind me honked and I lurched forward—then slammed on the brakes when a pickup truck in the right lane swerved to avoid me.

"Crap!" I couldn't back up and three cars zoomed by, glaring at me before I could inch out into the lane of traffic. By now I was so freaked out I turned into the first parking lot I found, on the other side of the McDonald's. I pulled in kind of crooked next to the garbage bin in the back corner, then just sat there shaking. And crying. I was the most screwed-up teenager in the whole world, and nobody—nobody!—gave a shit about me.

Except maybe Kim.

So I wiped my eyes and pulled out my phone and dialed the number I hadn't dialed in almost a year. "Hello, Kim? Oh. Miss Rita. Hi. This is Lisa. Lisa Haines? Is Kim there?"

CHAPTER TWENTY-SEVEN

VOICE MESSAGE FROM KRISTA:

Hey, Jim, it's me. I was so glad to get your message. I hope your meetings are going okay. I've had a lot of time to think and I realize now that you can never be totally done with Diane. I talked to Father John yesterday and he helped me put things in perspective. But hopefully we *can* be rid of this Roberta woman. Father John said if she needs to make her amends or whatever to Diane, then that's between them and you should just get out of the way. He said we can't always protect the important people in our lives. We want to, but sometimes it's not for us to do. He also helped me understand that you're still grieving for Alyssa *and* for your first marriage. But he said that doesn't mean you want to be married to Diane again. I wasn't so sure I believed him, but then I got your message.

I love you too, Jim, and I don't want to lose you. The minute I heard your voice I knew I had to fight for you. For us. So I've already called Father John and set up an appointment for us. Or just for you, if you prefer. We'll talk about it more when you get home. I love you.

From: Jim
To: Krista
Re: Coming home

I love you too. And of course I'll go to counseling with you. But not to a priest, okay? Father John's a nice guy but I'd rather not get religion mixed up in this, especially since a divorced guy like me doesn't even qualify to receive sacraments in his church. Besides, what does he know about being married?

From: Krista
To: Jim
Re: Coming home

The Catholic Church may be against divorce but that doesn't mean Father John looks down on you. But if he makes you feel uncomfortable I'll find a regular family counselor for us. When exactly will you be home? And why aren't you answering your cell phone? Love you.

From: Jim
To: Krista
Re: Coming home

I hope to finish up with my meetings tomorrow and leave the next day. My phone is acting up but I'll have it checked out when I get home. Love to the kids. And to you.

LISSY-LISA

Kim wasn't home, so I talked to Miss Rita. Not just talked, but spilled my entire guts like a big baby, crying, wailing, whining. I told her the whole sordid story—about who my real mother was, about Diane's first kid and why she adopted me, about how I'd just met my birth mom, and how Jim and Diane were up in a motel room right now, and Bobbie was going to see them both, and how I was so confused and mad and sad and ... and everything! I even let slip about Snake and my tattoo. And the whole time I cried like I was twelve years old again, so hard I could barely breathe.

"Your mom loves you, Lisa. I'm talking about Diane, *that* mom. And despite the boyfriend, despite the tattoo, she's not going to stop loving you. But that works both ways. You need to cut her some slack too."

"But she's been lying to me my whole life!"

"She's also loved you your whole life. If she pulled some strings to get you or bent some rules—even if in the beginning she might have wanted you for all the wrong reasons—well, that doesn't change the fact that she loves you. You, for yourself, not for her first little girl. I've seen how she is with you. You know, she and I talked about the difficulties of being adopted moms, and I can tell you, she would *die* to protect you. That's how strong her love is."

"I guess." I'd sunk down in the car seat, no longer crying, but trembling so hard I might shake apart. I dug my fingernails into the palm of my hand until it hurt. It was the only way to get myself under control.

"Well, I don't have to guess," she said. "I know that for a fact. I also know that her greatest fear—because it's *my* greatest fear too—is that the child she has loved and raised will one day reject her in favor of her birth mother."

"I would never do that!" But wasn't that what I'd been doing every day for the last year when I started talking back to her and breaking her rules, rejecting her? And that was even before I found out about her past history with my mom. I pressed my nails down even harder, until I felt the tiny snap of skin and the warm gush of blood. I took a big, shaky breath. "Why do I even have to choose between them?"

"You don't. You don't have to choose, sweetheart. There's plenty enough love in your heart to share between the two of them. But you *do* have to let her know that. She might not be operating on logic right now, you know? First you're acting out; then her ex-husband shows up. And now she's facing the woman who caused the death of her first beloved child—and who might be here to try to take *you* away from her, her second beloved child." She paused. "God bless her, she must be an absolute wreck."

If Miss Rita was trying to make me feel like the world's most selfish, horrible kid, she was doing an A-plus job of it. I knew that wasn't her goal, though. She wanted me and Mom Diane to be happy together. I wanted that too—and I'm pretty sure Diane did too. So why was it so hard for us?

I slid my fingertips in little circles in my bloody palm and stared longingly at the McDonald's, warm and bustling now with people. "Would you call her for me?" Even to my ears I sounded like a pathetic, whining little kid.

Rita chuckled, but not in a mean way. "Eventually, sure. But right now you're the one she needs to hear from. Go home, Lisa. Call your mom right now, and tell her you're heading home. You can tell her we talked if you want, and that she can call me later if she feels like it. But you both have to put in the effort to make your little family work. It's the only way to show how much you both love each other."

"But what about my other mom? I mean, for all I know they're up there scratching each other's eyes out like a Jerry Springer show."

"I hope not. But even if they are, that's between them. You're just a kid, honey. You can't referee their conflict. Besides, their problems started long before you were even born."

I hung onto her words after our conversation ended. I was just a kid, and this was their fight. When I called my mom on the phone, though, I was super-relieved when it went to voice mail. "It's me and I'm fine. I'm driving home, and I'll wait for you there." I paused and rubbed the painful, damp spot on my palm. "I guess you know I saw my birth mom. Everything's cool, though, and I really want to talk to you about that. About everything." I pressed my nail into the tenderest part of my wound, needing that exterior pain in order to stay calm inside. "Love you."

I felt better when I hung up. At least that was done. Now I just had to get back on the highway and drive home without being rammed by some giant truck. I found a tissue and pressed it into my palm. Then I started up the car, but I didn't pull out. The engine idled and feeble puffs of warmth wafted from the vents in a vain attempt to heat the frigid space.

Just put it in drive and go. In ten minutes you'll be home, all nice and warm.

But I couldn't go. If Mom was so worried about me, how come she hadn't picked up the phone when I called?

Maybe she turned the ringer off.

While I was missing? No way. I craned my neck to see past the wood fence to the motel. Some really big scene must be going down if she wasn't answering her phone. Maybe I should go back and check it out.

Except that I didn't really want to go. Like Miss Rita said, this was their deal to work out. Plus, whose side was I supposed to be on? And yet ... I just couldn't leave it alone. This was the best opportunity I'd ever have to hear the whole truth about my adoption. That's the reason I'd been looking for Jim in the first place, to bring him home and confront my mom with as much of the truth as I knew. But now my birth mom was here too. Everyone who knew anything about me was in that room on the second floor.

I turned off the engine and pulled the keys out of the ignition. It might be a super-ugly scene, but this was my big chance to figure out my whole mixed-up life. I was not going to blow it. So I forced myself out into the frigid, gray day one more time and headed back to the motel.

"It's for the best," I muttered as I trudged up the stairs. "Tomorrow you'll be so glad you did this." If I could just get through today.

I trotted down the open corridor, past the naked pervert's door and the vending room and started my knocking routine. Nobody answered at the first two doors. Then I heard someone yelling. Two someones. Heart hammering overtime, I stood outside room 227. Was the man I heard Jim?

Then I heard my mom's voice. "No, Jim. This is crazy. You can't be serious." Even muffled she sounded majorly stressed.

Caught between wanting only to eavesdrop and wanting to burst into the room, I just stood there stuck in neutral. Then I heard someone else—my birth mom?—say, "Just leave, Diane. Leave."

"Don't *you* even *talk* to me!" my mom screamed back. "Just ... Just shut up!"

That's when I shoved the door open and practically fell into the room. I don't know what I expected. Them all shouting and accusing each other. Screaming, yes, maybe even crying. But I never expected a gun. Jim held it in his right hand, and it was pointed straight at my birth mother's heart!

"Lisa!" My mom—Diane—practically tackled me and tried to muscle me out of the room.

But no way was I leaving. "What's going on? What's he doing?"

"Get out of here!" my other mom hissed. "Get her out of here," she told Diane.

"I'm not going anywhere!" I twisted out of my mom's grasp and pressed back against the wall by the door. It was so scary, like some cheesy movie, only a hundred times worse. Bobbie stood up against a dresser, her hands in front of her like she could ward off any bullets he shot. Jim stood at the foot of the bed looking all crazy and freaked out. His hair stuck out and his eyes were bloodshot, but he looked deadly serious. And the gun in his hand looked cold and big and deadly too.

"Don't hurt her." My words came out thin and shaky. I took a harsh breath. "Please don't."

"Who's this?" he barked. I could tell when he recognized me from last night. "This is *your* kid, Diane?"

"Yes!" I shouted at him. "And I'm *her* kid, too!" I pointed at my birth mom. "Roberta Fenner Davis's kid."

"What?" His head twisted back and forth from Diane and me, to Bobbie. "What do you mean?" Then he looked at me, stared really hard, and I could see when he saw the resemblance between me and Bobbie. The gun in his hand wavered, like he was shaking. I was so afraid it would go off that I must've winced. Diane too, because she grabbed me and twisted us so that I was behind her.

"I adopted her," she told him. "When I found out Roberta was going to jail and that she had a little girl, I found a way to adopt her child. It was only fair," she went on, turning to me now, her eyes wide and pleading. "I'm sorry. I never meant for you to find out."

I wrenched out of her grasp. "You were *never* gonna tell me? *Ever?*"

She opened her mouth, then closed it and only shook her head.

Jim started laughing, this weird, nervous laugh that made the hair on my neck stand up. "You got her kid!" He laughed again. "Way to go, Diane. Way to go!" Then his face seemed to sag, like he got twenty years older in one split second. "You got her. But that didn't bring Alyssa back, did it? She can't make up for what this bitch—" He waved the gun at Bobbie. "What this bitch did to our innocent baby."

Without thinking I grabbed for Mom Diane, bracing for the gun to go off. I could feel her trembling so bad. She was as scared as me. Jim kept staring at me. "You were at the town house last night, but you lied and said Diane didn't live there anymore." His eyes bored holes in me. "What's your name again?" he finally asked in this hoarse voice.

I didn't want to say. I just wanted to blink and disappear and go back to this morning, before I ever jacked Mom's car and found Jim and stumbled into this horrible mess. But then I wouldn't have met my birth mom, and when all was said and done, that had been my goal from the first. Trying not to stare at the gun, I straightened up and despite Diane's hold on me, edged out from behind her.

"My name is Lisa," I answered, digging my nails into my throbbing palm and struggling not to look as terrified as I felt. "But before that—before Diane adopted me—I was named Lissy."

It was like I had slapped him. He jerked back and his face

turned this awful mottled red. I prayed he would have a stroke or a heart attack, and fall down dead—or at least drop that gun. But he didn't.

Instead he advanced on Bobbie. "You low-life bitch! You kill my child and then you give your little bastard *my* baby's name?"

"She's *not* a bastard," Bobbie retorted, edging along the dresser until she hit the sidewall. She looked so scared, her face pale and her eyes opened real wide. But her voice was strong and steady when she switched her gaze to me. "You had a father who loved you. We were married, but Ken died when you were barely two—"

"That's just semantics," Jim bit out. "Was he a junkie too? Two junkies making another little junkie bastard."

I wanted to punch his lights out, but Diane jumped in first. "Lisa is a great kid, Jim. I've made sure of that."

He laughed. "So great that she stole your car? Sounds like a chip off the old block." He twisted his head to stare at me again. "So, kill any babies on the drive over, kid?"

"Jim!" Diane exclaimed in horror.

"No," I mumbled, then hated myself for even answering his disgusting question. I wanted to scream at him, to call him every curse word I knew. But I was too afraid of what he might do.

Then I realized that he was crying. He wasn't sobbing or anything, just these two uneven lines of tears dripping down his ruddy cheeks. I never saw a man cry before and it was unnerving.

"Look, Jim," Diane said in a calmer tone. "I'm sending Lisa out of the room—"

"I'm not going," I hissed. "No way."

"Yes, you are." She turned back to Jim. "I want you to put that gun away, okay? We need to end this."

He shook his head. "It's never going to end. Don't you get it? And now that I know about her kid, I realize that she was lying all along. She said she just wanted to make amends to you. Make amends. What crap! She was looking for her kid and now that she's found her—" He broke off with a gasp. "Oh my God! She found you and her kid by following me! Is that right?" His arm straightened with the gun only three feet from Bobbie's face.

"Don't hurt her!" I screamed. "Don't!"

"She came here to steal her kid back, Diane. What other reason would she have? I can't let her do that to you."

That's when Bobbie lowered her hands and seemed to relax. It was too surreal, like she was resigned to everything. She gave Diane this long, steady stare. "Take her out of here, Diane. Now."

"No!" I cried. "I just found you. I'm not letting you go."

"See?" Jim exclaimed. "See? She's stealing another kid from you. I can't let that happen."

Staying between me and Jim, Diane edged toward him. "If you shoot her, Jim, what happens to your new family? To Krista and your two darling children? You'll go to jail for a long time. How hard do you think that will be on them, growing up without their father?"

I saw him swallow hard.

"Don't you see," she went on. "Hurting Roberta—killing her—changes nothing from the past. But it changes everything in your future. It ruins *everything*."

In the awful stillness in that room, the only sound was his harsh, angry breaths. "I don't have a future," he said, so low and quiet that it scared me more than his screaming had.

"Get her out of here," Bobbie hissed at Diane. "This is between me and him." When Diane ignored her she added, "If you truly love Lissy, you'll get her away from here, Diane. Now!"

"What do you know about love?" Diane snarled the words at her.

I shrank away from Diane, looking back and forth between the two women, both my mothers. Diane was trying so hard to calm Jim, even though her hatred of Bobbie was just as strong as his. As for Bobbie, now that she'd found me it was almost like she decided it was okay if she died. But it wasn't okay with me!

"Lissy—Lisa—is the only thing I've ever loved," she said to Diane—and to me. "That's why I put her up for adoption, to give her a chance at a better life than I could ever give her. But I never stopped loving you, Lissy. Never."

"Yeah, right," Jim muttered.

"I wrote you letters." She stared past him to me, like I was the only thing she cared about.

"I never got them."

She smiled and shook her head. "Once you were adopted I lost contact with you. But I saved them. Ten years' worth of letters."

"She's a liar, kid," Jim broke in. "And a loser."

"*You're* the loser!" I screamed.

It was his turn to smile, this awful, broken parody of a smile. "You're right. I am a loser. I lost everything because of *her*." He waved the gun at my mother. "You should be glad you got Diane for your mother instead of her."

"I saw the letter," Diane blurted out. She was looking at my birth mother. "I saw it, when you gave her up."

Bobbie looked puzzled. "The letter to Child Protective Services? That letter?"

Slowly, almost like she was in some kind of trance, Diane nodded. Then she drew herself up and turned to me. "She said she wanted a better home for you than she could provide. And she specifically didn't want you raised by anyone in her family."

On the outside I didn't move at all. But inside my heart pounded so hard I thought my ribs would break. "That's what Toolie said."

"Toolie Fastbender?" Bobbie exclaimed. "You talked to her?"

"Shut up!" Jim shouted. "Enough of this crap! Out, Diane. Now. And take the kid with you."

"No, Jim. I'm not letting you do this. Your family needs you. You know they do. And ... " I heard her take a shaky breath. "And Lisa needs more time to get to know her birth mother. Her roots."

He snorted in contempt. "No she doesn't. She doesn't belong to her anymore. She belongs to you."

"I don't *belong* to anybody!" I shouted at them all. "I'm my own self!"

"You're right," Bobbie said. "You don't belong to anybody. You are your own smart, beautiful, strong self. But I belong to you and I always will, whether you want me to or not."

In the silence that followed I swear I could hear my heart beating, loud like a big marching-band drum. Outside I heard the faint sound of traffic. A horn honked. Tires squealed. Then Diane caught my hand in hers and said, "I belong to you too, Lisa. No matter how I got you, I love you and that will never change." She squeezed my fingers. Then she turned back to Jim. "I can't stand by and let you hurt Lisa's birth mother, Jim. Just like I can't stand by and let you ruin the beautiful life you have with Krista, Brad and Maylie."

He fell back a step when she said their names. Krista, Brad, and Maylie. I held my breath as she walked up to him, then sidled between him and Bobbie. A tear slid down his cheek, slow and heavy. Then another. Suddenly, even though he had a gun and was crazy, I felt sorry for him. He was probably a very good dad.

After all, he still loved his first little girl, Alyssa. "You know their names?" he said as Diane reached for the gun.

"Yes." She smiled at him. "I Googled you a time or two. For a long time I was so jealous of what you had, Jim. A lovely new wife, two beautiful children. But now I'm grateful for it. Your family needs you. They really need you."

That's when he broke. His chin sank to his chest, he lowered the gun they both held, and his whole body started to shake with these awful, heartbreaking sobs. Diane took the gun and laid it on the bed. Then she wrapped him in her arms and just held him while he cried.

It was so hard watching him cling to her, this man I'd always seen as a villain. I wanted to tear her away from him and have her arms around me as I cried. I don't know if it was relief that had me crying or just because there was so much emotion flying around in the room. So many years of rage and frustration and terrible, endless sadness. He was crying; I was crying; Diane was crying. And when I met Bobbie's gaze, I saw tears on her face too. Which made me cry even harder. I was blind with my tears, wiping my eyes with my sleeve when I felt her arms go around me.

"May I hold you?" she asked, her voice soft and shaking.

I nodded, and as she pulled me against her, it felt like something gave way, like when Peter Pan's shadow was cut away from his feet in the story my mom used to tell me. My adopted mom.

I didn't remember any stories my birth mom ever told me. But she *did* love me. She'd written me letters and she'd come all this way, tracked me down just to see me again. Now her arms were strong and warm, and they felt so right—and so familiar. I pressed my face to her shoulder and rubbed my cheek against her fleece jacket. A long time ago she'd held me like this—when I cried, when she carried me to bed. I wish I could remember, but I couldn't. I know it had happened, though. I know.

"Take her out of here," Diane said, my mother of the past twelve years.

I opened my eyes to find her watching us from over Jim's shoulder. Bobbie nodded and steered me to the door. But my gaze remained locked with Diane's. Her eyes were huge. It was like she was naked to the very bottom of her soul, like I could see all her pain and fear and everything her life had been since her little girl died. Surely she wasn't giving me up, giving me back to Bobbie that easy?

"Wait." I grabbed the door frame. "Come with us, Mom. Please."

She smiled then, and I saw all the love I always took for granted. But not today. Today I *knew* how much she loved me. "I'll be there soon," she said. "Just go."

"Okay." I nodded, then mouthed the words, *I love you*, as Bobbie hustled us out.

We were down the corridor to the bottom of the stairs before I could speak. "He won't hurt her, will he?"

"No." Bobbie had one arm around my shoulder. "He would never hurt her."

I led her to the car, then stopped. "We should wait for her. Just to be sure."

"No." She shook her head. "She wants you away from here, Lissy. Lisa." She gave a wry smile. "That's how much she loves you. She'd send you away, with me of all people, just to get you out of that room." Then she glanced around the parking lot. "You took her car to get here, right?"

"Yeah. She came in a cab."

"How about you leave her car over by the stairs so she'll see it. Then I'll drive you home in my car."

I guess I must have looked doubtful because she chuckled. "Don't worry. I have no intention of trying to skip town with you. You're just a little too old to kidnap. Besides ... " She paused, took a deep breath, then let it out. "Besides, you're her child as much as mine now." She pressed her lips together before she went on. "I never thought I'd say such a thing, let alone believe it. But ... " Her chin trembled and she had to take another breath. "Now that I've seen you, no longer the three-and-a-half-year-old of my memory, I see how much I missed—and how much Diane did for you."

Her gaze slid over me, from my snarled hair to my slept-in clothes, to my nicked-up deep-purple nail polish and my mangled, bloody palm, and for a moment I was embarrassed at how I looked. Then she smiled, and I swear it was just like my other mom's smile. "She obviously did a great job with you, Lisa."

Lisa.

Then she held out a hand to me. "Come on. Let me take you home."

EPILOGUE

INSTANT MESSAGE:

Kim: You are like the luckiest kid I know!! Even tho I e-mail my sister in Oregon all the time now, we don't know if we can ever find our birth mom in Korea. And no way will she ever be able to find us. I don't think they even have electricity in her village, let alone computers to Google us. It must have been so great when your birth mom just showed up like that.

Lisa: It was kind of cool. But it was weird too, because of her terrible history with my other mom. I mean, I love mom, Diane. She gave me a great life even if I never knew why we moved so much. But mom, Roberta, she's half of me, you know? And even tho we're just getting to know each other again, I already know I love her. But then I feel like I'm betraying mom Diane.

Kim: My mom always tells me that she loves both her kids, so it's ok for me to love both my moms.

Lisa: I know. Both my moms told me that too. It's freaky because they both say so many of the same things. Study hard, get good grades, go to college, no more tattoos. Yada, yada, yada. It would be easier if they could be friends. But I don't think they ever can.

Kim: Maybe in time. And once you're 18 and in college and they begin to see you as an adult, it'll be easier for them.

Lisa: Easier for them, maybe, but not for me. Sometimes I feel like those guys in Roman times, tied up to 2 horses and torn wide open when they gallop in different directions.

Kim: Just like kids in most divorced families.

Lisa: Yeah, only worse. So now I'm stuck seeing a therapist every week. My life has turned into a stupid cliché.

Kim: Why not just join an online adoptees group? I'm in one: teenadoptees.com. You should try it.

Lisa: Maybe. But I still have to go to therapy. I got into a little trouble and developed a few bad habits when I was so stressed out.

Kim: What kind of habits?

Lisa: Sex, drugs and rock-and-roll, girlfriend. With a little self-mutilation on the side.

Kim: Whoa. You must have been majorly stressed. How's it going now?

Lisa: OK. At least we're not moving again. And I know my real mom. But Mom Diane and I, we're just not the same.

Kim: Don't you love each other anymore? I can't imagine not loving my adoptive mother, even when she's super strict.

Lisa: I love her and all. But it's different and I can't explain it. At least we don't fight so much.

Kim: Well, that's something.

Lisa: Yeah, I guess.

Date: Jan 17, 2008
From: Toolie
To: Bobbie
Re: Lissy

I'm real happy you found Lissy. She seems like a nice girl and very smart. She was searching for you when she found me. Sooner or later she would have found you herself, but I'm glad how things happened to make it sooner. You know, you could have that Jim guy arrested. He could've killed you. But I understand why you didn't. It's funny how things work, that Diane stopped him from hurting you even though she hated you for so long.
So, when will you see Lissy again? Does she go by Lissy or Lisa now?

From: Bobbie
To: Toolie
Re: Lissy/Lisa

She uses both names. She said she likes it because she's had two lives and two moms and she's the living proof that it can work out. I tell you what, she is some great kid. Really great. But she's been screwing up in school and hanging out with a rough crowd. I told her there was nothing cool about getting loaded or drunk, and nothing smart about having sex when you're only fifteen. That boyfriend of hers–bad news. I told Diane she ought to put Lissy back in Catholic school. An all-girls Catholic school. Lisa did not like that. So I told her that she better shape up, then.

Can you believe that? Me powwowing with Diane on how Lissy ought to be raised. When I started looking for Lissy I just wanted to know she was okay. You know, from when she was sick that time. But now I want more. I need Lissy to be part of my life. If I could I would spend every minute of the day with her, only it's probably not the best thing for her just yet. I remember me at 15-1/2, how wild I was getting and I don't want to push Lissy down that road. Just the opposite. But kids are unpredictable. They'll play one parent against the other. Me and Diane, we're sort of like a divorced couple. We're not too keen on each other, but we have to be sure we're on the same page when it comes to Lissy. I'm waiting a while to give her all the letters I wrote to her too. Things need to settle down a little more before she'll be ready for them.

Listen, thanks for talking so much to Lissy. She told me you were sort of like a grandmother giving her advice and everything. Since she never had a grandmother, she really appreciated it. So do I.

From: Toolie
To: Bobbie
Re: Lissy/Lisa

So what are you going to do now that you found her? Are you moving closer to her? Or will she come to visit you?

From: Bobbie
To: Toolie
Re: Lissy/Lisa

I want to move right next door to her, but it's too soon. Besides, I hate to bail out on New Orleans. Nurses are in big demand and I know I'm needed here. What I was thinking was to have Lissy come this summer and volunteer, maybe with Habitat for Humanity or something. She needs to see how bad off some people are and get off her poor, pitiful me routine. Diane may have lied to her, but she did a good job raising her.

From: Toolie
To: Bobbie
Re: Lissy/Lisa

That sounds like a good idea. I haven't been to New Orleans in twenty years. It must be very different.

From: Bobbie:
To: Toolie
Re: Lissy/Lisa

You should come too. It would almost be like a family reunion.

From: Krista
To: Diane
Re: Jim

Thanks for your update on the whole Roberta thing. It's strange to write you as a friend because for a long time I've seen you as competition. I had no reason to think you wanted Jim back, but I was terrified that he wanted you back. He got home really late that first night like he promised and then slept through the next day, almost 20 hours. He got up, put the kids to bed, ate what I put in front of him, then went back to sleep. So we didn't get to really talk till the third day. If you hadn't already e-mailed me about what happened, I would have been a psycho bitch by then. But instead we sent the kids to my parents and we just sat and talked. He told me basically everything you already told me, except that he really was planning to kill her.

It's terrifies me to think how close he came to doing it. It would have destroyed our lives, especially the kids'. They love their daddy so much. Jim says he didn't plan on getting caught, so none of us would ever have known. But I know it would have affected him, and eventually that would have affected our marriage and home life too.

He never expected Roberta to show up while you were

there. And he didn't have a clue that your daughter was her daughter. But even after your girl showed up, he told me he still was going to kill Roberta. He cried when he admitted that, and he apologized for not thinking about our kids, for being so reckless with all our lives. The strange thing is, I think in some ways it was good. As awful as things must have been in that hotel room, it's like he finally let out all the poison in his soul.

The next day we talked to our priest, and Jim is meeting with him once a week now.

I hope this doesn't hurt you, Diane, but I think Jim is finally over you. I understand that he'll always love you, and what you and he and Alyssa had. He'll always mourn her loss and the loss of your family, because he's a good man. And that's why I love him. But for a long time I let his sorrow and unresolved anger be about me, when I really didn't have anything to do with it. I'm sorry for how I felt about you before. And I'm more grateful than I can ever say, that you talked him out of hurting Roberta and ruining all our lives. Thank you.

My only worry now is about you. It seems like everybody else has benefited. Roberta found her daughter. Lisa found her birth mother. Jim finally accepted the past and is embracing the future. And I got my husband back. But what about you? Are you okay?

From: Diane
To: Krista
Re: (no subject)

I'm relieved to hear that you and Jim and your children are on the mend. All I want for Jim is that he be happy. He was born to be a husband and father. He was great at it with me and Alyssa, and I know he'll be great at it with all of you.

As for me, it's a mixed bag. It's harder than I can say to see Lisa's excitement about finding her birth mother. I never wanted Roberta to find her and for the past twelve years I've done everything I could to make sure that never happened. I still believe I did the right thing by adopting her. But I did it for the wrong reason. I wanted to punish Roberta, to make her suffer forever. I wanted her to look her whole life for her child and never find her.

The truth is, a part of me would have been happy if Jim had killed her. Or so I wanted to believe. But once she showed up in that room with us, and he pulled out that gun, I knew it was wrong. Wrong for all of us. And I sure didn't want Jim carrying around that kind of load. For years he's been consumed with guilt for divorcing me. I see that now. How much more guilt would he feel for actually killing someone? Even the someone who killed our Alyssa?

When Lisa showed up, though, that's when everything I'd built our life around came undone. She loves her birth mother. It's as simple as that. She loves Roberta. They look alike; they share the same DNA. Their need to be together is like cellular attraction, and I can't fight it. I never thought I could love Lisa as much as I loved Alyssa, but I do. And that means I have to accept Roberta in her life.

In your e-mail you said that you let Jim's sorrow and unresolved anger be about you, when it really had nothing to do with you. That really stuck with me. I have to keep reminding myself that Lisa's love for her birth mother and her need to know her is not a betrayal of our lives together. It doesn't have anything to do with me at all.

So I decided to find a therapist. I'm also going to a grief group at this Unitarian church, and maybe between that and the therapy I'll finally let the past go too. Like Jim I'll always love and miss Alyssa. And I'll love him too. He's a wonderful man, and I'm so glad he's married to someone like you who's willing to work to make your marriage a success. You two belong together and I know you'll make it.

As for me, I don't know. I'm doing okay. I've actually been thinking about getting back into CAJA. Helping my CAJA kids really helped me once before. Maybe it would help me again.

But I worry about Lisa. For so long I was blind to her frustration and unhappiness.

I was strict and consistent and made sure she had consequences for improper behavior. But after our last move everything started to spin out of control. She's in therapy now too, and she hates it. But I have to do something. She got a tattoo and was cutting herself. I worry that she was into drugs and sex too. But she refuses to admit anything. At least Bobbie's on my side in this argument. I doubt Lisa would even go to her therapy sessions if Bobbie didn't back me up. She's back in New Orleans, but they keep in touch, although I don't ask Lisa about it.

I have to admit that Roberta is not as bad a human being as I expected. It seems like she's turned her life around, and she's taken a real tough line with Lisa about school and boys. And tattoos. So we'll see. I only have 2½ years till Lisa goes to college, and I'm determined to make them good years for both of us.

BTW I'm attaching some pictures of Lisa and me from our vacation in Chicago last summer. If you have any, I'd love pictures of your kids. I understand if you'd rather not continue to communicate with me. But if you want a new friend, I'm willing.

Give my best to Jim.

AUGUST 16, 2009

Dear Alyssa,

Today is your 25th birthday. I guess you must be up in heaven because what kind of God would send a little kid to hell? Anyway, if you can see everything that goes on down here, you probably know what a crazy couple of years it's been. I was so freaked out when I first found out about you. It was weird because I felt jealous of you even though you were dead. Our mom never talked about you, and I just wanted to forget about you. But I couldn't. And then everything exploded. But it's actually better now. We talk about you sometimes. Both of my moms do.

I hope you've forgiven my birth mom for the car wreck and everything. I don't know if mom Diane can ever totally forgive her, but if you can help her to do that it would be good.

Right after the "big event" things were pretty rough. But slowly it's getting better. I brought my grades up and I'm working a lot harder at school. At the spring arts camp at my school we did a section on poetry and I wrote a free verse poem to you. I hope you like it.

To A from L

Where would I be if you hadn't died?

What would I be?
A dropout?
A druggie?
A whore?

Who would I be?
A liar?
A thief?
A loser?

Why did it happen this way?
I don't know.
Maybe you do.

You died and I got a new life.
And so did my birth mom
And my new mom
And her ex-husband
And his new wife
And their kids
And their kids ...

The choices we make go on forever,
the good ones and the bad.
So thank you for the life you gave me
and for the good, brief life you had.

PS. I know free verse isn't supposed to rhyme, but that last part just came out that way.

PPS. I decided to quit cutting myself but I did it one more time, just to get enough blood to make us blood sisters. It only seems right. I took the blood, watered it down a little and then washed it over a copy of the poem so that it has this streaky pink background. Then I framed it and hung it inside my closet. I'm not ready to show it to our mother yet. But maybe I should since today is your birthday.

Happy Birthday, Sister
Love, Lissy